LIE
TO
ME

Claire

Tell me a good lie!

Natasha Preston

Books by Natasha Preston

THE SILENCE SERIES

Silence
Broken Silence
Players, Bumps, and Cocktail Sausages
Silent Night

THE CHANCE SERIES

Second Chance
Our Chance

STAND-ALONES

Save Me
With the Band
Reliving Fate
Lie to Me

YOUNG ADULT THRILLERS

The Cellar
Awake
The Cabin
You Will Be Mine

LIE TO ME

NATASHA PRESTON

Copyright © 2018 by Natasha Preston
All rights reserved.

Visit my website at www.natashapreston.com
Cover Designer: Sofie Hartley, Hart and Bailey Design Co
Editor and Interior Designer: Jovana Shirley,
Unforeseen Editing, www.unforeseenediting.com

No part of this book may be reproduced or transmitted in any form or by any means, electronic or mechanical, including photocopying, recording, or by any information storage and retrieval system without the written permission of the author, except for the use of brief quotations in a book review.

This book is a work of fiction. Names, characters, places, and incidents either are products of the author's imagination or are used fictitiously. Any resemblance to actual persons, living or dead, events, or locales is entirely coincidental.

ISBN-13: 978-1987412017

*For the wonderful ladies and gents in my reader group.
I love each of you!*

1

Savannah

THREE YEARS AGO, TO the day, I took off in the middle of the night. Leaving only a note behind.

I was nineteen and in so much pain. My family had no idea that I was planning my escape; they didn't have a clue how bad things were for me. Or perhaps they just didn't care.

I suppose, in the end, it doesn't matter.

I'm in my cosy little kitchen, a hundred miles away from home, and although I don't really have anyone, I'm better off. It's better to have a small group of genuine friends than dozens of surface ones, right? Well, that's me. Only, instead of a small group, I have one friend, who's also my boss, who I could be genuine with—but that would involve opening up.

Basically, neither of those is me. I don't have friends. I'm the hermit. That's me.

Placing my hands around my mug of steaming hot coffee, I drop my shoulders. Yes, okay, I might be better off, but it still sucks.

Things were so bad back then, and I had no one to turn to, no one who seemed to be on my side or at least trying to see things from my perspective. So, I did the only thing I felt I could, and I left.

I hate to admit that I still feel the ache in my chest when I think about the circumstances surrounding my total abandonment of my boyfriend and entire family. Sometimes, it takes my breath away, and other times, I can ignore it. The ache is like the moon—always there but not always visible.

My mum and my ex contact me often, but I do everything I can to keep them out of my life. I don't want to go back there. I don't even want to think about what happened.

In these last three years, my life has changed immeasurably. I used to live with my family in a large house on a respectable estate where everyone kept their grass cut at a scarily precise length. It was a beautiful and safe place to grow up.

It's where I met Simon—aka The Colossal Wanker.

It's also where I left Simon.

Now, I live in a small one-bedroom apartment on the outskirts of the city. It's a nice flat, built about six years ago, and I rent it from a sweet lady who bought it to hand down to her granddaughter when she turns eighteen. The apartment is also super close to work.

Sometimes, I barely recognise the person staring back at me in the mirror, but this year, I am determined to rebuild me.

The warm July rain hammers down on the window in my little kitchen.

In my old life, I hated the rain. I used to care so much about my appearance and would never leave the house without perfect makeup, flawless hair, and trendy clothes. When I closed the door to the old Savannah—or Sav, as I was nicknamed—I decided it was pointless to worry about such trivial things. When your whole world has imploded on you, it makes stressing over flat hair a little too superficial.

In an hour, I have to walk out the door for work. I'm ready, as I hate being late anywhere, not that my boss and only friend here would mind if I was a few minutes late.

LIE TO ME

Heidi is everything I want to be. She's strong, independent, and successful, and she seems to have everything together.

Her ducks are in a row. Mine are zigzagging.

Though, I suppose, leaving everything I knew at nineteen and building a new life on my own does make me independent, but I'm working on the rest of it. Most of the time, I feel lost.

My laptop is open on the table in front of me. I kept my old Facebook account, but I don't use it. Sav Dean is long gone. The picture of me barely looks like me. I was eighteen, and the photo was taken at Glastonbury. Even there, my dark blonde hair is styled in a perfectly maintained bun.

Why did I ever care so much about what people thought of me?

There are two unread messages in my inbox. I open every single one Simon, my family, and old friends have sent, but I never reply.

Here goes nothing.

With my heart racing, I click the first one.

Simon.

He can bugger off.

His messages have changed a lot over the years. They started desperate, then turned angry, and then were full of hurt and a million apologies where he said sorry but didn't actually take any responsibility. Lately, they've been more pleading, but in the last two weeks, he's thrown in some desperation again.

> **Sav,**
>
> I know it's been a little while since I last tried to contact you, but I hope I've given you enough space to really think about us getting together. You probably have questions, lots of them, and I want to give you answers.

> Please let me at least try to offer you some peace. Please. I need to do this, and you need to hear this. We can both heal if you just let me talk to you.

Nope. Not a chance in hell.

My finger hovers above the keys, and my eyes tense. I want to tell him where he can go—straight to hell—but three years ago, I resolved to never speak to him again unless the apocalypse happened, and we were the last people on earth. And then our only interaction would be me laughing as I threw him to a zombie.

Since that's not happening ...

With shaking fingers, I click off his message and open the one from my mother.

> Savannah, my darling Sav, please come home. I understand you were hurt, but we are all here for you. We love you. Mum and Dad.

I roll the grey eyes I inherited from my mother. *Lies.*

Although, deep down, I still love my parents and sister, Isla, I'm not entirely sure I'd help them in the apocalypse either. My feelings toward them change daily, depending upon my mood. If I'm near *that* time of the month, they have absolutely no chance.

Temptation tingles in my fingers, so I get up and grab my handbag from the table. I'll be early for work, at least fifty minutes, but Heidi won't mind. I can't stay here where the call to reply is getting stronger.

Spending some time with Heidi always helps. Her strength seeps into my pores, and I gain a little more clarity when I've spoken to her. She has no idea what she does for me. I've never told her the real reason I left. Of course, she knows that I'm not close with my family and that I moved away, but no one in my new life knows about my old one.

LIE TO ME

Not that I have many people around to hide my past from.

I stop off at Starbucks on the way to the studio to grab Heidi's skinny latte and my Americano. She's a bit of a coffee nut, and if she doesn't have at least five cups a day, she gets cranky. The rain has eased, so I'm going to turn up at work, looking like a drowned rat.

When I open the door to the studio, Heidi is sitting at her sewing table in the corner of the room. She looks up over a large pile of white-and-navy-chevron material and tilts her head to the side.

Her blue eyes swim with sympathy. I'm only ever very early when something has gone wrong. Meaning when my old life comes knocking.

"What happened, Savannah?" she asks, holding her hand out for the large drink.

I hand it over and drop down in a seat on the other side of the table.

Running my hand through my damp hair, I consider, for the millionth time, confiding in Heidi. She only has a very small portion of the real story.

"My mum," I mutter, sipping on my coffee.

"Oh, babes. I hate that she's still treating you badly."

Her words feel like broken glass rubbing against my skin. "I know. I do, too. It's hard not to let her bother me when she messages."

It's harder to read from my mum than Simon; it always takes me back to a time when I experienced the worst pain I had ever felt. She should have been there for me.

"Why don't you delete your old email account?"

Heidi thinks my mum contacts me via email. I haven't told her I have a Facebook account. She thinks I'm weird for not being all over social media, but that's fine. No one here calls me Sav, so I don't think she would find it anyway. Not that she would look.

I suck in a breath. "I've asked myself that same question dozens of times over the last three years. I don't know why."

Literally, I have no idea why I can't do it. Maybe I'm a masochist, and I secretly enjoy being hurt over and over again. Maybe I'm just as weak as I think.

Heidi raises her eyebrow and brushes her iron-straight brown hair behind her shoulder. "We should work on that."

"Speaking of work, what are you making right now?" I ask, eyeing the fabric.

"Order for mother and daughter skater dress in the zigzag that came in last night."

"Last night? You're already starting it?"

We have, including this new order, seventeen items of clothing that Heidi needs to make by the end of the week, and she's making the most recent one.

"Ugh, don't look at me with those judgmental eyes, Dean. I'll put this away at eight and work from the first order. Kent will be here soon, too."

My spine stiffens at the sound of his name. Heidi's younger brother, Kent, always puts me on edge. I've only met him around five or six times, and we've spoken fewer words than that. He's intense and arrogant, only talking to those he deems worthy.

"Why is he coming today?" I ask, my voice wavering, getting higher, like I suddenly inhaled helium.

After Simon's and my mum's messages this morning, I'm definitely not poised enough to be around Kent.

Brilliant idea, coming into work early.

Can I go back to bed and start the day again?

"Last night, I finally guilted him into putting together the new units and shelves in the storeroom. I wanted to get him in before he changed his mind, and I had to pay someone. We're running out of space, and we desperately need the storage."

"Yeah, of course."

When she mentioned asking Kent to put it together rather than hiring someone to do it, I hoped he would refuse. It's a menial job after all and not worth his time.

"He's not that bad, Savannah."

I shake my head in an attempt to appear surprised by her statement. "I don't think he's bad."

"Hon, you're a terrible liar."

Oh, that is so untrue.

"He doesn't like me, and I suppose that makes me feel a little uncomfortable. Ignore me though; I'm more emotional than normal. Do you need me to do anything other than the usual today?"

While Heidi handles the creative side of the business, I take on every other aspect. I deal with processing the orders through the website, social media, bookkeeping, packaging and posting orders, and all other admin jobs that need sorting. I love it.

She winces, and I know I'm not going to like this. "I feel awful asking now, but I need the storeroom cleared, so Kent can work. All of the stuff just needs stacking in the far side, near the door."

I smile, but I'm sure it looks more like a grimace because I'm certainly not going to enjoy being in such close proximity with the miserable one.

"No problem." The words taste sour, leaving my mouth. I'm going to need a really big glass of wine when I get home tonight.

"Are you sure, Savannah? You just said he makes you uncomfortable, and I don't ever want you to feel that here."

Raising my hand, I kick my legs out and sink back into the seat. "That was a bad analogy. Like I said, I'm ultrasensitive today, but honestly, I have no issue with working alongside your brother. It'll be good to get the storeroom organised." I add a smile to really sell my speech.

Heidi sighs in relief, the colour returning to her cheeks as she realises she can concentrate on creating amazing, handmade clothing rather than babysitting me and her brother.

See, I'm not a terrible liar.

I take a large sip of my coffee. At least I have the biggest caffeine hit Starbucks sells.

The front door to the studio bangs open. I feel him before I see him. The air changes, thickening to the point where I fear it might choke me. Heidi stands up and takes her latte with her as she greets her brother. My pulse hums.

Breathe, Savannah.

I've survived worse than Kent Lawson.

My legs are made of lead as I stand and turn to face them.

All right, so Kent might come across as angry or bored most of the time, but, Jesus, he is good-looking. He's easily over six foot with dark hair styled slightly longer on top, eyes that are closer to turquoise—changing from blue to green, depending on what he's wearing—and muscles that could turn any sane woman crazy.

But he's a massive knobhead. A *massive* one.

So, there's that.

He makes me feel as timid and insignificant as I sometimes feel. I can't ignore the change in myself when he's around, and, damn, I hate him for that.

Heidi starts talking to him and leads him towards the storeroom, but her words are just noise. Kent hasn't even acknowledged my presence. Not that I'm surprised, but sometimes, it's nice to be seen as an actual human being.

See, he's a knobhead.

"Fucking hell, Heidi, what have you bought?" he grumbles, looking into the storeroom.

It's a pretty big space, and we have shelves and cupboards that span the length and height of the longest wall, opposite the door.

"Thanks for agreeing to do this," she replies sweetly, totally unfazed by his less than charming manner.

"I'll start clearing the rolls of material away from the flat-pack boxes," I offer. My voice sounds normal, so at least no one in this room, besides me, knows how nervous I am around Kent.

"No, Savannah, finish your coffee first," Heidi says, giving me a look that I know means, *Do as I say*.

LIE TO ME

I pause, standing still and not really knowing what to do. On the one hand, I want to rush into it and get it over with, but I also *really* want this coffee.

"Yeah, it's not like I have anything else to do," Kent says, raising his eyebrow.

Gritting my teeth so hard, I'm surprised they don't snap, I count backward from ten.

You want to keep your job.

"Kent, don't be a dick! Ignore him, Savannah. He obviously got out of bed on the wrong side." She slaps his arm hard, but he doesn't even flinch. "Be nice to her," Heidi tries to whisper, but I still hear.

And, now, I feel like a child.

Seriously, I want my do-over.

Kent swings his arms behind his back and rocks back and forth on his feet. He looks around the room, but he's not really taking anything in; he's trying to make it clear that he's waiting.

I take a sip very slowly and narrow my eyes. My heart is racing as I challenge him because, although I want to stand up to him, he would definitely win if pushed.

Why does he make me feel even weaker than usual?

Because you know the old you would have taken him down in seconds. You wouldn't have let him make you feel meek.

I don't stand up to him because he's the sort of guy to push, and all I want is to keep people out. Kent isn't someone you're able to keep at arm's length. No, he would be all up in my face ... and other areas.

Kent's chest expands as he sucks in a breath. He stills, not letting it out. Watching me with his stunning eyes, he rocks back again. Heidi is oblivious of the battle I'm having with her brother, still looking into the storeroom with a frown. She's probably having one final debate about where things should go. She walks inside and doesn't look back at us.

I take another sip. God knows where I've found the confidence to face Kent, but I don't look away. Partly because

I'm tired of feeling weak and partly because Kent is like gravity. He's the car crash you can't look away from.

Kent lets out a long breath, eyes still staring dead at me.

I sip.

He tilts his head down, glowering. If his eyes shot bullets, I'd be gone.

I take the final sip, stretch my arm out, and let the cup drop into the bin.

Smirking, he drops his arms from his back to his sides. "Done?"

"Ready when you are," I reply, standing tall.

I want to high-five myself for holding my own, but I'm not yet entirely sure I won't faint. That wasn't a good idea.

Kent dips his chin in the direction of the storeroom.

He's letting me go first.

Well, fuck me.

Maybe he just wants to watch me fall over. But I don't. I walk ahead of him with my head held high, like a total boss.

2

Kent

I OFFERED TO PUT this shit together over two weekends, but Heidi was having none of it. She didn't want to come in on her days off, as she's big on downtime to improve productivity. What-fucking-ever.

Never mind that I don't want to be in the same room as Savannah Dean, which is currently where I am.

Heidi was stupid to employ her, only giving her a job because she heard some fucking sob story, no doubt. I'm proud of my sister, but we could keep her business in the family. One of our cousins could be doing what Savannah is doing here.

I ball my hands and breathe deeply.

Savannah bites her lip and gestures to the boxes with her hand. "Where do you want to start?"

Though she's always been boring as hell and a meek pushover, the coffee thing excluded, she is without a shadow of a fucking doubt the hottest thing I have seen in my life. Slim figure with a few curves in the right places, long dark blonde hair—which was almost brown when I saw her in winter, I remember—and big grey eyes that remind me of the sky before a storm. Someone with the personality of a Monday shouldn't look like that.

Heidi keeps telling me to give her a chance, but what's the point? She's not the type of girl I'd hang out with. I prefer someone who wouldn't jump if I called their name. I don't know why, but she seems so emotionless and shady.

"Clear a space, and open the first box, I guess," I reply.

"All right." Spinning, she heads over to the boxes and gets started.

I watch her as we clear a space big enough to put together this massive storage unit. Every move is thought out and precise, but she does almost bump into me a couple of times.

"Sorry," she mutters, shifting around me again.

For fuck's sake, she apologises every time we almost bump into each other. *Almost.* How pathetic is that?

Her arm grazes mine, and I jerk my head back. She spins around, her hair fanning around her back. Shit, her hair smells like coconut.

Abandon ship!

I grit my teeth. Clamping my mouth shut, I haul a large box out of the way and ignore her. She moves over to the other side of the room and keeps her eyes down, seemingly trying not to look at me.

I shove a stack of paperwork in a box half-full of other paperwork. They really need to get a handle on their filing.

Savannah moves materials and boxes of needles and thread out of the storeroom. Her long hair falls in her face as she bends down to pick up a small stack of fashion magazines. I now know how it smells, too.

My dick responds, stirring at the thought of that hair splayed out over my thighs.

Get it together. She probably doesn't even do blow jobs.

I bet her face would turn bright red at the mere mention of sucking a dick.

She picks up a large box, her fingers digging into the bottom. It's probably too much for her to carry. Why she doesn't put it down and leave it for me, I don't know. I fold my arms and watch her shuffle awkwardly to the door in her heels.

Ask for fucking help!

I'm not that much of a dickhead that I wouldn't help her. But, apparently, I'm big enough of a dickhead to watch her struggle with it.

Why doesn't she ask?

She turns to head out the door, and that's when I see it. A roll of fabric sticking a little too far out on the floor. I drop my arms and open my mouth, but before I can move an inch or mutter a word, she's falling.

Fuck.

With a short scream, she hits the floor, face-planting on the box.

"Shit, Savannah!" I shout, sprinting to where she's lying on the floor.

Pushing herself onto her arse, she hisses. "Oh God, my wrist. Jesus, it hurts. I think it's broken."

Well, that's great. She's probably going to sue my sister.

Savannah lifts her wrist with her good hand and winces.

I crouch down, and her grey eyes flick to me. I place my hand under hers, gently touching her slim wrist. "Show me," I urge.

"Why? Do you have medical training I don't know about?" she snaps.

Her words are completely unlike her. I blink, surprised that she's not only said more than a few words to me, but that they're sarcastic words, too. I'm half-impressed, half-turned on.

What the hell has gotten into her? The five or six times I've seen her before, she's been quiet and shy. Does pain make her argumentative? I don't know if she's withdrawn because that's just her or if she's hiding something. I don't like that I can't read her. That's how you get fucked over. I would know.

"Hilarious." I move my hand closer to her. "Now, let me see."

Removing her good arm, she mutters, "Fine. But don't touch it too hard; it's painful."

"Yeah, you went down like a sack of shit there."

"Wow, thanks." She winces.

For a good minute, neither of us speaks. I don't dare look up at her because I have no idea what I'll find. All I know is that I don't like her being in pain ... and I can smell coconut.

"I can't see any visible breaks, but it's starting to swell. We should get it looked at."

Growling, she narrows those pretty eyes. "This is just great. I should have known. Simon can bloody rot. I don't care if he gets eaten—" She clamps her mouth shut, mid-rant. Her pale skin turns pink over her cheeks.

"What are you going on about?" I ask. *Who's Simon?*

Shaking her head, she drops her eyes. "Nothing. Forget it. This really hurts, so I need to get to Accident and Emergency. Can you let Heidi know what's happened, please? I'll be back as soon as I can."

I'm still kneeling on the floor as she gets up. I should move.

"Kent? Hello?"

Snapping back to reality, I leap to my feet. "I'll take you."

"What? No, you don't need to do that. There's a taxi service just down the road."

"I said, I'll fucking take you, Savannah. Do you need anything? A handbag?"

Her slender frame jumps at my volume. She needs to accept help the first damn time and not try arguing against it.

"Yeah, I need my bag," she says, walking out of the room.

This is a bad idea. I should just let her get a taxi.

Jabbing my finger and thumb in my eyes, I groan.

Dropping my arms to my sides, I sigh and follow her out of the room. I should never have agreed to help Heidi.

I grab my keys from Heidi's table, and we head out the door. Savannah pushes it with her good arm. I slam my hand on the door above her, shoving it wide open so that she doesn't have to. Looking up at me through her lashes, she smiles in thanks.

Tapping my fingers against my palm, I ignore her. Or I try to at least. The scent of her hair is still intoxicating. I unlock my car and glance over the road at the café where Heidi is getting more coffee. I can't see her, but we don't have time to go looking. Savannah needs medical attention.

Tugging open the door to my Range Rover, I stand to the side, so Savannah can get in.

Her light eyebrows rise in surprise. "Um, thanks, Kent."

Is it really that surprising that I've opened a door for her again? How low is her opinion of me?

I jog around to the driver's side, get in, and start the engine.

"I should call Heidi and let her know what's going on," she says, digging around in her bag for her phone. She rests her bad arm on her leg, her eyes narrowing slightly through pain.

I speed down the road, eager to get her to the hospital and me away from this whole situation. Next time Heidi asks me for help, I'm going to hire someone for her.

Gripping the steering wheel harder, I listen to Savannah's soft voice as she explains to my sister why we left.

"Honestly, I'm fine, Heidi. I'll be back after I've had it checked."

She wants to go back to work. I'm no doctor, but I'm pretty sure she should rest it for a least a day. The words are on the tip of my tongue before I realise she's nothing to do with me, and I don't care if she goes back to work or fucks off and goes home.

I don't care about Savannah Dean.

"Yeah, I'll let you know as soon as I do. Bye, Heidi." Savannah lowers the phone and cuts the call. Her eyes flick to mine for a nanosecond before she's looking down.

I watch her pull her full bottom lip between her teeth and chew it like it's a piece of fucking steak. She's either in a lot more pain than she's letting me see or my presence makes her more nervous than I first thought.

I'm not a total wanker ... at least, not all the time.

"We're nearly there," I say, giving in to the need to fill the silence and maybe make her more comfortable with being in the car with me.

Her head rises, grey eyes seeking mine, and she gives me a stunning smile. "Yeah. Thanks again for driving me. It's a lot quicker than waiting for a taxi."

"That, and I don't charge as much."

Her eyes widen. "Of course. I'm going to give you money for petrol," she says, flustered as she digs in her bag.

"Whoa, Savannah. Chill. I was kidding." *What the fuck?* "I don't want your money."

She freezes with her hand in her bag. Her face is blank, like she's trying to figure out how to respond.

This is damn painful.

"It was a joke." My eyes widen. "A bad one clearly."

Clearing her throat, she sits back up in the chair. "Right. Sorry. Though I don't mind. You are doing me a favour."

"No money, Savannah."

Fucking hell.

I make a left, and the hospital is just up ahead.

She sighs. "I hope I don't have a long wait. The last time I was here, it took almost three hours to get my foot looked at."

"What did you do to your foot?"

"Dropped a kettle on it. Thankfully, it was filled with cold water, not hot."

"So, you're accident-prone in general."

Tilting her head, she cuts me a look. "I've only had to go to the hospital twice in my whole life. Well, three times after today."

"What was the other trip for?"

Turning away, her shoulders bunching over, she sucks in a breath. Well, I've hit a nerve. She doesn't say a word, but the walls go so high, I'm surprised she hasn't jumped from the car yet.

LIE TO ME

That was weird.

Her body is rigid as she stares out the window, like she's alone in the car. It's still awkward, so thank God we're here. I pull into the car park, and by some miracle, I find a space right away.

The second I stop, she takes off her seat belt. "Thank you for the lift. I appreciate it."

Am I really about to do this? "Look, I'll come in and make sure you're okay."

"You so don't have to do that. I'll be fine from here."

"How will you get back?" I ask.

"A taxi."

"And what if the driver attacks you? How will you properly defend yourself with only one good arm?"

Her lip quirks. "Really, Kent?"

"You never know."

"I think I'll be fine."

My chest burns with ... anger? Annoyance? I'm not sure, but it, she, or the fact that I've not been this attracted to a woman since my ex is pissing me off.

"Savannah, I'm coming."

"All right," she concedes and tugs the door handle with her good hand. I didn't think it would take long for her to back down. "Thanks."

I groan and look up. *What the fuck have I gotten myself into?* I could hardly go back to Heidi's office alone though. She'd have had my balls for leaving Savannah alone at the hospital.

Getting out of the car, I lock the doors and walk around the front where Savannah is waiting. With a little half-smile, she turns and walks toward the Accident and Emergency entrance.

"How's the wrist?" I ask, striding beside her.

She's got a proper march on. She must be in a lot of pain. I have to walk inhumanly fast to keep up.

"It hurts."

The double doors slide open as we approach, and Savannah heads to the reception desk.

The chick behind the desk, probably only a few years older than me, looks at me first. Her eyes linger a little too long.

Just do your job, for fuck's sake. I'll get to you in a minute.

"How can I help you?" she asks.

Savannah clears her throat. "I fell and hurt my wrist."

The woman—Carlin, according to her name badge—is totally my type, but coming on to her in the middle of her shift and in a busy Accident and Emergency room is probably a no-no. Not that I'm not up for the challenge.

"Okay," she says, averting her eyes and finally looking at Savannah. "I'll just need to take a few details."

Usually, I wouldn't let something such as work, public spaces, or human decency get in the way of a shag, and the vibes Carlin is giving me guarantees me naked time, but there's something about having Savannah right here that has me biting my tongue.

I'm supposed to go back and put flat-pack storage systems together for my sister, too. I don't want to let Heidi down; that's what it is.

"Thanks," Savannah says after giving Carlin all the details she requested.

I take one last glance at a missed opportunity and follow Savannah to find a seat.

3

Savannah

I SLUMP DOWN ON a plastic seat and clench my teeth together. *Why am I irritated over Kent and the receptionist making eyes at each other? They can do what they want, right?* I shouldn't care. Well, maybe I'm irritated because I'm the damn patient, and she was more interested in shagging him with her eyes.

Not that I blame her. It's difficult to look away from him.

Kent's gaze follows me as he leans back in his seat. He looks wary, scared of me almost. That makes for a nice change. Though, in reality, he's probably just wishing he were anywhere else.

"You okay?" he asks cautiously, his voice wavering, showing real emotion. In that second at least, he cares if I'm all right or not.

"Yes, I'm fine. You don't have to sit around with me, if you don't want to."

Bugger off, and speak to the woman who would undoubtedly take you into the restroom right now.

His eyebrows knit together. "Did I dream our conversation in the car? I thought we'd established that I was staying."

"We did, but you seem very ... distracted."

"The fuck? We've been in here for three minutes."

I'm acting like a crazy person. *Why does it matter what he does?*

He's staying to give me a lift home, not to hold my damn hand.

My God, today is a bad *day.*

Sighing, I try to get a grip on myself. "Sorry. I'm just in pain, and I don't do pain well."

He folds his arms and kicks his legs out. If someone were walking past, he would trip them. "Don't worry about it. I grew up with two sisters."

My spine instantly straightens. "Meaning?"

"Dramatic," he grunts.

Cheeky bastard.

"My gender has nothing to do with it! I'll tell you what; lay your arm on the floor, I'll stamp on it, and we'll see if it fucking hurts."

His head snaps back in my direction, and his mouth parts. I've shocked him.

I've kind of shocked myself, too.

My heart is thudding away, sending blood pumping through my body so fast, I might faint while sitting down. This is a little more like the old me. The part I actually liked.

He gave me a lift to the hospital, and he's waiting for me so that he can take me home, and all I've done so far is be bitchy. Oops.

"Do you want me to see if they have any pain relief? Or a fucking sedative?" he asks.

Despite myself, I can't stop the burst of laughter that erupts from my mouth. Kent chuckles, too, and shakes his head.

"I apologise for the"—I raise my eyebrow at him—"dramatics."

"That's all right. I understand it's hard to keep a cool head when I'm around. Many women suffer the same."

LIE TO ME

I roll my eyes. "Like the receptionist? And I don't lose my mind around you, Kent; you're not my type."

Actually, that's not the whole truth. Physically, I'm very attracted to him—my pounding heart can attest to that—but he doesn't need to know.

His jaw tightens. "Don't lie to yourself."

How did he ...

"I'm not lying to myself or anyone else. I don't want *any* man." *Ever again.*

His eyes search mine for a second. I don't know what he's looking for, but he clearly doesn't find it because he asks, "Are you a lesbian?"

"Are you for real? If a girl doesn't want you, that makes her gay?"

"You really are dramatic, Savannah. You said you don't want any *man*."

Oh. I blink and desperately rack my brain for something to say to get me out of this. "Well ... no."

"*Well, no?*" he repeats.

He's loving this.

I fidget in my seat. *Where the hell is a nurse?* If it could get me away from Kent and this conversation, I would break my other arm.

"I'm straight."

"What did he do?"

I cut him a look. "What did who do?"

"Your ex."

What did he do? Wow. That's definitely not a conversation for a hospital waiting room. Or anywhere else for that matter.

I shake my head and reply, "He didn't do anything. We just didn't work out. Besides, I've never had a proper relationship before. But with, what, forty percent of marriages ending in divorce and everyone cheating on everyone else nowadays, I think I'll pass."

"So, what's the plan?"

"Career. What's your plan?"

"Same." He grins. "And casual sex."

Of course that's his plan.

"Have you had a relationship before?" I ask. *I'm guessing no.*

"Yes."

Well, damn.

I feel my eyebrows rocket to the top of my forehead. *Way to keep the surprise off your face.* "You have?"

"We were seventeen. She turned out to be a fucking whore." His words are filled with venom, his teeth bared.

She must have done a real number on him.

"Can I ask what happened?"

"No," he replies tightly.

Okay then.

"Savannah Dean?"

I look up to find who called my name. A lady in blue nurse's scrubs looks around the room. Thank God. Standing up, I give her a smile.

"If you'd like to follow me," she says, returning my smile.

I don't look back at Kent because, honestly, the whole conversation since we got here was like a car crash. If he's gone when I get out, I won't be surprised.

I'd give anything to keep my cool around him—he wasn't exactly wrong when he said I couldn't—but apparently, I can't. Like, really can't.

He draws me in, and that's the last thing I need. I want to be in the background, forgettable.

The nurse asks me a series of questions and takes a look at my arm. When she's unable to get a diagnosis, she takes me for an X-ray. After that, I'm led back to the waiting room until a doctor has checked my X-ray.

Kent is sitting in the same seat with his legs kicked out and crossed at the ankles. He's transfixed on something on his phone, and he doesn't see me walking toward him.

Be normal around him.

"Hi," I say.

His eyes flick up. He sits taller and lowers his phone. *Jesus, he's gorgeous.* "How did you get on?"

LIE TO ME

"She's unsure. I had an X-ray and now have to wait for the results."

He dips his head in a nod. "Is it still hurting?"

"Not as much. She rocked and gave me paracetamol." I sit down beside him. "Can we forget earlier? I feel like we continuously get off on the wrong foot, and if we're going to be working in the same place while you put together the storage, we should be civil, right?"

"Sure," he replies. His answer comes a little too quickly, and it's just a touch too snippy.

Translation: I'll tolerate you if I have to.

I guess, after all my crazy toward him, that's probably more than I can ask. Besides, once he's finished helping Heidi, I won't have to see him again—or hopefully, not for a long time. He stops by the studio to see Heidi sometimes, so I'll probably still see him then.

I turn my head away when he raises his hand and falls back into his phone.

I regret taking my book out of my bag last night. I'm going to be bored as hell, sitting beside someone on their phone, until my X-ray hits the top of the pile.

Biting my lip, I tap my feet on the floor as the silence between us seems to take a life of its own. He doesn't seem to be bothered at all. He's perfectly happy to ignore me and play on his phone. I, on the other hand, want to fill the silence with anything. Or run away.

Running sounds like a plan. I'm good at it, too. It's kind of my thing.

After about fourteen hours—okay, twenty minutes—I'm called through by a doctor the height of a mountain. I crane my neck to see him as we walk into a curtained-off room. It's sterile in here, which isn't bad, but the smell stings the back of my throat.

"Okay, Miss Dean, I've reviewed your X-ray, and as you can see here, you have a small hairline fracture in your wrist." He points out the tiny line—thankfully, because I can't see a bloody thing.

Squinting, I lean in and can only just about make out a faint line beside his index finger.

Sitting back, I ask, "What happens now then?"

"You'll need to wear a splint for six weeks. We'll give you an appointment to have it X-rayed again before it can be removed."

He picks up a black splint from the table. It looks like it will span the length of my lower arm. It's going to be a pain, but at least it's not my right hand.

"I'm not going to be able to drive, am I? My car is manual." I won't be able to change gears.

"I'm afraid not. You need to keep this on."

After fitting the splint, the doctor goes on and on about things I can and can't do, and I'm handed a printout of the same information and a box of painkillers to take home.

"Do you have any questions?" he asks.

"No, I'm good. Thank you."

I'm on my feet and walking out of the room the second he nods, dismissing me. The splint on my arm is mega tight, but I suppose it has to hold my bones in one place.

This time, when I walk out into the waiting room, Kent looks up. He's probably done that with everyone who walked out because he is bored and wants to leave. He stands up, his eyes trained on my wrist.

"Is it actually broken?" he asks.

"Small hairline fracture. I have to wear this for six weeks … and I can't drive."

"Sucks. You have family around to help you though, right?"

Has Heidi not told him that I have no family? Or has she, and he's pretending he doesn't know?

"There's just me, but I'll be fine. I don't live too far from work, so I usually walk anyway." I'll bet that it rains for six solid weeks now though.

"Just you?" he whispers.

I know a little about Kent's family from Heidi. There are three siblings, and they're all close, as they are with their parents and the extended family.

Must be nice.

"Yep. It's fine honestly. I'm perfectly happy, being by myself."

That's not a total lie. I'm definitely much better off alone than I was before. Can't say I don't miss having people around, but I like that no one knows my past, and that's how I want to keep it.

"All right. But is there anyone to help while you're getting used to only one hand?"

We start to walk out of the building, and I feel the stress starting to ebb away. I don't like it in there. "I'll be fine. It's my weaker hand anyway, and I'll live off takeaway for a few days until I get more used to it. Ha, there is a plus side to fracturing your wrist."

"Hilarious, Savannah," he says as we walk to his car.

"Thank you again. It is actually nice to have someone here."

"Even me, huh?" He unlocks his car and opens the passenger door for me.

Laughing, I grin at him. "Yeah, even you."

I drop my bag in the footwell and sit down. I'm about to reach across and shut the door when Kent slams it shut. A smile tugs at my lips, but it dies as he gets in the driver's side.

Kent drives us back to the office, and it isn't as uncomfortable as before.

Heidi is on her feet as soon as we walk through the door. "Savannah, are you okay?" Her eyes fall on my wrist. "It's really broken?"

"Fractured."

"A small fracture," Kent adds.

"Let me fracture your wrist, and we'll see how you get on," Heidi says.

"Wow, that's both of you threatening physical harm. I'm going to get on with this unit," he says, heading into the storeroom.

Heidi steps closer. "You should go home and rest."

"I'd rather be here." After visiting the hospital for the first time in thirty-eight months today, I'm definitely not ready to be home alone. "I've taken painkillers anyway, so I'm feeling fine."

"Savannah, I really think you should be home."

"I'd go crazy, sitting indoors, after the weekend. I promise not to do too much, but I can catch up on emails just fine."

Sighing, she chews on her lip, debating on whether to believe I'm all right or make me go home. "Okay, but if your wrist starts hurting, you're out of here."

"Deal."

I'm just not going to tell her if it does. I can't be alone right now. *Who knows if I'd be strong enough to resist the messages from Mum and Simon?* Today is a massive pile of shit, plus the injury, and I don't want to risk letting it all out in a ranty reply.

"Sit down, and I'll make you a cup of tea."

"Mine's a coffee!" Kent shouts from the other room.

Heidi rolls her eyes. "Did he behave himself while you were at the hospital?"

Mostly. It was me who was the idiot. "He was great."

She smiles. "I'll go make that drink."

I sit down and log in to the computer.

In the background, I can hear Kent moving things again. My heart beats a little faster.

4

Kent

SAVANNAH'S ACCIDENT MEANS THAT I'm way behind where I want to be. I planned three days to put the storage together because Heidi had bought so many shelves and different units with stupid smaller shelves and drawers inside them. I'll now be there for a fourth day, possibly fifth, because I no longer have Savannah's help with moving all the shit my sister has from one side of the room to the next.

I called the guys for an emergency night out because I'm in a foul mood, and I know only alcohol and those dickheads will be able to cheer me up.

A woman would usually cut it, but it was a woman who constantly aggravated me all day. After her performance at the hospital, I'm not sure if I still think she's just meek, hiding herself—*but why?*—or if I think she's fucking insane.

She definitely acted insane. We've never spoken much, and she's never snapped back at anyone. Even Heidi says Savannah needs to stick up for herself and not let people walk all over her. This morning, she definitely stuck up for herself, but there was more, and it was weird. So, I need this drink tonight.

Plus, I can still smell coconut.

Fuck coconut.

Toby sits down opposite me at the table and lifts his black eyebrow. Max is with him. They both look at me like they're about to interview me.

"What did she do? I want details," Max says.

"She … I don't even know, man. I don't want to talk about her."

Max chuckles. "Sure, you don't."

Toby picks up one of the three beers I ordered. "So, you broke her wrist, and now, you're pissed at her?"

"I did *not* break her wrist."

He looks at Max. "You said he didn't take the heavy box for her."

Max nods and replies to Toby as if I'm not even here, "That's what he told me."

"Hey!" I snap, and two pairs of eyes flash to me. "I didn't realise the box was *that* heavy, and that wasn't the problem anyway. She tripped."

"Doubt she would have if she hadn't been carrying a heavy box though," Toby says, putting his beer down.

Max shakes his blond head. "I think Kent's here to ease his guilt, and he wants us to do that."

"Will you two fuckers stop talking as if I'm not here? I don't have any guilt over Savannah Dean."

"Huh. That sounds like something a guilty person would say," Max jests.

"Why did I think you two would help?"

Toby chuckles. "How is her wrist?"

"Hairline fracture. She went back to work after, so it can't hurt that bad."

Max snorts. "I have a week off work when I get a cold."

"I doubt Savannah has ever pulled a sickie in her life. She's too good."

"I don't really know what to think about this. Toby, Kent hasn't had women troubles since that bitch, what, six years

LIE TO ME

ago, and now, we're being called to meet for *Monday* night beer over some chick."

"Again, stop with talking like I'm not here, Max. And will you grow a pair over the Monday drinking?"

"Why *did* you call us here?" Toby asks.

"She's just frustrating and infuriating."

"*Ohh*. You like her," Max says.

"No."

That is not the case. I'm not even lying to myself. Savannah might well be the most stunning thing on the planet, but that's it. If I'm ever going to like someone again after the last time, it's going to be someone with personality, who won't randomly snap at me for no apparent reason.

Actually, I don't mind the snapping thing.

Max draws his eyebrows together in a frown. "Are you sure?"

"Really sure." I rub my forehead. "As a rule, I've stayed away from women, you know, besides a shag, since Freya, and today has just reaffirmed how right that decision is. Today just threw me off, spending time with Savannah and generally being pissed off because she's such a pushover."

Toby takes a swig of beer. "Maybe you're just not giving the girl a chance. What's her story?"

Frowning, I reply, "I don't know really. She doesn't have family around; she said it's just her but didn't want to talk about it. I'm not sure of anything; she just doesn't seem herself."

Not that I know who the real her is.

"Well, maybe there's something there," Max says. "You have issues from Freya. Maybe Savannah has issues from her family."

I didn't think of that. "Heidi said Savannah doesn't share much, but she might know a bit."

Toby holds up his beer. "There you go. Ask your sister."

"Hold on. I'm looking her up." Max taps away on his phone.

I lift my eyebrow. "You're social media–stalking her?"

"Don't say that as if the whole world isn't doing it. What's her surname again?"

"Dean."

This feels wrong, but I want to know more.

"Okay, Savannah Dean, let's see what you've got in your closet."

Toby and I watch Max as the seconds stretch on.

"Well?" I ask.

He shows me profile pictures, but I shake my head at each one. None of them is Savannah. We move to Twitter and Instagram but nothing.

"I can't find her on Facebook, Twitter, or Insta." Max looks up. "Something ain't right about her, bro. Where does she live?"

"We're not stalking her for fucking real!" I snap.

Max rolls his eyes. "You're such a fucking pansy."

"Dude, I think that's illegal. Actually, I know it is." Toby rubs the stubble covering his jaw. "Has this girl gotten to you this much?"

I shake my head. "Nah. You know, let's just forget her. She's not important, and after this week, I won't have to see her again."

Max lets go of his phone, and it drops to the table. "So, I'm not stalking her anymore?"

"You weren't doing it before. She's not on social media," I reply. That is weird in itself.

I think the thing that bothers me is, no one really knows much about her, and Heidi trusts her with her business. Our family has been burned before—*fucking Freya*—and Heidi hasn't hesitated in diving in, assuming Savannah isn't going to double-cross her.

"Tell me you guys had a better day than me."

"I had sex with a coworker in the restroom," Max says.

I nod. "The one you've been wanting for a while?"

"No, her friend."

Toby playfully punches Max's arm. "Close enough."

LIE TO ME

I listen to the guys talk about how much of a slut Max is, much more than me and Toby combined, but my mind is still on Savannah. Something is off about her, something I don't trust, and I won't be able to relax until I know my sister's livelihood is safe.

I get to Heidi's office a little after nine in the morning. She's behind her desk, sketching something that looks like a dress or a long top. It's fucking ugly, but it's not really aimed at me.

"Morning," she says, looking up from her work. "There's a coffee on the kitchen counter for you."

"Thanks. Where's Savannah?"

"In the storeroom."

"What's she doing in there? She's only got one good arm."

"Kent, enough. She's not moving anything."

Then, what the fuck is she doing?

Heidi keeps all her accounts and banking information in there.

"Well, what's she doing then?"

Heidi's blue eyes fire daggers. "She's getting the banking together to pay some in cash."

She does that?

"And you check what she's done, right?"

"Kent!"

"What? How much do you really know about her? You have to check that she's doing what she's supposed to."

"Okay, don't tell me how to run my business, and don't assume that Savannah is a bloody thief. I know enough about her, as much as any employer knows about their employee, so back off."

Raising my hands, I take a step back. "All right." *Jesus, what's up her arse?*

I walk around the partition to the kitchenette area and pick up my coffee.

She might think she knows enough about Savannah, but I don't. My gut is telling me that something is wrong with her.

I'm getting Freya vibes from Savannah.

I take my coffee into the storeroom where Savannah is sitting on the floor. She's wearing leggings and a long top with the slogan across her boobs, reading, *#NOPE*.

She's cross-legged with a cardboard box in front of her and papers scattered around. Between her legs is a mug of tea. Looking up, her stormy grey eyes drink me in. She's gorgeous.

"Morning, Kent," she says. Her voice is barely above a whisper, making her sound scared.

"Morning," I grunt.

Does her hair still smell like coconut?

I want to punch myself.

"I'll be out of the way in a minute. I didn't think it would take so long to find the paying-in book for the bank."

"Why is it hidden?"

That's something a business has handy, not chucked in some box.

What's Savannah really up to with my sister's banking documents?

Heidi needs to be more careful with who has access to those.

"It's not usually. Heidi threw it in one of the four accounting boxes last week, but with the reorganisation, she forgot which one."

I grit my teeth. That does sound like Heidi. She's an incredible designer, but when it comes to the business side of things, she's a nightmare. But that doesn't mean that Savannah isn't up to something she shouldn't be.

I don't think she's being true, and I don't like her because she could easily take advantage of Heidi's kindness and scatty approach to business.

Swallowing a sick feeling, I say, "I'll help. It'll be much faster with someone with two hands."

Her full lips curve in a smile. "You know I still have my arm, right?"

I kneel down and put my coffee on the floor. "Which boxes have you been through so far?"

"This is the first. I might still have the arm, but it's slow-going without the use of it."

I lift the lid off the second box. "How is the wrist?"

"Painful. Much more today than yesterday."

"You taking those pain meds the doctor gave you?"

"No, I thought it would be more fun without."

Whoa.

She shakes her head, and her cheeks tint pink, like she's embarrassed by her outburst. "Yes, I take them every four hours."

I find myself grinning despite not wanting to. *Is this who she really is? Is the dull personality an act?* I'm not sure yet. "And I see they've turned you into a comedian. How strong are they?"

"I can't drive on them, but then I can't drive with this either," she replies, raising her injured arm.

"Well, that's what happens when you don't look where you're walking."

Her mouth drops open, but I can tell from the light in her eyes that the action is playful. "I couldn't see over the damn box. I thought the floor was clear."

"It wasn't."

"Yeah, no shit." She dips her stunning eyes and picks up her tea. "How much are you hoping to get done today?"

All of it. I want out of here.

"Not sure. I'm starting with the fucking full-height cupboards first, as they'll take the most time. I should be out of your way by the weekend."

"You're not in my way, Kent. Technically, I am." She gestures to the box and papers over the floor and raises her eyes to me again.

I dig in the box in front of me. "It's fine. You're the one who has a job to do. I'll work around you."

"Ah, here it is," she says, lifting the paying-in book out of the box. She puts it down and brushes her hair off her shoulder, revealing her neck.

Yep, she washed her hair this morning. I clear my throat, my gut tightening.

"I'll just tidy this stuff away and let you get on. I'd offer to help, but I'm not sure how helpful I'd be," she says.

Fire rages in my chest, and my hands clench. "You'd be more of a fucking hindrance than a help anyway. I'll wait outside for you to finish up and leave." Grinding my teeth, I rise to my feet and leave an open-mouthed Savannah frozen on the floor.

Fuck. Fuck it.

5

Savannah

I CAN FEEL MY face burning, and my mind is trying to make sense of what just happened. Only it doesn't make sense. We were fine one second, and the next, he was telling me I was in the way.

Kent is an arsehole, and I shouldn't have ever thought we could be civil. I mean, for the first thirty seconds there, it seemed like we could work alongside each other for this week without another incident but obviously not.

I'm already over trying to be nice to him, and it's only day two.

Scooping the papers with one hand, I shove them back in the box, not caring that I'm moving slow. He can wait. There was no need for him to be such a wanker back there.

But I guess he can't help it.

Very awkwardly—because I'm one-handed here—I manage to get the paperwork away. He's absolutely tripping if he thinks I'm moving them out of the room for him. I no longer feel guilty that Heidi and I didn't manage to get around to clearing the room before he started.

In fact, I feel like messing it up even more. And hiding his tools.

Clutching the banking documents I need against my chest, I head out into the office. I left my empty mug on the floor. Oops.

Kent is standing by the kitchen, drinking. He's leaning against the countertop with his legs crossed at the ankle, like he owns the place. He seems to think that, just because this is his sister's business, he has more right to be here. Or maybe he's just an entitled prick who thinks he owns everything. I don't know what he does for work, but his clothes are nice, and his car is an expensive, new Range Rover, so he must earn a decent amount. Maybe money has ruined him.

I think his family is wealthy. Heidi said they own their own business and have a decent-sized house on a lot of land, but I don't think they're rich enough for him, a grown man, not to have a job.

Anyway, I don't care what he does.

He probably doesn't do anything. I bet he claims money from the government while spending his days stealing sweets from children and pushing over old ladies.

I keep my eyes on my desk as I walk through the main studio. My handbag is on the desk, which has the money inside to be paid, so I focus on getting that and getting out. The air is thick, though I don't think Heidi senses the tense atmosphere. It wouldn't surprise me if Kent didn't either.

He has to know that snapping at me was out of order, right?

Yeah, unlikely.

Heidi looks up and smiles. Her blue eyes are almost identical to Kent's when his look bluer, but hers look at me with kindness, not contempt. "You found it?" she asks.

"Yes. I won't be long."

"Do you want me to write out the paying-in slip?"

I shake my head. "That's okay, thanks. I have to get used to using one hand." My right hand is fine, but I've found it difficult to write without being able to hold the paper still.

LIE TO ME

"I'll drive you," Kent says.

I almost fall over. Like proper drop-to-the-floor falling over. My legs are weak. Twisting around, I gawp at him with my jaw wide open.

Did he forget what he said two minutes ago? Perhaps he's planning on running me over with his car.

"No, that's fine. The bank is only a few minutes away. I always walk." I turn away because I don't want to look at the bastard. Ever again.

"Yeah, but you were told to take it easy and rest your wrist to begin with. I'll walk with you, and I can help if you need it."

"He's right, Savannah," Heidi says, putting her pencil down. "He can help get everything ready or be there just in case you need it. You really can't use that arm at all right now. It's not even been twenty-four hours yet."

"I don't think there will be an issue. The door at the bank is automatic, and I can put my bag down on the counter to get everything out." I can hear the hysteria building in my voice, but Heidi doesn't blink, so thankfully, she doesn't realise how much I bloody do not want Kent with me. I would rather struggle or sit down and use my feet to get the money out of my bag.

"It's really not a problem," Kent adds gruffly.

I can't see his expression because my back is still to him, but I have the distinct feeling that he's smug.

Why does he want to come anyway? Did I dream what happened in the storeroom? No, it definitely happened. I'm not losing it.

"That's settled. And, while you're out, Kent, you can grab me a vanilla latte."

"Do I look like your errand boy?"

She grins. "Yes, you do."

"I've taken time off to do you a favour, you know."

Oh, so he does work. Loan shark? Drug lord? Pimp?

I sling my bag over the shoulder of my good arm and turn to face the prick. "Are we going then? I'm sure you're eager to get on with all your flat pack."

Kent raises his eyebrow. "Ready when you are, Savannah." His voice is overly sweet and quite clearly knobbish.

I really don't care what he thinks of me, but I would rather we didn't bitch at each other in front of Heidi. It could get uncomfortable, considering she's his sister and my employer. I need to keep this job, and she's the only friend I have. Sad but true. I left the old ones behind, and considering it took most them only three weeks to stop trying to reach me, I don't think they were all that cut up about me leaving. Unlike me.

Pressing my lips tightly together, I walk past him and hold my head up. My instincts are still to keep to myself, to look away and not get involved in anything with anyone ever again—whether that involvement would be good or not. Kent is obviously the not.

He is hot on my heels. I hear his long strides thudding on the floor behind me, but I just hope he stays a step back because I don't want to even look at him.

I shove the studio door open, and Kent catches it at the top, but I'm out just as he touches it, so technically, he didn't hold the door for me.

We walk along the path toward the bank, and unfortunately, he doesn't keep his distance.

I wait for the apology he owes me, but there is only silence between us.

"Which bank?" he asks.

"The one up here," I snip back.

"What's up with you?"

Are you fucking kidding me?

My God, he makes me so bloody angry. I curl my fingers around the handle on my handbag. I don't want him to have any power over me. I don't want to let him get to me, and I don't want to argue or snap at him. Nothing he does or says matters to me in the long run.

"Nothing's wrong with me."

He snorts. "Yeah, all right."

LIE TO ME

I might have made the decision to ignore him, but that doesn't mean I can't kill him in my head. I think I'll need to do that regularly if I'm going to survive this week.

Over the last three years, I've kept my emotions in check. There was a massive blowout, and I left home. Since then, I've been in perfect control. I don't want to lose that control again. With Kent, I sometimes feel it slipping, like when he's being a dickhead, so I need to try harder. Letting someone in again, in any respect, leaves me open and vulnerable to being hurt.

I won't let that happen.

Kent sighs beside me, and I'd like to think it's because he's realised he acted like a knob and he feels bad, but I know better. People like him don't care what they do or who they hurt.

As we approach the bank, the door slides open. Even if I need help, I'm not going to ask him. I'd rather struggle. Hell, I'd rather use my fractured arm and end up breaking it fully.

"No queue," Kent muses as we head to the cashier desks.

No shit, Sherlock.

I chew on the inside of my cheek and walk to the nearest available cashier.

The guy at the other side of the glass smiles. "How can I help you today?"

Know a hit man?

Sliding my handbag off my arm, I place it on the desk. "I need to pay some money into a business account, please."

Behind me, far too close behind me, I can hear Kent's breath. He doesn't say anything, but I can feel his intensity. My heart flutters with so much nervousness, I barely make it through a conversation with the cashier.

I clear my throat and take the money and paying-in book out of my bag. It's awkward. As I lift the envelope of money out, the corner catches on the strap. With my splint-covered arm, I steady the bag, so it doesn't fall off.

Kent doesn't say anything or move an inch. He's waiting for me to ask for help.

Unlikely.

I unhook the envelope, and it almost drops. Slamming my body against the low wall, I trap the envelope before it falls and grab it. Raising my eyes, I push it through the opening at the bottom of the glass with the paying-in book.

See, no help needed. I might have looked like someone trying to escape from a paper bag, but I did it alone.

I turn my head a fraction to the side, so he can see my triumphant smile and know he's completely redundant here. The cashier taps away on his computer. I watch him work, pretending to ignore Kent when he's fucking everywhere.

Sliding the paying-in book back under the glass, he asks, "Is that all today?"

I snatch the book up and shove it in my bag. "Yes, thank you." Slinging the bag on my shoulder, I turn around and stalk out of the bank.

Kent catches up with me. "You did well." His voice is soft almost. And that touches a nerve. Actually, it jumps all over every one of my nerves, does a dance, and then spits on them.

The patronising little wanker.

I step back onto the street, seething. My hands twitch, causing my fractured arm to throb. The pain is welcome; it adds to my anger, ensuring I won't cave and forgive him.

You did well. What am I, six?

Control yourself.

With every ounce of anger I have building inside, coursing through my veins, I imagine him getting run over by passing vehicles.

Of course, I wouldn't actually wish death upon him, but it wouldn't suck if he were in pain right now.

My blood is boiling, and I feel like crap for keeping my mouth closed. But I know I will feel worse if I snap back. I've gone through too much to have Kent screw it up. It's Tuesday, and he wants to be done by the end of the week. I have to put up with him for only three more days at the most. I can do that.

LIE TO ME

Just kill him in your head. Stab, stab, stab.

Kent's pace slows until I can no longer see him in the corner of my eye. That's just fine with me. I grip the handle of my bag and push my legs faster, eager to get back to the studio where Kent will go into the storeroom.

How is Heidi so nice, and Kent is so … not? They have the same parents, same upbringing.

I guess he was born an arsehole.

Kent stops briefly to get coffee. I decline because he won't take money from me, and I don't want to owe him anything.

We approach the office, and Kent catches up with me. His posture visibly relaxes, and I realise what that was about. He came with me because he didn't trust me with Heidi's money.

Of course that's it. He couldn't care less if I was struggling or not. He just wanted to make sure I didn't pocket some cash.

I press my hand to the burning in my stomach and blink fast. *Do not cry.*

Kent means nothing to me, he's a bastard, and I'm quickly growing to hate him, but the thought of not being trusted with my employer's money—hell, anyone's money—makes me feel like shit.

I'm not a thief.

Why would I steal from someone who's given me a job, someone who helped me find another apartment I could afford, someone who has been my only friend and doesn't push the things I don't want to talk about? I wouldn't.

I shove the studio door open, eager to get away from Kent and calm my frayed nerves. Heidi doesn't look up from her sketch as we walk back into the office. When she's really into a design, she probably wouldn't notice a bomb going off.

I put my bag on my desk and take the paying-in book out, much more successfully than I did in the bank. Kent stops by my table and takes a deep breath. I'd love to know what's going through his mind right now.

Is he telling himself to play nice?

"I can take the book and put it away," he says. His voice is low, and he kind of sounds like a kid who's been forced to be kind by his parent.

"Thanks," I say, but in my head, I'm screaming, *Fuck off.*

"Knock, knock!"

I turn toward the voice. I've not met Kent and Heidi's sister, Brooke, but if this isn't her, then someone has cloned Heidi. The only difference is, Heidi's dark hair is longer.

"What're you doing here, Brooke?" Kent asks.

Heidi is still completely absorbed in her design, but she does acknowledge her sister's presence with a quick raise of her eyebrow.

"Wow. Hi to you, too." She rolls her eyes. "I wanted to see how Heidi was getting on with my wedding dress. You must be Savannah. It's lovely to finally meet you. I hope your arm is okay," she says, walking past her idiot brother and holding her hand out.

I shake her hand. "Good to meet you, too. It is, thanks. Your dress is almost finished, and it looks amazing."

Heidi finally looks up, her pencil suspended midair in her hand. She smirks at her sister before regarding me. "Savannah, can you help Brooke into it? I'll be with you both in a minute when I've finished this."

Brooke beams at me and claps her hands together. "Let's get me in it!"

Kent wrinkles his nose and walks into the storeroom.

Good.

"Sure, follow me."

Through a door next to the storeroom is a larger space with a sofa, table, and curtained area. It's where Heidi takes the few clients she's done bespoke work for. One of the long sidewalls is also where we have the photographs of the clothes taken.

"How do you like working for Heidi?" Brooke asks.

"I love it. I love clothes." I walk to the end of the room and swing the curtain open.

LIE TO ME

Hanging up on the hook on the wall is Brooke's dress. Heidi usually takes it to Brooke's house for fittings, but I guess Brooke couldn't wait.

Brooke gasps. "God, it gets better each time I see it."

The dress is made of lace with a short train and sweetheart neckline. At first, I thought it might be lace overload, but it's not. It's gorgeous.

"I think so, too. Heidi is a genius."

"She sure is. Though, growing up, she was proper annoying."

I laugh as I carefully take the dress off the hanger, one-handed. "You're the eldest, right?"

"Yeah. I hated them both growing up. Heidi was my shadow, trying to do everything I did, and Kent did everything he could to aggravate me."

He's not changed.

I lift my eyebrow and hand her the dress.

She tilts her head. "He's not that bad anymore, I swear. Not when you get to know him and realise why he's so ... intense."

Not exactly the word I would have used right now. But, I'm intrigued.

"Something happened to him?"

Her lips purse. "Let's just say, he didn't always expect the worst in people."

I nod because it's clear she's not going to spill his secrets, and I don't want to pry. Even though I totally want to pry.

What happened to make him so sceptical of people?

"Do you need help with the dress?"

"I can get into it, but would you mind buttoning the back ... if you can?"

"Of course. I can button one-handed," I reply as I step back and close the curtain.

I walk to the other side of the room and take a seat as Brooke gets changed. My mind is whirling with Kent theories. He must have been hurt by someone. Cheated on maybe? Clearly, his trust in anyone is gone.

It's hard to have sympathy for him when I don't know what happened, and he's done nothing since after we got back from the hospital but be horrible.

Still, it's a shame he's turned so bitter.

I know something about having your life, your personality, your whole soul changed because of an event outside of your control.

Don't go soft on him. He's still a dick.

He might have been hurt by something so bad, it transformed him, but that doesn't mean he has to be nasty. I choose not to take out my past on the people around me.

So, yeah, he's still on my shit list.

The curtain slides open, and Brooke steps out, beaming with happiness. Her eyes, a little greener than Kent's, shine.

"Wow, you look incredible," I say, rising to my feet.

I walk over to her, and she turns.

"Thank you," she replies as I start to button up the back of the dress.

I've gotten used to buttoning one-handed after working for Heidi. There have been plenty of times where I've had to do something up while holding pins or fabric.

"Your fiancé is going to lose it when he sees you."

She laughs. "I hope so!"

"When is the wedding?"

"Just over two months away, mid-September."

"Is everything ready?"

"Pretty much. Just the dress now, and it's almost there."

"It looks like it fits perfectly. I don't think Heidi will have to make any more adjustments."

Brooke looks over her shoulder and gives me the biggest smile. "I can't wait to wear this all day."

I can't imagine getting excited over marriage. But then Simon royally fucked up romance for me. I wouldn't know where to start with trusting another man with my heart again. Not that I even want to yet.

"I'm sure it will be perfect."

"Oh, it'd better be."

LIE TO ME

I finish the last button and drop my hand. "There, all done."

"Thank you."

"Heidi, Brooke's in the dress," I call out.

Heidi pushes the door open and presses her hand to her heart. "You look more stunning in that each time you put it on."

"What's the dress like then?" Kent says as he walks into the room, too.

I'm not sure if he's meant to be in here, but obviously, he doesn't care about that.

Ignoring him is annoyingly impossible as I witness the pride in his eyes at seeing his big sister in her wedding dress.

At least that shows he's not totally dead inside.

Not like me.

"Brooke, you look beautiful," Kent says, smiling at her.

It's the first time I've seen a softer side to him. Even when he took me to the hospital, he was less than warm and fluffy. It makes him more attractive.

"Thank you. Okay, I need to get this off and go meet Freddy. I'll see you both tonight, yes?"

Kent and Heidi both nod.

Brooke gasps and turns to me. "You should come, too. We're having dinner with our parents and Freddy's brother, and I'd love for you to join us."

"Oh no, that's fine honestly. You don't need to invite me along." My face heats. *Oh God, I don't want a pity invite.*

"No, I want you there. Please, Savannah," she begs, placing her palms together.

I open my mouth to protest when Heidi cuts in, "She'll be there. I'll make sure of it."

I grit my teeth and force a smile.

Brooke squeals, "Great."

Yeah, great.

6

Kent

BROOKE LEAVES ON A high, like she's not just fucked me over. It's bad enough that I have to see Savannah every day this week, but now, I have to spend the evening with her, too. I can't keep my cool with her, and it's doing my head in.

Max and Toby would love this.

I'm back in the storeroom, unpacking yet another box of fucking flat-pack crap. In the studio, I can hear Heidi and Savannah talking. I can't quite make out what they're saying, but I think Heidi is telling Savannah that it's fine she comes tonight.

Why she doesn't think it's fine after being invited, I'll never fucking know.

Something isn't right with her. After Freya, who I didn't see through until it was too late, I'm always on high alert.

"Kent, do you want a coffee?" Savannah asks.

I look up from the pile of cardboard. She's holding on to the doorframe, peering around the corner. Her dark blonde hair is around her face, falling halfway down past her breasts.

Gulping, I reply, "Please."

She disappears, and I sit back on the floor.

Why does she wind me up so much?

She's nothing to me; I barely know the woman, but every time I see her, I want to punch something. And I want to tangle my hands up in all that hair.

Gripping the corner of a box, I rip it open and grind my teeth. I need a drink. Tonight, I will definitely need to drink. A lot.

Savannah comes back in a few minutes later as I'm laying out the wood planks on the floor. She puts my coffee down on one of the shelves I've already put up.

"Ha, it's holding," she teases.

Her comment, giving me a glimpse of a personality again, makes me smile. "Of course it's holding. I'm basically a carpenter now."

"I'm not sure flat pack qualifies as carpentry."

"I think you're wrong."

She tilts her head, and her hair falls to the side. "Don't add carpentry to your CV, Kent."

When she's like this, I can totally get on board.

"I don't need a CV."

"You work for yourself?" Her voice is higher than usual, portraying her surprise. I'm not sure how to take that.

"I don't like people telling me what to do."

The soft sound of her laughter fills the room.

Wow, she laughs.

"Neither do I. Thankfully, Heidi isn't super bossy."

She takes a breath, and her eyes meet mine. For a second, my heart stops.

Savannah shakes her head. "Anyway, I need to get on."

"Okay …"

Did something just happen there?

It was almost like she realised we were having a civilised conversation, so she bailed. Or maybe I'm reading the situation wrong, and she just has work to do. Either way, I suppose I don't really care.

LIE TO ME

I arrive at the restaurant after receiving a text from my mum. She and Dad are waiting at Brooke and Freddy's because Brooke is still getting ready, so they're going to be late. The only person sitting at the table we reserved is Freddy's brother, Bobby. I don't like him.

Bobby looks up and raises his hand. I give him a smile, pissed off at myself for not pretending like I didn't see him and heading to the bar.

I slowly walk over. *Where the fuck is Heidi?* Hell, even Savannah would do at this point.

"Hey, Kent," Bobby says, adjusting the black cap on his head. His clothes are about three sizes too big, making him look like a lanky prick.

I dip my head and take a seat on the other side of the table, a couple down from him. "Bobby, how's it going?"

"Not bad, brother. Parents are still on me to get a job."

You're twenty-two. You should have a fucking job!

My parents are paying for dinner tonight, which is the only reason this leech is here.

I grin at him, seething inside. I fucking hate people who sponge off my relatives.

Bobby's eyes light up, staring at someone behind me. "Dude, what I would give for a night with that."

My heart sinks. *Don't be her. Don't be her.* I crane my neck over my shoulder.

Savannah. Of course it is.

She looks around the room and then settles on me.

"You know her, man?" Bobby asks as Savannah makes her way over.

I turn back around. "She works for my sister."

Savannah stops at the table, and I stand up.

"All right?" I ask, ignoring my dick's reaction to the fitted black dress she has on.

"Yes, thanks. You?"

My eyes drop to the hint of cleavage. *Why does her body have to be so ... perfect?*

When I pull myself together and look up, her cheeks are pink. She purses her lips, looking away.

This is getting weird.

I tug the chair out next to mine and nod toward it with my chin.

"Thanks," Savannah whispers and sits down.

It's only when I drop back to my seat that I realise I've made her sit next to me. Bobby's mouth is wide in a huge grin. He slips into the chair beside his, so he's opposite Savannah.

Reaching across the table, he says, "I'm Bobby, Freddy's brother."

Savannah looks up, blinking in surprise that someone else is there. My traitor of a chest aches at the thought of her only seeing me.

I swallow sand. *What is going on here, and where the hell is the server?* I need something strong to drink.

"Hi, I'm Savannah," she replies, shaking his outstretched hand. She retracts her hand and looks at me. "Are we early, or are the others late?"

"Brooke isn't ready, so my parents will be late with her. I've not heard from Heidi, but she's never on time. I thought you would have come with her."

"She offered, but she would have to come past the restaurant to get to mine, so it seemed stupid. I took a taxi."

"You're drinking tonight, Savannah?" Bobby asks, gaining her attention again.

"I'll have a couple, but I can't drive anyway."

Bobby's eyes fall on her arm covered by the splint. "What happened to your arm?"

"Tripped and fell."

I don't like the way Bobby looks at her, like she's a meal. Cracking my knuckles under the table, I clear my throat. Thankfully, the waitress stops by our table and takes our drink order. We get single drinks and two bottles of red wine for the table, as that's all my parents, Brooke, and Freddy will drink.

LIE TO ME

Savannah surprised me by going for a gin-based cocktail. I thought she would drink pissy white wine or something with bubbles.

Should she even be drinking at all while on her painkillers?

Bobby ordered the same beer as me, which annoys me more than it should.

Savannah reaches into her bag and pulls out her pain medication from the doctor at the hospital.

Lifting my eyebrow at her, I ask the obvious, "Should you take those with alcohol?"

She purses her lips again and turns the bottle around to read the instructions stuck to the side. "I'm not sure. I don't think they're particularly strong though."

"You can't get them over the counter, so I think they're strong enough that you shouldn't drink on them."

Her lip pulls to the side in a smirk. "You sound like a dad."

A dad? Weird of her to say a *dad and not* my *dad. Her family isn't around, I know that much, but what happened to her dad?*

She grips the bottle and pops the lid open with her thumb. If I'd done that, they probably would have flown everywhere. She's adjusted to using only one arm well.

The waitress puts our drinks down on the table, and Savannah eyes her cocktail. She chucks two pills into her mouth and takes a long sip of her drink.

That's excellent self-care there. Take the pain meds with alcohol. I'd probably do it, too, but it does annoy me.

"Ah, Heidi is here," Bobby says, lifting his eyes above my head to my sister.

Savannah's shoulders relax, and she turns her head. She's relieved to have someone else here. Can't say I blame her. She's not my biggest fan, and Bobby constantly looks like he wants to attack her.

I'm not entirely convinced he wouldn't either.

Savannah stands and hugs Heidi.

"You good?" my sister asks her, and Savannah nods. "Sorry I'm late. Traffic was bad."

She takes a seat next to Savannah. I watch them talk. Savannah is so much more comfortable around Heidi; her posture is relaxed, and she's more animated. She's almost normal. But that's probably because Heidi's a woman, and Savannah popped pills with booze.

I look over to Bobby, who's still staring at her.

"Mate, you good?" I say, lifting an eyebrow.

If he's trying to flirt with her, he needs to step it up. Right now, he looks like he'd be waiting for her down a dark alleyway.

Bobby shifts his eyes to me. "I'm fine. So, Savannah, how is working in the fashion industry?"

"It's great, thanks. I love it. What do you do, Bobby?"

I smirk.

"I'm looking for the right gig. I want a career, not a job."

Savannah nods and presses her lips together. She knows what that means, too. She knows he's a lazy shit, waiting for the perfect job to fall in his lap. News flash: it ain't gonna happen.

She brushes her hair over her shoulder, and a blast of coconut almost knocks me off my chair. I ball my hands.

"Right. So, what do you do all day?" she asks him.

When I recover from the hair incident, I snort at her sarcastic comment laced with judgment that she asked so innocently.

"I live with my parents."

"Oh," Savannah replies, not mentioning the fact that he answered a completely different question to the one asked. "Well, I hope you find something soon." She doesn't elaborate, but I can almost hear her mind shouting, *For your parents' sake.*

"Thanks. Good thing I'm single, right?" He kicks his eyebrows up.

I'm not sure if he's dissing himself or trying to tell her that he doesn't have a girlfriend. Either way, I don't think she's going to be impressed by him.

Not that I know what kind of guys she's into.

He's clearly into her.

She wouldn't go for someone like him though.

I look between them. She doesn't seem interested.

Not that I give a fuck.

"Ah, here's the happy couple," Bobby says.

We all get to our feet, besides Bobby, and greet my parents, my sister, and her fiancé.

My mum instantly makes a beeline for Savannah. Heidi has friends, but she's never been close to anyone or had a best friend; she's always been too into her clothes designs and researching how to make it as a fashion designer. She talks about Savannah a lot, so my mum is over the moon that Heidi has a girlfriend to talk to.

"It's lovely to meet you, darling," Mum says to Savannah.

"You, too, Mrs Lawson," Savannah replies.

I wince.

"Mrs Lawson is my mother-in-law." Mum rolls her eyes. "Please call me Judy. So, Heidi tells me you're doing fantastic at the studio."

"I'm glad. I really love working there."

"You girls need to get out more though. Heidi never goes out."

"Mum!" Heidi groans from beside Savannah.

"Oh, don't *Mum* me. You're only twenty-eight. You should be out in the evenings, looking for Mr Right. When dinner is over, you girls should hit a club."

Growing up, Mum and her best friend, who is still her best friend, would go out almost every evening. They still go out a couple of times a month.

I agree that Heidi should do more than work, but I'm sure as hell not encouraging her to go out and meet lots of random men.

We take our seats again. Mum boots Bobby out of his seat, so she's now opposite Savannah, much to Bobby's disgust.

"What about that club that just opened on the corner, opposite Nandos? Junction, I think it's called."

"Judy, will you give them a break?" Dad says.

"That's what I'm trying to do, Harrold. Look at your menu, and stay out of women's talk."

Dad shakes his head, discouraged, but he still grins. He knows what Mum is like—fucking interfering. Though I enjoy it when it's not my life she's meddling in.

"Maybe we'll do that, Mum," Heidi says through gritted teeth to appease our mum.

"Are you single, Savannah?" Mum asks.

Savannah freezes, cocktail glass to her lips. She blinks, swallows, and then lowers the glass. "Yes, I'm single."

"Mum, relax," I say, picking up my beer.

"Relax? Why are you telling me to relax, Kent? I am relaxed. I just want to get to know the beautiful girl sitting next to *you* a bit better."

I grip the neck of the bottle harder. It's fun when Mum is doing this to my sisters but less so when it's to a practical stranger. Besides, I didn't like the look in her eye when she asked Savannah if she had a boyfriend or the emphasis on "you" when speaking to me. She has a plan, and I have a feeling it's not one I'll enjoy.

The fact that Savannah is still here is a miracle.

Shifting in her seat, Savannah takes another sip of her drink, a longer one this time.

"You okay?" I ask her when Mum's attention is taken by Brooke.

I'm leaning closer, and I instantly regret it. *Why does she smell so good?*

"Er, I think so."

Heidi leans over Savannah's shoulder. "Sorry, she's crazy."

Savannah turns back to my sister, and it's only then that I realise how much she turned toward me, too. Her whole body was practically facing straight on.

"No, she's sweet. It's nice that she cares so much about you."

Did Savannah's mum stop caring about her?

LIE TO ME

Heidi's eyes widen, but she laughs. "I suppose she means well. Are you up for getting wasted here tonight? I think I'm going to need to."

Savannah laughs, tilting her head to the side. She holds up her cocktail. "I'm definitely up for that." Twisting back, she adds, "Kent, are you getting drunk with us?" Her mouth snaps shut, and she goes statue-still, like she's just realised that she basically asked *me* to get drunk with her.

I swallow.

Her stormy grey eyes stare back at me.

"Sure," I breathe, somehow finding myself agreeing.

"You three are going out?" Mum says.

I jump, startled, and my gaze snaps away from Savannah.

"No, we're staying here longer." I clear my throat since it feels like I swallowed concrete. "When I take my sister to a club to meet strangers, I won't be drunk. I need to make sure they're not dickheads."

"Language," Brooke sings, smirking at me.

She looks between me and Savannah with a look she got straight from Mum. They both look happy. Mum is beaming, her eyes wide and fucking glowing.

I turn away from them all.

Nope. Not *happening.*

7

Savannah

WHAT IS GOING ON tonight?

Between Heidi's no-boundaries mother and a couple of moments—or what I perceive as moments—with Kent, I'm ready to run away. There have definitely been some looks between us; I'm not imagining that.

Judy keeps the cocktails coming though, which I'm extremely grateful for, as she has absolutely no problem with asking personal questions. I don't know how long I can be around her because I have no clue how I will handle it if she asks questions I can't answer. Some things that happen in life are too much to bear. Some people can work through any obstacle or heartache and come out stronger, but for others, all you can do to keep breathing is pretend.

I'm counting on Heidi or Kent to stop her when she asks something I sure as hell won't be answering. So far, she's not touched on my family. No one knows the truth. They all think I'm just not close with my parents and that I cut them out of my life.

It's not a total lie. They don't know I have a sibling, grandparents, and an aunt and uncle. Hell, they think I've only ever dated once. I've had a very serious relationship.

Just the one. Never again.

I glance at the kitchen door on the far wall. *Come on, bring our damn food. How long have we been here? We put our food order in about twenty minutes ago. It must be coming soon.*

Kent has been weird with me since our most recent moment. I don't think anything would have happened if we hadn't been interrupted, but I can't be sure. He jumped away from me, and since then, all I can see of him is his shoulder and the back of his head. He's deep in conversation with Freddy.

Though I have a feeling, the football conversation Kent initiated is a smoke screen. He's worried his mum will pick up on what happened. I saw her delighted expression though. Thankfully and probably by some miracle, she hasn't made a comment.

I won't relax until we're out of here though.

"You seem tense," Heidi whispers as she leans in.

She's perceptive.

Giving her a fleeting smile, I grab my cocktail. "I'm fine. Just hungry."

And waiting for your mum's questions makes me anxious as hell.

If I refuse to answer, they'll know something is up.

"Yeah, the food doesn't usually take this long to come out here."

Great.

In front of us, Bobby stretches his arms over his head. "So, ladies, is it invite-only to drinks after dinner?"

I stiffen. The guy is a lazy creep, and he keeps staring at me, so I have no desire to spend any time around him when he's drunk.

Yes. Heidi, please say it's invite-only!

Kent bumps into my arm as he straightens up, and out of the corner of my eye, I see him turn our way.

"Nah, you can join us, bro," he replies. His mouth tightens as he glances at me, like he knows how awkward I feel around Bobby.

Did he do that on purpose?

Why would he? I mean, he's not my number one fan, but surely, he wouldn't be that spiteful. As if anything he does or says still surprises me. He blows hot and cold constantly.

"Ace!" Bobby cheers, his eyes landing on me as he dips his chin. I think he's supposed to look seductive, but he looks psychotic.

Yeah. Ace.

Heidi strikes up a conversation with Bobby, so I turn to the devil himself.

"What was that?" I hiss.

God, he makes confrontation, something I usually hate, so bloody easy.

"It's not a private party, Savannah."

"I know that, but I've seen you press your lips together so that you won't react to him. Why would you want to spend more time with him? Unless it's because you know I don't want to."

His eyes darken. "Oh, it's all about you, isn't it?"

"I never said that."

"Get over yourself, Savannah," he snaps. His voice is quiet, but there's no mistaking the malice.

"Whatever," I mutter, shaking my head and turning away from him. I rub my forehead, relieving the tension.

Is there something wrong with Kent to make him so back and forth? If there were, Heidi probably would have mentioned it, so Kent wouldn't seem so cold and, well, dead inside.

"How long have you lived this way, Savannah? You're not from around here originally, are you?" Judy asks.

I lick my lips. "About three years. I love it here. This city is quite small, but there's so much going on."

Judy shakes her head. "Heidi and Kent love the city, too. We're just outside, where there's a hell of a lot more greenery."

"Heidi said your place is amazing. Is it on a farm?"

"Not quite. We just have a lot of land. No animals. I'm not an animal person. You must come next week for dinner."

Beside me, Kent freezes.

He doesn't want me to go, so against my better judgment, I find myself nodding. "I would *really* like that."

To be honest, it is nice, spending more time with Heidi and her family, besides Kent. As long as her mum doesn't push, I'm more than happy to be alone less often.

I'm not too ashamed to admit that I miss having people around. Not necessarily my family—they suck—but I've missed the family dynamic. It's nice to see even if it does make me long for it.

Again, not the ones I was born to.

"Great!" Judy claps her hands together. "Kent lives closer to you, so he can drive you."

I grit my teeth and smile at her. I'm not going to get into it with her, but I'm definitely getting a taxi.

"I don't know if I'm coming yet, Mum," Kent says.

I bloody bet his sudden indecisiveness is a direct result of his mum inviting me.

Arsehole.

Judy's lips purse, and her eyes tighten. It's the look my mum used to give me and my sister when we did something wrong in public. It's the substitute-for-yelling look.

Kent grinds his teeth but makes the intelligent decision not to bite back to his mum. It's a bit strange, seeing his interaction with his mum. Before I met her, I would never think there was a person in this world who could make him back down.

She's great.

After eating, we order more drinks, two each actually, and I sip my fifth—I think it's the fifth—cocktail as the atmosphere around me warms and turns kind of fluffy.

Yes, everything is fluffy.

Heidi is hilarious, more so after many of the fruity pink drinks like the one I have in my hand.

LIE TO ME

Kent is sitting a bit closer than usual. He's angled his body toward me, and I can smell his aftershave. It's very nice, very manly, and kind of going to my head more than the alcohol.

Brooke and Freddy are currently arguing over whether they should feed each other cake at their reception or not. Judy, Harrold, and Heidi get involved, but Kent and I stay out of it.

"What would you do?" I ask Kent, tilting my head to the side.

He shrugs. "Eat the cake."

"Right! I personally don't see how anyone wouldn't want to be fed cake."

Chuckling, he necks a long swig of beer, his forehead creasing, almost like he doesn't want to be laughing with me. We're getting on—at this particular second—and I don't know if I'm just paranoid, but it seems almost like he feels like we shouldn't.

Or maybe I just need more to drink.

"You don't look like you love cake."

"What's that supposed to mean?"

His eyes rake over my body, lingering on my breasts.

Well, the cake isn't going to go to them!

"Hey!" I snap, clicking my fingers in front of him.

With a smirk, he looks up. "Apologies." He doesn't look sorry.

"These are really good," I say, holding up my drink.

"I can tell. How are you getting home?"

"Uber."

"You're going to Uber drunk?"

"Yeah. Why not?"

"You know that Uber is just people off the street, right? I could sign up," he says.

"Yes, but you're not people off the street."

He rolls his eyes. "My point, Savannah, is that someone could take advantage of you."

"Someone could do that when I'm sober, too."

"Okay, we'll Uber together and drop you off first."

"Didn't you drive? You can't drive now. You've had a lot to drink."

"I took a taxi. In fact, we'll take a taxi."

I raise my eyebrows. "Yeah." I giggle. "I want to Uber. That's a funny word."

"Definitely not going home alone," he mutters, shaking his head but grinning.

I take another sip and smile. He smells good. And his eyes are nice; they're bluer today. I like them bluer. And greener.

Work is hell. Drinking is hell. Well, the morning after drinking is hell.

Staying after dinner to drink was a stupid idea. It's nine in the morning, but it feels like the middle of the night, like I should have at least another thirteen hours to sleep.

This morning, I feel like I shouldn't have stayed out last night. *What was I thinking?*

I used to be able to go out and drink way more than I did, and I would be fine. In the last few years, I've only had wine and gin occasionally in the evenings, so I've not been drunk.

Jesus, I'm seriously out of practice because my head feels like someone has a mallet smashing around in there.

Groaning, I rub my temples as Kent crashes around in the storeroom. He's doing it on purpose because both Heidi and I are dying. He can hold his drink.

"I'm going to kill him," Heidi mutters, laying her head on her desk. She wraps her arms around her head and adds, "I'm going to get his drill and shove it through his chest."

Okay, maybe I do hungover a little better than her.

"He hasn't been this loud before, has he?" I ask just as Kent walks into the main studio.

"Suffering, Savannah?" He looks up and sees Heidi. "Oh, come on, not you, too."

LIE TO ME

"Go away," she mutters. "Better still, make coffee, and then go away."

"Strong black coffee," I say.

Kent rolls his beautiful turquoise eyes. With the grey on his top, his eyes are definitely leaning more toward blue today. "You two should be ashamed. You're in your twenties."

"Savannah's worse. She's only twenty-two, and I'm twenty-eight."

"You need more practice. Want to come out tomorrow night?" he asks.

"No," Heidi and I reply simultaneously.

My heart races at his offer, but right this second, I genuinely do not ever want to leave my apartment again. I wasn't at all prepared for a hangover. Sometimes, I've woken with a dry mouth and dull headache before but nothing like this. *How do hungover-prone people do this every week?*

"You know you're doing your twenties wrong, don't you?"

I lift my eyes to his, wincing as the bright spotlights above me burn my eyes. "How should we be doing it?"

"You should be going out more than you're staying in."

"Okay, so we're doing it wrong," I say, turning to Heidi. "Not that I care."

"You're a real ray of sunshine, aren't you?" Kent says. His voice is light but holds a little tightness.

It's hard to tell if he's teasing, but I think he is. Right now, I care even less than usual about what he thinks of me.

"I'm hungover. There will be no sunshine today."

He laughs. "You should change that."

I can't say I don't agree with him. There is so much I should do, so much work I have to do on myself so that I can be somewhat proud of the person I am, but I don't know where to start. Adding light to a shadow just makes it disappear.

It's been hard enough, picking myself off the floor and building a new life from nothing, let alone holding on to the happy-go-lucky person I once was.

"I agree; we should do it more often," Heidi replies. "But I need to recover first. I don't want to even think about alcohol for a couple of days." She stands up. "I should get to this meeting with the landlord. Fingers crossed, he doesn't raise the rent ... or I don't throw up in his face."

She grabs her bag and heads out. Then, I'm alone with Kent.

"Did you want that coffee?" he asks. "I'm making."

What? "Er, yeah. Thanks."

"Why are you surprised by that?"

I clear my throat and get to my feet. "Well, you're hardly full of sunshine either."

"I am a fucking delight," he replies.

He tries to be serious, but his lips kick at the sides. It makes me smile, too.

Laughing, I grab my empty mug from the desk. "Oh, yeah."

Kent follows me around the wall into the kitchen area. I fill the kettle, and he grabs himself a mug from the cupboard. He seems to know his way around here, making himself at home.

"So, what do you do? You know, when you're not building storage units for your sister."

"Software," he replies, too busy messing around with coffee and sugar to give me more information than that.

"Okay," I mutter. "Do you like what you do?"

"Sure."

I fold my arms and turn to him. "Do you think I should take my top off?"

His hand freezes midair as he was about to pour a spoonful of coffee into my mug. Beautiful eyes peer over at me. "You think I wasn't listening?"

"Well, you were only giving bored, one-worded replies."

"You were asking *boring* questions."

"Fine," I huff. "What age were you when you lost your virginity?" My eyes widen the second the words escape my lips. *Did I actually ask that? What the hell business is it of mine how old he was when he first had sex?*

Kent's eyebrow lifts. "Much better, Savannah. I was fifteen. How old were you?"

"Fifteen," I reply.

I had been with Simon for eight months, and it was about two months before my sixteenth. We were going to wait, but ... well, things happened. At the time, I didn't regret it, but boy, do I now.

"Really?" His voice picks up, portraying his surprise.

"Yes, really."

"Did you come?"

"What the hell, Kent?" I gasp.

Who asks that question? It's private, and the very fact that he asked shows how arrogant he is.

Chuckling, he leans against the counter and crosses his arms. "We're asking interesting questions, remember? Not many women come the first time."

"I don't think you understand the definition of *interesting*."

"I do, and I also know it's subjective."

Jesus, arguing with him is exhausting.

"Did you come, Savannah?"

My cheeks prickle with heat. "No," I admit. *And I didn't come the next three thousand times we had sex either.*

Simon wasn't bad in bed. I always had a good time, but I needed a little more to get me off. I'm not sure why that's any of Kent's business though.

"I would have made you come."

Rolling my eyes, I drop my arms and pour water from the kettle into our mugs. "Of course you would have."

"You disbelieve me?"

"I so don't want to go down this road. It doesn't matter because, one, I can't get my virginity back, and, two, I'm not going to sleep with you."

"Don't be so sure, sweetheart."

"If you think the cocky thing impresses me, think again. Being an arrogant prick isn't the way to get into my pants."

His smile grows. "What makes you think I want to get in your pants?"

"You're not exactly subtle, Kent."

"Neither are you."

I put the kettle down. Staring at the steam rising from the mugs, I ask, "What does that mean?"

"It means, you're not fooling me."

I stir our coffee, my heart racing a hundred miles an hour. *What does he mean by that?* "I'm not trying to fool anyone."

Kent doesn't respond. Seconds tick by as I stir the coffee for much longer than necessary. His silence only makes me more nervous.

How much does he know about me? He can't know my whole story, or he would have definitely said something about it.

From now on, I need to keep my distance from him.

8

Kent

I STEP BACK AND admire my handiwork. The cupboards and shelves are done. Two walls in this room are completely covered by storage. Heidi will barely be able to fill half of it, so hopefully, I won't have to come back anytime soon to put anything else together.

I chuck the few tools I needed to do the job in my holdall and head into the studio.

"Where's Heidi?" I ask Savannah.

My sister was sitting down ten minutes ago when I went for a piss.

Stormy grey eyes peek up at me over the top of an A4 piece of paper. I can see Heidi's sketch through the paper.

"She's gone out for a lunch meeting. Do you need anything?"

"Just to tell her I'm done."

Savannah puts the sketch down and flicks her blonde hair out of her face. I'm sure it smells like coconut. "Great. That's so great."

Yeah, I think so, too.

The last couple of days, she's been keeping her distance while I've been here. At first, it pissed me off that I was being ignored, but then I realised it was for the best. I don't want her in my life either.

I'll be fucking glad to see the back of Savannah Dean for a while. Well, until Wednesday when I have to pick her up for dinner at my parents' house. My damn mother would not let me out of it. No woman will ever tell me what to do—I'm *always* in control, the one in charge—but when it comes to my mum, I do what I'm fucking told.

Hey, what can I say? I'm pretty sure the woman is either crazy or a witch.

I tilt my head to the side. This morning, Savannah was wearing a dress, I'm sure. It was mid-thigh length; I definitely remember that. Now, she's wearing jeans and a black T-shirt.

"Did you change?"

"Huh?" She looks down. "Oh, yeah, I spilled my drink. You noticed that?"

"I have eyes."

She takes a deep breath through her teeth. "I'll let Heidi know you finished."

Where's your dress? Did you get changed here?

"I can wait for her."

Were you naked merely meters away from me?

"It might be a long meeting."

I shrug one shoulder and let my bag drop to the floor. "I have time."

Actually, I don't. It's one p.m. on a Friday, and by now, I'd be out with Max and Toby, lining up tonight's fuck. Instead, I'm waiting at my sister's work with the blonde whose naked body I cannot stop thinking about right now.

If I spill something on her, will she have another outfit to change into?

Savannah's mouth purses, and her grey eyes cloud like they're about to thunder. "Of course you do." She stands up. "Take a seat. I'll be in the storeroom."

LIE TO ME

When she walks past me with her eyes on the ground, my chest clenches.

Why do I turn into a bigger dickhead than usual around her?

Closing my eyes, I tip my head back.

Since she met Brooke, she's been more involved in my life, too. My mum loves her, both my sisters love her, and she's been invited to two family events in the space of a week.

I can't have her as a permanent fixture in my life. She makes me angry and horny.

Fuck Heidi, I need to get out.

So, I leave without saying another word to Savannah.

Wednesday rolls around way too fast. I have a whole evening with Savannah. It's been really nice these past four days that she's been out of my life. Yet, the whole time, I've been craving the way we snip at each other.

I need help.

I cut my engine outside her building and look up. Apparently, she lives up on the first floor and faces out toward the road.

Is she looking at me right now?

Why I feel the need to get out and buzz her apartment, I don't know, but somehow, I find myself getting out of the car and walking toward the building. I stop at the front door, realising that Heidi told me what floor Savannah is on but not the number. Or she might have told me, and I just didn't listen.

This is a great start.

I'm about to call my sister when I see Savannah through the glass, walking down the stairs to ground level.

Fuck me.

Has she always looked like that?

She's wearing a pair of dark blue skinny jeans and a grey off-the-shoulder shirt, but she looks sexier than any other woman I've ever seen in a little dress.

Why don't I like her again?

Her steely eyes, looking even more prominent with the colour of her top, warily eye me. Our last encounter wasn't exactly pleasant.

She opens the door and smiles. "Hi, Kent."

My back stiffens. "Savannah."

"Are you sure you don't mind taking me tonight? I can Uber."

And there it is. This is why she fucking bothers me so much. I feel like telling her to call a fucking Uber then. She always sounds so unsure of herself, like every tiny thing a person does for her is some massive inconvenience. *Why?*

"It's fine," I spit.

She folds her arms, carefully because her fractured arm hasn't healed. It does take away a little of the dramatic flair she was going for. "Do you need to take a nap before we go?"

"What?"

"You're cranky."

"You're too polite."

"Being polite is a bad thing?"

I flex my jaw. "Yes."

"Fine. Get in the car, and take me."

The intent behind her words is clear; however, I hear it completely different and laugh.

She rolls her eyes. "Don't be a knobhead, Kent. Take me to your parents' house, I mean."

"Knobhead. I've not heard that one in a while."

Savannah takes another long breath. "I really don't know why I thought accepting a lift from you would be a good idea. In fact, I didn't. I *still* think it's a bad idea."

"You always follow through with bad ideas?"

"Tonight, I am."

Fuck yeah. I love this fighting side of her. It's like, when I rile her up enough, the cover slips, revealing the real

LIE TO ME

Savannah. I'm not sure if she's hiding something the way Freya was.

"You should work on that. I don't do anything I don't want to."

She tilts her head to the side, fire and determination in her eyes. "Oh, you wanted me to come tonight? And you wanted to be the one to pick me up?"

"You're hot when you're angry, Savannah."

Actually, she's hot all the time. It's just, right now, she's the whole package.

"You always use bullshit like that to deflect from someone calling you out?"

"You're the first woman to call me out."

"Why doesn't that surprise me?" she mutters.

"Do you want to argue on your doorstep all night or get to my parents' for dinner? I'm cool with either, just checking to see which way you're leaning."

She drops her arms, one still bound tightly in a splint. "I'm hungry."

"Excellent, let's go then."

I walk around to the driver's side, and Savannah heads to the passenger.

"Ah, remember that time you were a gentleman and opened my door?"

Shaking my head at her, I get in, and she does, too.

I slam the door. "You had a broken arm."

Holding her bad arm up, she replies, "Still do."

"You manage just fine. I'm sure your medal is in the post."

The engine roars to life when I turn the key. I pull onto the road, and we drive toward my parents' house.

The whole drive is silent, but it's comfortable. We're about five minutes out when Savannah shifts in her seat. Up until now, she's been a statue, and I've been enjoying the peace. I don't like talking when I'm driving.

"It looks really pretty around here," she says, staring out the window.

We're surrounded by forest. My parents are out in the country. They have a lot of land and no neighbours. I want to settle there when I'm older.

"It is."

"What was it like, growing up here?"

"Fine."

"I've always loved the countryside, but the city is where I feel at home. Was it hard to transition to the city after this?"

"Nope."

She rolls her head toward me. "Are you sulking?"

"What?"

"You're grunting one-worded answers again."

"My first answer was two words."

I feel her roll her eyes. "If you'd rather we didn't speak, that's fine."

I don't know if she's being polite now or bickering back. "Why do you want to talk anyway? You hate me."

"I don't hate you, Kent," she replies, her voice low and breathy.

"Bollocks."

"No, I don't hate you."

I glance at her, but her face is emotionless. "Well, you sure hide it well."

"I could say the same for you. Can't pretend that it's always a pleasure being in your company, but I don't hate you."

"It could be a pleasure if you wanted it to be."

She snorts. "Has that line ever worked on anyone before?"

"I've never had to use a line on anyone before."

"You sleep around a lot, huh?"

The judgment in her words feels like sandpaper against my skin.

I clear my throat. "I'm single, and everyone I sleep with knows the score."

"You don't have to justify it to me."

"I take it, you don't sleep around a lot?" I ask even though I really don't need to.

"Nope."

I raise my eyebrow. "Have you ever had a one-night stand?"

"No, but you already know I'm not a virgin."

"I know, and I think it's a shame. I would have loved to be your first."

She laughs, twisting her body toward me. I like that she's finally feeling comfortable enough to move.

"What makes you think that, if I were saving myself, I would let you take my virginity?"

"Babe, I'd clearly be the one you were saving yourself for."

"Right. I would wait twenty-two years to give it up to my boss's brother, who mostly acts like I'm constantly pissing him off."

"I don't have to act."

"Nice. All I'm saying is that a one-night stand wouldn't be my first encounter."

I pull onto my parents' drive, and Savannah's mouth opens.

"I got something you can put in there," I say, smirking at her.

She clamps her mouth shut and glares at me. "No, thanks. How do you go from looking like you want to throw me under your car to trying to get in my pants?"

"It's a talent. And I don't ever want to run you over."

"Can you tell your face that? You're always glaring."

Shit, she's noticed. "That's just my face."

"You don't glare at everyone else, not as much anyway."

"Well, maybe they don't piss me off as much."

"Because they're not as polite or because they won't give you a blow job either."

I laugh, thumping my head back against the headrest.

"What is so funny?" she demands.

"I thought you were too proper to say *blow job*."

"Too proper? Why would you think that?" She frowns and looks genuinely confused, not understanding why I would reach that conclusion.

I need to tread carefully here. I'm not at all scared about telling her straight, but, believe it or not, I don't actually want to hurt her. "The polite thing doesn't help. But you always seem on edge and controlled. The only time you're yourself is when I piss you off so much, you snap back, and you just generally seem like you think you're above everyone else."

Her mouth drops open.

Surely, I'm not the first person in her life to be saying this?

"That is so far from the truth. I don't think I'm better than anyone."

I nod. "Okay. That's good to know."

"Do people think that?" Her eyes gloss over like she's trying not to cry, and her face falls.

Fuck, I can't do crying. If she starts bawling, I'm going to throw myself under my car.

"No, everyone else seems to love you." She dips her head, and I feel like the biggest piece of shit to grace the earth. "Savannah, I'm sorry."

"No, it's okay. That's how you feel, and I want you to be honest."

"Me, too. I fucking despise liars," I spit. Freya's face appears in my mind, grinning at me, the smug bitch.

Savannah flinches at my tone.

I'm not doing well here at all. "Sorry, that wasn't directed at you at all. I don't hate you, not even close. I'm confused by you." *And how I really feel about you.*

"Kent, Savannah, are you going to sit out there all night?" Heidi shouts.

Snapping my head up, I realise we are in fact still sitting in my car on the drive.

Savannah uses my distraction to get out of my car like it's on fire.

Why do I even bother opening my mouth at all?

LIE TO ME

I follow suit, catching up to her, and we walk the long path to the front door. It's on a slight incline, so Savannah is a little slower than usual.

Heidi laughs at us from the front door. If we get much closer, she will be able to hear us.

"Hey," I say, touching her back, "I am sorry."

I can smell Savannah's hair as it blows lightly in the warm breeze, and all thoughts of my ex disappear.

Coconut.

"You don't have to be sorry."

"I still am. I just don't know you."

Her eyes lift to mine. "You don't want to know me."

"Who said that?"

"That's how *you* come across." She stops walking and turns to me. This conversation is now not at all inconspicuous, but Heidi has turned around, talking to whoever is standing in the hallway. "You act like I'm beneath you and not worth getting to know. You think you know me, but you've just admitted you're confused by me."

I hold my hands up. This is getting us nowhere. "Truce? Let's put whatever preconceived ideas we have of each other aside and start again."

She bites her lip, considering my proposition. Finally, she smiles. "Okay, that sounds good. Arsehole."

"Now, that was uncalled for. I'm the one—"

Laughing, she turns back and starts walking. "I was kidding."

She probably wasn't, but I deserved it. I catch her again just as Heidi looks back at us both.

"Seriously, could you drag this out any longer?" she says sarcastically.

Savannah slows her pace.

"How old are you?" I say.

"As if you didn't think about doing it, too. You're just annoyed I got there first. Arsehole."

"Okay, you need to drop the arsehole thing, princess, or I'm going to make you."

"How?"

We're now in earshot of Heidi, so I clamp my mouth shut. Savannah looks at me over her shoulder and lifts her eyebrow in challenge.

Oh, it's so on, girl.

"Kent!" Mum shouts, running from the kitchen into the large, open hallway. She runs at me and wraps me in a death hug.

"Jesus, woman, I saw you only a few days ago."

Pulling back, she slaps my arm. "Less of the *woman*, and days feel like months when it's your children." She turns from me and addresses Savannah, "Darling, I'm so glad you could make it."

"She didn't have a choice," I mutter.

Mum ignores me and hugs Savannah with the same intense grip that she hugged me.

Crazy woman.

"You coming through to the kitchen?" Heidi asks me while Mum and Savannah are talking.

Damn it, I'm standing here, watching Savannah, like a fucking creep. She looks different now.

"Sure," I say. "I need a drink."

"Kent Lawson, you are not having anything to drink if you're driving," Mum says, following us through.

But I think I'm going to need one tonight. "Fine."

"What are you two drinking?" Mum asks Savannah and Heidi. "I have a bottle of white open."

Savannah walks past me and smirks. "Sounds good to me."

Little fucker. She had better not get drunk.

Dad is in the kitchen, stirring what smells like his famous pasta sauce. He looks up from it for a brief second and says, "Hey."

He'll not interact until it's done. I think he loves cooking more than us.

Mum pours three glasses of wine.

"I'll grab a Coke then," I say.

"Good boy."

"Are Brooke and Freddy coming?" I ask, taking a can from the fridge.

"No, they can't make it now."

I close the door. "I wonder what they're doing instead."

Mum points at me, but her mouth smiles anyway. "Don't."

Savannah takes a sip of wine, and her stormy eyes flick to me. Watching her lips press together as she swallows is agonising. I stand closer to the massive island in the middle of the kitchen as my dick starts to swell at the thought of those lips around my cock.

Is she doing that on purpose?

I glare in warning, but that only seems to spur her on. She sits on the stool next to where I'm standing, and Heidi sits next to her with Mum opposite. I would go and pretend I'm interested in Dad's cooking, but if I move, everyone is going to see the raging fucking erection I've got going on.

I can smell Savannah's hair from here, and it's quickly becoming my new favourite scent. Swallowing hard, I open my can of fucking Coke and swig. My throat is dry as hell. She looks at me with her mouth slightly parted and eyes full of heat.

I don't think I'm confused about how I feel anymore, but I do think I'm in trouble here.

9

Savannah

SO, I DEFINITELY MOVED too close to Kent. It seemed like such a good idea when he was looking at me like he wanted to rip my clothes off. It was a massive change from the way he usually looked. I should have stayed put and kept a little distance.

Now, I'm so close, I can feel his body heat and smell his aftershave.

He laughs at something his mum says, and his arm brushes mine. The touch is electric. I bite my lip.

What the hell is going on? How can I go from disliking him one second to wanting to be under or on top of him the next?

One look from him is all it took to get my pulse racing.

I've not been this turned on in forever, and he's not actually done anything yet. Sure, I've been physically attracted to him since we first met, but since we cleared the air and I've let go of negative feelings, it's made way for how I really feel.

Which is wanting to jump his bones.

I'm hot, and my insides feel like mush. My God, I'm pretty sure my vagina is on fire.

Calm down. His fucking parents are in the same room!

I take another long sip of wine and wish Judy had just given me the whole bottle.

Thank heavens I'm not driving.

He is though, so he can't drink. That might not be an issue. I might be feeling this alone. That does sound right. It would totally be my luck to want a guy this bad for the first time ever, but he doesn't feel the same.

Kent isn't exactly saving himself for marriage though.

Am I seriously talking myself into a one-night stand with my boss's brother?

"Savannah?"

I jump as Heidi's hand flashes in front of my face.

"Yes?"

She laughs. "You were miles away then."

"Oh." *Great, she was talking to me.* "Sorry."

"Spa day sometime. You in?" she asks.

Not going to say no to that. "Definitely."

Judy claps her hands. "Great."

Kent leans forward, resting his forearms on the counter. He waits for Judy and Heidi to strike up another conversation before he looks at me.

"What?" I whisper. My voice is hoarse, even to my own ears.

His lips curl into the smuggest grin that lights his eyes. "Nothing."

Okay, he's fully aware of the situation then.

"You okay?" he asks.

"Yep." If you call a pulsing between your legs and nearly hyperventilating fine, then I'm all dandy.

He turns to the side and hops up on the stool he was standing near. The movement is quick, but I catch a glimpse of the bulge in his jeans. Averting my eyes, I sip my wine. White isn't my favourite drink, but right now, it's my best friend.

Oh Jesus, that is not helping.

I grip the stem of the glass harder when Kent leans in close.

LIE TO ME

"Still okay?"

No. No, I'm bloody not.

"Yeah, you?" I ask, raising my eyebrow but glancing south where he is still very much hard.

He murmurs, "Follow me to the bathroom, and I'll sort this out."

My mouth parts. *Is he serious? We're in his parents' house!* "Thanks, but I'll pass," I whisper.

"What're you two whispering about?" Judy asks.

My mind goes blank. Literally blank.

Say something.

Not the truth.

"Savannah was trying to get me to go to the bathroom with her."

Eyes widening, my head turns to him. *Stay calm, and fix this!*

Summoning every ounce of cool I have, I reply, "You wish." Okay, my voice was even. *I got this.*

Kent laughs, and he actually seems ... impressed with how I handled that.

I am, too, because, until the words came out of my mouth, I had nothing.

"Get your head out of the gutter, son," Harrold says. He doesn't even look around or stop stirring whatever he's got cooking. It smells amazing though.

"I can't help it. She's offering me all sorts over here."

I whack him with my good arm and scowl. "Heidi, your brother is annoying."

"Tell me about it," she replies, rolling her eyes.

He laughs, blocking another whack. "Why do you think we took so long to get here?"

When I turn away from Kent, Judy is smiling.

Oh no. I bite my lip, knowing we've taken it too far.

We opened the door to civility, and lust came pouring out. His mum is kind of a force, and she's definitely going to say things if she thinks we're getting close ... or if she just wants us to get together.

We've only just agreed to start over. Yes, I want to follow him to the bathroom, but that doesn't mean I'm going to. I don't have to act upon this attraction, and I'm really not up for being another notch on his post.

Even if the constant throbbing disagrees. Clearly, it's been a long time since I've had sex.

"Ignore him, Savannah. The rest of us do," Heidi says, waving her hand in his direction.

I wish I could but, hello, vagina on fire here.

"Dinner is almost ready," Harrold announces, stepping back. "And I agree that you should ignore Kent. He's still under the illusion that he's God's gift to women."

Kent scoffs while Heidi, Judy, and I laugh. I really, really like Harrold right now.

"I got that impression, too," I reply.

"If you haven't tried the goods, don't leave a review, sweetheart."

I tilt my head in his direction. "That's gross."

"Kent, find your manners," Judy says, giving him the tight-eyed look again.

He laughs and shrugs.

"Make yourself useful, and set the table, Kent," Harrold instructs.

When he gets down from the stool, I see that he's calmed himself down a bit. He salutes his dad and heads into the room off the kitchen, which I assume is the dining room.

"You'll have to excuse my son. We raised all of them the same, but I must have forgotten that I dropped him," Judy says, making me laugh.

"I heard that!" he shouts from the other room.

I shake my head. "That's fine. I can handle Kent." And I finally feel like I can.

We each assumed things about the other before getting to know one another, and it made us hostile, only feeding what we thought was true.

Now, he doesn't seem so intimidating. Actually, he's not intimidating at all.

LIE TO ME

I bite my bottom lip as I feel my smile grow, feeling a touch more like the old me. No one could make me feel small or unworthy before.

People are supposed to get stronger as they grow, but I seemed to have gone backward. Not anymore though. Kent is right; I'm not being myself. It's through fear of letting my guard down too much, but I can't live like that.

Ha, I'll probably change my mind about that one tomorrow. I hope not though. I want to grip hold of the strength I feel entering my body and never let go. I'm so tired of just existing.

"We can tell that you can handle him," Heidi says, wiggling her eyebrows.

"Don't get any ideas," I hush.

Judy bends over the counter. "I already have *a lot* of ideas."

Why doesn't that surprise me?

"He's not my type."

Now, that much is true—in the relationship sense anyway. I've never gone for the kind of guys who are arrogant and sleep about, hoping I'll be the one to change them. If someone wants to be with me, they'll stop shagging other women. Though maybe I've been looking at it all wrong because Simon was quiet and reserved, and that hardly ended well.

So, maybe I just need to die alone.

Okay, that's a touch dramatic.

"We are ready," Harrold says, tipping something into a large serving bowl.

There are tons of dishes along the counter over by the cooker. He has pasta dishes, salad, and breads. It all looks amazing, but I don't know how we're going to eat everything.

"Ooh, I'll top these glasses up. You two go through," Judy says.

"Can I help with anything?"

Harrold looks up. "Just grab something on your way and tuck in."

I take a dish and follow Heidi. I'd have picked up two, but my arm still hurts when I carry something with a little weight. Heidi has the bread and is looking at it like she wants to run off with it.

I put my dish down in the middle of the table. "Where should I sit?"

"Next to Kent," Judy says over my shoulder as she places a large plate on the table. "I'll go back for wine. You all sit."

When I turn, Kent is looking at me with his eyebrow arched. I don't want to sit next to him now, but if I don't, it'll look like I pussied out. Old me wouldn't have backed down, so the new old me can't.

I walk around the table, ignoring his goddamn smirk, and sit next to him. Heidi is opposite me with Harrold and Judy on either end of the table.

"What?" I say, keeping my eyes on the food.

Shit, that is a lot of food.

"Nothin'. Want a sausage?" He holds up a plate of sliced sausage. I look at the bowl with a frown. "It's not weird really. Dad wants to put it in every pasta dish, but Mum won't let him, so they compromise."

Okay, that makes sense. "Hmm… no, thanks. I don't like tiny sausages."

Kent lowers the plate and narrows his eyes. "Oh, I know you didn't mean what I think you mean."

Nope, I've seen your bulge.

"Head out of the gutter," I say, using Harrold's words.

Judy comes back in with wine, and she takes her seat. I immediately take a sip. God, I feel a bit too comfortable in their house. It warms my heart at the same time as scaring the living crap out of me.

Losing my family—well, walking away from them—was hard enough, but these people don't owe me anything. We aren't related, so there's nothing stopping them from never talking to me again.

I'd hate that. The very thought leaves a nasty taste on my tongue. I love Heidi and her family. I can't go there with

Kent. It'd be too awkward, and I know I would hate seeing him with other women after.

He bumps my arm, thankfully not my fractured one. "Dig in. They hate it when there are leftovers."

My eyes widen. *Are they expecting five people to eat seven dishes of food plus a ton of bread?*

Kent chuckles. "Kidding. You'll be sent home with a tub full though. It's the only reason I keep coming back."

"Kent Lawson!" Judy snips. I love it when she uses his surname, too. "You had better be eating properly. If I find out you're living off leftovers and takeaways ..." Judy doesn't finish her sentence, and although her intention is clear, I really wish she had said something about slapping his arse.

"Mum, do I look malnourished?"

No, he looks mighty fine to me.

I press my lips together, so the words can't slip out.

Judy squints, looking at him like she's trying to find something about his appearance to pick at. "You'd better not be, or you'll be moving back home."

He rolls his eyes. "I'm twenty-five, for fuck's sake."

"Language!" Judy and Harrold say at the same time.

I shake my head at him. "Honestly, the amount of F-bombs you drop."

"I knew this would happen, Harrold. As soon as they move out, they think they can swear."

"The fact that I'm an adult means I can choose to swear."

Oh my God, I love their family!

I wonder if they want to adopt another child. Though that would be weird with the way I've been feeling about Kent.

"I'm your mum, and I don't care how old you are."

There was a lot my mum cared about that she shouldn't have. I admire Judy so much for loving her children unconditionally. That's what you're supposed to do, isn't it? There's this bond between a mother and her child that nothing could break. My mum is an exception to that rule.

"Fucking hell," Kent mutters under his breath.

Neither of his parents hears though as Heidi starts talking about Brooke's wedding dress.

I dish a spoonful of every pasta onto my plate and take a piece of rosemary bread. I'm not sure what's in every one of these pasta dishes, but they all look and smell great.

Kent piles up his plate like he's trying to make a food mountain.

"Are you going to eat all that?" I ask.

He grins. "Of course I am."

"You'll be sick."

"Are you planning on us doing anything particularly *active* after dinner?"

I roll my eyes.

"If you are, I won't eat as much."

"Pile it up, buddy, because, unless you're planning on going for a run after this, you'll be just fine."

He laughs, and it makes my insides squirm.

10

Kent

MY STOMACH IS SCREAMING when we finish up the desserts. My parents are feeders. It's a miracle Brooke, Heidi, and I aren't all massive.

Savannah looks at the empty serving dishes in the middle of the table with wide eyes.

"We should get going. We both have work tomorrow," I say before Mum can offer a final course of coffee and biscotti.

Savannah looks so full, I don't think she'll need to eat for the rest of the week.

Nodding, she stands up with me. "Okay."

"Are you sure you don't want to stay for coffee?" Mum asks.

"No, thanks," I reply, ushering Savannah around the table.

When you decide to leave my parents', you have to just leave. If you hang around, Mum will start a conversation, and you'll be stuck.

"Okay, I'll grab leftovers before you go," Mum says, getting to her feet and heading back to the kitchen.

Heidi left a few minutes before us because she is at the other side of the city and takes a different motorway.

Mum heads out of the house with two tubs full of food.

Dad, Savannah, and I follow her outside.

It's warm out tonight, and the sun has almost set, turning most of the sky pink. We reach my car with my parents close behind, like they're trying to soak up as much Savannah time before she goes. They love her, and Mum definitely wants something to happen between us.

They've both been waiting for me to find someone else for a while, not that they will ever admit to it. Savannah has been chosen as the woman to change everything.

Apparently, I don't get a say.

Savannah clutches a plastic tub full of food that Mum handed over.

I hold my door open, waiting for my mum to stop talking so that we can leave.

"You'll come back soon. I won't take no for an answer."

Savannah laughs. "I would love to. Thank you so much for tonight."

"It was so lovely to have you with us, darling," Mum replies. She then turns to me. "You make sure you bring this one next time you're here."

I'm not her boyfriend, but okay.

Biting her lip, Savannah looks at me over the roof of the car.

"Let's go. See you guys later. Dad, hold Mum back, or we're never going to get home."

Mum raises her hand and steps back from the car. Dad puts his arm around her waist as they smile at us.

Savannah and I get in the car, and I lock the doors.

"Was that necessary?" she asks, putting the tub down by her feet.

"My mum seems to love you, so I wouldn't put it past her to come for one last hug."

I reverse on the drive and turn around.

"Your mum is awesome."

LIE TO ME

"If you say so," I reply, but I know she is. As interfering as she is, I wouldn't swap her.

"Oh my God, I'm so full," she groans as I head toward the main road.

"Me, too. I don't think I could do you right now, sorry."

With a little laugh, she swats my arm with her hand.

"Okay, I don't think you should hit the driver."

"You're an idiot."

"An idiot who could leave you to walk home."

"I wouldn't walk home. I would call your mum and tell her what you did."

"You wouldn't be able to call with no tongue." Savannah's eyebrows shoot up, and I frown. "Yeah, sorry, that went a bit darker than I'd planned."

She nods. "Yeah. Besides, you wouldn't cut my tongue out because then you wouldn't get a blow job."

I nearly crash the fucking car as I join the road from the track to my parents'. As I grip the steering wheel, my head snaps to her while my dick stands to attention. "Don't say shit like that if you're not serious."

Laughing, she tips her head back.

"I'm not joking, Savannah. That's just cruel. Tell me you want my cock in your mouth, sweetheart." I'm hot. It's too hot in here. I jab my finger into the air-con button.

Shit, I really am going to crash the car.

"Kent, I'll be honest; this conversation has backfired a little."

Cutting her a scathing look, I growl, "You're such a tease."

Grinning, she tilts her head toward the road. "You need to look where you're going."

"You need to ..." *Don't say it. Just don't even think about her mouth or what you want it to be doing right the fuck now.* Groaning, I look ahead and take a breath.

Why am I like a horny teenager again? I thought getting hard at inappropriate times was over. I'm an adult now. Shouldn't I be spared that embarrassment?

"Sorry, that was mean of me." She doesn't sound sorry. Her voice is light and packed full of amusement.

"No more blow-job talk unless you're going to do it, okay?"

"Deal," she agrees. "But don't hold your breath."

"I thought we were getting on now?"

"You get blow jobs from every woman you get on with?" She pauses and frowns. "Right. Of course you do."

I feel uneasy under her judgment of my sex life again. "Savannah, I'm single, and—"

"And they know the score," she finishes. "I got that."

"Then, why the look of disgust?"

"I just don't get it, but casual sex isn't for me, so I'm not going to."

Fuck's sake. My dick shrivels up and dies at her words. I'm not going to get in her pants if she's sticking to that.

"You've never done it, so how do you know?"

"Trust me, I know." She sounds so sure of herself.

Arsehole ex? Bad experience? I don't know why she's so against a night of no-strings sex, but she needs to sort it out. I've got blue balls over here, and I'm fucking *dying* to be inside her.

"Have you ever had sex with someone you love?" she asks after silence drags into minutes.

I clear my throat. "Yep."

"Didn't end well, I take it?"

"Nope."

"Would you want to again? Let someone in, I mean."

I cautiously eye her, not really sure if her question holds any weight or if she's asking out of curiosity. "Probably. Why?"

"Just wondering."

I don't know what to think of that. *It's a bit of a weird thing to wonder, isn't it? Why would she care if I were open to a relationship again?*

"You missed the turn," she says casually, sinking back in the seat.

"Fuck," I mutter, braking so that I can make a U-turn.

She puts her hand out on the dashboard as I swing the car around. "Where is your mind?"

"You don't want to know."

Rolling her eyes, she says, "Blow jobs again?"

"I think I remember telling you not to bring that word up unless you're going to do it. And you agreed, babe, so away you go." I hook my eyebrow at her.

"One day, I'm going to do it, Kent, and you won't know what to do."

I snort. "Oh, I'll know what to do, but I'm game if you want to test that theory."

"Is sex all you think about?"

Not usually. "You make me hard as fuck. What can I say?"

She turns her head, but I can see the pink in her cheeks from the glow on the dashboard.

"You're not used to people being so up-front, are you?"

"No," she mutters.

"No one has told you how painfully sexy you are?"

Her head turns away a bit more. "No."

"Come on." As if I'm buying that one. I mean, look at her; she's the hottest thing I have ever seen.

Her shoulders hunch, like she's trying to protect herself.

Is she embarrassed?

"You're serious?" I ask.

"Yes."

"Look at me, Savannah," I demand.

She turns, widening her eyes. "Look at the road, Kent!"

"I'll look at the road when you open up."

"I know we called a truce, but that doesn't mean we have to be besties and share everything."

I ignore her bitchiness. She's only saying that because she wants to hide away from something.

"What about the guy? The one you were with for a little while?"

"That was nothing really. It was a long time ago, and the whole thing was a mistake."

"He's an idiot."

"Yeah, he really is."

What did he do to her? She's lacking in confidence—when she's not trying to drive me crazy, that is—so was he a dick to her?

I don't know how anyone can find a fault with the way she looks.

"Well, that was a conversation killer," she mutters. "Sorry, but I don't really know how to handle compliments."

"You could say, *Gosh, Kent, that really turns me on when you tell me I'm stunning. Take me now.* That would be an appropriate reaction."

"Your mum really did drop you, didn't she?"

Laughing, I peek back at her. Her pink lips are pressed together, smiling. I want to lean over and take her mouth, see if her lips are as soft as they look.

Down, boy.

"You're hilarious," I reply dryly. "Are you going to the summer festival?"

Why am I asking her that?

"I wasn't planning on going. Every year, I say I will, but I never do."

"Heidi will probably make you come along."

"You go? Doesn't seem like your thing."

"Beer and food. What's not to like? Brooke, Freddy, and Heidi love it, so I tag along with them."

"Until you find the beer?"

"Exactly. You should come, too … if you want?"

Biting her bottom lip and making me fucking crazy at the same time, she nods. "Yeah, I would like that."

Did I make that sound like me asking? Well, fucking obviously. I asked her somewhere. Fuck.

If she tells Heidi I invited her, my sister is going to say things. Then, she'll tell our damn mum, and she will say lots more things.

Why couldn't I have just left it to Heidi? She definitely would have made Savannah come along.

LIE TO ME

I'm losing my touch. She is making me turn into some sappy twat, desperate to spend more time with a girl I barely know.

No, I'm not desperate to spend time with her. I'm desperate to fuck her.

Those are very different things. Very goddamn different.

"Kent, do you want the whole road to yourself?" Savannah snaps, holding her good arm out in front of her.

Shit. With a sharp intake of breath, I veer the car back into my lane. We were right on the line, so I wouldn't have stacked it in the ditch, but how could I have let my car swerve?

She's going to kill me. Literally.

"Sorry," I mutter, my heart sinking.

I have got to get her out of my head, but I don't think that's going to be easy. I need someone. Anyone.

I need her, but that's not going to happen.

"Are you okay? I would offer to drive if you're tired, but—"

I cut in, "But fractured arm and four glasses of wine."

"Three glasses of wine."

"It was four, Savannah."

Her lips purse, and my eyes flit from them to the road and back again.

Jesus, concentrate on driving. If we die tonight because I can't keep us on the road, I'll have no chance of getting in her pants.

"Oh, it was four," she says. "Please tell me your mum and Heidi had four, too. I don't want to be the only wino."

"No idea," I reply with a shrug and turn onto the motorway.

I watch the road for once, but I feel her grey eyes burning a hole in the side of my head.

"What?" I ask.

"Why do you know how much wine I had and no one else?"

Shit. Busted.

"You were sitting next to me, and I had to judge the chance of you throwing up in my car." The words spill from my mouth so smoothly, I'm seriously impressed. That sounds plausible, too. I don't know what it is about her, but I notice everything. Like the smell of her hair, the darker grey flecks in her eyes, and the way she tilts her head when she's flirting. It all seems to automatically register with me without any effort on my part.

"I've never been sick through alcohol."

"Never? Isn't that like some rite of passage that everyone has to experience once?"

"I'm not going to worry about never having puked up vodka."

"One night, I'm getting you absolutely shit-faced."

She laughs and turns her body in my direction. "Shit-faced?"

"Yep. Don't worry; I'll hold your hair back."

"Wow, such a gentleman."

"Believe it, baby. I've never held a girl's hair back before."

"What? Do you usually let them vomit all over themselves?"

"Hell yeah, I do. They got themselves into that state, and I'm not risking getting it on me."

"But you're making an exception for me?" she slowly speaks the words, like she's thinking hard about each one.

I grit my teeth. Yeah, I seem to be making all sorts of exceptions for her. It's doing my head in, but I can't help the way she makes me feel. Admittedly, that's pissed me off half the time, but the other half is good. Real good.

"That's what I said," I reply tightly.

"Well, thanks."

"You're actually looking forward to this, aren't you?"

We turn into the city, and my heart drops. I've only got her for another ten minutes.

"I think I am. I'll probably not say that in the morning. What does that say about me?"

"That you want to catch up on all the fun things you missed from being so perfect, growing up."

"I'm not perfect, Kent."

Could've fooled me.

"You certainly won't be when you're puking your guts up in my toilet."

"Your toilet? What makes you think we'll be at your place?"

I roll my eyes. "I'll be on my best behaviour. No matter how much you beg me to take you, I won't put my dick anywhere near you."

She snorts. "Thanks."

"I'm more than happy to get you off with my tongue though."

"Oh, there it is. I was wondering when you'd turn it dirty."

"It's only a matter of time, babe."

Her eyes dance. "I would really love to watch you come on to a woman."

"Where were you all night?"

"I don't mean me. I'm curious to see why women go for all that arrogant bullshit."

"I'll show you next time."

There is something seriously hot about her watching me put the moves on someone else. Would she be jealous? Yeah, she'd definitely be jealous. Would she get turned on, knowing I was only doing it for her? There's no way I could leave with someone else when there was a chance of getting up close and personal with her.

Her eyes turn stormy, and she takes a ragged breath. "Oddly, I'm looking forward to that."

You're not the only one.

We reach her building.

"Thank you for the lift, Kent. Tonight has been great."

I dip my chin. "That's all right."

She opens the door with her good hand, slips her handbag over her shoulder, and grabs the tub on the floor.

"Do you need me to carry that?"

"Oh, I've got it, thanks."

"Savannah," I call as she swings one leg out.

Looking back over, she replies, "Yeah?"

Am I actually doing this?

I hand her my phone.

Her eyes drop to it and then back to me. "Huh?"

"Your number. I can't get you shit-faced one night if I can't reach you." I could, of course, find her at work.

I want her number.

She sees right through me but doesn't make a comment. Instead, she rests the tub on the chair between her legs—fantastic place to be—and taps her number on my screen.

"Don't use my number to sign up to daily sex position subscriptions or anything like that."

I laugh and put my phone back in the cup holder. "I swear."

With a smile, she picks up her stuff and gets out. "Good night, Kent."

"Night," I reply.

When she's inside and climbing the communal stairs, I leave. I can't see her once she's past there anyway. I drive home, which doesn't take long, as I'm only twenty minutes from hers. At this time of night, the city isn't rammed with traffic.

I take the lift to my apartment and let myself in. My phone, now in my pocket, feels heavier. I want to take it out and text her.

She's drunk, so I should make sure she got in okay.

Fuck it. I'm not the type to overthink talking to a woman.

> *Kent: You get in okay? Not passed out in the hallway?*

> *Savannah: Couldn't make it. Going to camp on the stairs tonight.*

She's joking, of course, but I kind of need confirmation.

LIE TO ME

Kent: Get in bed, and send me a dirty pic.

Okay, so although I wouldn't say no to a picture of her, that's not exactly what I'm after here. I want her to tell me she's in a certain part of her apartment. She'd better not be outside.

Savannah: Sorry, just put my PJs on.

Good. I walk to the fridge to get a bottle of water to take to bed. It's still too early for me to sleep, but I feel like I need to lie down. Trying to figure her out is just as exhausting as trying to figure out why I want her so badly.

Kent: Next time. ;) Night, Savannah.

I wince as I press Send. I already said good night when she got out of my car.

Savannah: See you at the carnival. Night.

Shit. Sighing, I scrub my face with my hand and close my eyes. *I'm looking forward to it.*

11

Savannah

IT'S SATURDAY, AND I have plans. I feel like I should mark it on the calendar or make an announcement in the newspaper. This past week, I've gone out more times than I have in the previous three years.

Yep, I'm a loser.

Heidi is dragging me to the summer festival—or so she thinks. Kent invited me on Wednesday, but I've obviously not told Heidi that.

The streets are lined with stalls selling food and drinks and crafts. There's music and dancing, and I'm finally going to get to experience it from the ground rather than watching a small part of it out of my window.

Hello, having a life.

I chuck my phone and keys in my bag and head out to meet Kent, Heidi, Brooke, and Freddy.

Since dinner at Harrold and Judy's three days ago, Kent and I have been texting. A lot. It's mostly been flirty texts and teasing each other, but it's been fun. I've not flirted in years, and it has taken me by surprise how much more confident I feel, knowing someone is interested in me. It shouldn't. I know confidence should come from within, but after the way Simon made me feel, I was sure no one would ever find me attractive again.

I lock my door and head down the communal stairs to the front door. My building is quite small. I don't know any of my neighbours but the old couple opposite me. Everyone else keeps to themselves, which is good because I do, too. There's nothing I would find worse than small talk out in the hallway.

Heidi is walking toward my building when I get out. Her sister and future brother-in-law are behind her. And Kent is trailing behind, looking at a group of women in short shorts and sports bras.

He's already annoying me.

It's hot today. I have on a light-yellow summer dress and gladiator-style sandals.

Heidi grins. "How awesome is this! We're getting our faces painted. I just walked past this stall, and you can have glitter and—"

"Are you drunk?" I ask. This is so unlike her to be all bouncy and wanting to get something painted on her face that isn't makeup.

Kent laughs and runs his hand over his dark hair. He looks edible in a plain white shirt and denim shorts. "She actually is."

"Heidi, it's eleven in the morning!"

"Hey, don't judge. We also passed a stall selling the most amazing gin cocktails." She points at me. "*You* will love them."

She's drunk before lunch.

"I don't know what to do with you right now," I say, laughing as she throws an arm over my shoulders and hugs me.

"We're going to get some food," Brooke says, leaning her head on Freddy's shoulder.

I don't miss anything about Simon, but I do miss having someone there who cares. I miss the affection of being in a relationship and being held. Being in someone's arms, feeling

LIE TO ME

the beating of their heart and the rise and fall of their breath, gives you a sense of belonging. Everyone wants to belong somewhere, to someone or something.

But am I seriously letting my mind go to Kent? He's not all that fluffy.

He was at one point; he has an ex. An ex who hurt him and made him want to keep interactions with women strictly strings-free.

Sex is something I've been missing, too. Three years and nothing. Before now, I just ignored it because I didn't want anyone near me. But Kent has me constantly hot under the collar, so I've not been able to avoid wanting to get physical for the last week. I've been a nun for too long now.

Simon was my first and last, the only person I've ever been with. Now, *that* makes me pathetic.

Maybe I should have a one-night stand.

I wrap my arm around Heidi's back since she's not letting go of me. "Where to then?" I ask.

"Tequila!" Heidi shouts, gaining a cheer from the surrounding crowd.

Okay, I wish I were drunk, too.

"Where's the nearest restaurant?" Brooke asks.

"There's a nice Mexican on the corner," I reply, tipping my head in the direction of the restaurant.

"Let's go then. I'm starving," Kent says, walking off ahead.

Brooke and Freddy are in front of us. Heidi is slowing us down, but I don't care because, one, I love her drunk, and, two, I have a nice view of her brother's butt from here. He might be a massive dickhead most of the time, but he's very easy on the eyes.

"Kent's jolly today," I say sarcastically. "You should have made him have some of those gin cocktails, too."

She giggles and then pointedly stares at me. "He's moodier than usual."

"And that's my fault how?"

"You two rub each other up the wrong way—which is funny to watch, by the way—but the sexual tension is palpable."

"There is no sexual tension," I say as we walk around three women dressed as flamingos.

Heidi stops dead, and I almost pull her over. We let go of each other in the process, and I turn to look at her.

"What're you doing?"

"I know you've been out of the game for a while now, but please tell me you're aware that you two want to jump each other's bones." She scrunches her nose up. "It's totally gross because he's my brother, so I don't ever want any details."

Oh, I'm acutely aware.

"Okay, let's get you some food and coffee because you've stopped making sense," I lie.

Heidi rolls her eyes but starts walking with me again.

We both know she's making sense. Kent might make me want to stab him, jump him, and run away from him, all at the same time, but I can't lie to myself. I would run my tongue all over that body.

We're seated as soon as we get inside. The festival and street food means that restaurants are quieter than usual.

Heidi smirks at me as she sits next to Brooke, meaning I'm between her and Kent. He's on my left, too, so I can't even whack him if I need to, not without being in pain anyway.

"Can we have five shots of tequila to start?" Heidi asks as the server hands out menus.

"Okay, I don't think we're going to be successful in sobering her up," I say, opening my menu.

"Nope, but I'm going to be successful in getting you as tipsy as me."

Brooke and Freddy break off into their own conversation. They're so cute, only having eyes for each other. I don't remember having that with Simon, not even in the early days.

"I'm up for that," I find myself saying.

LIE TO ME

Hell, I should be having fun like her. I'm only bloody twenty-two. Somehow, I seem to have aged thirty years in only three. It's time I act like I'm in my twenties.

Kent grunts. "So, you're getting drunk, and I'm going to be looking after you all."

I look over, steeling myself for the reaction. My eyes meet his, and my heart jumps. He's wearing grey, and it makes his eyes look more on the blue side today. I can't help staring.

"Why can't you drink, too?" I ask, my body kicking up a few thousand degrees.

"Freddy and Brooke will head off early to have their *alone time*, so I'll be left with two drunk women."

"Hmm, why do I think that's never been an issue for you before?"

He glares. "If you want to ditch my sister and find another woman to get trashed with, I'm totally there, sweetheart."

"I would rather never have sex again."

"We don't have to find another woman, if you don't want."

"Where's the tequila?" I mutter.

To my right, I can see Heidi smirking as she pretends to read her menu. I need to stop this flirty banter with Kent in front of her, or she's only going to get more stupid ideas. Right now, I'm doing a crap job of convincing her I don't want in her brother's pants.

The warm feeling in the bottom of my stomach and my fluttering heart make it impossible for me to fool myself. I want him. I want him over me, under me. I want his mouth and hand and cock.

I can tell he'd be good in bed. He's had enough practice, and I really need mind-blowing sex.

"I didn't hear a no," Kent mutters.

He's watching me. I can feel his stare burning a hole in the side of my head.

"No," I say, making my voice very clear when inside my head is a fuzzy haze of lust.

"Keep telling yourself that."

Tequila. Tequila, tequila, tequila!

I ignore him and concentrate on picking something to eat, but all the words on the menu seem to blur into one. Kent presses his leg against mine under the table, and my breath catches.

Read. The. Menu.

"What're you all having?" Brooke asks.

I don't know because it might as well be written in fucking Spanish!

Words aren't making sense.

What's Mexican? Quesadilla! That'll be on the menu. Just ask for one of those.

Freddy, Heidi, and Kent reply, already having theirs picked out.

"Savannah?" Brooke presses. I look up, and she smiles. "What's it between?"

Everything. Every-fucking-thing.

My foggy brain can't read a word right now; it's too busy doing all manner of dirty, naked things with Kent.

"Um …" Frowning, I look back down.

Kent leans forward, resting his arms on the table, and chuckles.

The bastard knows the effect he's having on me.

"Chicken quesadilla," I say, my voice sounding like one of the bloody Chipmunks.

"That's what I'm having, too," Brooke replies. "Shall we get nachos to share?"

"Sure," Heidi replies.

The server comes over with a tray of tequila, and I want to kiss him.

He puts five glasses down in the middle of the table. "Are you ready to order?" he asks.

We place our order and take our shot glasses.

"Can we have five more of these?" I say over my shoulder before the server can get too far away.

"There a reason you want to drink a lot at lunch?" Kent asks.

LIE TO ME

"Yes, you're being your usual annoying self."

He presses his leg harder against mine. "Is that right?"

Fuck off.

With a deep breath, I snap, "Yes."

Why am I not moving my leg? His touch makes my brain short-circuit, and I want to forget all the aggravating or shitty things he's said to me and sit on his lap.

Jesus, calm down, Savannah.

Is it hot in here?

Kent leans in and whispers, "You're looking a little flushed."

"There is a knife in front of me, Kent; keep talking."

Laughing, he sits back up as Heidi raises her glass.

I down my shot, wincing at the burn, and put the tiny glass down. Yep, I definitely want more of these.

"So, Heidi," Freddy says, "how is business?"

I listen even though Heidi is very open with all aspects of the business with me. I know what's in the bank accounts, what comes out, and what is yet to be invoiced. Heidi is doing well, really well. She deserves it.

Kent's hand comes down on my thigh, and I freeze. My body seizes up and bursts into flames.

What the hell is going on?

If I bat his hand away, one of them might see, but I can't exactly leave it there. He's waiting for me to react and shove him. This is a test, and I don't want to lose … but how far will he take this?

I literally can't just sit here while he fingers me under the table.

I push my hair behind my shoulder and pretend to listen to what they're talking about. Their mouths are moving, so I know words are being spoken, but all I can focus on is Kent's hand. His fingers dig lightly into my flesh; it's maddening. I want him to remove his hand, and I want him to go higher.

He pushes me further, gently grazing my skin with the tips of his fingers as he moves closer to where I *really* want them right now. I've never done anything like this before. The throbbing in my clit makes me want to scream. Simon was a very safe, in-the-bedroom-with-the-door-locked kind of guy. Kent pushes every boundary I've set for myself, and, bloody hell, I love it.

The danger of getting caught doing something in public has my body begging for him.

I slowly part my legs just enough to give him better access, and his reaction sends my heart into overdrive. His fingers grip my leg, cutting down into my skin, and he takes in a sharp breath.

What am I doing?

He didn't expect that, and knowing I'm now affecting him as much as he's been getting to me spurs me on.

I'll be mortified if we actually get caught, but right now, that's not enough to stop me.

We're only at lunch, too, so we have ages left of the day. I want to take him home. My apartment is so close to this restaurant.

Kent leans closer as the others laugh, completely engrossed in their conversation to notice us. "You're so fucking hot. I've never wanted anyone this badly before," he whispers in my ear.

I shudder.

Thank God we're sitting with our backs to a wall. Brooke, Heidi, and Freddy might not be able to see what's happening here, but if anyone were behind us, they would. The lighting is low, but I'm not sure if it's low enough to hide the blush that is probably lighting up my cheeks like a fucking Christmas tree.

I squirm in my seat, desperate to relieve some of the tension building inside my body, too turned on and frustrated that this can't lead to anything in a restaurant. Kent has other ideas though. He stops gripping my thigh and trails his hand higher until he's right between my legs.

Groaning quietly as he reaches his goal, he hooks his finger around my underwear and slides his finger beneath the fabric.

I almost come off my seat. Clenching my jaw, I focus on trying not to fucking scream. Clenching my fists, I breathe through my nose, clamping my mouth shut so that I don't moan.

Breathe.

Forcing myself to sit still is a mission in itself. I want to move, rock against his hand, kiss him, or climb on his lap. I want to do something. I'm going out of my mind.

My body ignites and tightens. He moves his finger, sweeping it over my clit, and I bite back a moan.

Shit, I need more.

Carefully arching my butt, I widen my legs. Kent's side presses against mine. He moves his hand, slipping a finger inside me while his thumb presses down on my clit.

He's too good at this.

I'm close. So, so close.

I grind into him.

The friction of the pad of his thumb against my skin is too much. I bite down on my lip, my body trembling, heart racing. Then, I fall apart.

Dipping my head enough so that my hair falls in my face, I close my eyes as I contract around his finger.

My body loosens as the last wave passes over me. I take a breath and open my eyes. Kent moves his hand, smiling at me like he just won the lottery. I don't dare look at the others, but I can finally hear them talking, so I know they haven't noticed us.

Bringing his hand to his mouth, he pops his finger in while staring at me.

Why the hell is that so hot?

I look away as Kent chuckles and adjusts himself in his jeans. Neither of us says anything, but there is little to say right now.

I can't believe I let him do that. And I can't believe I had the most intense orgasm of my life, sitting around a table in a bloody Mexican restaurant.

"Heidi, you know you're going to be making adjustments to Brooke's dress up until the day," Kent says, slotting himself into the conversation so seamlessly.

Brooke disagrees and starts to tell Heidi how perfect the dress already is and that it doesn't need any more work.

Kent uses that distraction to his advantage. "You taste better than I imagined," he whispers when the others delve into another topic of conversation.

I'm sure my face is bright red.

"You imagined how I'd taste?" I ask.

"Daily. Tell me you haven't."

"Kent, will you stop harassing her?" Heidi says, peering around me to glare at her brother.

"I'm not harassing her. I'm making conversation."

What kind of conversation was that?

Sure, the best kind, but still.

"You'd better not. I know what you're like." She narrows her eyes at him.

"Savannah," Kent says so smoothly, it sends a bolt of electricity straight down south, "have I been anything but a gentleman today?"

I swallow. It's really hot and dry in here. *Where's my other shot?* "He's been fine, Heidi. Nothing I can't handle."

"Apparently," Kent mutters behind his hand as he rubs his lips with the finger he just had inside me.

He's going to have to stop doing that.

Over the years, I've perfected lying. I've always hated that trait, but once I ditched my old life, I had to lie. So, Heidi doesn't even blink when I look back at her.

"All right, but I'm watching you," she says, pointing at Kent.

Yeah, so am I.

12

Kent

I CAN'T CONCENTRATE, NOT on a single thing. There is stuff I need to do, like walk and breathe and contribute to the conversation, but none of that even registers when I can still feel Savannah's heat, see the pink shade of her cheeks, and hear the deepness of her breath.

That was singularly the hottest thing that has ever happened to me, and I want to do it again—right now.

But I can't because we have finished lunch and paid the bill. Now, we're outside, walking along the stalls. I feel like I'm in some alternate universe. Never in a million fucking years did I think Savannah would let me get her off in the middle of a restaurant.

I knew I was pushing my luck, and I expected her to kick me or something, not open her legs wider to let me in.

Fuck.

"Oh my gosh, that smells amazing," Savannah says, pointing to some stall that must sell food or something else fragrant.

I don't give a fuck.

The festival is huge. Dozens of streets take part, and every year I've made the most of sampling food and booze from almost all of them. This year, I'm pissed off with how big it all is, and I just want to get her home. I don't even care whose home it is.

Savannah and Heidi are walking in front of me, and all I can focus on are Savannah's legs in that short yellow dress. It sits teasingly mid-thigh, driving me insane. I know how those legs feel beneath my hands, but now, I want to feel them around my waist.

"Ooh, we need to get crepes for dessert!" Brooke says, tugging Freddy off to a stall up ahead.

Heidi drops her arm from Savannah's and dashes after them. "I want Nutella!"

I'm alone—sort of, as there's a shitload of people around—with the girl occupying my mind again. "You okay?" I ask.

Folding her arms, she peeks up at me through her lashes. "What were you thinking back there?"

"You didn't like it?" I arch my eyebrow. "You seemed to like it."

"That's hardly the point, Kent."

"You could have stopped me at any point. I didn't hear much protesting."

She stops walking, planting her feet in the ground, and cocks her eyebrow. "That's not going to happen again. I don't sleep around; I told you that."

"Keep telling yourself that." I step closer, getting in her personal space. "Whatever rules you've made for yourself, they're slipping."

"You don't know that. We haven't had sex."

"I do know that. I'm doing it myself, letting my own rules slip. Get out of your head, Savannah, and let yourself go with the flow."

"Go with the flow? If I did that, we would be in my apartment right now." She snaps her mouth closed, not meaning for that to be spoken aloud.

Her eyes stay focused on mine though, and I love that she's not backing down anymore.

"You're preventing that, torturing us both, because you don't want no-strings sex?"

"It's a good reason, Kent. I wouldn't expect you to understand."

"I understand." I'm not an idiot. My mouth opens to offer her strings attached, lots of strings, really big ones, all woven together. But, thankfully, I realise what I'm about to do before I say anything.

I wouldn't even know how to do anything more than sex. Freya was a long time ago, and I was younger. I'm pretty sure women don't like exclusive dates to McDonald's and the local bowling alley.

I've now established that Savannah isn't stuck up, but that doesn't mean she's going to want to slum it on a date.

And why am I even considering dating again? Getting involved with my sister's friend and employee also adds another level of no to the equation.

"Good. I'm glad you understand where I'm at."

"You still want to watch me come on to another woman?"

"You still want me to watch you come on to another woman?"

Grinning, I reply, "Well, I am curious."

"Well, maybe you should come out with us tonight then."

God, I love these games with her.

"You're on."

"Kent?" she breathes.

"Yeah?"

"You're not going to tell anyone about what happened back there, are you?"

"As much as my boys would love to hear about how I got you off in a restaurant, a gentleman never tells."

She blinks. Then, she asks, "So, you never talk about conquests to your friends?"

"All the time." My heart quickens. "You're different."

"Oh." She takes a step back and looks around. Either she doesn't know what to say or she's looking for Heidi.

She shouldn't be different, but I can't lie to myself anymore. The whole time I was hating Savannah, I was really hating Freya. Savannah's reluctance to be anything other than a robot made me think she was hiding something the way Freya had.

They're not the same person, and I happen to like the person standing in front of me.

Savannah lifts her eyes and whispers, "Well, thanks." She really can't take a compliment.

Rather than act like a dick and call her out again, I say, "Want to get a crepe before Heidi makes you paint your face?"

"Sure."

After we all split, I meet up with Max and Toby. They would absolutely love to hear about today. Max and Toby would probably give me some sort of medal. Max would *definitely* give me some sort of medal. He would also do it in front of Savannah.

I'm meeting her and Heidi again tonight, but I need to start early with the guys because I know I'll go crazy if I'm home alone.

When we got outside the restaurant, Savannah put the walls up again. All of a sudden, she was listening to her head. I couldn't imagine not acting on emotion. It'd be a boring, cold way of living if you never handed yourself over to something you wanted.

But, after telling her that she was different, she spent the rest of the afternoon flirting ... at a safe distance. About two minutes after we dropped her off at her apartment, I sent her a text.

LIE TO ME

I don't know what happened to playing it cool, but I've been very uncool and probably a bit desperate.

She replied straightaway though, so maybe a bit desperate is just our thing.

"He has girl trouble," Toby says, cautiously eyeing me.

"He does," Max agrees, resting his elbow on the arm of the chair and rubbing his chin. "But he's not pacing and swearing like he did with Freya, so this Savannah chick hasn't lied to him or stolen his money."

I raise my hands. "I'm right fucking here."

They're so aggravating when they talk about me like I'm someplace else.

"Then, you do the talking. What's up your arse?" Toby picks up his pint and tilts it toward me. "Open up to your buddies."

"I hate you both. Nothing is wrong. We always drink on Saturdays."

"Not usually at four in the afternoon though, mate," Max replies.

"Fucking hell, can we not have an earlier session without it meaning something?"

They look at each other and frown.

"Toby, what do you think? I'm voting no."

Toby nods. "I'm voting no, too. There's definitely something wrong."

I need new friends.

"What's she done, Kent?" Toby asks.

Sighing into my beer, I start to question what I actually like about these dickheads. "She hasn't done anything."

Max points at me. "And there is the problem. We knew it. We've said this before; you want the blonde."

"How do you know she's blonde?"

He rolls his eyes. "They're always blonde."

"That's not ..." My sentence dies off when I realise that is actually true.

I have a type. Savannah physically fits my type, and after this afternoon, there's no part of her that I think doesn't fit.

I honestly thought she would push me away. It was such a turn-on to watch her internal battle before she gave herself over to me.

I won that battle, but the war is still up for grabs. And I don't intend to lose.

Toby grins. "You like the fairer hair. I do, too."

"You like all the hair, mate," I reply.

Toby isn't fussy.

"That's true. Heidi is dark brunette."

Taking a breath, I glare at the fucker. Sisters are left out of shit. Unfortunately, Toby didn't get the memo.

Max grips his heart. "If you marry Heidi, Kent will be your brother, and there will be no time left for me."

I roll my eyes. "Dude, have you been taking oestrogen pills?"

"Fuck off, Kent."

"Do you like her?" Toby asks, cutting through the bullshit.

"I didn't," I reply.

He deadpans. "So, you do now."

"Not how you think. I want to fuck her, and I no longer think she's a stuck-up bitch. You know I'm not interested in getting into anything."

Am I? I was willing to offer her strings before. I didn't even think about it. I just almost blurted it out. We talk all the time—well, flirt over text—and I can honestly say that, each time we're messaging, it's the best part of my day.

"Dude, you were nineteen when you said that, and the whore had just fucked you over. If you spend the rest of your life alone because of her, she wins."

I know all that. For the longest time, I've been okay with being alone because I'm young and hot, I have a successful business and my own apartment, and I have plenty of sex, but the further down the road I look, the more that doesn't seem like enough.

LIE TO ME

That's not to say that Savannah is the one or any shit like that, but the way we are together, the banter and bickering, yeah, it makes me miss being more than a shag.

Fucking woman is royally screwing my life.

"Toby's right; don't let that bitch Freya win. I fucking hate her with a burning passion. Her mum should have swallowed."

"Lovely, Max," I reply, but I can't disagree. I wish I had never met Freya. "I need whiskey."

Max stands. "Yeah, ya do."

Toby waits until Max is at the bar. "When can we meet her?"

Fuck. "Tonight."

He sits up straighter and smiles. "Yeah?"

"We're going to a club."

"Mate, you can't take me and Max on your date."

"It's not a date, dipshit. Heidi is going, too."

"Hell yeah!"

"Stay away from my sister."

Chuckling, he reclines in the armchair. "Don't worry; I'm only teasing."

"You'd better be. I know where you've been, and Heidi doesn't need someone to walk out on her."

"Ouch, bro!" He shrugs. "You're right though; I'm definitely not down for the relationship thing yet. Did you know you could get married at *eighteen*?"

Rolling my eyes, I reply, "Of course I knew that."

He looks me dead in the eye, nose scrunched in disgust. "Why would you want that? You're practically still a kid."

"No, *you* were practically still a kid."

"Oh, right. I forgot I couldn't count on you to agree with bull like this anymore, not now that you're pining for Savannah."

"I am *not* pining for anyone."

Or maybe I am. I miss her. I damn well miss her.

"Yeah, all right. I can't wait to meet her tonight." He laughs darkly. "What are you going to do if she likes me or Max more than you?"

I give him a look. "Have a word with yourself, Toby."

That's never going to happen.

"I'm just saying, buddy, it's not a guarantee just because you're hung up on her."

His smile widens, and he kicks one foot up on the low table in the middle of the four armchairs. I turn away because he's smug as fuck and pissing me off.

I am not hung up on her. Much.

13

Savannah

I DRAG MY LIGHT-PINK Mac lipstick across my lips and press them together. I'm half-drunk, thanks to two large glasses of pink gin and tonic, which isn't normally part of my going-out routine—mostly because I don't really go out—but Kent will be there tonight, and things got a little weird after lunch at the Mexican restaurant.

Then, things got a bit hot over text.

Heidi rings my doorbell. I know it's her because she jams her finger into it for, like, five solid seconds. *Don't I regret telling her the keycode for the communal front door!*

Where's the bloody fire, Heidi?

Jogging from my bedroom to the front door—which, to be fair, doesn't take long since my apartment is small—I tug the door open. "What is wrong with you, woman?"

She laughs and raises her arms in the air. "I'm here!"

"I've noticed," I reply dryly.

Her arms drop. "What's wrong?"

"Nothing." I smile, shaking my head. "Come in. I have a bottle of gin waiting."

"Predrinks, Dean? I like it."

I close the door, and Heidi heads to the kitchen area in the corner of my open-plan living area. She's wearing a gorgeous emerald-green dress, clinging to all the right places, and her hair is sleek and straight.

"I think predrinks are necessary."

Tomorrow is Heidi's birthday barbeque at her parents' house, and I plan on having predrinks before that as well because Kent will be there.

She spins on her toes, eyes narrowing with suspicion. "Why?"

Because I like your brother, and him texting, telling me he wants his mouth on me next time, has made me rather bloody horny!

There. I'll admit it to myself. I like him, and I'd like to know more.

"Isn't that part of doing your twenties right? Shouldn't you be half-drunk before you even leave?"

Silence hangs in the air. She suspects my drink is because of Kent. Of course she does; she's not stupid. I've seen her watching us. Thankfully, she wasn't looking too hard in the Mexican restaurant.

"I guess," she replies, pouring herself a glass. "No other reason you need alcohol before we go out drinking?"

"No," I reply, my heart racing at the lie. I shake my good hand and pick up my drink.

You would think lies could roll off my tongue without a second thought now. After all, I've been hiding the truth from Heidi for years now. But I never enjoy it. To be honest, it's exhausting, and I hate lying to people I care about.

"Hmm," she murmurs, bringing her glass to her lips.

"We should have just enough time to drink these and then go to meet Kent and his friends."

Light-blue eyes peek at me as she takes a sip of gin.

I feel like I'm under interrogation. Her gaze comes thick with speculation.

"Okay, just get it all out, Heidi."

She lowers her glass and blows out a puff of air. "All right. What's going on between you and my brother?"

"Nothing. We've just decided not to hate each other. It makes situations, like tonight, much easier on everyone."

"Really?"

"Yes. Nothing is going on."

Her eyes narrow, like she doesn't believe me. I'm sure as hell not telling her about the Mexican-restaurant incident and the fact that we text multiple times a day. She doesn't need to know that anything has happened between us.

"It would be okay, you know."

I hesitate before answering, "What would?"

Sighing like she's frustrated with me, she replies, "You and Kent. It wouldn't bother me. After Freya, I didn't think he would find someone he liked until he was in his fifties or something dramatic like that. He tends to hold grudges, so I thought he would be too stubborn to let anyone in."

"Heidi, you're reading into things a bit too much. Just because we decided to get along doesn't mean that he likes me beyond a friend." Or beyond getting me off in a restaurant. That was just him proving that he could.

"Uh-huh." She lifts her manicured eyebrow and takes a sip.

"Okay, drink up. We're going," I say, frowning.

She had better not be like this all night.

"I've always wanted a sister," she teases.

"You have a sister."

"Not a younger one."

I roll my eyes. "Don't say shit like this tonight," I whine.

"Oh, please, I know my brother."

What does that mean?

You know what? For the first time in forever, I'm not going to overthink this.

I tip the rest of the gin down my neck and put the glass down on the countertop. "Let's go."

Heidi follows suit, and we head out of my apartment. Arm in arm, we walk the ten minutes deeper into the city, to the club that Kent suggested. Obviously, being a hermit, I haven't been before.

There's no queue, so we head straight inside.

Although it's dark, my eyes immediately seek Kent. It takes me seconds to find him. He's by the bar with two other guys, laughing. He's easily the best-looking man in here. Hell, he's easily the best-looking man on the planet. Shame he's a massive womaniser and allergic to relationships.

Not that I want a relationship with him.

You definitely do not, Savannah!

"Over there!" Heidi says, pointing to Kent and his friends.

"Oh, yeah," I reply with a smile, pretending like I haven't already seen him.

We weave through the crowd, and my heart beats harder with every step closer to him I take. Heidi is practically bouncing; her steps are animated, like a child out trick-or-treating. She's looking forward to tonight. I was until I got here. Now, I have butterflies in my stomach.

"Hey," Heidi says as we reach the guys.

Three pairs of eyes turn to us. Kent's instantly snap to mine. He straightens his back, eyes widening a fraction and nostrils flaring. Usually, I'd think that look is down to him liking what he sees, but with Kent, I can never be sure.

It depends entirely on what his mood is.

"Ladies," the friend with jet-black hair says. "Lovely to see you again, Heidi." He turns to me. "You must be Savannah. I'm Toby."

"Hey, Toby."

"Hey, I'm Max," the blond friend says.

"Nice to meet you."

"What are you two drinking?" Max asks. "It's my round."

Heidi puts her bag down on the bar. "I'll have a white wine, please. Savannah?"

I tear my eyes from Kent, who's still looking at me. "Er, gin and tonic. Thanks, Max. Are Brooke and Freddy still coming?"

"If they get back from his parents' early enough," Heidi says. "So, Toby, who's tonight's lucky lady?"

LIE TO ME

I turn away from Heidi and Toby as they get into a conversation about how he's waiting for her before settling down. I'm not sure if he's serious because she rolls her eyes, and Kent doesn't say anything. He doesn't strike me as a guy who wouldn't care that his friend and sister were getting it on.

Kent is still standing in the same spot. Max is leaning over the bar, giving our order, and Heidi and Toby are now sitting on stools, focused on their conversation.

Kent and I probably look really odd, standing near the bar, facing each other but not speaking. It should be awkward to look at a person for this length of time, but it's not. My heart thumps in my chest as he watches me like he's ready to pounce.

I offer him a smile. "Hey." One of us has to talk first, right?

He blinks and then nods his head. "Savannah."

My name is a whisper and sends a bolt of desire down south.

Don't even think it.

"How are you?" I ask. It seems like such a stupid thing to say after he had his fingers inside me this afternoon. Despite seeing him only a few hours ago, I've missed talking to him. Well, arguing with him. Flirting with him.

God, I thought I was pathetic before.

His lip quirks. "Good. You?"

I nod. "I'm fine. Looking forward to tonight."

Is he really going to try it on with another woman in front of me? I shouldn't want that, right? But there's something about him chatting up someone else when I know it's me he wants to take to bed that makes me all hot.

Unless he likes her and takes her home.

Oh God, this could backfire.

Narrowing his eyes, he leans in like he's trying to figure something out. "Are you drunk already?"

Why would he ask that? I didn't stumble, and my breath can't smell of alcohol. I had a mint on the walk here. "What?"

"Your eyes look drunk."

"Oh." My mind empties. Literally every word I know fucks off, and I'm left with no response. There's not really much I can do about my eyes.

Kent's light eyebrow arches.

If you're waiting for me to say something, you'll be waiting a while. I've got nothing here.

He sighs, and his eyes flick to the ceiling before landing back on me. "You look nice ... stunning."

I laugh. His voice is gravelly, half-sounding like that hurt him to admit and half-sounding like he's a bit turned on.

Again, I have no idea which one.

"Thank you." His compliment sends my mind into a bit of a spin. "Don't look too bad yourself."

And that was the understatement of the year. His plain black shirt perfectly highlights his sculpted chest and arms. The sleeves are rolled up his forearms. I'd love to know how long he spends working out. Hell, I'd love to watch him get all sweaty.

"Savannah?"

My body jerks at the sound of my own name. *Oh, dear God, no.* I feel my eyes widen as I look away from his chest. I was staring. Pressing my lips together, I ignore the burning in my cheeks, super grateful that it's not all that light in here.

Besides a smirk, he doesn't call me out for openly gawping at him.

It would seem that Kent's nice side is out to play tonight. *Good.*

Max hands Kent two drinks. One is mine.

"Thank you," I say to Max as Kent passes it to me.

Max wiggles an eyebrow and turns back around.

Oh, he so has the wrong impression. For anything to happen between me and Kent, we would have to get along for longer than ten minutes ... and he would have to stop being a dickhead to me. Or, apparently, we'd have to share a meal.

"Your arm okay?"

"No more pain. It's just annoying, wearing the splint."

LIE TO ME

"If you need help getting changed, I volunteer," Max says, spinning around so fast, I'm surprised he didn't trip.

I tilt my head to the side. "Wow, thank you for the kind offer."

Max looks at Kent and shrugs. "I didn't hear a no."

Kent's jaw hardens.

"Hmm, not familiar with sarcasm," I say, and Max laughs. "No."

"You wound me, Savannah. I guess I'm not the one you want to unzip that beautiful, tight dress."

My hand tightens around my glass. *Don't throw it at him.*

"Right. I already have someone for that," I reply. I mean, it's me. I'm the only one taking my clothes off, but Max doesn't need to know that.

"You have a boyfriend? You said you were single." The muscles on Kent's forearms bunch.

Rolling his eyes, Max turns around. Great, he's the catalyst for this conversation, and he bails out when it gets awkward.

"I am single." Very, very permanently single, just how I like it.

Kent doesn't believe me. His eyes stare straight through me.

"I didn't lie," I add. Not about that anyway. "There is no one but *me*."

With a nod, his posture loosens up, as he understands that I do everything for myself.

Jesus, uptight much? Why would it matter to him if I lied anyway?

"Table!" Max shouts. He dashes between me and Kent, holding his drink out in front of him.

"Is he okay?" I ask, my eyes following him power-walking to a table in the corner.

Kent laughs. "We're not sure, but we should follow him, or he'll get lost."

"Dude, I'm marrying your sister," Toby says as he and Heidi also pass us.

Kent rolls his eyes. "Of course you are, dickhead."

Okay, Toby's definitely trying to wind Kent up. Doesn't seem to be working. He might actually have to marry Heidi.

I turn to follow the others, but Kent doesn't move.

"Are you coming or standing there the whole night?"

"After you."

I take a swig of my drink and walk. *I wonder if he knows how weird he is.*

The seating area in the club is along one side, heaving with people walking back and forth from their table to take a drink before returning to the dance floor.

A group of people to my left moves into my path. I turn away from them to protect my fractured arm, but it's not needed because Kent's arm reaches around me, blocking a guy who bumps into him rather than me.

What?

The bumper apologises and walks around the back of us.

I look up at Kent over my shoulder. "Thanks."

He takes a small step back and lowers his arm. "It was nothing."

Kent sidesteps me and walks over to everyone else, who is now sitting down. They've left two chairs free—next to each other, of course. I take a seat between Kent and Max.

Max leans over. "So, Savannah, tell me about yourself."

"Not much to tell."

"Oh, there's plenty. You just don't want to."

Correct.

I shrug. "I moved here three years ago from a small town, and I've never looked back. I like pizza, coffee, wine, gin, clothes, and summers spent in pub gardens. I hate arrogant men," I say, looking directly at Kent.

Kent smirks. "You keep telling yourself that, babe."

Toby slaps Kent's arm with the back of his hand. "You definitely don't want this arrogant prick, Savannah. I'm much more of a gentleman."

"I just watched you trying to bed your best mate's sister," I reply flatly. "Doesn't exactly scream gentleman. You've not even offered to take her out."

Toby sits back in his seat, mouth popping open a fraction.

"Yeah, she talks back," Kent mutters, lifting his eyebrow at his mate.

I smile because I'm starting to. Slowly, Kent is bringing me back, and I'm not sure what that means. If it even means anything. Maybe he's just the one to piss me off enough to snap me out of my funk.

I've missed having a group of friends like Kent has. In my teens, I was surrounded by people. Becoming a shadow was my choice, but I never realised how much I'd faded until I saw people carefree, and I started behaving like the old me.

I'm basically a sixty-year-old woman.

Toby flicks his index finger up in the air. "I said I wanted to marry Heidi, not just sleep with her."

"You said that to wind Kent up. I bet you've never even had a girlfriend before."

"I've never had a girlfriend, but at least I'll have more than one night with a woman."

I don't need to ask, but I do anyway. "Who can't have more than one night?"

"Kent. He thinks they'll get attached if you spend too long with them," Max says, injecting himself into the conversation.

"I don't see how that's possible," I tease, grinning at Kent.

Max chuckles and points at Kent. "The lady has a point. You're hardly a catch."

"Why are you two talking about my love life?" Kent grunts.

"Spending two nights with a woman isn't going to make them fall in love with you. It doesn't make sense to me," I say.

"Hmm, interesting. Why do you think he has only one night then?" Max asks.

"Micro penis?"

Max throws his head back and laughs at the same time Kent bellows, "What the fuck, Savannah?"

I grin triumphantly.

"I do *not* have a micro penis. I'll show you right now!" His hand reaches down to the zipper on his jeans.

"Whoa!" Heidi flails her arms. "You keep that in your jeans."

"Savannah, follow me to the restroom," Kent snaps.

"Absolutely not," I say the words, but I don't think I put enough disgust into them. Mostly because I don't totally hate the idea of being somewhere private with him. Unless he's in a shitty mood. If he'd asked that after the restaurant incident, I probably would have gone.

He makes eye contact, and it's the kind that hooks me and demands I don't look away. I lick my dry lips, and Kent's chest puffs. Okay, that wasn't meant to be teasing, but I'll take it.

"Are you ready to hit on someone in here?" I ask.

He watches me for a second before replying, "Yeah, you."

Laughing, I shake my head. He's persistent; I'll give him that. It feels really nice, having someone chase me. It's been a long time since I've felt desired. A bloody long time.

"Fine." His head dips, and he whispers, "Which woman do you want me to talk to while you sit here and watch, getting wetter and wetter until you're begging for my cock?"

I bite my lip. *Why is this so hot?*

"Any. I don't care. And it's going to be you doing the begging."

He leans back, shrugging. "I'll do it now if it'll work."

"Go, Kent!"

With a wink, he gets up and walks to the bar. I don't miss the bulge in his jeans.

Every encounter with Kent, whether good or bad, is foreplay. I know I'm not supposed to have one-night stands, but that rule seems so stupid now. But I don't know how I'll feel the morning after, and I vowed to never allow a man to hurt me again, not if I can help it anyway.

Kent screams heartbreak.

LIE TO ME

I watch him, feigning interest in the conversation Heidi, Toby, and Max are holding, but I have no idea what they're saying.

Kent stops by a woman, and she does a double take. She obviously likes what she sees because she twists her body and arches her back, so he gets a better view of her cleavage. Obviously, he picked the woman with big boobs.

Mine aren't big.

Kent steps closer, but I notice that he makes sure I can clearly see his profile, so right now, I'm still on his mind. The woman, who I decide I don't like, laughs, throwing her head back.

I bet whatever he said wasn't *that* funny. *He's not a fucking comedian, love.*

Still, he has her eating out of the palm of his hand even while his eyes flick back to me.

He moves closer again and touches her arm. That's like throwing a bucket of cold water on a flame. My stomach churns. There wasn't supposed to be touching. Okay, I'm definitely enjoying it less now that there's been physical contact. It was hot, knowing that she wanted him and he was trying to get into my pants, but he's making it seem like she can have him.

His eyes move to me again, and a frown pulls across his forehead. I look away as ice settles in my stomach. This isn't fun anymore. It was much better when it was just a fantasy. I guess some things shouldn't be acted upon.

I run my fingers down the stem of the oversize gin glass. *Why did I ever think that was a good idea?*

He's made me lose my mind. I've not been this stupid in forever. Coming here tonight was a mistake.

I'm such an idiot.

"At what point did that experiment fail for you?" Kent whispers in my ear.

My breath catches. I turn my head, and yep, he's back.

"Well ..." I say, composing myself. *He came back.* My heart leaps. *He came straight back for me.* I take a breath to calm the thudding in my chest. "About the time you got hands on."

Kent smirks. "Noted." He sits back and grabs his beer.

Oh. He thinks I'm jealous. I did sound jealous just then. But I'm not. I mean ...

God. I'm jealous, and he came back because he knew that.

14

Kent

TOBY SLAPS MY BACK, and that's when I realise I'm still looking at Savannah.

I honestly think we should just sleep together and get all this sexual tension out of the way. She was jealous when I was talking to that woman. I was turned on, thinking about her watching me chat up someone else. In my head, I thought, when I came back to Savannah, she would be so horny, she would jump me.

However, I'm more than happy with how things turned out. Savannah is jealous.

"You good, bro?" Toby asks, grinning like a fucking prick.

"Fine," I spit.

I wish he would go back to trying to hit on my sister. Heidi would never go there. Plus, Toby is only after one thing, which Heidi isn't into. At least, I damn hope not.

"I'm sure she doesn't really think you have a micro penis," he replies. "You could always send her a dick pic if Heidi's getting all precious about not wanting to see it, too."

Heidi slaps Toby's arm. "Precious? Would you want to see your brother's penis?"

I turn my body, so they're more behind me.

Savannah is smiling and looking around the table. I don't think she has anyone besides Heidi. So far, she's fitting in with my friends, and I'm not sure how I feel about it.

Who am I kidding? I like it.

"Right. I think I've done enough small talk for now," Max says. He gets up and walks into the crowd on the dance floor.

"What was that?" Savannah asks.

"He's done talking to the group and going to look for a lady friend."

She rolls her pretty grey eyes. "I should have guessed. Is that what you all do?"

Yes.

"Not always."

"Not always? Sometimes, you don't feel like finding the girl you're bedding *once*?"

Leaning closer to her, I smile. Shit, I can smell her hair from here. "Tonight, I'm all yours."

I sit back to see her response. Her lips part.

God, it does not help me wanting to fuck her when I know she wants me as well. I don't know if she would agree to one night. I'm thinking not.

She recovers her shock and adjusts the strap of her dress over her shoulder. "You wish."

Yeah, actually, I do.

"You're going to deny you want to be under me?"

Lifting a single eyebrow, she shakes her head. "I don't think so. I'm not a one-time kind of girl."

Damn it.

"What's wrong with a one-night stand?"

"Nothing, if you *want* a one-night stand."

Savannah tries to be angry. Her grey eyes are narrowed, but she's leaning as close to me as I am to her, which dampens her fire a bit. She blinks heavily. Yeah, she wants me.

LIE TO ME

I need her to make the first move since she's the one saying no.

"I still can't believe you've never had sex with a stranger."

"Believe it, and you're not a stranger."

"Wow. You're sure you've definitely had sex before, right?"

Her cheeks turn pink. "Yes! Very funny," she hisses. "Not that it's any of your business."

"Was he shit in the sack? Lie there like a sack of potatoes and make you do all the work?" Smirking, I add, "Did *he* have a micro penis?"

Her eyes dart away.

Oh God, is one of those things true?

"I don't really want to talk about the guy I slept with. It's in the past."

"Did he break your heart?"

She looks back and stares me dead in the eye. "No. I've told you before, I've never had a proper boyfriend. He just messed with my head a little."

"So, micro penis or rubbish in bed?"

"Why are we talking about the guy I slept with?"

Yeah, why am I?

I raise both hands, conceding. "Want to dance instead?"

What the fuck? Dance? Why am I asking her to dance?

She jerks her head back, shocked. "What?"

I don't know why she asked that after she clearly fucking heard what I'd asked.

Tapping my foot on the ground, I spit out, "Dance."

"Well ... yes. I mean, yes, but you don't seem like the type to get out on the dance floor to dance."

"What do you think I do on a dance floor then?"

She playfully nudges my arm. "Dry-hump."

"Very funny, Savannah."

"Come on. Show me how you dance without rubbing yourself against me."

I stand up as she rises. "Where's the fun in that?"

"Where are you two going?" Heidi asks.

"To dance," Savannah replies. She bites her lip like she's suddenly realised I'm Heidi's brother, and she's not sure if she needs permission.

Heidi's eyes widen. "Oh my God, Kent, don't just dry-hump her!"

Savannah laughs and bumps my arm with her bad one. I don't want to wish pain on her, but I hope that hurt.

I tilt my head in Savannah's direction. "It's not funny."

"Yes, it is."

"We'll come with you. Toby, you can totally dry-hump me if you want," Heidi teases.

Fucking sister. I think I preferred it when she lived to work.

I lead Savannah onto the dance floor, being careful that no one knocks into her arm. This probably isn't the place for someone whose fractured arm is still healing. She's got another three weeks in the splint.

Turning around, I place my hands on her hips and groan as the feel of her makes my heart race. She doesn't seem to care that I'm touching her since nothing sarcastic comes out of her smart mouth. Her hands reach up and land on my chest.

Jesus.

She has better use of her fractured hand now. Before, she was holding it pretty still, but she's moving it as much as the splint will allow.

I wonder just how much she is able to do with that hand.

I close my eyes, feeling myself grow hard. It doesn't help that her body is all pushed up against mine in that tight little dress. I want to fuck her so bad, it's taking over my rational feelings for her.

Why can't I push her away and go find some girl who doesn't do my head in and who is very up for coming home with me tonight?

Savannah reacts to me just the way I want her to when she's not hating on me. Her body arches into mine, her stormy eyes hooded and pink lips slightly parted. She has never looked so beautiful before, and I want to kiss her so much.

I pull her closer, and I'm sure she can feel my erection against her stomach, but she doesn't address it. Not sure if that's a good thing or not. The fact that she looks like she wants to jump my bones is a good sign though.

Leaning in, I brush my lips against her ear and whisper, "You have no idea how desperate I am to slip my hand under that dress."

Even over the sound of the music, I hear her gasp. I back up an inch, so I can see her. She presses her lips together, but her cheeks are flushed.

"What makes you think I'd let you do that?"

Smirking, I reply, "Really? You're plastered against my chest, giving me looks that make me want to fuck you right here."

With a heavy blink, she moves back a little, so we're not pressed against each other. I don't really mind because I know why she's doing it, and as much as I want to tug her back, I love how hard she's fighting this.

"We're just dancing," she argues.

"That's how you always dance with men?"

Her light eyebrows pull together. "I don't usually dance with men."

"Oh God, please tell me you dance like this with women. Can I watch?"

Her mouth pops open, and her good hand whacks my chest. Laughing, I hold on to her tight in case she tries to get away. I'm so not done with her.

"I think we should go and get another drink," she says.

"Why? Because you're scared of what will happen if we keep dancing?"

We're going to end up in bed together eventually; it's inevitable. We both feel it, but I don't know if she's going to allow herself to act on it.

I would act right now if she were game. I'm over obsessing about being inside her to the point that I'm sorting myself out in the shower every day.

We're terrible together, but in bed, I know we'd be dynamite.

She glares, but the effect is lost somewhat by the fire in her eyes. "Drink, Kent."

"As you wish." I let go of her, and she drops her arms. Before she can walk off, I take her hand and lead her toward the bar.

I don't hold hands, so this feels weird. It's not a bad weird, but it makes my chest tight. Savannah doesn't tell me to fuck off either. Her fingers are between mine, curled tightly into the back of my hand.

We fit.

We approach the bar, and I pull her in front of me. Letting go of her, I place my hands on the black graphite bar. With my arms on either side of her, I've trapped her in. She leans her back against my chest—and there's the coconut—and I don't know how she can even try to deny the way she feels.

Denying us naked time is hurting her as well as my dick.

"What're you drinking?" I ask, leaning into her back.

"Something different. What are you having?"

"Beer."

She nods. "Then, I want beer."

Fuck me, I would love to taste beer on her tongue.

"I'm hard," I murmur into her ear.

She looks up at me over her shoulder. "I know."

"Fucking tease. Let me take you back to mine. I have beer."

She turns around between my arms, and we're now face-to-face. "Is that how you get women?"

"No, I don't usually have to try."

She scrunches her nose up, but it's true. I'm awesome, great in bed, and hung like a fucking elephant. Women are happy to be under me. Savannah is making me work hard for it.

And I love that.

"You're disgusting, Kent."

"No, I'm honest."

"See, now, I don't want to sleep with you because I'm afraid I'll catch something."

I roll my eyes. "I'm clean, and you know it."

"How would I know it?"

Taking a deep breath, I battle the urge to either take her over my knee or strangle her. Instead, I step closer and press her up against the bar. "You just do."

I've always been careful and had the necessary checks. I might sleep around, but I always wrap up.

"Do you think this is a good idea?" she asks, lifting her eyebrow.

"Us?"

She nods.

"No, I don't, but that doesn't mean I'm going to stop." I graze my lips against her jaw and up to her ear. "When I want a woman, it's only a matter of time before I sleep with her. Granted, you're dragging this out so much, I've been left with permanent blue balls, but that doesn't change the fact that I'm going to be inside you soon."

I pull back. Her eyes blaze with anger, but her chest heaves with passion. She's having a massive internal debate, and I'm so looking forward to finding out whether she'll focus on hating me or getting into my pants.

"You're very sure of yourself," she rasps.

"After this afternoon, yes, I am sure."

Shoving my chest, she frees herself. "Don't be. I'm not like the rest of them."

Don't I know it?

Storming past me, she heads in the direction of our table.

I bite back a smile as I wait to place our drink order.

When I walk over to our table with our drinks, Savannah is sitting there, talking to another guy.

The motherfucker has his arm over the back of the booth, leaning in.

I stand over them and slam the glass bottles down on the table so hard, half of the alcohol spills.

The fucker's little beady eyes look at the drinks and then at me. "Can I help you?" he asks.

"Yeah, you can fuck off."

"Kent!" Savannah chastises.

Is she fucking serious?

"What are you doing?"

The guy shifts in his seat. "Is this your boyfriend?"

Savannah snaps, "No."

He holds his hand up. "I'm not looking to get in the middle of anything."

Neither Savannah nor I look at the prick as he gets up and walks off; we're too busy glaring at each other.

"You spilled the drinks," she says.

I laugh, but there's no humour behind it. I don't care about the fucking drinks. "That's all you have to say?"

Slipping out of the booth, she puts her hands on her hips. "I don't know what your problem is, but you need to back off."

"My problem? You're the one coming around my fingers and practically fucking me on the dance floor and against the bar, and then I come back to find you with that dickhead!"

"I was not nearly fucking you, and you're the one with the massive head, assuming I want you like everyone else."

"Savannah, you admitted it."

"Oh my God, you're so annoying!"

"Are you drunk?"

"No!" she snaps.

"Suffer from severe short-term memory loss?"

She growls, and her face turns red. "Fuck off, Kent!"

"You fuck off."

"Oh, good one."

Jesus, what the hell is her problem? My chest burns, temper ready to bust. "You know what, Savannah? Go back and find that guy."

Dismissively waving her good hand at me, she replies, "Maybe I will, and you go find someone nice and easy to sleep with tonight. Big tits at the bar seemed up for it."

"I will."

"Have fun with your syphilis."

I turn around, burning with anger, and scan the crowd. *Fucking syphilis.* I can't deny that her comeback was much better than mine, but I'm sure as hell not going to admit it to her.

Ignoring whatever she's doing behind me—I don't care anyway—I head over to a woman at the bar. She was eyeing me earlier, so she's the easiest bet tonight.

Smiling as I lean on the bar beside her, I say, "That dress is really working for me."

She turns to the side and smiles. I know I've got her. "Is that right?"

I drag my eyes down her body. "Oh, yeah."

All I can think is how much better Savannah's dress and her body work for me.

Well, she can get the fuck off my mind.

What am I thinking? If she was easy to expel from my head, I would have done it a long time ago.

I'm so over Savannah. This new chick is coming home with me.

15

Savannah

MY HEAD HURTS. THE previous night's events come flooding back the second I open my eyes in the morning.

I pull my legs into my stomach and groan. *What the hell was I thinking with Kent last night?* Well, he asked me to dance, and he was being nice and flirty, so I thought we were getting on. He was the one coming on to me. Until I told him where to go, and he moved on to another woman, that is. Though he left alone.

I got jealous, and we argued like a damn married couple.

Oh my God, can the ground swallow me up, please?

How am I supposed to face seeing him at Heidi's birthday barbeque today?

Maybe I can pretend I'm sick. Heidi wasn't around to see my argument with Kent last night, so she won't know I'm lying.

Kent will though. But I'm firmly back to not caring what he thinks.

I reach for my phone to text Heidi and warn her that I'm not well, so I might not make it today. I'll give her the gift I bought when I see her at work on Monday.

Unlocking my phone, I see three missed calls from an unknown number.

My finger hovers above the screen to ring it back. Unknown numbers always make me nervous since I left my parents' house.

I should just ignore it and call Kent. There's some damage control that I should work on since I've become friends with his whole family. A part of me wants to do that. I want to call him and say everything that's on my mind, but the other part doesn't ever want to see him again. I'm so stupid for thinking he actually liked me, that our rocky start was over.

I always run from confrontation. I keep to myself, so I can't be hurt again. I've become a shadow of my old self because of my past. I don't want to keep running. I want to be strong again.

The old me wouldn't take any crap.

Jesus, I can't believe I'm doing this.

With a deep breath that has my heart thumping, I call the landline number I'd missed.

"Savannah?"

I drop the phone like it's on fire, and my hand flies to my throat.

"Sav?" My name is quieter this time because my phone is facedown on my bed, but his voice is unmistakable.

Simon.

How did he get my number?

No.

My heart drops.

I flip it over and end the call.

When I ran away, I changed my number. I'm going to have to do that again. Heidi is going to ask why, so I'm going to have to tell another lie.

My phone starts ringing again, so I flick it on silent.

This is just fucking fabulous.

My doorbell rings. I rub my temples.

Whoever it is needs to go away. It's Sunday, and after last night, I don't want to see another human for at least twenty-four hours.

Everything can go to hell.

Fuck Simon.

Tears sting my eyes. He wasn't supposed to find me. I can't have him calling.

The bell rings again.

Sighing sharply, I shove the quilt off me and get up, leaving my phone flashing with another call from Simon.

Not happening, arsehole.

I stomp through my apartment like a kid having a tantrum and yank my door open.

Kent looks up, and apparently, I can't catch a fucking break.

"Yes?" I say as a greeting. I'm on edge, my hands shaking from the shock of hearing Simon's voice.

Kent doesn't speak. His eyes trail down my body.

I'm still wearing an oversize T-shirt. I'm wearing *only* an oversize T-shirt.

Perfect.

Folding my arms over my chest, I glare. "What do you want, Kent?"

His eyes find mine again. "I wanted to see how you were."

"Why?"

He shrugs.

"I'm fine. Take care."

I grip the edge of the door and close it, but Kent shoves his arm in the way. He slides through the gap, and he's in my apartment.

"I'd kill for a coffee."

"If you don't leave, the only thing being killed will be you."

"Your place is nice," he says, looking around, ignoring me.

I want to be madder at him than I already am, but I can't. He doesn't look out of place in my living room.

I slam the door shut. "I'm putting shorts on. You make the coffee."

"I don't know where everything is."

"You're a big boy. I'm sure you'll figure it out." The very second the words leave my mouth, I know I've messed up.

Kent laughs. "Yes, I am, baby."

I roll my eyes as I walk away from him and into my bedroom. I'd love to kick him out, and I will, but I do want to hear what he's got to say first. Kent doesn't seem like the kind of person to go apologising to a woman, so this, whatever it is, will be interesting.

I throw on a pair of shorts and dash into my bathroom to brush my teeth. My reflection in the mirror is awful. Hair is a wild mess, matted at the side, and I didn't properly remove my makeup because I have two thin black lines under my eyes from my mascara.

Excellent.

At least Kent was too fixed on my semi-naked body to notice my face.

Dragging a brush through my long hair, I manage to tame it, so it looks somewhat decent. I don't care about dressing up in front of Kent though, so I take a wipe and run it under my eyes. I'm not putting makeup on today.

Closing my eyes, I grip the edge of the sink. *Keep calm. Everything is going to be okay.*

Unlocking my bathroom door, I walk through my bedroom and into the kitchen/living area.

Kent is pouring boiling water into two mugs when I make my way over.

"You have milk and no sugar, right?" he asks.

It's such a weird and domesticated question, which sounds odd, coming from him.

"Milk, no sugar, yeah."

What are we doing?

LIE TO ME

I stop beside him and watch him tip a spoonful of sugar into his mug. He glances at me, his eyes drinking me in.

Why does he have to be so good-looking? I've not been this attracted to a man in … forever. Physically attracted. Beyond skin deep, I just think he's a massive twat.

"You're staring, Savannah."

"I've not seen you look away yet, Kent."

His eyebrow rises, and the corner of his lip quirks. "You're fun in the morning."

"Just finish the coffee, so you can be on your way." I turn away and go sit on my sofa.

I don't like him being here. He's too close to my life, being in my apartment. Heidi has only been here a couple of times.

Although he went off and spoke to a woman, he didn't actually do anything. He calmed down, said good-bye to Heidi and his friends, and left alone. Toby didn't say anything, but he was the one to witness our argument. Heidi had been dancing with a guy, and Max had taken off with a woman he'd met.

Kent joins me and puts the drinks on the coffee table. "Hungover?" he asks.

"Nope."

"You're angry. Why are you angry?"

Is he for real?

"I'm not angry. I'm annoyed."

Annoyed at Kent for leading me on, annoyed at myself for falling for it, and annoyed at Simon for being such a massive prick. My phone is in the bedroom, and I don't dare look at it yet. Simon is forcing me to change my number. I don't know who he'll tell, but my parents haven't tried to get ahold of me yet, so he must have kept it to himself. Unless, of course, my parents aren't really that interested in contacting me.

"Why are you annoyed?"

"You woke me up," I quip, lying through my teeth.

"That's it?" He shifts his body, and his leg presses against mine. "I'm sorry about last night."

"You have nothing to apologise for."

"I don't?" he asks.

I nod my head, diverting my eyes. "Nope. Most of the time, you can barely stand me, so I really don't know why you feel the need to say sorry."

He's not even voiced what he's saying sorry for.

"Savannah," he whispers.

Defiantly, I ignore his plea and reach for my coffee. I cannot wait to get this damn splint off. This morning, the restricted movement is proper pissing me off.

"I don't dislike you."

Rolling my head, I look up at him. "You don't?" My words are sarcastic because he certainly does dislike me.

"No. You irritate the fuck out of me, but I don't dislike you."

I get the impression he silently added *anymore* on the end there.

"Why do I irritate you?"

"Because you're not being you. I see you hold back so much that you want to say."

How the hell does he see that?

I clench my teeth.

"Why are you holding back?" he asks.

Fuck off.

"I'm not holding back. I just have very little patience for bullshit, so I prefer to keep to myself." That is true. Since Simon, I have no time for most people.

He watches me for a minute. I'm not sure if he's going to push the matter or let it go.

"All right." He nods. "So, if we're not arguing, I'll get the real Savannah? Like the first part of last night."

Ah, the part before we argued in the middle of the club.

"Maybe. If you can manage not to piss me off."

Chuckling, he throws his arm over the back of my sofa. The tension in his muscles is gone. I think he believes me.

He smirks. "I'll try my best. Do you want to talk about me getting you off with my fingers or us almost having sex on the dance floor?"

My back stiffens. "No."

What the fuck? Who brings that up? Well, Kent does.

"Are you sure? I'm trying not to piss you off, so to do that, we should talk about what happened."

"You know nothing about women! That's the exact opposite of what will not piss me off."

How is an intelligent man, who is also a successful business owner, so fucking stupid?

"I wanted to take you home, too," he says.

"Oh my God, Kent, stop." I don't need his pity. This whole thing is humiliating enough as it is.

"What's your problem? Why don't you want to discuss this? I don't like holding back. I hate secrets and fucking lies."

The venom in his words makes my heart slow. *What?*

"Are you still talking about last night?" I didn't lie last night.

His chest caves with a sharp intake of breath. He slowly breathes out. "No, I just ... I'm sorry. I prefer to have everything out in the open."

Yeah, that worked amazingly the last time I had everything out in the open ...

Can't say I'm loving out in the open.

"We both had a few drinks, and it happened. Or didn't happen. Whatever. It's done, so don't worry."

"Don't worry?" he asks.

I nod. "Yep. Let's forget it."

Kent frowns. "All right."

"Good. It's forgotten then," I confirm.

Kent's eyes linger on mine.

Nothing is forgotten.

16

Kent

FORGET. SAVANNAH WANTS US to forget. I know we probably should since things go from inferno to ice cold with us in a nanosecond, and that's not good with her being my sister's friend, but I can't—not the part where we were dancing and flirting, and it felt as natural as breathing. Everything was going well, and we were getting on. I got to see that side of her that made me genuinely like *her* and not just her body.

Of course it wasn't going to last.

We fucked things up. *I* fucked things up.

"So, is that all you came here for?" she asks.

I came here to pick up where we'd left off before I made a mess of things. But I can't tell her that. She wants to forget it.

"I wanted to clear the air before Heidi's barbeque."

She kicks her legs up underneath her. "Yeah, I'm not sure if I'm going to go."

"Why not?"

"I'm not feeling well."

She just looked me square in the eye and lied.

My hand tightens around the handle on the mug, and I resist the urge to snap. It's a white lie, one she feels she has to make because of my behaviour last night. I might hate lying, but I can't hold this one against her, not when it's me she wants to escape.

"Really? You didn't have that much to drink last night."

"It's not alcohol-induced. I'm just not feeling great."

I sigh, closing my eyes. "We're cool now, Savannah."

"Yeah, I know. This has nothing to do with you."

When I open my eyes again, she's nervously biting her lip.

"Bullshit." I take a sip of my coffee.

Savannah glares at me, her naked face impossibly beautiful, even when she's angry. "It's not bullshit."

"Heidi really wants you there. So does Brooke and my mum."

"I'll invite them out to lunch one day."

Fuck, she's impossible.

"It wouldn't suck for me to have you there either."

There, I said it.

Jesus. I like Savannah. Despite knowing very little about her and only seeing her true personality a couple of times, though she's always herself in messages, I like her. And not just in a wanting-to-get-her-naked way. I just wish she would drop the false side of her that she was so determined to show the world. It's like, if she portrays herself as someone in the background, she won't be bothered.

After everything I've been through, I still know I don't want to live a lie.

"Why? So, you can come on to me all night and then leave with one of Heidi's friends?"

"Yes, to the first part, and, well, you're the only friend going, so yes to that, too."

She rolls her eyes. "You're not coming home with me."

"I'm home with you right now."

"You know what I mean, dickhead!" she says, nudging my arm.

"Can we call a truce again? No more arguing."

"That sounds easy." The sarcastic tone in her voice makes me laugh. "It's not worked the other times we've tried."

"Yeah, we're not good at that."

She lifts her eyebrow. "Perhaps because you keep bringing up screwing each other's brains out every five minutes."

I hold my hand up. "Sorry, it's hard not to when you constantly make me hard."

"Didn't we *just* say we're not going to do that?"

"Sorry." I grin.

"I'll come to Heidi's barbeque," she concedes. "You'd better be on your best behaviour, Lawson!"

With a salute, I reply, "I'll be like a Boy Scout. Or a monk."

"I'm surprised you even know what a monk is."

"Come on, I'm not that bad."

"Have you only ever had one girlfriend?"

Why is she bringing this up?

"Yeah. Why?"

"Just wondering if there's a reason for the man-whoring or if you're a genuine one."

Laughing, I tip my head back. "A genuine one?"

"You know, one who just likes lots of sex and isn't trying to get back at anyone or the memory of someone."

I'm not a genuine one.

"Honestly?" I ask, and she nods. "Freya. We got together when we were seventeen, and by nineteen, it was all done."

She doesn't need any more information than that right now. She already knows way more about me and my family than I do about her.

"And, after that, you decided to sleep with everyone else?"

Laughing, I nod. "Something like that. I wasn't up for another relationship."

Her eyes round at my use of past tense. I wasn't up for another relationship, but now, I am. With her.

Would I really *start something up with Savannah?*

"What about you? Are you ready for the serious stuff?" I ask.

She hesitates, biting her bottom lip. Slowly, she dips her head in a reserved nod, like she's unsure. Or she's sure but scared.

"Now, is that because you're getting on a bit or because I'm too awesome?"

Her shoulders slump, and she loses the heat in her eyes. "What makes you think I would want a relationship with you?"

"I don't know how you're even trying to deny it. Do you often let men make you come in—"

"Okay, you're no longer allowed to bring up the restaurant thing either!" she snaps.

"Good luck with that. It was the most amazing moment of my life."

She rolls her pretty grey eyes.

"I'm taking you to the barbeque," I tell her. "How long do you need to get ready?"

"You trying to say I look like trash, Kent?"

"Your hair is messy as fuck, and you're wearing tiny shorts with a T-shirt that really doesn't hide the fact that you have no bra on."

With a glare, she wraps her forearms across her chest.

"Hey, I like that about your outfit. You look great."

She glares some more.

"Come on, you could never look like trash. But Brooke and Freddy are bringing Bobby with them, and I don't want him seeing those perfect tits."

"What if I want him to see them?" she says defiantly.

Sighing, I ask, "Do you, Savannah?"

I already know the answer, but I still wait for her reply.

"No, of course I don't."

"Drop your arm, babe. I don't like you hiding from me."

Why the fuck am I talking to her like she's mine?

Very slowly, her arm drops. Her eyes stay fixed on mine. I almost pass out.

LIE TO ME

Since when does this girl follow orders?

She's sitting beside me, bare legs crossed on the sofa, nipples popping against the thin material of her top, no makeup, and a fucking bird's nest on her head.

My idea of perfect.

"Why are you really here, Kent?"

"To clear the air after last night. It started off so well and then—"

"No, why are you really here?" she repeats more forcefully.

I know.

I'm here for her.

We've been building up to this since the first day in Heidi's studio. I've tried to deny it, but what's the point in delaying the inevitable? She is the first woman I've wanted to spend time with, be real with, since Freya, and I'm not about to ignore that any longer.

"I'm already tired of going back and forth, Savannah, and I've only known you for around three weeks."

She plays with her fingers, squirming awkwardly on the sofa. "I thought we talked about casual sex. I'm not going to be your fuck buddy, Kent."

I press my lips together because laughing at her right now isn't going to get me what I want. What I need. "I'm not here to get you into bed."

Her eyes lift, and her hands still as she tries to process what I mean. "What are you saying?"

"I want more than sex."

"Wait, say that again, so I can record it." She grins.

"Can you be serious for one minute? And, no, because you'll let Max and Toby hear the recording, and they'll never let it go."

"I wouldn't."

Yeah, right.

She laughs and shakes her head. "Sorry, what were you saying?"

Folding my arms, I say, "I'm not sure if I want to tell you now."

She untangles her legs and stands up. There is so much bare skin, I don't know where to look first. I breathe heavier as she slips down onto my lap. Her eyebrow lifts when she feels how hard I am for her.

She'll have to get used to that. I don't think it's going away anytime soon.

"Tell me, Kent."

I sit up straighter, so we're chest-to-chest, and I wrap my arms around her back. Her hair falls in front of her face as she leans closer to me. My dick turns to steel at the feel of her slim body pressed against mine and at the smell of coconut.

Grey eyes the colour of a stormy night burn into mine.

"My God, you're beautiful, Savannah."

Her lips part. "Please tell me why you're here."

Her fingers desperately dig into my shoulders. She needs to hear the words; it's not enough that it's damn obvious what I want.

"I'm here for you. I'm here because I can't get you out of my head, and I'm done trying. I knew I would want a relationship again at some point. I just didn't think it would be so soon. But I'm ready. You make me ready." I look down her top. "And this body is certainly making me ready."

When I look back up at her, she has tears in her eyes.

"Kent, I—"

We don't need any more talking. I press my mouth to hers, effectively shutting her up. Her response is electric. She grips hold of me and moans, arching her body into mine. There is no distance—the way it should be.

Fuck, she feels good. Why haven't we been doing this the whole time?

Her lips are as soft as I imagined they would be, but she kisses me back with the same desperation I'm kissing her. My hand finds her hair. I tangle my fist in her locks at the back of her head, the way I've been desperate to for weeks, and hold her exactly where I want her.

LIE TO ME

Crying my name against my lips, she grinds against my dick, and I nearly fucking go off. I feel the orgasm building, my heart hammering and hips rocking against her.

Savannah whimpers, mashing her mouth against mine as her body shudders. The sound of her coming is my undoing. Ripping away from her, I throw my head back, groaning as I come harder than I have ever done before.

Fuck.

What the fuck was that?

My chest heaves. Savannah collapses down on me, and I hold her closer.

I just came in my boxers. That's not happened since I was about fourteen.

"You're amazing," I whisper, my heart jackhammering against my chest.

"Hmm, back atcha, Lawson."

"The third time I make you come, it's going to be while my tongue is inside you."

Laughing, she splays her fingers out on my chest and pushes herself up. "Sounds good to me." Her eyes dance. "Shower?"

My eyes widen. "Fuck yeah, a shower!"

17

Savannah

I DRAG MY BRUSH through my damp hair. Kent is lying on my bed, watching me like a hawk. He's naked, I'm naked, and we're together. We haven't necessarily said the words, but we don't need to. We both know what this is.

When I woke up this morning, I did not expect that, today, I would be with Kent. Now, I'm not going to get too ahead of myself, as this is all very new, but I'm happy.

My heart is aching in the best way, phone call with Simon forgotten for now.

"You okay?" Kent asks.

Smiling at him in the mirror, I reply, "Yep. You?"

He smiles back. "Yep."

Taking a breath, I focus on brushing my hair out before it dries a mess rather than all the ways this could go wrong. Plus, it's hard to concentrate on anything when my mind is on Kent using his tongue on me in the shower five minutes ago. My legs still feel like jelly.

"We need to go soon," he says, glancing at the clock on my bedroom wall.

"You want to go?"

"You would let me blow off Heidi's barbeque?"

I turn to him and frown. "No way."

"Then, we need to go soon."

"You would blow off your sister's barbeque?"

"Absolutely. There is still so much I want to do to you."

I put my hairbrush down on the vanity table and walk over to him. He sits up, back straight but arched a little forward, like he's getting ready to pounce.

"There's still so much I want to do to you, too, Kent, but we can't miss Heidi's birthday."

"She'll understand."

I tilt my head and deadpan.

"Fine, we'll go," he concedes with a sigh. "But, as soon as we get back to your place, I need to finally be inside you."

We haven't had sex yet. He was very focused on me, and then we washed each other. Although I do very much want to have sex with him, I loved the sensuality of having his hands lather soap over my body. He was showing me that not everything was about sex to him, like it used to be, like I assumed.

"And, as soon as we get in the car to drive back to mine, I want you in my mouth," I say.

"Oh my God, Savannah, don't say things like that unless you really mean them, baby," he whines, sitting up on his knees and pleading with me with wide eyes.

"You're so cute." My legs hit the edge of the bed. "I mean it. You've been very nice to me so far."

"Yes, I have. I *really* deserve a blow job."

Laughing, I bat his chest with my good arm. "Ugh, I got my splint wet. That's going to take ages to dry."

Kent takes my arm, eyeing the black splint stretching from my wrist to elbow. "Does it hurt?"

"Not really. Well, a little after the living room thing." I smirk. "But it was worth it."

"Do you need painkillers?"

"No, it's fine."

"Orgasm? That'll take your mind off it."

LIE TO ME

The word *yes* is on the tip of my tongue, but there's no time. If we don't leave very soon, we're going to be late. And, if we're late, Heidi will ask questions. Or Judy will.

"Later. Get dressed." I step back, and Kent pouts. "You're such a baby."

"I'm hard again." He looks down at his erection.

I don't want to look because we do need to go, but when Kent wraps his hand around the base, I can't help it.

"What're you doing?" I breathe. "Kent, stop. We need to get ready."

"I'm not stopping you from getting ready."

"You're wanking on the middle of my bed!"

A burst of laughter explodes from his mouth. He drops his hand, using it to tug me onto the bed. "Wow, babe." Bending his head, he kisses me. "You have such a way with words."

"I want you," I murmur against his mouth. Watching him touch himself is so hot, I'm throbbing. "I need to come again."

He moans against my mouth and pulls back. "No more orgasms until we get to mine."

"What?"

With a laugh, he gets off the bed. "You've been teasing me for weeks. It's time to taste your own medicine."

"That's not okay, Kent."

What the hell is he thinking?

"I think I'm going to enjoy this," he says.

"You're still hard," I point out.

"Oh, I know it's going to suck for me, too, but I'll deal with it."

I fold my arms. "I've wanted you the last couple of weeks, too, you know. Do you have any idea how many times I've woken in the night, thinking about you, and had to take care of myself?"

His nostrils flare at my words. "You don't play fair, woman."

"No, I don't."

He steps into my space and cocks his eyebrow. "I guess we'll see who cracks first."

The bastard.

"I guess we will." I walk away, knowing he's watching, and bend down to get underwear from my drawer.

He takes a sharp intake of breath, and I smile.

I'm so winning this.

We arrive at Harrold and Judy's house with minutes to spare. They knew Kent was picking me up, so it's not suspicious that we've arrived together.

Though I don't know if we're supposed to keep us a secret or not. We've not discussed the details yet. We were too busy getting naked ... and not having sex.

Kent cuts the engine and looks across at me. "So ..."

Okay, looks like he wants to have that conversation now.

"So?" I prompt.

"If for any reason you don't want to tell anyone about us, let me know now."

"You plan on telling them?"

"Yeah. Why wouldn't I?"

Shrugging, I grab my bag from beside my feet. "I don't know. It's new."

"That means it has to be a secret?"

"No, of course not. I just haven't even had a second to process everything, and as much as I love your mum—"

"She's going to be very into this," he says, completing my sentence. "All right, why don't we agree to keep it to ourselves for today?"

"Okay."

"Just today, Savannah. I'm not hiding us any longer than that."

"Me neither. Besides, it'll make the game more interesting."

His eyes light up. "You still think I'm going to give in before you?"

"Oh," I say, opening the car door, "I know you are."

Kent follows me along the long path, carrying presents for Heidi.

"Your arse looks amazing in those shorts," he says, looking straight ahead, acting like he's not uttered a word.

"My arse would look better on your lap."

He purses his lips, but it fails to stop him from grinning.

I won that one at least.

What have I even turned into? My head is filled with all things dirty.

I've never felt this need to have a person all the time before. Old friends would confess to feeling the same when they got into new relationships, but I always thought I was different, or they were exaggerating because I didn't have that with Simon. Sure, we had sex, but he never made me feel like I was burning and like I had to have him right then and there.

So, I guess we weren't compatible sexually either.

"Mum, Dad!" Kent shouts as we let ourselves into the house.

"Everyone's out back!" Brooke shouts from the kitchen.

"Hi," I say to her as we head into the room.

"Savannah, hey." Brooke gives me a hug. "What are you drinking? I've made mojitos."

"Sounds perfect to me."

"Oh, hi, Brooke," Kent says sarcastically, dumping Heidi's presents on the table.

Brooke rolls her eyes. "Hi, Kent."

He heads out the back, running his hand over my butt as he goes past. I bite my lip. Every touch from him ignites my nerve endings.

Why did I hate him at first again? I can't imagine it now. I mean, I know he was a dick, but that seems like a different person.

"How are things?" Brooke asks, bringing me back. She pours me a glass of mojito from a massive jug.

"Thanks. Things are good. How's the wedding planning?"

"I swear, I'm never doing it again."

"That's the plan, right?"

She looks up. "Well, yeah. But you know what I mean. Whenever you get married, elope. It'll be much less stressful."

"Is there anything you need help with? Not sure how good I'd be at anything wedding-y, but I can try."

"Sure, I need a table plan sorted."

"Why don't you just let people sit wherever?"

She scrunches her nose. "Like a school canteen?"

I shrug, not knowing if that's the right thing to do or not. "Er, I don't know. Be easier for you though."

She frowns, weighing up the stigma I didn't know existed of having no plan with the irritation of having to do one. Surely, people are able to sit themselves down without being told where.

"Clearly, I'm no help," I say, taking a sip of my drink.

"No, you've given me something to consider. I'll see what Freddy thinks."

"Will he care?"

She laughs. "No, probably not, but I need him to tell me no plan is fine."

"That's cute."

"He helps me to stop second-guessing myself. It's stupid."

"It's not stupid." I needed to hear Kent say he wanted me because, if I'd let actions do the talking, I would have worried that he hadn't said anything, so he would have walked away.

There's a certain amount of reassurance we all need at times.

She smiles. "Thanks. Don't tell Heidi about this conversation. She's all about the strong, independent woman."

"Wanting Freddy's opinion or reassurance doesn't make you weak, Brooke."

"You know that, and I know that, but …"

Dipping my head, I reply, "Right. Well, my lips are sealed."

I take my phone out of my bag and check my messages while Kent is out of the way. There's one from Simon.

> *Simon: Let me know when you're free. We need to talk.*

That'll be never.

Deleting his text, I chuck my phone back in the bag and smile at Brooke. "Shall we join everyone else?"

"Let's do it," she replies, raising her glass and clinking it against mine. "Has my idiot brother been behaving?"

I blink at her question, my mind switching into overdrive. *Does she know something?* I can't see how she would know. We've been together for a couple of hours, and Kent hasn't been on his phone since. If she can sense it, she's a witch.

"He's been behaving," I confirm.

So not true. He behaved very badly in the shower.

I can't keep the grin from my lips.

18

Kent

WHEN SAVANNAH WALKS OUTSIDE with Brooke a few minutes after me, I can't take my eyes off her. She's carrying the cocktail Brooke made in her hand, and she's laughing at whatever my sister just said.

The way Brooke smirks over at me has my interest. She's probably ripping me. I never used to care what anyone said about me, whether it was joking or not, but I don't want my sister putting Savannah off. I'm sure she'll realise she can do a fuckload better soon enough anyway.

No, shut up. She won't. We're perfect together.

I'm going to try my damn hardest not to screw this up, but I'm not confident. All I know is that I really like her, and I'm not going to give up without a fight.

I don't have the energy to focus on what they're saying and think of some witty retort because my mind is still very much back at her place. Particularly her bathroom. Watching water cascade down her body while I was on my knees was incredible. I can still picture her fingers, white-tipped and practically digging into tiles. It must have hurt her fractured arm, but she was too lost to feel pain.

"Savannah," Mum says, getting up from the chair beside me where she was just talking to me.

I guess we're done now that Savannah is here. Mum fucking loves her, and hopefully now, I'll be able to keep her around permanently. She fits right in with my family.

"Hi, Judy." Savannah puts her drink down on the table and returns the hug Mum is going for. When she lets go, Heidi is right there. Savannah wraps her arms around my sister. "Happy birthday, Heidi!"

"Thank you. Those are to die for. I'm already on my third," she says to Savannah, pointing to the cocktail.

"I have some catching up to do."

She'd better not get drunk. We can't do anything if she's drunk, and I *really* want my blow job on the drive home.

I can still feel her soft and wet skin under my hands.

"Absolutely, girl. Today, we're getting drunk!"

"Don't get drunk, Savannah." The words slip from my mouth before I can stop them.

Wide grey eyes slide to me.

"You can't tell her not to get drunk," Mum says, frowning at me. "I raised you to respect women, not—"

"Calm down, Mum. I just don't want puke in my car."

Savannah takes a long sip of her drink. "I won't puke in your car."

She knows exactly what I mean when I told her not to get drunk. She also knows that nothing naked will be happening while I'm sober, and she's not.

"I hope not."

With a private, knowing smile, she turns back to my sister. "One night, I'm taking you out to that new cocktail bar near my street."

"You're on," Heidi replies.

"Brooke, you in?" Savannah asks.

"Absolutely. We'll arrange something."

Great, a girls' night out, getting drunk. If she's trying to drive me crazy, it's working. Men will probably try it on with her, and I won't be there to tell them to fuck off. Not that she can't do that for herself, but the thought of another guy touching her makes me angry as hell.

I slam my bottle down, and beer erupts from the opening, spilling over the top and running down the neck. "Shit," I mutter.

Mum gasps and grabs a pile of napkins.

Savannah shakes her head at me, grinning behind her cocktail glass.

Shit. She might win this.

"I've got it, Mum," I say, taking the napkins and chucking them on the spilled beer.

"Are you all right, love?" she asks. Her hands land on the table, and she leans in. "You seem a bit on edge. Has something happened?"

A lot has happened. I've let someone in, and I'm equal measures scared and excited.

"I'm fine. Just wasn't looking at what I was doing."

"Hmm," she replies, lifting an eyebrow.

Mum is naturally suspicious. While we were growing up, she accused us of way more than what we had actually done.

I look away from her because she'll probably guess if I hold her gaze for much longer. Goddamn woman knows almost everything.

"I think I know the problem," Brooke says. Savannah and I both freeze. "He's not had a lady friend round to play in a while."

Mum throws her hands up. "I'm not listening to this. I'm going in to help your dad."

Laughing, Heidi, Savannah, and Brooke take a seat around the table.

Freddy, sitting at the end, finally puts his phone down and pipes up, "What's the longest you've gone again? Was it three days?"

"Fuck off. I'm not that bad."

This really isn't a conversation I want to be having in front of Savannah.

Brooke points. "I think about a week. You're out every weekend with Toby and Max, and I bet you don't go home alone every Friday *and* Saturday."

Savannah's eyes are trained on me, but I don't dare look at her yet. She knows I've been with quite a few women, but I don't think either of us planned to discuss the details. I have no desire to work out how many it's been, let alone tell my girl. There are certain things that don't need to be shared.

"When did you break up with your girlfriend?" Savannah asks.

She knows when.

Heidi puts her drink down. "I get where you're going with this. He was nineteen, but the whoring didn't start until he was twenty. He's now almost twenty-six." She shakes her head. "Kent, that's a lot of women."

"There hasn't been one a week!" I snap.

My sisters laugh, but Savannah doesn't. She's very quiet.

I catch her eyes and hold her gaze. *I only want you. Please believe that.*

She *is* all I want. It's happened so suddenly and completely out of the blue; I never got a second to think or breathe. But she makes my pulse race and my body heat. I want to spend every possible second with her. I want to know everything that makes her the incredible person she is. And I want to protect her from whatever pain she keeps deep inside of her.

My heart stops until she smiles and wraps her hand around her drink. She got it. She knows there isn't anyone else I want to stick my dick in. I need her to understand that I'm all in. It might be terrifying, handing myself over to someone and trusting her when I've been burned in the past, but she makes me want to give her the fucking world.

I'm ready for a relationship. I want to be with her.

She turns her attention back to me and smirks. "There was a girl at the club."

"She wasn't my type. I prefer the girl from today."

LIE TO ME

Brooke mutters a distasteful sound. "Really? Before you came to your family home?"

"I had a shower, Brooke," I tell her.

Savannah presses her lips together, slumping a little lower in her seat. If she doesn't want this thing to be obvious, she's going to have to learn not to react.

Not that I dislike the way she reacts.

"You're disgusting," Heidi huffs.

Her eyes go to Savannah, like she's trying to figure out what she's thinking. I am, too, since her face is blank.

"Can we stop talking about how gross I am now, please?" I ask. This is a bad conversation to have while no one knows I'm with Savannah.

"That would be good," Heidi replies. Her jaw is tight as she looks away from me.

What the hell have I done to her?

Savannah's hand lands down on my knee. I hold my breath, gripping my beer. God, I love how bold she's becoming. Is it bad that I really want her to reciprocate what happened in the restaurant right now? I mean, my fucking sisters are only ten feet away, but I don't care about any of that right now.

I want her hands all over me, I want her mouth on mine, and I want her tight pussy wrapped around my cock.

"You okay?" she asks as Brooke strikes up a conversation with Freddy and Heidi.

"Uh-huh," I mutter through gritted teeth. "Fine."

"You seem jumpy." Her voice is light and flirty, but the innocence in her words isn't fooling me.

Plus, there's the fact that her hand is slowly working its way closer to my aching erection. I would give anything to have her right now.

I narrow my eyes at the little tease, which only makes her smile.

Fuck me, you're beautiful.

Her hand slips higher. I grit my teeth as her fingers grip my cock. My God, I want to unzip my jeans and give her full access. I feel like I'm going to come out of my skin. My chest tightens.

The command to unzip is on the tip of my tongue, but her hand moves. I snap my head to her, and she looks up at me through her lashes. There are too many people around to say what I want to her.

She doesn't speak, but she doesn't need to. I can see how smug she is and how much she's enjoying getting me all worked up and leaving me hanging.

"You're evil," I growl under my breath.

Her smile grows, and I can't say that I hate it. I've seen Savannah's smile, but it's never seemed so easy and genuine before.

She works hard to keep up appearances and hold people at arm's length, so I love being the one to break through all that bullshit. Under the armour is a woman who could easily bring me to my knees.

Savannah turns her head, joining the conversation with my sisters, not caring that I'm sitting here with a raging hard-on and the desperate need to come. I take a swig of beer and force myself to focus.

My mum comes back out and sits down.

"How many single people are coming to the wedding?" Heidi asks Brooke.

"Yes, darling, we need to find Heidi a nice man."

"And a dozen women for Kent to work his way around," Brooke adds, distaste dripping from her words.

Okay, fuck this. "That won't be necessary. That's all done with, no more one-night stands."

Mum gasps. "Why is that? Have you met someone? Who is she?"

Heidi instantly looks at Savannah and then back to me. She sits up taller. "Are you serious?" she squeals.

Everyone else looks at Heidi like she's lost it because they haven't figured it out yet.

"Serious about what?" Brooke asks.

LIE TO ME

"Savannah!" Mum replies, the ball finally dropping for her, too. She reaches in front of Heidi to wrap her arm around Savannah.

"Shut up!" Heidi says, squished back in her seat. "How did you manage that, bro?"

Mum moves back, and all eyes are on me.

"I'm charming."

Savannah laughs, not caring that I've told my family when we decided not to. "Yeah, you're a real gentleman."

"Worked on you, didn't it?"

"Why didn't you say anything?" Mum asks, cutting off my conversation with Savannah. "You've been here ages. When did it happen? How?"

Oh, she does not want me to say how.

"We were spending more time together and texting, and I guess I realised he's not actually *that* bad."

"Wow, that was so heartfelt," I tell her, clutching my chest.

She deadpans. "That's exactly what happened."

I lift an eyebrow. "Exactly?"

"Yes." Her reply is a warning.

I haven't even told Max or Toby what's happened between us, so I'm certainly not going to tell my family.

Heidi pours more of Brooke's homemade cocktail into her glass and then tops up Savannah's. "Well, have you been on a date? Did he ask you out?"

"Not yet," I reply.

"Kent! That's not how you woo a woman," Mum says, folding her arms.

"Woo?" I repeat, smirking.

"Don't get smart with me."

"Mum, we *just* got together," I tell her.

Mum looks back at Savannah. "This is your first time out as a couple? Kent, you should have taken her somewhere special."

"How is my birthday not special?" Heidi interjects.

"You know what I mean, darling." Mum puts her hand over Heidi's.

Savannah is grinning, amused that I'm getting shit from my mum.

"Anytime you want to jump in here and tell my mother that I'm not a totally shit boyfriend, that would be great." I realise what I said the second I finish.

We've only been together for a couple of hours, and I've dropped the boyfriend bomb. That's what I am though. We're together. No one else is in the mix—or they'd better not fucking be.

Savannah purses her lips, a light blush tickling her cheeks. "He's not *totally* shit," she says, not taking her eyes off me. The way she's watching me has my chest tightening. "Besides, there's plenty of time for dates. I was so not missing Heidi's birthday."

"Well, at least someone cares about my birthday," Heidi says, smirking at Mum.

"Stop being dramatic," Mum tells her. The attention is back on me seconds later. Mum isn't going to get bored of me and Savannah for a while. "Where are you going to take her on a date?"

Don't say, In the back of my car.

Grinning to myself, I steal a look at Savannah. She cautiously eyes me.

"I don't know, Mum," I reply.

"What do you mean? You need to think about these things, Kent," Dad says, coming up and showing that he's firmly on Mum's team here.

"Fine. McDonald's and bowling," I joke.

Mum gasps, but before she can yell at me, Savannah says, "I prefer KFC."

"You two might just be made for each other," Mum says, shaking her head, discouraged by the both of us.

The more time I spend with Savannah, the more I know we were made for each other. She makes me forget my past. I

LIE TO ME

have a clean slate with her. And I think I'm good for her, too. She's certainly not taking any shit from me anymore.

We lock eyes again, and she smiles.

I can't believe there was a time when I didn't want to be around her. Now, I can't get enough. When I text her, I stand still and wait for a reply. When I'm trying to focus, my mind flicks back to her. She's constantly on my mind, in every thought. It feels incredible.

For the rest of the evening, Mum is super fucking annoying. She's determined to make sure I treat Savannah right. I have no plans to mess around on her. I don't want to screw this up. There is nothing any other woman on this planet could do to make me stray.

At ten p.m., we're finally on our way to her apartment. Although Savannah had quite a few cocktails, she did eat a lot—because you have to at my parents'—and switched to water and coffee an hour ago.

She's not drunk, and I'm hard as fuck, waiting to see if she goes through with the blow-job thing. I don't want to say anything, almost as if I could jinx it. But she might still be up for it, just forgotten.

What the hell do I do?

Savannah rolls her head on the headrest, looking at me. "You look like you're deep in thought."

How do I get you to blow me?

"Just concentrating on the road," I tell her.

"No, you're not."

"How do you know that?"

"I'm not blind, Kent. I can see."

Huh?

I'm about to ask her what she means, but then I feel myself straining against my jeans. She knows I'm thinking about her.

"I can't help it."

"I like it," she confesses. "It's been a long time since I've caused this." Reaching out, she rubs my erection.

I hiss through my teeth, hands tightening on the steering wheel.

"Savannah, men have gotten hard over you; they just haven't told you."

She shrugs off my comment, and it makes me start to wonder why she doesn't think she's desirable. Of course, she knows I want her—that's been very clear—but does she somehow assume I'm a one-off?

"I'm going to unzip your jeans now," she says, tugging her seat belt loose, so she can reach.

I groan. "Hell yeah, babe."

Blow job is a go!

19

Savannah

EARLY THIS MORNING, KENT took me to my doctor's appointment to remove my splint. It feels so good to have full movement in my wrist and hand again. I get back to my apartment to grab my forgotten lunch. Kent didn't come in with me; he took off straightaway, something about a possible disciplinary for an employee. He was tense and snippy, and I could tell he really hated having to deal with crap like that. As the boss though, he has to.

He is meeting the office manager to discuss the details and tell him how to proceed, and then he's coming to the studio, as arranged, to bring Heidi and me breakfast.

After the spending the evening at Kent's parents' house, we got back to mine…and didn't have sex. It's bothering me.

Not that he doesn't want to, but last night, I fell asleep after getting a splitting headache shortly after we got back to mine. Kent got me tablets, and then held me in bed until I fell asleep.

I think it made me like him even more.

He's not pestered me for sex now that we're together, and I don't think he would, but he must be as sexually frustrated as I am. I'm a little worried that he's not making the first move because he wants to prove he's into this relationship thing. I might have to be the one to make the first move, and that doesn't seem like such a daunting idea, as I thought it would be.

Tonight, I'm staying at his. I'm not going to drink cocktails and get sleepy, and although my head feels fine, I have a pack of paracetamol in my bag, just in case. I will take pills at the first sign of pain.

I need him.

Dashing around my apartment, I grab my bag and slip my shoes on.

I'm running late. For the first time ever, I'm leaving the house ten minutes after I should, and it's the day that Kent is bringing breakfast to the studio.

I slam my front door and run down the stairs to the ground floor. Shoving the communal door open with my good hand, I dash out onto the street.

My world comes to a crashing halt.

No. No, no, no.

No. This is not happening.

"Sav."

He's come here. I didn't reply to any of his texts, so he's shown up.

His eyes bore into mine, and I feel like I'm going to pass out, like his gaze is squeezing my lungs.

"No!" I snap in Simon's face. "Go home, and get out of my life. I don't ever want to see you. Ever!" My voice is high, very accurately portraying how desperate I am to get him the hell away from me.

"Sav, stop," Simon says, lifting his arm to block me as I try to get past.

His use of my old nickname makes my skin crawl.

His arm touches my stomach, and I leap back. "Get off! Don't touch me!"

The thought of him touching me is revolting. I swallow back down bile.

LIE TO ME

"Don't be like that."

Heat blasts through my veins. "Don't tell me how to be, you prick! I think I made myself very clear when I left three years ago and changed my number. You never picked up on hints easily, Simon, but even you must get that one."

"We need to talk."

"No, I need to get to work, and you need to go home."

"I can't yet," he says, his eyes wide and bloodshot. He looks like he hasn't slept in days. Not that I care. "I need to talk to you."

I wave my hand. "Nope. Whatever you have to say, I'm not interested, and you can't be surprised. Leave me alone, Simon."

He growls, and his eyes darken. "It's not that simple, Sav, is it?"

"It is. Turn around, and walk away."

"You're not even going to hear me out?" he asks, his voice tight as he runs his hand through his messy blond hair.

"No. There is absolutely nothing you can say to make what you did better. I will never forgive you, so go away. Don't follow me, and don't come back here. I mean it. Go. Please, just go!"

He grits his teeth, wringing his hands. "Fine!"

This time, I shove past him, knocking him off the path, but unfortunately, he doesn't fall into the road and get run over.

He doesn't chase after me or even call out, so I take that as a good sign. I'm not going to hold my breath though. He's been messaging more, there was that missed call, and now, he's shown up. I doubt he's going to give up whatever he wants to do or say just because I told him to do one.

Power-walking down the road, I look over my shoulder, checking out both sides of the street.

He's not there. It's okay.

My heart slams into the floor. He can't come back here and potentially meet Kent. I have to think of a way to permanently get rid of Simon because I can't have him messing up my life again just when it's getting really, really good.

The studio door comes into view, and I feel like crying. My throat clogs, like I swallowed a golf ball. *This is not happening.*

I round the corner, getting lost in a crowd of people hurrying to work. My back aches from the tension in my muscles.

At the end of the road, Kent steps outside the studio and looks along the path. His eyes land on mine, and his shoulders drop.

He's looking for me.

My heart skips as he walks toward me, but my nerves are frayed. Kent's face is expressionless, but his eyes portray everything and make me weak.

"Hi," he says, stopping a meter away from me.

"Hi back," I reply, the shock and stress of seeing Simon ebbing away as Kent's turquoise eyes stare into mine. "I'm late."

"Yeah." He smirks. "Heidi is pissed."

Gasping, my hand flies to my chest. *Shit.*

"Calm down," Kent says with a chuckle. "I'm kidding."

"What the hell?" I slap his upper arm with the back of my hand, and we walk to the studio. "That's not funny. I don't want to let her down."

I walk through the door, and Heidi looks up at me, smiling. Thank God she doesn't look pissed off.

"You okay?" she asks.

"Yeah. I'm so sorry I'm late. I don't even know what happened. I was rushing around and—"

She lifts her hand. "Savannah, don't worry about it; happens to us all. Your wrist okay?"

Nodding at Heidi's question, I feel Kent behind me. The close proximity steals my breath.

"You should give her a formal warning, sis."

He places his hand on the small of my back. I didn't think it would be long before he touched me; he's very handsy.

LIE TO ME

"Do you not have any work to do?" I say over my shoulder. *Is my voice normal?* To me, it sounds high.

Grinning like a Cheshire cat, he shakes his head. "Perks of being the boss."

"What food did you bring?" I ask, turning to face him. "I'm starving."

He's really close. "Bacon."

"Just bacon?" I ask.

Heidi laughs. "In bread rolls. Go and serve them, Kent."

"I'll make coffee," I offer, walking to the kitchen area with Kent.

Shaking my trembling hands, I fill up the kettle. Kent hungrily watches me, and as much as I want to sink into his arms, I'm at work, and that wouldn't be appropriate.

"You okay?" he asks. He takes a step and wraps his arms around my waist.

I instinctively lean back, pressing my back against his chest.

This is exactly what you shouldn't be doing at work!

"I'm fine, just annoyed that I was late."

"Like Heidi said, it happens. Is there anything else?" he asks, pressing a kiss to the top of my head.

I swallow the words. I want to tell him everything about Simon and my family, but that would open old wounds that I'm not ready to feel again.

Turning in his arms, I run my hands up his chest and close my eyes. God, I missed him this morning. "No, I'm fine now." The lie tastes sour on my tongue.

He presses his forehead to mine and closes his eyes.

I need this.

"I want to take you home now."

"Me, too, but some of us have work to do."

His eyes blink open, and he smirks. "Come and work for me. I'll give you more time off."

"Hey!" Heidi shouts. "Stop trying to poach my employee. You can't have her."

"You can have me tonight," I whisper so that only Kent can hear.

He groans and kisses me. All too soon, he backs away and turns to Heidi. "I'd be a much better boss."

I slap his arm. "Get the food, you."

Kent busies himself, plating up the bacon rolls, and I make us all coffee.

Heidi clears dozens of sketches off the meeting table, and we set up breakfast.

"You need to bring breakfast more often, Kent," she says, sitting down and grabbing a roll. "Can't think why you decided to do this now."

Kent rolls his eyes. "Just eat, Heidi."

They start a conversation about Brooke's wedding in two weeks, which I'm now invited to, but I sit in silence and chew my food while my phone vibrates in my handbag.

I feel like the worst person in the world for not telling Kent the truth.

He values honesty above everything, and I'm lying.

I wish I knew how to talk about it. If there were a way of telling him without actually talking about it, that would be great. I'm not ready to go to that place again. It was too much then, and that's not changed.

Kent doesn't live too far from me. He offered to pick me up from work, but it's only a fifteen-minute walk to his place. I've always enjoyed walking when the weather is nice. It clears my head, and right now, I need a good clear-out. It's sunny and hot, so it's the perfect conditions for me to take a stroll and hopefully get my mind straight.

Besides, driving into the city centre is always a nightmare. With the traffic, it's much quicker to walk.

LIE TO ME

I'm not sure when I'll get the opportunity to properly deal with Simon. He's not shown up again since earlier, but he has sent me a text, which I have yet to read.

I'm going to have to call him at some point and have a conversation. Until I'm satisfied that he has gotten the message and will stay away, I can't relax. He knows where I live.

I take my phone out of my bag as I walk down the street. Time to rip the plaster off, I guess. I read the message from Simon.

Simon: I'm not going anywhere until we talk.

Savannah: Tell me what you want, and then go.

Simon: Not doing this over text!

Savannah: You don't get to make any demands! Text or nothing.

Simon: Meet me.

What does he not understand about him not being in a position to ask anything of me? Stupid arsehole. I grip the phone tight in my hand and grit my teeth.

Simon: Please. I need to see you.

Savannah: Phone is going off. I'll contact you soon. DON'T EVER show up at mine again if you want the chance of me talking to you.

That should drive the point home. I flick my phone on silent and hold it as I walk. I pass shops and restaurants as I head deeper into the city. This will be my first time at Kent's, and I'm really looking forward to seeing what his place is like.

It's probably a bachelor pad with lots of gadgets, black leather sofas, and perhaps a pool table. He would have removed any posters of half-naked women if he had any ... I would imagine.

I look over my shoulder, my eyes trained on looking for Simon. He's not here, and I've made it abundantly clear that he's not welcome, but I can't help feeling like he's going to pop up again.

If I can't keep him away, then I might lose everything I've worked for. Everyone would know what happened, and I would be expected to talk.

It's too much.

Turning my head again, I wrap my arms around myself and go faster, trying to outrun my past that seems determined to catch up. I'm running from Simon to Kent. He is my present, and if things go the way I'd like them to, progress how they have been, he will be my future.

Kent's building comes into view, and it's massive. I knew where it was, and I've seen it in passing, but I've never paid attention before. It's nestled between other high-rises, but Kent's is taller, of course, and covered in black-out glass. It's intimidating and very masculine, just like him. Not that I find him intimidating anymore.

My phone vibrates. I look down, holding my breath, until I see Kent's name.

Kent: I hope you're nearly here.

Savannah: Almost. I can see your building.

Kent: Tell me you're not wearing underwear.

Savannah: See you soon, pervert.

I shove my phone back in my bag, grinning like an idiot as I approach the door to the building. There's a long list of buzzers by the double glass doors. I press the one with *LAWSON* written in copper letters.

That's a bit pretentious.

"Savannah?" Kent's voice through the speaker makes me smile. He sounds like he's been waiting to answer that ring for a while.

"Yeah, it's me," I reply.

I hear a buzz, and then the front door clicks. I step toward it, and two large black panes of glass slide open, disappearing behind the wall.

How much money does Kent have?

I know he owns a successful business and has a shiny new Range Rover, but he's never been that flashy with his cash. He insists on paying for everything, but he doesn't eat at fancy restaurants or drink at exclusive bars.

He seems too normal to be rich enough for this building.

I call for the lift as I contemplate what his financial status could mean for us. *What if things go really well, and we want to buy a place together? I won't have much money to put down, and I don't want him paying for everything.*

Oh my God, am I actually worrying about this? There's no point in stressing over that stuff unless it happens.

The lift opens, and the second I get inside, I press the top floor.

Shit, he lives in the penthouse.

Money doesn't have to be a big deal though, right? Certainly not since we're at the beginning stage of our relationship.

I need to chill and enjoy this. If anyone can make me forget my ex, it's Kent.

Enough now. Forget money and the threat of Simon coming back, and enjoy tonight.

20

Kent

I'M PACING. I HAVE been for the last ten minutes. It's irrational how much I miss her when we're not together. We've not been in a relationship long, but I don't give a shit. She makes me want to jump headfirst into commitment.

She's my second chance, and I know, this time, it's real.

The knock at my door steals my breath. Seriously, the effect this woman has on me is insane. It's the strongest, most terrifying, beautiful thing I have experienced.

I stride to the door and let Savannah in. She's wearing a turquoise dress. I'd smirk at her or make a comment because she's mentioned how much she loves my eyes before, but her eyes are wide and darting around my apartment.

So, I might have left out that my place is the penthouse. It's huge, way more space than I could ever need, but I started earning a shitload of money when I was twenty-one, and a big-arse penthouse seemed like the perfect buy.

Maybe it was also a big *fuck you* to Freya. She had taken almost every penny I had when she stole my bank details, but I still succeeded, and now, I'm loaded.

The ground floor is mostly an open plan; the living, dining, and kitchen are all one area. There's also a gym, cinema, and sauna. The second level is smaller, housing three bedrooms and a rooftop terrace.

I'm not big into showing off with cash, so I don't publicise the fact that I have a lot of money. I don't ever want to attract the wrong people again. That was a lesson I learned the hard way.

Walking deeper into the room, she turns to me. "Oh my God. My apartment can literally fit into this room ten times."

"Literally? It can *literally* fit in here *ten* times?"

She tilts her head, deadpanning. "You know what I mean. Jesus, look at that view!" Strutting to the glazing that stretches all around the apartment, she admires the city. "I feel like I shouldn't touch anything."

My heart sinks at her words. I knew it was more than she was used to, but I hoped it wouldn't be a big deal. "You're not comfortable here."

Turning back around, she's shaking her head before she speaks, "No, it's not that. I just didn't expect this."

"It's just space and stuff, babe."

I'll move right now if I have to.

"Yes, but it's a lot of stuff and a lot of space." She lightly shakes her head, making her hair sway. "Sorry, it's stunning. Everything is amazing." She smirks. "I knew you would have leather sofas."

If I'm honest, it took me a long time to feel comfortable here. My parents' house is a decent size, and we never went without growing up, but my bank account is on a whole new level, which, at first, was as scary as it was thrilling.

I'm not scared anymore. Now, I just fucking love it.

Walking even further into the open room, she looks around the massive dining table, which I've never used, and the ultra-modern white-and-black kitchen.

"I didn't see this when I pictured your apartment. Besides the huge flat screen and sofas."

"I bought it at a time when I needed something like this."

"What do you mean?" She puts her bag down on the sofa.

Now is the time for this talk, I guess. "You remember me mentioning my ex, right?"

"Sort of."

"Her name is Freya, and she stole all of my money."

Savannah's mouth pops open. "What? When was this? I thought you were together when you were teens."

I know what she's thinking—that Freya must have only stolen a couple of quid. "My grandparents, my dad's parents, passed away when I was little. They were really wealthy and left forty thousand each to me, my sisters, and our three cousins. I wasn't able to touch it until I was eighteen, but I had a lot of plans for it."

She moves closer and leans in.

With her so close, my brain short-circuits. I want to reach for her, but if I do, we'll end up in bed, and I can tell she wants to know more.

Her lips part, and I want nothing more than to kiss her.

Hold it together.

I ignore how she's making me feel, how my heart is racing, how I'm desperate to hold her, and I do the talking thing.

"I was with Freya before that, but after she took off with it all, I realised she'd heard about it before we got together. Her mum did shit like that a lot, taught her everything she knew. I didn't know at first. I'd planned to start a business with the money, but at nineteen, I wasn't sure what that was going to be, so I didn't touch a penny."

I shake my head as I reveal how stupid I was back then. "I stopped getting bank statements, but I'd only chucked them, unopened, in a pile anyway, so I didn't have a clue. Freya had been taking money over the course of six months, and then she left one day without a word. I was so worried at first. Her house was empty, and she and her mum had vanished."

"Oh my God," she whispers, reaching out and taking my hand.

"Yeah." I rub my thumb over her knuckles and breathe a little heavier at the way this simple touch is electrifying. "I couldn't work it out at first. I called everyone, trying to find out where she was. It was only a few days later that Dad mentioned money. I checked my bank, and that's when I knew."

"I can't believe she did that to you. Do you think her mum made her?"

"At first, yes, but then, through Max and Toby stalking her online, we found someone who had been burned by Freya, too."

"I'm so sorry, Kent."

"It's fine, babe. I started a business with a lot less, and it's a bigger success than I could have ever imagined."

She dips her head in a nod. "So, you needed a big apartment to show you'd done well despite her."

"It's stupid, I know, but it's what I needed."

"You don't like it?" She arches her eyebrow.

I hold my arms out, and she steps straight to me, no hesitation. "I do, but I don't see myself here long-term."

"Why not? If I lived here, I would never go outdoors again."

Don't tempt me.

Smiling, she sinks into my embrace.

I press my forehead against hers. "I love the space and everything else this apartment has to offer, but this isn't where I'm supposed to settle down and start a family."

"You want to live in the country." Her words are a statement rather than a question, something she knows after she's been at my parents'.

"Yeah. I loved growing up with tons of outside space. Heidi, Brooke, and I would ride our bikes around our land almost every day. We'd camp out and build dens in summer and sledge in the winter. It was the perfect childhood."

Savannah is a city girl, so I don't know how that fits with her, but I would love to take her away in the middle of miles of fields and see no one else for days.

LIE TO ME

She purses her lips. "That actually does sound good."

Damn, she's perfect.

I can see it, too. I can see us in the future, living in the country, surrounded by greenery and children.

Freya has been forgotten, and we're back to us. We've had the conversation, albeit brief, but then that woman doesn't deserve any more of our time.

"Do you want a drink?" I ask before I propose she runs off with me.

I need to cool it, or I'll scare her off. We're so new. I keep forgetting how new because I feel like I've known her my entire life.

We still have so much to learn about each other. This could very quickly get out of hand.

"I would love one. It turned out to be a very long day." Savannah follows me to the kitchen.

"Why? What happened?"

"We had a bride in. She'd heard about Heidi through one of Bobby's friends. I really feel for Heidi if this woman wants her to design her dress; she's definitely going to be a bridezilla."

"You should leave there and come work for me," I say, taking a bottle of Savannah's favourite brand of tonic water out of the fridge to mix with the gin she likes.

She eyes the bottle and smiles. "And what would I do if I were working for you?"

"That sounds like a trick question," I reply, twisting the lid off the bottle and pouring her a large gin and tonic.

"Thank you. I so need this. Isn't it illegal to pay for sex?"

Smirking, I grab a beer. "What makes you think you would be working for me in the bedroom?"

"I know you; that's why I think that."

Laughing, I walk over to her and press my lips to hers. "Hi," I whisper.

We forgot the greeting when she arrived, mesmerised and a bit scared by my apartment.

Her eyes dance. "Hi."

God, I love seeing her in my place. I don't want her to go home.

Calm down again, Kent.

"How was your day?" she asks. "Did you sort out the bad employee?"

"He wasn't bad; it was just a misunderstanding—thankfully, because I would hate to fire someone."

"You're a big softie really."

I'm not, but I don't exactly relish the thought of cutting off someone's income.

"Feel, babe," I say, pressing myself against her chest.

She moves her arm, so I don't spill her drink, and she takes a heated breath.

"You're always hard for me," she murmurs.

"Even at the most inconvenient times."

She pushes her breasts into my chest and looks up at me through her eyelashes. I grow impossibly hard.

"I can help you out with that right now."

"Oh, can you?"

"Uh-huh … if you want, that is?"

"Your use of *if* is entertaining, babe."

She closes her eyes and breathes, "Take me to bed, Kent."

I don't have to be told twice. I take the gin glass, which I only bought a couple of days ago because I knew she liked it, and put it down on the counter along with my beer.

Reaching out, I offer my hand. Savannah takes two small steps and places her hand in mine. I am so ready for this. It's been agony, not being inside her each time we've fooled around.

The time wasn't right though. She had to know that I wasn't just after her body, especially since she'd told me she wasn't into casual about thirty thousand times.

I lead her to the stairs, and neither of us speaks a word while we climb them and enter my bedroom. I turn and watch her, expecting her to say things about the size of my room and, particularly, my ginormous bed. A bed that I've never had anyone else in. But she doesn't.

LIE TO ME

Her eyes burn into mine, and her chest rises and falls with quick, shallow breaths.

"Savannah," I groan, closing the short distance and moulding my mouth to hers.

She grips the back of my neck, pasting herself to my chest. This morning, her splint came off, so when we kiss, she's much grabbier. I fucking love it.

I curl my arms tightly around her back and lift. Her legs wrap around my waist as I walk toward the bed. Her hot mouth doesn't leave mine the entire time. Soft lips move against mine with a desperate hunger I know all too well myself. Knowing that she wants me as badly as I want her makes me hard in the most excitingly painful way.

I've had a lot of sex, but the way Savannah makes me feel is completely new. This is addictive, and I thought it would be scary—the intensity of my feelings for her—but it's not. I'm jumping into this headfirst without a shadow of a doubt.

"I want you so bad," I murmur against her mouth.

She whimpers as I lay her down, covering her body with my own. Her legs stay glued around my waist, like she's scared I'll run away.

No fucking chance.

I pull away, and she takes a deep breath. Her lips are beautifully swollen, and her grey eyes stare at me with so much passion, it sends a bolt of red-hot desire right down to my dick.

Digging my fingers into the sheets on either side of her head, I bite out, "Clothes off now."

She shimmies her jeans down with a smile and raises her eyebrow. "How are you going to fuck me while you're dressed?"

Right. I need to be naked, too.

I rip at my clothes like they're on fire and undress in two seconds flat even though I fumble to get my jeans over my feet. Savannah throws her bra onto the floor, and then there she is, in all her stunning, bare glory.

I have never seen anything so beautiful before.

She's got you by the balls.
"You're perfect, Savannah."

Pearly-white teeth bite down on her bottom lip. I don't know if a guy has knocked her confidence or if her rocky relationship with her parents means she never really had much, but I'm determined to build it with her.

"You are," I press. "Remember, never hide this body from me."

With a gulp, she dips her chin in a shy nod of agreement. I'll take that for now. But I plan on telling her how incredible and beautiful she is on a daily basis until she believes it herself.

I reach into my bedside table and grab a condom. I tear the foil packet so eagerly, it rips open in half, and the condom almost flies out. She watches me with heated eyes as I slide it into place.

"Kent, please," she mutters, squirming under me. Her hands land on my forearms and sweep up to my shoulders. "You're still not inside me."

Point taken.

I lower my hips. She lets go and grips my condom-covered erection. I've never wished I didn't have to wear the goddamn rubber before. I want to feel her heat, her skin against mine.

She squeezes my cock, and suddenly, I don't really care about the condom. Hissing through my teeth, I close my eyes and arch into her touch. She gently pumps me—I assume so that the condom doesn't move—and then guides me inside her.

Her moan dies under the sound of my own as I enter her warmth.

Jesus. Fucking hell.

"Kent," she breathes, her fingernails cutting into my shoulders. It's the hottest thing that's ever happened to me.

The thought of her drawing blood only spurs me on. I rear back and thrust into her hard and crash my mouth down on hers.

My body is on fire, orgasm building at an alarming rate.

I want to come, but I want to make this last for hours.

No fucking chance of that with the way her tight little pussy is gripping my dick.

"God, Savannah," I groan, pressing my forehead against hers. Hooded grey eyes stare up at me. "You feel amazing."

"Don't stop," she pleads, her forehead creasing. "Kent, don't stop."

"Wasn't planning to, babe. I could sink my cock deep inside you all day."

She whimpers, eyes flitting closed. "I want that. God, I feel you everywhere. Please just ..."

Just what?

"I'm so close, Kent. I'm going to come."

She arches her back, and I slam into her harder with a desperation that shocks me. Moulding my mouth to hers, I kiss her with a burning desperation to be as close as possible.

She's too much. My dick is about to fucking explode.

Fuck.

Savannah wraps me in a death grip with her legs, and her nails cut deeper. I lose it. With a growl, I'm coming so hard, my mouth leaves hers, and a long groan rips from my throat.

In my haze, I hear her calling my name as she contracts around my dick, milking every last drop of come.

I drop my forehead to hers, panting. Her eyes are closed, and she has the most stunning smile on her face, her cheeks tinted pink.

Perfect.

I could get used to this. I'm not letting her go, not ever.

Well, I might let her get up in the morning because she has work. But, metaphorically, she's never going anywhere.

21

Savannah

IT'S BEEN A WEEK since Kent and I had sex. Since that first time, we've barely left the bedroom. I can't get enough, he can't get enough, and there's absolutely no reason we both shouldn't go at it every time we're alone.

And I love it because I'm finally experiencing good sex. Like, mind-blowingly good sex. It's not just all the orgasms I'm loving either; it's being so close to him, having him all around me, inside me.

My splint was removed last week, too, so that's made exploring Kent's body and holding on for dear life much easier.

I'm walking home late from work because I've had a sea of messages to reply to on my the business' Facebook profile since Heidi ran a giveaway. We've had thousands of new likes, and while that's fantastic, it means a lot of extra work to get through the messages and comments.

The city is still buzzing with activity as people make their way home, but the closer to home I get, there are fewer people around. Kent lives right in the centre, where I always wanted to be but couldn't afford. Now, it seems a bit too busy for me.

I pull my leather jacket around my chest as the temperature drops. The days are still nice, but after six p.m., it gets much cooler.

A small crowd of people burst out of an office building across the road. My eye catches the profile of a man, and the hairs on the back of my neck stand.

Simon?

My steps falter, the sight of him sending my mind spinning.

A guy behind me gasps and then spits, "Watch it," as he moves around me.

I'm still, almost causing people to crash into me.

"Sorry," I mutter halfheartedly as I sidestep to the curb.

I try to look around people to the other side of the road, but there's now too many to see properly. The man sure looked like Simon. Same short, light hair, same slightly lanky build. But he wouldn't have been in an office building.

It couldn't have been him. Still, I watch with my heart in my mouth as the crowd starts to disperse, people going in different directions to home.

Where are you?

More people tut as they have to avoid me, but I don't care. My eyes scan both sides of the path, left to right and past the office doors. I can't see him.

Because you're paranoid, and it wasn't him.

I let out a breath. *This is stupid.*

Turning again, I hurry home, feeling like a bit of a nutjob for seeing my ex in strangers. Simon wouldn't be here, watching me. He might be a bit desperate to get me back or explain his actions away, but it would look even worse on his part if he'd taken up stalking, too.

I key in the code on the door and let myself into my building. Once the door clicks shut behind me, I sag my shoulders in relief of being off the street. Climbing the stairs, I take one last look back. No one is at the door.

LIE TO ME

Kent is out tonight, so I'm home alone for the first time since we got together. It's going to be weird, but I suppose we need to spend some time apart. He might get bored if I'm with him constantly.

As much as I was up for him spending time with his friends, my nerves are now raging, and I could really do with him holding me. He can make me relax with just a look.

But I can't rely solely on Kent for that; it's unhealthy. So, I let myself into my flat and lock the door. I'm okay here. This is home. It's my escape.

Kicking off my shoes, I move deeper into the living area. The first thing I'm going to do is get changed into something cosy and comfortable. Since I'm not seeing Kent or anyone else tonight, I don't have to look presentable. I'm not quite at the point in our relationship that I want him to know how much of a slob I am when I'm home. I don't think I usually wear normal clothes indoors for longer than it takes for me to walk to my bedroom and get changed.

I've missed my favourite pair of joggers and oversize T-shirt.

After the incident out in the street, I know I have to deal with Simon. That might not have been him, but that doesn't mean he can't show up again. And he could show somewhere Kent is.

Simon has been messaging again, every day, asking to meet, demanding to meet. Right now, I need to sort out dinner though, which is going to be Chinese, and pour a very large gin and tonic.

I take off the skirt I was wearing for work and tug my sleeveless shirt over my head. I fling my bra and sigh as it hits the floor. My favourite time of the day has to be when I remove that thing.

When I'm changed, I call the Chinese restaurant and place my order.

It's strange to be home alone. Even though I've not been with Kent long, we've spent almost all of our free time together. I have very quickly gotten used to him being around. I love it.

Hanging up the phone, I pour my gin and tonic and then sit down on the sofa. My apartment is quiet. It's too early to hear people in the street heading out for the evening, but most people have already gone home. It's a rare, calm parcel of time in the city when everything is still.

As much as I love the hustle and bustle of city life, I love the peace, too. I'm beginning to think I love the peace more than the busy.

I'm so used to being alone now. I've grown accustomed to my own company.

Being alone is something I used to fear. Maybe that's why I stayed with Simon for so long even though we had been drifting apart. I planned a life with him, but deep down, I knew it wasn't right. We weren't as in love as some of my friends and never had been. If I had been honest with myself about that at the time, my world wouldn't have fallen apart months later. Simon must have felt the same, only he decided to move on before he ended things with me.

Wanker.

His number is on my phone from his last call, but I refuse to save it to my Contacts. It's not like I don't know it anyway. When I was a teenager, I adored the fact that I'd memorised his number, but now, I wish my brain would forget it.

His first few texts after I told him to wait for my lead were reserved, even a little off. Every single one was the same.

Simon: MEET ME, SAV.

For two days, he sent those same three words fifteen times. Creepy. But, since then, after me not replying, they've been desperate. Like his last one, which I received this morning.

Simon: FUCKING GIVE ME A CHANCE.

LIE TO ME

I assume he means a chance to explain why he's such a massive knobhead because him asking for another chance with me is too gross to imagine.

My finger hovers over the call button. I should really eat first. I need to be calm enough to have a conversation with him rather than shout, so I can get through to him. If I'm hangry, that's not going to happen.

I don't know why he's suddenly popped up now— whether it's just taken this long to find me or if something happened, so he's come for me now. It has just been the anniversary but not the first one, so it must be more than that.

There are so many possibilities, but surely, if something bad happened with my family, my mum or dad would be the one contacting me.

Not that I expect anything from them anymore. Especially not my dad.

The air in my little apartment shifts, darkening like a storm, and it feeds the anger burning in my stomach.

Screw waiting. I need this over with.

I tap the button and put the call on speakerphone. I'll probably chuck it if he pisses me off, so it's best not to be holding it.

"Sav?" he whispers. In the background, I hear a door being opened and closed. "Are you there?" His voice is now louder.

"I'm here. Start talking," I snap. The sound of his voice makes me want to punch something.

"I'm glad you called."

I hear the smile in his voice and cringe.

"What do you want, Simon?"

"We didn't really talk about what had happened before you ran off."

"Shocking I didn't want to discuss the details, considering you were screwing my sister!" My hands make fists.

Who the hell does the wanker think he is?

He didn't sleep with someone random. He didn't go out one night and sleep with some woman he'd met that night. He chose my sister! My fucking sister.

"I'm sorry, Sav."

"Oh, you're sorry. Well, after three years, that's nice to hear, Simon, but it will never make up for what you did."

"Not if you don't let me try," he replies.

So, he does want to try to make it up to me.

My mouth falls open. "I don't want you to try. I don't want anything to do with you."

"You're angry," he tells me.

"You're as sharp as ever." *You're supposed to be calm, Savannah.*

"Can we meet face-to-face?"

"No."

He sighs. "You always were stubborn."

"What makes you think I would want to meet you? Have you lost it? You slept with my *sister*."

"That. Was. A. Mistake."

Finally, he admits that.

"Yeah, a big one." I run my trembling hands through my hair. "There's nothing you could ever say that would make me want to forgive you, so I don't know why you're trying to get in touch."

"Things aren't okay. You haven't seen your family in years. This needs to be sorted, Sav."

My blood simmers faster, faster, faster, until I feel like screaming. "Why do you care about my relationship with my family?"

God, I hate this knobhead.

"We have a long history, and I still care about you. A lot actually."

"Well, stop because all I feel for you is hate and disgust."

"You don't mean that," he rasps as if my words are a massive blow.

"Don't tell me what I mean," I snap.

LIE TO ME

What did I ever see in him?

"If you could let go of this grudge, we could all move forward."

"I don't want to move forward with you or my family. I'm done."

He sighs again, like he's annoyed with me. "Maybe we can talk when you're in a better mood."

"My mood is never going to get any better when I'm speaking to you. I'm done, Simon. I thought I made that clear."

"You never said that."

"I left three years ago and never came back!" I exclaim, throwing my hands up. "How is that not clear?"

There is something seriously wrong with him if he thinks for a second that I could ever forgive what he did. Though he saw nothing wrong with switching to my sister, so he's obviously a twat.

"Look, I don't want to argue with you. I just want you to leave me alone. We've not been in each other's lives for three years, and that's the way it should be. You can't contact me again."

"I don't think you mean that."

"Well, you're going to have to take my word for it because I'm so over this, and I'm not going to change my mind."

"You don't miss your family?" He fires the question at me like he's trying to keep me on the line, keep me talking.

Sometimes, I think I do. I miss the family unit but not the people. "No, I don't. Not anymore."

"You were close to your mum." He sounds genuinely baffled.

I was close to my mum, we did a lot together, but when Simon and my sister slept together, multiple times, she didn't react in the way I'd thought. There was also the thing right before that. At that time, I needed her more than ever, and she let me down.

There is no length of time that will help with that. Our bond was broken, and I know I could never trust her again. So, there's no point in trying.

"Yep, *was*."

"Sav, I don't know what to do when you're like this."

"You don't have to do anything."

"I want to help."

"Then, promise you'll leave me alone. Don't call me or show up again."

I can't have him in my life, not now that it's finally getting good. If I hadn't met Kent, I probably would have just changed my number, taken off, and started again somewhere else.

"How can I do that when I think you're making a mistake?"

I want to shout down the phone exactly what I think of him and then tell him to drop dead, but I'm so close to getting rid of him for good.

"I'll tell you what; if I change my mind, I'll contact you. Until then, you back off."

The line is silent for a minute. He thinks I'll want him back, so let him wait. He'll die of old age first, but that's just fine with me.

"All right."

"Yeah?" I ask, a little shocked that he's agreed.

"Well, I know you have to get there on your own. You've always had to do things in your own time. You're not ready yet."

I barely listen to his words, but it all sounds good. "That's right. So, I'll call if I want to make amends, like you assume I will."

I need confirmation.

"I know you better than you know yourself, and I can wait. Try not to leave it too long," he breathes, as if he really believes me.

He hangs up, and I slump back into the sofa.

LIE TO ME

Hallelujah.
My shoulders feel lighter.

22

Kent

WEDDINGS BRING OUT THE crazy in people. My whole family, besides me and my dad, is running around like lunatics, making sure every last detail is spot on.

That's the job of the wedding team at the hotel, but whatever.

I've been ready for the last hour. Freddy begged me to get my tux on even though we had ages, so now, I'm sitting at the bar with my dad and a couple of other guests, bored fuckless.

Max and Toby are coming in the evening to eat a buffet and get drunk.

It's now midday, and we have an hour and thirty minutes until the service. Savannah is supposed to be here anytime now. Brooke insisted she attended, and at first, that irritated me to no end, but now that we're together, I'm constantly watching the door to see when she'll walk in the bar.

The more time we spend together, the more I like her. She's not what I first thought, and I love that. And let's face it; I more than like her. I'm crazy about her.

I love that she doesn't back down. She challenges me often. I've never been excited to see a girl the way I am with her. Not even my ex made me feel like a fucking idiot. Savannah is something else.

"Waiting for someone?" Dad asks, pushing a pint toward me.

I wrap my hand around the glass and take a gulp. He knows I am. "Why don't you go and see if Mum needs help with anything?"

He laughs a deep belly laugh that makes a few people look up from their drinks. "Not a chance, son. What time is she supposed to be here?"

Now. We're going to have a drink together first.

"Anytime now."

"She's different you know."

My eyes slide to him. I was just thinking the same. "I know."

Savannah is nothing like my ex, but there is something about her that I'm unsure of. She's not shared much. All I know is that she's estranged from her parents, she isn't close with any other family members, and she moved here three years ago from her hometown.

I have no details about her childhood or what her parents were like—or are like—whether she misses them, if she ever sees them, or if she wants to build bridges. I don't even know if she's still in contact with friends from school; she's not mentioned them, and it's a bit too soon to grill her. Even though I really want to.

Savannah walks into the room, and I get tunnel vision.

She's wearing a full-length dark grey dress that clings to her body. It has a plunging V-neck that makes my heart race and dick harden. Her hair is in a plait to the side, a few tendrils hanging out.

I'm at my fucking sister's wedding, in the bar with my dad, so, my God, I can't get hard!

Her eyes lock with mine, and she smiles, her cheeks tinting pink.

LIE TO ME

Dad looks over his shoulder, and then I hear him laugh. He stands up. I feel his palm land on my shoulder before he walks off.

I'm still staring at Savannah, and Dad is going to rip me apart for that one later, but I can't bring myself to care.

She takes agonisingly slow steps toward me. I stand up, but my mind is empty.

"Hi," she whispers.

"Hi. You look ..." *Words. I need a word!* "Yeah ..."

Giggling, she drops her eyes. When she looks back up, her bottom lip is between her teeth, and her grey eyes are stormy and filled with desire.

"Well, thank you. You look *yeah*, too."

Why am I such a dickhead?

"Drink?" I ask her because I clearly need a few more.

Freya never made me feel nervous. Savannah is the only person to make me forget everything.

"I'd love a glass of rosè, please?"

"Wine tonight?"

"I'll hit the hard stuff after I've eaten, or I'll be lying on the floor."

"Well, let's not discount having the harder stuff right now. I wouldn't mind you lying on the floor. Or any other surface you want."

She tilts her head, arching an eyebrow. "Oh, really?"

I'm desperate to take that dress off and run my hands and tongue over every inch of her body.

"Kent!" She nudges my arm.

"What?"

"I just asked what you were having to drink. Where was your mind?" She grins, stepping closer, as she knows exactly what is going on in my mind.

"I can show you where my mind is."

"I bet you can."

Her lips are pink, and as much as I hate lipstick, unless it's leaving rings around my dick, I lean down and kiss her. She responds by gripping my upper arms and pressing her body against mine.

This could quickly escalate, so I reluctantly pull back.

Savannah presses her lips together, smiling.

"Did I mention yet that you look—"

"*Yeah*," she cuts in, using my embarrassing word from earlier.

That can't stick.

"Well, I meant to say stunning, perfect, edible."

"You know, I'm not sure if I prefer stunning or perfect to *yeah*."

"Really?"

She leans forward again, so her chest is all pressed up against mine. "Uh-huh."

Having her body glued to mine is doing nothing for the erection currently wedged against her stomach. I'd think she would back up, but she hasn't.

"Are you going to get me drunk today?" she asks.

"That depends."

"On?"

"Are you planning on letting me get inside you?"

Her eyes glow. "Why does my alcohol consumption affect that?"

"Because I can't have sex with you if you're off your pretty little face."

"Don't you mean my *yeah* face."

I drop my chin to my chest.

"Okay, I'm sorry." She laughs. "Say I get drunk tonight, but in the morning, I'm sober?"

I lean in and whisper in her ear, "Then, in the morning, I'm burying myself inside you and making you scream my name."

Her breath catches, and her body sways harder into mine.

Groaning, I drop my forehead to her shoulder. "I'm hard, Savannah."

With a giggle, she pushes me back and tugs me to a stool at the bar. "Down, boy. Drinks first."

LIE TO ME

"I don't want drinks first."

Looking over her shoulder, she replies, "Tough."

This woman is going to be the death of me.

I press my chest against her back and whisper in her ear, "I want you."

"Tell me something new, Kent," she teases. "What are you drinking?"

"Rum."

"You can't be drunk at the ceremony. How many beers have you had?"

"He's had three," Dad says, sitting down beside us. "Rum *after* the ceremony. Savannah is right."

But she's driving me crazy, and I need something to stop me from thinking about how perfect she looks in that dress.

Not that I can say that to my dad.

"Fine. I'll have another beer then."

Dad grins. "Good boy. Now, put her down."

"No."

Rolling his eyes, Dad orders our drinks, getting Savannah the glass of wine she requested.

"How are you feeling about walking Brooke down the aisle?" Savannah asks my dad.

"Hmm," he replies with a frown. "I'm not thrilled about letting her go, but Freddy is a good guy."

"She moved out years ago, Dad."

Savannah elbows me in the chest.

What?

"I wouldn't expect you to understand until you're waiting to give your daughter away, Kent."

I've not thought much about having kids. Of course, in the back of my head, I've always assumed I would—maybe with Savannah, when I'm older and settled down. I'm settling down now, and to be honest, the thought of tiny people I'm solely responsible for is terrifying.

Savannah looks up at me, biting on her lip like she can read my mind. Well, I can't read hers, and I have no idea how she feels about kids. She's still really young. She's in her early twenties and career-orientated right now. There's no way she wants children soon ... right?

Fuck, what if she wants them soon?

"You're freaking out," she says.

I shake my head, but holy shit, I am.

Dad laughs and sips his beer. He's loving this.

"I don't want children for a very long time," she says, settling the horror in my chest.

I blow out a long breath. "Okay."

Good.

Dad pipes up again, "Your mum is going to be so disappointed."

"I don't care. She can pester Brooke for grandkids. Even Heidi is older than me."

"She *has* been pestering Brooke for grandkids, and Heidi is still single."

"Can we talk about something else, please?" I ask.

Savannah and I have been together around six weeks, I think. We don't need any pressure to provide bloody grandkids yet.

She tilts her head. "It's funny how much children scare you."

"Children don't scare me. Having them does. Drink your wine, Savannah."

Dad leaves as soon as he finishes his beer, popping a mint as he goes in search of Brooke.

"Do you need to be doing anything? The ceremony starts in thirty minutes. Aren't you an usher?"

"If people can't find their way into a room and sit on a seat, they shouldn't be allowed to leave their house."

"Kent! Take this seriously. It's your sister's wedding."

"I'll usher you in there."

"You're impossible," she says on a sigh. "Come on. Let's go and see if we're needed anywhere." She puts her empty glass on the bar and grips my hand.

"We're not working this wedding, you know."

Tugging my hand, she looks back at me. "Don't be lazy. You can't sit in the bar and drink when your sister might need us to do something. That's what family is for, right?"

"Apparently," I grumble.

I've been to a few weddings before, and they only start getting good in the evening. Though I'm not single for this one, so I don't have to wait until the party starts to have fun.

I wonder what the chances of getting Savannah off during the meal are.

She would fucking kill me if I tried that here.

I tug her back and let go of her hand. Gasping, she stumbles back into my chest where I wrap my arm around her waist. That's better, she's back in my arms. I can't get enough.

"Fancy a repeat of the Mexican restaurant today?"

Her eyes widen. Tilting her head, she warns, "Do not dare."

Grinning, I lean down and press my lips to her forehead. "I'll be on my best behaviour ... until we get up to our room."

We walk into the ceremony room, and Mum is rushing around, straightening flowers attached to the end rows of chairs. Guests have started arriving, milling around outside.

"Judy, the room looks perfect," Savannah says, trying to calm my mother down.

When she looks up, Mum's shoulders sag. "Oh, I needed to hear that, darling."

"How is Brooke doing?"

"Better than me. I just want to make sure everything is perfect."

"Everything is perfect, Mum. Brooke isn't going to notice if a few flowers are out of place. She just wants everyone to have a great day," I tell her.

"You're right," Mum replies, smoothing her hair. "Okay, let's do this."

Mum walks past us without another word. I don't know what she's going to do now, but she seems much calmer, so Savannah and I don't follow.

A few of the guests—some I recognise and others I don't—start piling into the room.

"Where should I sit, Mr Usher?" Savannah asks.

I shrug. "Wherever you want."

"Well, do Brooke and Freddy want his family on one side and hers on the other?"

I shrug again.

"You're a terrible usher."

"They didn't tell me I had to separate people."

"They must want people to sit on any side then."

I follow her as she finds a seat on the third row from the front.

"You need to be at the front, Kent."

"I'm sitting with you."

She frowns like I'm doing this all wrong.

How am I the one doing this wrong? As if I'm going to fuck off to the front and leave my girlfriend behind.

"Do you think my sister or my mum would want you sitting back here while I'm up there?" I ask, pointing to the reserved row.

Her mouth parts, ready to argue, but she presses her lips together when she realises I'm right. I'm always right.

Standing up, she walks round the rows to the front.

"Good girl," I mutter.

"I'm looking forward to meeting more of your family."

"Don't. They're all weird."

"They are not."

"My cousins share a woman."

"What?" she hushes, leaning closer. "Like, they're both with her, *with her?*"

I nod. "It's always the elephant in the room because they go places together."

"Are they all here today?"

"Yep."

"Where?"

I take a look around the room, and it's filling up quickly. My grandparents sit down at the other end of the row and wave when they realise I'm there.

"Three rows back. Two blond guys sitting on either side of the red."

"Are they brothers?"

"No, they're cousins. My mum has two sisters."

"That's less weird but still weird."

"Oh, I know."

"Do they live together?"

"They all rent separate places. I don't know if they plan to buy together."

Her mouth drops. "Why don't you know this? How could you not have asked?"

"It's not my business, and I don't really care."

"Well, start caring!"

"Ask Heidi. She probably knows."

"Oh, I'm planning on befriending the red! What's her name?"

I laugh. "You're so nosy."

"I'm curious. Her name?"

Rolling my eyes, I kick back in the chair. "Louise."

"Talking about Louise?" Amie asks, sitting down beside me.

Amie is my cousin, sister of one of the little threesome.

"Savannah was curious," I mutter.

She nudges me.

Amie reaches across and shakes Savannah's hand. "I'm Amie, Kent's cousin. It's nice to meet you."

"You, too, Amie," Savannah replies. "We weren't gossiping. It was just a surprise."

Amie laughs. "Don't worry; I've asked all the questions you've probably thought of and more. I don't know how Tom can share, but he does."

Savannah sits frozen, like her mind can't comprehend the situation. Or she just has too many questions whizzing around in there.

Before she can ask anything though, Freddy and his best man—his idiot brother, Bobby—walk down the aisle, saying hello to the guests.

Bobby heads along our row, and I brace myself.

If he hits on Savannah ...

"Hey, guys. Glad you could make it, Savannah."

"Hi, Bobby. How's it going?" she replies.

"It's going good. You look incredible."

He doesn't wait for a reply. With a wink, he wanders off to the front to stand with Freddy.

I bet I end up punching him at some point.

23

Savannah

THE REST OF THE wedding guests find their seats, and then we're asked to stand. I rise to my feet, feeling a bubble of excitement as I prepare to see Brooke in her dress. Not that I haven't seen her before, but this time, it's for real.

She's about to get married.

At one point in my life, I was so sure I would marry Simon. If he weren't a colossal wanker, we might be married now … and I would never have met Kent. I shudder at the thought. As much as Simon and my family gutted me back then, I wouldn't change it.

What I have now is so much better.

Simon has stayed true to his word and not contacted me. At first, I jumped every time my phone rang in front of Kent but not anymore. Now, I can enjoy my life the way it is right now—perfect.

I twist my body as music starts to play, signalling Brooke's entrance. God, I'm so excited for her. We've gotten quite close. I don't see her all that much, but we text a lot.

Kent takes my hand, watching for his sister, too. That simple action holds so many promises. We're together, in this for the long haul, and maybe, one day, we'll be here, Kent waiting for me at the end of the aisle. The image seems too flawless to imagine, like, if I let myself even think about it, I'll jinx everything.

Seven weeks with him, and I'm mentally planning our wedding.

Call me obsessed.

His hand tightens around mine as Brooke comes into view. She looks stunning. Stretching onto my toes to get a better look, I tug Kent's hand. I love weddings, and I love Kent's family, so this one is going to be amazing; I can feel it.

He looks over at me and cocks his eyebrow, amused by my excitement.

The wedding registrar instructs us to take our seats. Kent doesn't let go of my hand through the entire ceremony.

Once Brooke and Freddy are married and walking down the aisle, hand in hand, we start to filter out. There are drinks outside in the gardens while the photographer captures their day.

"That was beautiful," I say, blotting the damp skin under my eyes. My heart is racing for them.

"Really?" he asks. "I thought it went on a bit."

I nudge his arm with mine, my hand still tucked in his. "You're so grumpy."

"It takes three minutes to read vows, exchange rings, and sign a piece of paper. How they drag it out over twenty is astonishing."

He's a little ray of sunshine.

"Want a drink?" he asks, steering the conversation to safer grounds.

"Oh, I do now."

"Ugh," he says, turning his nose. "I think it's all fizzy wine shit."

"Prosecco or champagne?"

"I dunno, but it all tastes like piss."

"You know what piss tastes like?"

LIE TO ME

"No, but I know I don't want to drink it. Same goes for that stuff," he says, nodding to the table packed with champagne flutes.

I pick one up. "Well, I like it."

"Keep drinking, babe. You're hilarious when you're drunk, and I still owe you a puking session, remember? I still can't believe you've never drunk so much you were sick."

"Yeah, not too sure I want to do that in front of your family."

"Why not? They're all going to be shit-faced later anyway. At my mum and dad's wedding anniversary, my nan got so drunk, she threw up in a bowl of punch and then did the Harlem Shake."

My mouth drops. "She did not."

"I have a video."

Kent's family *is* weird.

"Nope, don't look at me like that," he says, circling my body with his arms. "You're stuck with me now. There's no getting out."

"Your nan dances to hip-hop, and your cousins share."

"Tip of the iceberg, baby."

I don't think I want to know.

"There anything weird about you?" I ask and take a long sip.

His smirk grows. "I'm not telling you."

Great, something to look forward to.

"If I ever walk into the room to see you parading around in my underwear ..."

Kent laughs and presses a kiss to my forehead. My heart soars. I love it when he does that.

I look up at him through my lashes and smile. "If I get really drunk, are you going to stop me from doing things to you?"

He narrows his eyes. "You test me, woman."

Kent will not touch me if I'm drunk—it's his one thing—but if he were to be just as off his face ...

"Wait, what if we're both drunk?"

His eyebrows knit together. "What do you mean?"

"Have you never had drunken sex?"

"No. Have you?" he asks the question, but the hesitation in his voice doesn't convince me that he wants to know the answer.

"Yeah. He wasn't very good ... but you are"—I lean closer, so my chest is flush with his—"very. Good."

His eyes are saucers, and his Adam's apple bobs as he swallows. "Drink up, babe. I'll go to the bar."

I watch him leave ... so I can stare at his arse obviously. It's a very nice arse. He reaches the bar and stands next to one of his super-generous cousins who shares a girlfriend.

The idea of Kent touching another woman makes me feel a bit stabby. I definitely couldn't do it, but they seem to do it just fine. It can't be fine though, right? All three of them must have moments when it royally sucks. Her less so than them.

I want to grab the girlfriend and fire thousands of questions. I'm so curious to find out about their lives together, but that's probably not going to make Kent's family like me.

"I can see your mind working overtime," Heidi says, handing me another glass of Prosecco.

"Thanks," I reply, taking the glass in my other hand. I have two drinks.

"Kent told you about our cousins then?"

"What makes you say that?" I ask from behind the almost empty champagne flute, looking up at her with the aim to appear innocent. I'm not usually a gossip. The subject has to be *really* good to pull me in, and this, holy hell, is really good.

She laughs. "You keep looking between them."

Shit, I do?

My eyes widen, and that only makes Heidi laugh even more.

"Hon, you have got to stare more casually."

Is that even possible?

"I'm sorry. I didn't mean to be rude."

"You're not being rude. Get Kent to introduce you to them. They're all very open about the whole thing."

"Well, clearly!"

"No, I didn't just mean with each other." Shaking her head, she laughs at me some more. "They don't mind talking about it and answering questions. Actually, I think she kind of likes it."

"I'm willing to put my entire savings on that. What do you think she would do if one of them wanted to add another woman to the mix?"

Heidi shrugs. "They've all said, no one else."

"Do you think they will all move in together?"

Way to not be a gossip, Savannah.

"Probably. I don't really know."

Kent turns from the bar and walks over to us with two drinks in hand. He looks at the new Prosecco in my hand. I put my old glass on the table. "Glad to see you're getting a head start."

I shrug. "Just trying to keep up my end of the deal."

"I don't even want to know," Heidi says.

She saunters off toward one of Freddy's ushers. She's on the prowl. Good for her.

"I hope we eat soon. I'm starving," he grumbles, taking a long sip of his beer.

"Kent Lawson!" his nan shouts from across the room.

I haven't met her yet, but I recognise her from photos at Kent's parents' house.

Kent looks over and groans. "Here we go."

"Here we go, what? What's wrong with your nan?"

"Nothing, but I failed to mention you to her on the phone."

"Charming," I reply.

He rolls his eyes. "Don't you start. This was just after we got together." When he turns to greet her, his back straightens. "Don't be difficult, Nan."

Her mouth lifts at the side. "I'm as easy as they come. Your granddad loves that about me."

"What the fuck, Nan?"

I almost fucking choke. Plastering my lips together, I cough, Prosecco sloshing around inside my mouth. *Oh God, don't laugh.* I press my free hand to my chest, not giving a single shit that my wrist aches in response. Even though I've had the splint off for a little while now, it still aches sometimes.

Air fills my lungs as I take the deepest, most careful breath I have ever taken and swallow the mouthful. I put my drink down, step in tow with Kent, and smile. "Hi, I'm Savannah," I rasp, still trying not to choke.

Her eyes snap to me, and I feel her judging me, trying to work out if she thinks I'm worthy of her grandson. It's an agonising few seconds of waiting to see if I fall short or not.

Finally, she smiles. "It's lovely to meet you. Call me Nan, okay? We've been waiting for you since that slag fucked him over, and he started sleeping with everything that breathes."

What?

I don't even know what to say.

There aren't many times in my life where I have been completely, utterly speechless, but hearing Kent's sweet-looking nan swearing like a trooper, particularly using the word *slag*, has left me with nothing. Nada.

"Okay," I eventually manage to mutter.

"Nan, will you act normal?" Kent growls. He looks at me. "We think she's a bit senile."

"The only good thing about getting old is being able to speak your mind with no repercussion. I'm not senile."

I kind of love her. "I can't wait until I'm older," I say.

Wow, Kent's nan is so much cooler than me. I know I have a life and actually leave my flat now, but I'm nowhere near saying the things she does in public.

"See, Kent, Savannah doesn't think I'm senile. How old are you, love?"

"Twenty-two."

"Practically still a baby. Kent is pushing thirty soon."

"I don't think twenty-five is pushing thirty, Nan."

LIE TO ME

Kent will be twenty-six in November, almost a month to the day after my birthday. Not exactly thirty.

"It's a slippery slope." She takes a quick swig of whatever clear liquid is in her tumbler glass. Something tells me it's not water. "You two come and find me later. I'm off to get your granddad to buy me another one."

Without another word or letting anyone else speak, she walks away with purpose.

Kent turns his head. "So, that was my nan."

I grin up at him. "She's amazing."

"She is. Fucking embarrassing sometimes though. Hey, look, they're calling us through for photos."

I watch from a short distance while photos are being taken, even being pulled in for a couple of them. When they're over, dinner is announced.

Kent nods his head and leads me off toward whatever room we're eating in.

He puts his hand on the small of my back and leads me into the room filled with beautifully laid tables and stunning flower arrangements. There are four bottles of wine on each table.

Kent smirks at me.

We're getting shit-faced tonight.

24

Kent

So, I'll admit, weddings aren't that bad. I used to dread them unless there was some hottie in the evening I could take back to the hotel room. Now, I've had a hottie all day, and I definitely can't wait to get her back to our hotel room.

My parents are drunk, my nan is wasted, and Heidi is chatting to one of Freddy's friends at the bar. Somewhere, probably in hotel rooms, are Max and Toby. I think they both said about three words to us before heading off to chat women up. I'll give it to Brooke and Freddy; they know some beautiful women, all of whom pale in comparison to Savannah.

She's tipsy, too. Leaning against me, giggling at my nan dancing with my granddad. They're a disgrace, gyrating on the dance floor, but I can't help but laugh, too.

"I want to spend every day with your grandparents," she says, speaking slower than usual, as the effects of all the Prosecco have started to hit.

"No," I reply, lifting my eyebrow as she pouts. "Come and dance with me ... not like my grandparents though."

Her smile hits me right in the gut, stealing my breath. *How was there ever a time when I didn't like her?*

"You're going to slow dance with me, so you can press your body up against mine?" Her eyes turn to thunder.

"That's the plan, babe."

"Well, okay then. I like this song. Come on."

"Sex on Fire" by Kings of Leon is playing, and never before has there been a more perfect song for her. She turns around and takes my hand. We walk, not in a straight line because she's past that, to the dance floor.

I swing her around and pull her body flush with mine. Her dark grey dress matches her eyes right now as she stares up at me with a heated look that makes my dick swell.

Bending my head, I whisper, "I'll never get enough of you."

With a drunken smile, she replies, "Good. I never want this feeling to end."

Fuck me.

I tangle my hand in her hair and suck in a breath. *What the hell is she doing to me?*

Savannah stares into my eyes, lips parted and body pushing against mine like she can't get close enough.

My heart goes into overdrive, and I can't breathe.

Fuck, I am so in love with you.

"Savannah," I whisper. The words are on the tip of my tongue, but I don't want to tell her for the first time here, not when we're surrounded by people and she's drunk. So, I kiss her.

She responds instantly, parting her lips and sliding her tongue against mine. My hand grips her hair. The alcohol has done wonders for her inhibitions, but I've not quite had enough to let things go too far in front of my whole family.

"Babe, we're in public," I say as I remove my mouth from hers.

Biting her lip, she shrugs one shoulder.

"Oh, you want to put on a show?"

LIE TO ME

"No, not really. I don't want anyone seeing you come when you're inside me; that's just for me."

"Keep talking like that, and you might not have a choice," I reply, pressing my erection into her stomach.

"I think we should leave."

Hell yeah!

"Sold."

I lead her toward the door, but before we make it out, Max steps in front of us. "Going somewhere?"

"Yep," I reply.

"No, you can't. The girl ditched me, and I need a drink."

"How's that our problem?"

Savannah nudges me for being insensitive. Still don't see why I need to be involved in his drinking.

"What did you do to her?" Savannah asks him.

"Nothing. I was giving her my best lines, and she excused herself and walked off." He shakes his head, like he can't believe this happened.

Savannah reaches out and touches his arm. "She just doesn't want to sleep with you."

"No, that's not it," Max replies.

Sighing, she drops her arm and nods toward the bar. "Come on then. Let's get you drunk, too."

Max throws his arm around Savannah's shoulders as they walk to the bar. He looks back and smirks, but it really doesn't bother me. There is no way either of them would do the dirty on me. In fact, I love that she gets along with my friends. As much as I want to punch Max and Toby, which is often, I love them like brothers.

If his hand reaches around her front though, I'm going to break his arm.

Max and Savannah find two stools at the bar. She waits for me. I get on, and she perches on my lap. Max orders two double whiskeys each for us and three glasses of Prosecco for Savannah.

"Really, man?" I say.

"Hey, she wants to get drunk."

Her eyes widen at him. "I'm going to have to pee, like, a thousand times."

"Suck it up and drink," he responds.

She picks up the first glass that was put down and takes a sip.

"You did want to get properly drunk tonight, babe."

Turning her head, she looks at me over her shoulder. "Yes, I did."

I pull her a bit closer when she goes back to her drink. The smell of her hair is maddening, not to mention the fact that she's sitting on my lap.

"You two make me sick," Max mumbles, making me and Savannah laugh.

"You know, if you stop looking for a shag, you might find someone you're crazy about, too."

Her words make me groan. I so badly want to tell her that I love her.

Max turns his nose up. "Nah, not yet."

"We're going to end up having to adopt him, aren't we?" she says, shaking her head.

"I think so."

"Hey! I'm right here!"

"Yeah, annoying, isn't it?" I reply. "You fuckers do the same to me all the time."

"I really like this," Savannah says to no one in particular, holding up her now-empty glass. She puts it down so carefully, as if it were a bomb, and picks the second glass up.

Max laughs, tipping his head back. "She's so puking tonight."

"I do owe her one. She's never been sick from drinking before."

"How is that possible?"

I shrug while Savannah works on another Prosecco.

We stay talking with Max right until he sees another woman walk past, who is just his type—alive.

"Later, fuckers," he calls, leaping off the stool and following her.

LIE TO ME

Savannah slips off my lap and turns around. She has finished the three glasses and now has another one that I ordered for her. I'm not sure at what point I'm going to have to cut her off, but I think it's soon.

She stumbles to the side and frowns.

Yep, cutting off right now.

I take the drink from her hand and put it on the bar.

"Is she okay?" Heidi asks, stopping on her way back to the guy she's been with all night.

"She drank all of the Prosecco and is now suffering the consequences," I reply as I catch Savannah in my arms when she stumbles forward toward me.

"We should dance, Kent," she says, raising one arm in the air. "I want to dance with you, and then I want you inside me!"

"Okay," Heidi responds, "I'm out of here."

"You are very drunk, babe."

Giggling, she theatrically nods her head, her chin almost touching her chest. "I know."

"Savannah, dance with me!" Nan says, taking her hand and pulling her away from me.

"Nan, don't let her fall!"

Nan waves her hand and doesn't even look back at me. My girl and my nan sway to the dance floor because neither of them can walk in a straight line anymore.

"You look happy," Mum says, stopping beside me as I watch Savannah.

I tear my eyes away from the blonde who's got me by the balls and smile at my mum. "I am happy."

"Good. That's all I've wanted for years. Savannah is lovely. I'm glad you found her."

"I don't even want to think about where I'd be if I hadn't."

She smirks. "You'd be chasing women around this room like Max and Toby."

"No way in hell I'm going back there."

"I'm glad of that, too."

"I fucking love her."

Mum wraps her arm around my back. "I know. And don't swear."

25

Savannah

EVERYTHING HURTS.

Groaning, I roll over in bed and hear Kent chuckle. *Wanker.*

It must be morning. I can see some light behind my eyelids, but I have no idea how far into the morning it is.

My head throbs, and I feel it worse between my eyes. I'm not opening them.

"Morning, babe," Kent says, drawing shapes on my naked back with his fingers.

I still don't open my eyes, but I don't miss the humour in his voice.

"Is this what it feels like to die?" I mumble into the pillow, gripping my head with the hand that's not caught under my lifeless body.

"You can cross *drunken puking* off your bucket list."

Oh God. I groan again, trying to recall the incident, but there's nothing. After shots and dancing with Kent to "Sex on Fire," I don't remember anything. Not a single thing.

Shit.

"No." I don't want Kent to have seen me throwing up. *Where did this happen, too? Please, please, please let it be in our hotel bathroom. If his family saw this …*

Laughing, Kent throws his arm over my waist and kisses the top of my head. "Don't worry; I held your hair back."

Great, he saw.

"Oh my God," I slur.

"You really put it away last night. I'm kinda proud."

Yeah, but apparently, it all came back out.

"Enjoy it because I'm never drinking again."

"Of course you're not."

I lift my head off the pillow, and it's instantly the worst mistake I've made in my whole life—besides drinking. My head pounds as I drop it back down.

Best not to move.

"I need water and pills. Or to die," I whine.

Laughing, Kent kisses my head again. "I'll be right back. Let's sober you up, so we can go eat."

"Fuck off," I moan.

There's nothing I want to do less than eat right now. Before I do anything, I need pain medication and to burn off all the alcohol. *Evil stuff.*

I shut my eyes and feel myself being pulled back into glorious sleep when the bed dips.

Great, he's back.

I'm crazy about him and all that, but right now, I want to sleep for about another six hours.

"Can you sit up?" he asks.

"No."

"You need to take these."

I assume he has pills for me to take, but I can't open my eyes or move.

"Savannah, you need to sit up. I can help."

"No, you'll move me too fast."

He laughs. "I'll move you slowly."

I push up, wincing as pain slices through my skull. Twisting myself, I sit up against the headboard and crack my eyes open. Thankfully, Kent has kept the room as dark as he can. I look across at him ... smirking.

"This isn't funny."

"Depends on where you're sitting, I guess." He holds his hand out. "Swallow."

I take the pills and pop them into my mouth. Kent gives me the water, and I proceed to drink it like I've not had anything in a week. My throat is so dry, the water feels like razors, but after a few gulps, the pills slide down. Now, I wait.

Kent takes the glass from me and puts it on his bedside table.

"Please tell me I didn't do anything embarrassing last night," I plead. "Well, apart from being sick."

"You were perfect. My family loves you, even the drunk version of you. The puking didn't start until we got up here."

"Thank God," I whisper, closing my eyes.

How long until those pills kick in?

"I think you must have vomited about three litres of Prosecco."

"Okay, I accept that you saw me being sick, and I love that you're still here right now, Kent, but we can't ever talk about it."

His mouth kicks up at the corners. "Why not?"

"Because it's embarrassing and gross. Can we pretend it never happened?"

"Sure. As soon as I've ditched my puke-stained shirt, I'll forget it."

My eyes widen. *Oh fuckity fuck! I was sick on him?*

"Shut up. Tell me you're lying."

He frowns, his eyes darkening, and he growls out, "I'm not lying."

Bad choice of word. He hates lies.

"Tell me you're just trying to wind me up."

"Sorry, babe, no can do."

No!

"Why are you still here? Seriously, there must be something wrong with you."

"Savannah, it doesn't bother me. I mean, I don't think we should make a habit out of it, but I don't care. Plus, the shirt came with the hired suit."

"You keep the shirt when you hire a suit?"

He shakes his head. "Not this time."

"I want the ground to swallow me whole."

"Forgive me, but I think I enjoy you hungover."

I deadpan, "I think I hate you."

"I don't think you do."

Right now, I'm not too crazy about him.

"Are you ready to eat yet?" he asks just as my eyelids flit together.

My stomach churns at the thought. "No."

"You should soak up that alcohol."

"I know … just not yet."

Kent scoots closer and slides his arm around my back, pulling me against his side. I lay my head against his and sink into his embrace. Okay, so I still feel like I might die, but I love it when we're this close to each other.

I never thought Kent would be much of a cuddly person, but I have been pleasantly surprised. It rocks because—and I know this is going to sound super dramatic—but I don't ever want to let go of him. He's like the big, shiny prize after surviving a monumentally shit three years. Like, well done for building a whole new life after your unforgivable betrayal; here's a man who would give a Calvin Klein model a run for his money.

It's very much appreciated.

Kent lets me doze on him for the next hour, but then his stomach starts to rumble, and my guilt over starving him takes over the need to remain very, very still.

I roll off his chest and sit up in bed. My head swishes sideways.

"What're you doing, babe?" Kent asks.

I feel the bed dip behind me, like he's rolled onto his side to face me.

LIE TO ME

"It's time for food. I just need a minute to adjust to being vertical."

"Do you want me to help you in the shower?"

I crane my neck to look at him, keeping my torso still because my stomach is super delicate. "There is no way I can do that right now. You'll have to keep it in your pants until later."

His mouth hooks into a smirk. "Out of the gutter, Savannah. I meant, help you wash, and that's it."

"You wouldn't get carried away?"

"Some of us have self-control."

"Some people, yes. Us, no."

He collapses down on his back. "All right."

"No," I whine. "I need you to help me."

As he keeps his head perfectly still, his eyes slowly roll toward me. I smile.

"You suck at hangovers."

"I believe getting me wasted was *your* idea."

"And I don't recall hearing *you* protest too hard."

With a sigh, I ask, "Are you going to help me or not?"

Kent kicks his legs over the bed and gets up. I plant my feet on the ground and use my arms to help myself rise. My head spins, and I squeeze my eyes shut.

Don't puke again.

Oh my God, I can't believe I was sick on him. My first boyfriend since Simon and the big betrayal, and I fucking puked on him. Just perfect.

Kind of his fault though.

Kent takes my hand and leads me into the bathroom. He opens the shower door and turns on the water. Steam rises from the spray. I'm already naked, so I don't have to worry about trying to wrestle clothes off my uncooperative body or, even worse, having Kent undress me like I'm a child.

I stumble forward and drop his hand as I step under the spray. Kent gets in behind me and flicks open a bottle of shower gel. Closing my eyes, I tilt my head back as he tenderly washes my whole body and then moves to my hair.

Yep, this man is perfect.

Chuckling, he presses his chest against my back and holds me, the water spraying our bodies. I could stay here forever.

26

Kent

WHEN SAVANNAH AND I got home, we spent the whole day lying around in my apartment while she got over her hangover. I've decided against ever assisting her in getting that drunk again because she cannot handle it. Alcoholically, she's old. In your early twenties, you're supposed to be able to bounce straight back in the morning. It's now nine at night, and she's still feeling a little delicate.

She is lying on my chest as we binge-watch *Peaky Blinders*. This part of her hangover I don't mind. Anytime I can have her lying all over me I'll take. Her body fits against mine perfectly—whether we're clothed or not.

I can feel her chest rising and falling with each breath. Her head is tucked under my chin, her hand lying over my racing heart. I run my fingers through her coconutty, long dark blonde hair, and she moans quietly.

"I like that," she murmurs.

"I know; you've been liking it for the last hour." I'm not complaining.

"Well, don't stop."

"First time you've said that to me when I've not been inside you."

She's facing the TV, but I know she's rolling her eyes. "I don't want to go back to work tomorrow. I want to stay here and have you play with my hair."

"Let's get this straight; I'm not playing with your hair."

Her petite body shakes above mine as she laughs. "Okay, well, however you want to put it so that it sounds manlier, I want to stay here for you to keep doing that."

"Call in sick tomorrow. You won't be hungover then. We can spend all day having sex, and then I'll do manly things to your hair," I reply with a ghost of a smile.

She sighs. "I can't do that. And you couldn't have sex *all* day."

"Want to bet?" I've been hard all day, and I want her all the fucking time, so I'm confident I wouldn't get bored of being inside her.

"Hmm, I think I'll make that bet next weekend."

Good.

"Did any of your family say anything about me after yesterday?" she asks.

"They all love you, babe. Everyone thinks you're a hilarious drunk."

"Great, that's just the impression I want to make," she retorts sarcastically. "Next time I see them, I'm not drinking."

"I don't think they'll let that happen. Brooke is already plotting to get you drunk when we're next at my parents'."

Groaning, she presses her face into my chest. "We can never go back there again."

"Sorry, no getting out of it. They're all crazy about you, too, so you're part of the family now."

Her body freezes.

Shit. The words spurted out of my mouth before my brain had a chance to engage.

She doesn't have family anymore, so I planned on bringing her into mine much more softly than just telling her she was stuck.

LIE TO ME

Is this going to be a big deal for her? Especially since it's so soon.

I can't believe we've been together not quite two months yet; it feels like so much longer. As soon as I realised that I liked her, that was it. I was hooked, obsessed, infatuated.

"You okay?" I ask, wrapping both arms around her back, so she can't bolt.

"You count me as part of your family?" Her voice is weak, and I'm not sure if the thick emotion in it is a good one or not.

I tighten my arms, willing her to understand how much she means to me. "Yeah, I do. After Freya, I never thought I would want to let someone into my life, my home, and my family so completely again. There's not been a second since we got together that I've wanted to keep you at arm's length."

She lifts her head, and her grey eyes fill with tears. "I think that's the nicest thing you've ever said."

"Probably is actually."

"Take me to bed, Kent. I don't care if I'm tired or still a bit fuzzy. I really need you."

Shoving myself to a seating position forces her to kneel on the sofa. I take full advantage, hook one arm under her knees and the other behind her back, and carry her to my room. I don't plan on coming back out until morning.

At the crack of dawn, I carry the tray of breakfast into my bedroom. Savannah is sitting up with her back leaning against the headboard. She's awake and now wearing my T-shirt from yesterday.

"That smells good," she says, eyeing the tray.

I've made coffee and pastries. Or rather, I've made instant coffee and warmed croissants in the oven. Either way, Savannah is smiling like I've just made her whole life.

"Of course it smells good. I'm basically Gordon Ramsay."

"Well, you do say *fuck* a lot."

Laughing, I climb onto the bed, put the tray down in front of us, and kiss her. "Should I have done something else with this? Like fruit?"

Lifting her eyebrow, she tilts her head in question. "Do you have any fruit?"

"No, I don't like it."

"That's what I thought. This is perfect anyway."

"Are you going to tell me you've decided to take the day off and spend it with me in bed?"

She picks at a croissant. "Kent, I need my job. We're not all rich, you know."

Smirking at her, I reply, "I told you, I'd give you a job with me."

"I like working with Heidi, and I'm not getting myself fired because your sex drive is through the roof."

"Please, you initiate sex just as much as I do."

"That's untrue," she argues.

"It's not. I might talk about it more, but the one making the first move is usually you. Not that I'm complaining." I give her a stern look. "Don't you ever stop doing that. I love that you want me inside you so much."

She glares, holding a chunk of pastry midair, trying to think of a comeback. There's nothing she can say because we both know the truth. Savannah is as into me as I'm into her.

"Whatever," she mutters and shoves the food in her mouth.

She's conceded. That used to be her thing, but since we got together, she will argue until she drops from exhaustion.

"Wow, I've not seen you back down in a long time."

"I can admit when I'm wrong, Kent." Her voice is tight, like it hurt her to speak those words.

Grinning in amusement, I shake my head, and the words fall from my mouth before my brain has engaged, "Fuck, I love you, Savannah."

Her mouth parts, and she gasps.

Clearing my throat, I reach across and run my fingertips down her cheek and along her jaw. Fuck it, I'm not sorry I said it, and I don't care that I probably shouldn't feel it yet. "So, I didn't plan on how to say that, but I definitely wanted it to be cooler than that."

"Do you want to take it back?" she asks in a whisper.

"Definitely not. I've fallen so in love with you, I can barely think straight."

Dropping her eyes, she puts her croissant down and then looks back up. Her grey eyes shine. "I love you, too, Kent."

Fuck me, I thought hearing those words before were everything. Coming from Savannah, it's unexplainable. I take a breath, my chest caving.

"Yeah, I know how you feel," she breathes.

"Tell me you don't want to sit here and eat." My heart feels like it's going to break through my chest. It hurts in the best way possible.

Slowly, she shakes her head. "Not hungry anymore."

Thank God for that because I can't wait. I move the tray to my bedside table because fucking her on breakfast and scalding her with the coffee isn't the mood I'm going for.

When I twist back, she launches herself at me. I laugh as we hit the mattress, her body pressing into mine.

Savannah and I spend the next two weeks in a loved-up haze of sex. It's amazing.

I pull up outside Toby's house after dropping Savannah at work.

I can't believe it's been two weeks since I realized at the wedding that I loved her. Everything was so fucking perfect. She fit in with my family like she was supposed to be there, and my God, she looked so beautiful, it hurt. I couldn't take my eyes off her, and when we were dancing and those pretty grey eyes were staring back at me, I knew.

She is everything.

Since then, at every opportunity, she tells me she loves me. I'll never tire of hearing her mutter those words or the way she looks at me while she's saying them.

"All right, mate," Toby says as he opens the front door.

"Hey, bud, I need a beer."

"It's nine in the morning, Kent."

Lifting my eyebrow, I stop beside him on my way in.

He raises his hands. "Yeah, I just heard myself, too. There's plenty in the fridge."

I close Toby's door and head to the kitchen. His place is huge, but he takes the term *minimalist* to a whole new level. See, Toby doesn't like to tidy or clean, so he has nothing to personalise his house. It's plain and empty, and he has a cleaner come twice a week. The lazy shit.

Raiding his fridge, I grab two beers and pop the lids.

"Thanks, man," he says, taking a bottle from me. "So, it's Savannah's birthday this weekend?"

"Yeah."

"You get her something nice?"

"Not yet. I have plenty of time."

"Three days. That's not a lot of time."

"How many days does it take you to buy a present? You go to the shops, and you get something."

He lowers the bottle from his mouth. "Kent, you love this girl. You need to put more than two seconds' thought into what you're getting her."

So, he might have something here. Obviously, I know I need to get her a gift that's thoughtful and, let's face it, shiny, but I have no idea what. She wears white gold jewellery, but she has a lot of it.

Would she want another piece?

But what else could I get?

For Freya, I just bought her the phone she was desperate for. The bitch was already stealing my money, so the expensive gift only added insult to the injury.

LIE TO ME

Savannah deserves something more personal. I want to get her a present that will mean something, not end up on a scrap heap the following year.

What the fuck is meaningful to women though?

Toby laughs. "You're worried now, aren't you?"

"Yes, you arsehole! What the fuck am I going to get her?"

He shrugs one shoulder and mutters around the neck of the bottle, "Just go to the jewellers."

"Isn't that what everyone does though?"

"You don't think she wants jewellery?"

"No, she likes it, but I want something different."

"Dildo?" He gasps. "Two-way dildo!"

"Nah, they're all smaller than me anyway."

Toby rolls his eyes. "You wish, bud. What are you doing for her birthday?"

"We're staying at my parents' the night before, so she can experience a birthday breakfast cooked by my mum."

"She's going to end up puking."

I nod. "Likely." My mother goes *all* out for birthdays. "We're doing the usual walk-and-pub lunch, and my mum was talking about a cocktail class or some shit like that."

He cocks his eyebrow. "After that?"

"After that, I'm taking her home and doing all manner of naked things to her."

"Good boy." He takes a sip, unspoken questions flashing past his eyes.

"What, man?"

Lowering the bottle, he says, "It's going really well with her."

"Yeah," I reply with an air of caution I've become accustomed to when Toby only gives half a story. Like when he called to tell me he was having a little trouble and needed to borrow some money. Turned out, the money he had to have immediately was to bail him out of jail after he got into a fight with his conquest's husband.

"Good."

"Spit it out, Toby. There's more going on in there." *What's he about to tell me? He's seen Savannah with someone else? No. No way. She's not like that. But, fuck, that was a shitty image to have.*

"Just checking in. Wasn't easy to watch you so beat down after Freya stole all your money, and I have a feeling that, although Savannah wouldn't steal from you, if she took off, you'd be worse."

"Yeah. It would be worse," I confirm. It would be unbearable.

Freya's betrayal left me bitter and unable to trust anyone for a long time. I thought that was the worst thing anyone could do to me. Honestly, I would have preferred she cheated; it would have been easier to handle. But she took almost every penny I'd inherited; she took what I'd thought was my future. That money was supposed to set me up if I used it right, and as immature as I was back then, I intended to use the money wisely.

Savannah wouldn't steal my money or cheat—that much I'm sure of—but she could decide that she didn't want me, and that would sting way worse than Freya being a robbing bitch.

"You're not worried about anything going wrong?"

I swig. "Should I be? This is getting a bit weird now, mate."

"When you were just coming out of your lowest point, you made me promise to always make sure you kept a cool head where women were concerned. I think you're hot."

"Don't swing that way, sorry."

"Fucking hell, you know what I mean, Kent, you dickhead."

Chuckling, I sit down on his sofa. "I know what you mean, and I appreciate the talk, but I trust her. She's different. I just wish she would let me in a bit more."

He sits down opposite me. "That doesn't ring alarm bells?"

"She's cagey about her past, and she doesn't like talking about it."

"There a story there?"

"Well, I don't think her parents are grifters, like Freya's mum, but they weren't there for her. She said she's not spoken to them in years."

"You're thinking she just doesn't like talking about it because it's painful?"

"I can see the pain in her eyes whenever I bring it up."

"I get that," he replies, closing his eyes and taking a long swig.

"Sorry, man. You all right?"

"Yeah." He opens his eyes and gives me a ghost of a smile.

Toby's parents were always more interested in booze than him. His grandparents raised him most of the time. Maybe he would be a good person to talk to Savannah when she's ready. As much as I want to be the one she opens up to, I just want her to be okay. Toby understands, whereas I don't have a fucking clue because my parents are, thankfully, very much involved.

Occasionally too involved.

"As long as everything is on the level and she's not about to screw you over."

"She wouldn't. She might be reserved, but she's not a liar."

She's not.

27

Savannah

KENT AND I HAVE fallen into somewhat of a routine. We go to work, then one of us will head to the other's apartment to spend the night. I don't think we've spent more than two nights apart since Brooke's wedding last month.

It's almost my birthday, and yesterday, Kent and I celebrated being together for three months. I do use the term *celebrate* pretty loosely since he had no idea, and I only realised late in the afternoon. Still, we then celebrated with dinner at *that* Mexican restaurant and then back to mine for a lot of sex.

Being with him, even for just three short months, has been the best time of my life. I'm so comfortable with him. We have similar tastes in music and film, and we pretty much finish each other's sentences. He doesn't care if I can't be bothered to put on makeup. He tells me how beautiful he thinks I am whether I have my face on or not.

We arrive at his parents' house mid-afternoon on Friday, ready to spend some birthday time with his family ... who are kind of mine now, too.

Heidi tried to give me the whole day off today, but I hate leaving her when we're busy, so I worked until twelve. I don't want to take advantage, and she's already been really nice to me when Kent has made me late.

He has been smiling like a moron the whole journey here, mostly due to torturing me over my birthday presents. He has them in the boot of his car and keeps taunting me with how awesome they are, but of course, I won't know until tomorrow. I love seeing him with a big smile on his face and laughter in his voice even if it's at my expense.

Kent's parents are out, but he still has a key, so we let ourselves in. I've not spent my birthday with humans in a few years, so I'm really looking forward to this weekend.

So far, I haven't received any emails from my parents, not that my dad would email anyway, or texts from Simon.

My parents have emailed every birthday and Christmas, usually the night before, so I doubt they'll miss it. It would be easier if they did though. A clean break is what we all need.

I'm still waiting, still holding Simon off. I don't know if he will eventually get the message and give up or if he'll try again. Until I know for sure, I can't completely relax.

I follow Kent into the kitchen, and he heads straight for the kettle to make tea.

"Want me to bring the bags in while you do that?" I ask, blinking innocently.

He tilts his head. "Nice try. I'll do it later."

Damn it.

I've never been this impatient before, but actually, I've not had a birthday present since I left home. Well, Heidi bought me a bottle of wine last year, and I had only been working for her for a few weeks at the time. Before that I had nothing.

I don't really want or need anything materialistic, but it does feel nice to have someone make a bit of a fuss over me turning a year older. Strike that, it feels phenomenal.

God, I really was lonely.

Kent hands me a mug of tea, the handle pointed toward me so that I'm not the one getting burned. My heart swells. It's little things like that, that make me so bloody happy.

LIE TO ME

"Thanks. What time will your parents be back?"

His eyes light up. "Why? Want me to make you scream?"

"No, idiot, I was just wondering."

"Dad is working until five, and Mum is shopping with my nan."

"Is your nan coming here?"

"I'm not sure."

"I hope so. She's brilliant."

His lips purse. "Hmm."

We're standing by the island in the kitchen, looking out the pane of glass. The garden is absolutely massive. So peaceful, so much greenery.

"I love it here," I say, gazing out at the scattering of trees lining their land.

"When my parents are dead, we can have it."

My head snaps to him, and my mouth drops. *What the hell was that?*

Tipping his head back, he laughs. "I'm kidding. We'll have to split it with Brooke and Heidi, too."

"You're a terrible son, Kent."

Grinning, he replies, "I know. So, would you really want to leave the city?"

"If you had asked me a month ago, I would have told you never. But your childhood sounds amazing, and I love the space out here. Hmm ... then again, I do love the fast pace of the city and being able to get takeaway at any hour. I don't know; maybe I'll have to split my time between a place in the city and one in the country."

"You want two houses? So, you are with me for my money." He grins wider.

"Well, it's not for your wit," I quip.

Kent laughs. "You wound me, Savannah."

"You love it."

"Why are you with me?"

"Fishing for compliments isn't cool," I retort.

Smirking, he stalks toward me like I'm his prey. "You're with me because I'm hot and hung like a fucking elephant, and I can get you off with my tongue in three seconds flat."

I lift my eyebrow. "Yeah, it's actually the money thing."

His arms wrap around my waist and cage me against his chest. I'm not complaining. I put my tea down, place my palms on his chest and admire the solid muscles underneath his T-shirt.

"Bollocks. You're obsessed with me, and you were before you even knew I had money."

His lips touch the top of my head, and my heart leaps.

Damn, he has me there. I couldn't care less how much he has in the bank. He makes me feel safe, and he makes me want to open up even if I've not been brave enough to yet. But I'm closer. I want to open up, and soon, I will.

I tightly held on to my heart since the day of the betrayal, and as scary as it was, I willingly handed it to Kent.

"I'll give you that … but I'm not obsessed."

Kent narrows his eyes. "Savannah, no lying."

He's so intensely against anyone lying to another person. And I'm lying all the time.

I press my thumb and finger across my lips, zipping them.

"I'm obsessed with you, too. There, I have no problem admitting it," he says.

"Good boy. You know how I feel about you."

He tugs me against his chest. "I do, and I like it."

"I think I've changed my mind about the tea."

"Oh?"

"Prosecco. Since it's my birthday week and all."

His eyebrow lifts. "Birthday week?"

"Yep."

Backing away, he kisses my head again and goes to the fridge where, as Judy informed me, there's a lot of Prosecco. "You're becoming high maintenance, I see. Not sure I signed up for that."

"You signed up for me, buddy, and that's exactly what you're getting."

He looks over his shoulder and gives me the widest grin. Yeah, I like it, too. I like that I'm feeling like my old self again; only this version of me is stronger. I know what I'm worth, and I won't ever allow anyone to make me feel shitty about myself again.

Every second I'm with him, I'm growing. Not literally—that would suck—but knowing someone could care about me and want to be with *me* means everything. Simon made me feel like I was worthless. I mean, he cheated on me with my sister, for fuck's sake. But Kent has made me realise that I'm not.

Having him want me for me and not just my body has made my confidence soar.

Fuck Simon and fuck ever feeling like I'm not desirable again.

No dozen cats for Savannah. Win.

Kent opens the fridge and holy Prosecco. I only get a quick glimpse as he pulls a bottle out and shuts the door, but there is a lot in there, maybe twelve. Judy is either expecting more people over or she's going to get everyone well and truly wasted tonight.

Probably the latter since it will just be Kent's immediate family here.

I can't think of a better way to spend the evening than with the people who are very quickly becoming so important to me.

"Here you go," he says, stretching to hand me a very full glass.

"Trying to get me drunk?"

"Absolutely." He rounds the island in the middle of the kitchen and stops right in front of me. "Now, what do you want to do?"

"I'd like to go for a walk."

His nose scrunches up like I just suggested the worst idea known to man. "You want to what?"

"Your parents live in such a beautiful area, and I'd like to see more of it. Besides, it's my birthday."

Rolling his eyes, he sips his tea. "Right, of course."

"Cool. Let's go."

"You're taking the drink?" he asks as I walk back toward the front door.

"Obviously. Come on, Kent."

It's still warm outside. October is such a weird month. My birthday is either warm or cold, and this year, the decent weather has really been holding out. The mornings are getting sharper though, so it's only a matter of time until autumn finally boots summer's arse.

Growing up, I remember always having a bouncy castle; only some years, it was outside, and others, it was in a hall my parents hired. They were good with that at least. I've often wondered over the past three years where they lost that unconditional part of their love for me. Or was it just a case of them loving Isla more than me? Not that it really matters anymore, I guess.

Things are good with me now. I'm happier than I have ever been, so I don't really need to keep obsessing over where everything went wrong or if I did anything … which I didn't.

Kent shuts the door, but he doesn't lock it. The house is fairly central on the three acres, but I still find it weird, not locking the door. There's no way I could do that in my apartment.

He throws his arm over my shoulders, holding his tea in the other. I have my Prosecco in my hand.

"It's so peaceful out here," I say as we head down toward the stream, which runs along the back of the property.

"Until my parents get back, and my mum's fussing over you."

"Your mum is amazing."

He gives me a smile. Although she does drive him crazy sometimes, he does know how lucky he is. I would envy their relationship if she didn't treat me like one of her children, same as Freddy.

I sip my drink. "Do you think we'll still be here on my next birthday?"

LIE TO ME

"We'll have to go home between, Savannah. I can't live with my parents for longer than a couple of days."

Rolling my eyes at the idiot I love so much, I carefully bump against his side, as I don't want to risk spilling my alcohol. "You know what I mean. I've not really allowed myself to look too far ahead."

"We can be wherever you want to be in a year."

Okay, he said we. That's good. I mean, I know we're not just messing around here, but sometimes, I really need to hear it. I love knowing that he's on the same page and planning a future.

He's probably not planned our wedding—guilty!—but I think he knows we're headed there if things continue the way they have been. It's a natural progression, right?

"I think I would like to come here again. Spend some time with your family ... and then fly to Paris or the Maldives."

"Paris or the Maldives?"

"I've always wanted to visit the Maldives and stay in one of those rooms on the ocean. But it's super expensive, so Paris it is."

Kent's lips purse.

"What?" I ask. *Where's his head?* "Oh." *Okay, duh!* "You have all the money."

"I do not have *all* the money, Savannah," he says, laughing. "But I have more than enough to whisk my girlfriend to the Maldives for her birthday."

My stomach ties in a very big knot. I turn to Kent and press my palm against the ache in my stomach. "I don't expect you to pay for everything."

"I know ... but I like to."

Why the hell did I mention expensive holidays? And is it bad that I want to casually mention my love for Lamborghinis?

"I'll let you take me on an expensive holiday if you let me pay for a dinner."

His eyes narrow as he realises I have him there.

"You can't love my independence and want to pay for everything at the same time."

His eyes become slits. "You're being impossible again."

"No, I'm not. Let me treat you to dinner, and I'll let you take me away."

"Can I have anal, too?"

My hand flies before I really register what I'm doing. I slap him on the arm. Laughing, he steps back, but it's too late.

"I'll think about it."

"You'll think about it?" His voice is about a bazillion octaves higher than usual.

Simon wasn't adventurous in bed. I've never really tried anything in *that* region, so the idea is a little intimidating.

"I will think about it," I confirm.

"Hell, babe, I'll take that!"

"What a surprise."

Taking my hand, Kent leads me down to the stream. It's about three meters wide, so I could jump it, but I don't know who owns the land on the other side. I don't want to piss off his parents' neighbours ... or be eaten by dogs.

"Come here." He takes my drink from my hand and places it on the grass. He lies down and looks at me. "You going to stay up there?"

I have a dress on, but, yeah, whatever. I sit down and then lay my upper body against him. His arm winds around me, holding me close. Trees next to the stream blow gently in the light wind. It's so peaceful. I close my eyes and cuddle into Kent's chest.

His hand finds its way into my hair. He seems to like my hair a lot.

"Growing up, we spent a lot of time here, in the stream. There's a tree farther down that we tied a tyre to. You couldn't jump in though, as it's shallow and you'd probably break your back."

Note to self: don't jump into the stream.

"I'll give that a miss then."

"No way. Next summer, you're getting in with me."

LIE TO ME

A smile tugs at my lips. "You just want to see me in a bikini."

"Yeah." Laughing, he kisses the top of my head. "When we have kids, we'll have to bring them here."

My heart leaps ... and then kind of hides. He said the words so casually, like he was telling me what he had for lunch.

So, he's, like, *really* all in. More in than me because I haven't moved past our stunning outdoor boho wedding yet. But I have a feeling it's not going to take me long to catch up.

Two kids. Or maybe three.

Bam, I'm there.

He kisses the top of my head again, still running his hand through my hair. "I love you, babe," he whispers as the sun shines down on us.

"I love you, too," I breathe.

We stay like that for a while, not talking but not needing to. After a while, the breeze starts to overtake the heat coming from the sun, so we get up and head back to the house, ready for everyone to arrive. Judy and Harrold are there when we enter the kitchen.

"Hey," Harrold says.

"Savannah, there you are, darling." Judy dashes around Harrold and opens her arms.

I manage to put my empty glass down before she reaches me.

"Hi, Judy," I say, hugging her back. "I found the Prosecco. You sure meant it when you said you'd grab a load of bottles."

She pulls back. "I never joke about alcohol, darling."

"Hi, Mum. I'm fine, thanks," Kent says sarcastically.

Judy ushers us into the living room with drinks, and then she and Harrold cook. When Heidi turns up, we outnumber Kent and get to put on a chick flick.

Although he hates the movie, he hasn't moved from my side. His hand is playing with my hair and massaging the back of my head. It's the most blissful distraction. Sighing, I lay my head on his shoulder and curl into his side.

I feel him smile against the top of my head as he kisses me.

"Dinner's ready!" Judy announces shortly after the movie finishes.

"Good, I'm starving," Kent says, getting to his feet. He bends over, takes my hands, and pulls me up. "Come on, birthday girl, let's get you fed before you get hangry."

Falling against his chest, I squeeze his hands. "I do not get hangry."

"Oh, yeah, you do." He presses his lips to mine, but before things can get out of control, which they often do, I back away.

"Come on, put her down," Heidi says, laughing on the way past.

"I don't want to," he replies, wrapping his arms around my back, so I can't move.

Laughing, I push onto my tiptoes and kiss him again. "I'm getting hangry," I warn.

"All right, I'm letting go." He does, but then he takes my hand, and we walk into the dining room. They have a table in the kitchen, too, but so far, I've not eaten at it.

I take a seat between Kent with Judy and Harrold at the ends. Heidi sits opposite me.

"This all looks ... like a lot," I say, eyeing the six dishes in the middle of the table.

Kent and Heidi laugh.

"You can't have a small pre-birthday dinner, darling," Judy says.

"No, *you* can't have a small pre-birthday dinner," Harrold teases, lifting his glass to his wife.

I wonder if this is how me and Kent will be one day. I see a lot of similarities between his parents and us already. Let's hope so because they're close, and they always have each other's backs.

LIE TO ME

"How are you feeling about being another year older?" Judy asks, ignoring Harrold.

"Er, fine, I think."

"Of course you are. You're still in your early twenties," Heidi pipes in, pouting.

"Time to find a husband, darling," Judy tells her daughter.

Heidi rolls her eyes. "I don't need a man, Mum."

"No, but it would be nice."

"For me or you?"

Judy smirks. "Me. I want grandbabies. Lots of them."

Kent tenses beside me. He has nothing to worry about because, although we want children, it's a long way off. I'm so not ready to be pregnant.

I turn to him. "Breathe."

He gives me a look. "I'm fine."

"No, you weren't," I reply, digging in as everyone else does. "You were freaking."

"*You* were freaking," he mutters in reply.

"Good comeback."

"Eat, Savannah. You're becoming even more impossible."

I dump a spoonful of mashed potatoes on my plate and catch Judy watching us with tears in her eyes. I reach out and put my hand over hers, making her take a deep breath. A silent understanding passes between us. I won't break his heart.

28

Kent

SAVANNAH IS STILL ASLEEP beside me. She's only the second woman I've had in my room back at my parents'. I thought that Freya's memory would be everywhere in here forever, but the second Savannah stepped over the threshold, Freya disappeared.

Savannah's chest rises and falls softly, the back of her head resting on my chest.

Last night was amazing. She's never said much about being part of my family after I blurted it out a while ago, but I know she truly felt it last night. The way she kept looking at me and then at my parents and sisters made my heart swell. I don't care that she never wants to talk about her family anymore—maybe she will want to one day—but I'm not going to wait for it or waste another minute with worrying what happened. She's mine, ours, now, and that's all that matters.

She stirs beside me, and then two grey eyes flick open. "Morning," she whispers.

"Happy birthday," I reply. "How does twenty-three feel?"

Frowning, she replies, "Hmm, same."

"Yeah? What if I give you your first birthday present now, and we see how you feel after that?"

"Savannah! Are you awake yet?" Heidi shouts from outside my door. "Happy birthday, hon!"

Sighing, Savannah sits up. "Thanks. I'll be out in a minute, Heidi."

I grip her arm. "Wait. No, you won't."

"Your sister is calling me."

"Go away, Heidi!" I yell.

"No, it's Savannah's birthday, and we're ready to start the festivities."

"Well, we're not."

"Oh my God," Savannah snaps, whacking my chest. "I'm not having sex with you when your family is waiting downstairs for us."

"Why not?"

"That was rhetorical, yes?"

"Breakfast is almost ready," Heidi says. Her voice is muffled, like she's right against the door.

Fucking family.

I close my eyes and groan. "We should have stayed at mine and driven here after sex."

"Come on. Get up, sunshine. It's clearly time to celebrate my birthday."

My eyes are still closed, but I feel the mattress dip as she rolls out of bed.

"Can I at least give you your present before we go down?"

"Kent, we're not having sex!"

I flick my eyes open. "I mean, your real present."

"Well ..." she says in a flirty voice as she saunters around the bed toward me. She's still totally naked, so I can't guarantee I won't get carried away. "That you can do."

Reaching into my bedside table, I pull out the shoebox I stashed there yesterday. "Okay, so I didn't really know what to get you, and Toby and Max just kept suggesting sex toys, so ..." I hand her the box, and her eyes widen in fear. "There are no sex toys in there, Savannah."

Shrugging her shoulder, she replies, "Shame."

"What? You were just scared."

"Of what they would suggest, not of you picking some things. I have faith that you wouldn't get some double-ended dildo and expect us to use it."

Flopping back against the pillows, I laugh. "That was Toby's suggestion."

She rolls her eyes and climbs back onto the bed. "Of course it was." Lifting the lid, she drops it on the quilt, and her breath catches in her throat. "Kent. Oh, wow. This is ..."

She clamps her mouth shut and looks up at me from the box. I've not known her too long but long enough to know a few of her favourite things. Believe me, I've been paying attention.

Inside the box is a voucher for a spa day with treatments included since she said she'd love to do that. It's for two, and I'm hoping she's going to want to take Heidi. There's also her favourite dark grey nail polish and light-pink lipstick, a DVD of *Twister*—which she told me was her favourite movie when she was a teenager—a new iPod since hers is ancient, a Tiffany bracelet that she and Heidi were gushing about in a magazine when I was fitting the storeroom out, Haribo, and Dolly Mixtures because those are her favourite sweets.

Her eyes zone in on the smaller pale blue box. "Kent ..."

"Just open it, Savannah."

She lifts the lid. "How did you know?"

"I'm observant." Even when I thought I didn't like her, I was watching. Everything she said or did, I remember. I guess I should have figured it out sooner.

"I love it. *All* of it."

Her grey eyes gloss over like she's fighting emotion. It feels fucking great, I have to say.

"You're welcome."

"You didn't need to get me so much, but thank you for not going ridiculously crazy."

I playfully narrow my eyes. "It wasn't easy," I tell her. "I want to give you the world."

"Kent," she breathes, shaking her head, "I just want you."

I lean over and kiss her because, fucking hell, she's amazing. "Are you ready for your birthday breakfast?" I ask against her soft lips.

She sits back and takes the bracelet out of the box. Slipping it onto her wrist, she nods. "I am now. I'm looking forward to seeing what your mum's done, but I'm concerned that I won't be able to eat it all."

I get out of bed and reach for my clothes. "Oh, you definitely won't be able to eat it all."

No one would be able to. Mum could cater for eating contests, and they wouldn't be able to finish it.

She looks over her shoulder and grins. Her back is to me as she stands to get dressed. But, right now, she's naked, and her soft, lightly tan skin is begging to be worshiped.

I love it when she's like this. It's not even just the fact that she's naked; it's how confident she is while she struts around in her birthday suit. It's sexy as hell.

Bending down, she scoops up her bra.

I squeeze my eyes closed. *Jesus.* "Any chance you want to be extra late to breakfast?"

With a laugh, she spins around and covers her breasts with the damn bra. "No, your mum is an awesome cook."

"Hey"—I frown—"I'm an awesome fuck."

Savannah shakes her head in discouragement, but she doesn't disagree. She can't because we both know I'm killer in bed. All the scratch marks on my back prove it.

"When we get back to mine, I expect you to provide me with a lot of birthday orgasms. Right now, we have things to do."

She slips on a pair of jeans and a top, and I do the same. I tug socks onto my feet in a huff. We might have had sex twice last night, but I want her again, and it's going to be ages before we're alone.

I want to spend the day making her come.

LIE TO ME

"Kent!"

Looking up from her arse, I mutter, "What?"

"Let's go down."

Right. I round the bed and hold out my hand. "Sorry, I got distracted."

"I like you getting distracted." She presses her body against mine and rises on her tiptoes until we're the same height. "I love knowing that you're desperate to get inside me, and I love it more when you have to wait. Makes you way grabbier when we're alone."

"Way grabbier?" I repeat, smirking and pulling her flush with my body.

Her cheeks blush. "Yeah."

"You like when I'm grabby, huh?"

"A lot. It makes me so hot when you can't wait. The second we're alone, and you slam me against a door or wall or tug my clothes off ... yeah, I like that."

I clear my throat as my dick swells in my jeans. "Right. Well, after that, I don't think you'll be disappointed later."

She backs away, putting a foot of distance between us. "You never disappoint, Kent. Let's go eat our body weight in food. You're going to need a lot of energy."

I follow her out of my room and onto the landing. "Oh, baby, you're the one who's going to need a lot of energy."

I'm so fucking excited right now. I watch her walk down the stairs, knowing how today is going to end, and I just want to press fast-forward. My heart thumps as she looks over her shoulder on the way down. She's fucking beautiful.

We enter the kitchen, and I see Mum has outdone herself again.

"Wow, this looks amazing," Savannah says, her eyes wide as she takes in the food on the kitchen table. "I thought last night's dinner was big."

"This is how birthdays are done, babe."

She turns to me, smiling. "We're eating here?"

"Yep, closer to the coffee."

My mum always goes way out for birthdays. And Christmas. And Easter. And Halloween.

The table is full of freshly baked pastries, stacks of toasts, platters of bacon and sausages. She has bowls of beans and rosti potatoes, mushrooms, and a warm plate of fried eggs.

There will be seven of us for breakfast, but there's enough food for double.

"Happy birthday, darling," Mum says, turning from the fridge and embracing my girl in a hug that's probably preventing her from breathing.

Savannah hugs her back though, a smile warming her face. "I can't believe you went to so much trouble, Judy. You didn't have to."

Mum lets her go and waves her hand. "It was no trouble. Come and sit down."

I take Savannah's hand and lead her to the seat next to mine. My parents are creatures of habit, so we all have our usual places around the table. Thankfully, the chair next to mine has yet to be claimed.

My dad, Brooke, and Freddy wish Savannah a happy birthday, and we dig in. There are so many choices, but I waste no time in making a mountain of greasy food on my plate. Savannah is a little more reserved in her selection than me, but she puts more food on than I would have thought.

She's either very hungry or being polite.

"So, after breakfast, we'll go for the walk, have lunch at the pub, and then on to something else," Mum says, spooning beans onto her plate.

Heidi nudges her arm. "Mum, Savannah might not want to do that."

"Right. Of course. I forget that she's not been with us the whole time."

Yeah, that's how I feel, too.

Savannah looks up at Mum over the sea of food in the middle of the table. "No, I'd really like to. Kent has told me all about your birthdays, and I don't have any traditions, so I'd love to experience yours."

Mum beams, her glossy blue eyes shining. "Wonderful. That's settled then."

I wonder what her birthdays were like. *If she's not close to her parents, did anyone bother celebrating her life while she was growing up?* I've always had over-the-top shit every year, and as irritating as it got, especially in my teenage years, I'd rather have a big fuss than nothing at all.

"I'm so glad you're here," Brooke says. "We will make up for every year you've had without tradition. Literally. Mum is way OTT."

"Hey!" Mum says, laughing. "You love birthdays and holidays at home."

Brooke widens her eyes at Savannah. "Wait until you see her at Christmas. It's like a grotto in here."

"I can't wait. I love Christmas."

"That's good. You definitely can't be a grinch around my mother," Heidi adds. "Now, hurry up and eat, so I can give you presents."

Savannah looks to me for help. She's not used to having a lot of attention or being showered with gifts, but I shrug because she's ours now, and she's just going to have to get used to it.

29

Savannah

TODAY HAS BEEN THE best birthday ever, and it's only two p.m. Kent's family is awesome. Their birthday traditions are designed to make the birthday person feel super special. I don't think there is anything his parents wouldn't do for their children.

They would never betray him.

I've been accepted as one of them, and they already treat me like one of the family. Being part of something again makes my heart warm. It's lovely to be around people who care so much about each other.

Before everything went to shit with my family, we were like that. We spent a lot of time together. We made a big deal out of each other's birthdays and took holidays together.

Most of my friends hated family holidays when they were teens, but I loved them.

I never would have thought we'd be here now.

Mum hasn't even tried to call me. She must have gotten my number from Simon unless he wanted to talk to me first. I wonder if he'll get Mum to call next and let her try. I don't really want to think about the possibility of her having my number but not wanting to call.

I think my lack of communication over the last three years speaks for itself. I don't want anything to do with them ever again.

Kent takes his card from the server and slides it into his pocket. He insisted on paying for lunch for me and his family. Even though he has plenty of money, I hate him constantly spending it on me.

"Thank you," I say, trying not to be difficult.

He grins triumphantly. "You're welcome."

If it wasn't my birthday, I would have pushed harder to pay at least part of the bill. Not that it would have gotten me anywhere.

Simon never let me pay for anything, and back then, it didn't bother me. It was what I was used to, just how we did things, but now, I have money of my own, and I want to pay my way.

And the fact that I hate him now has probably changed my views on women paying.

"Kent hasn't had to pay for a birthday lunch in years. It was definitely overdue," Heidi teases.

"You've never had to pay for a birthday lunch," Kent counters.

Brooke adds, "We're waiting for her to get the cats."

"I'm not going to be an old spinster!"

"Keep telling yourself that," Kent says.

I stand with everyone else. "She has Toby."

"Ha!" Heidi points at Kent. "I'll marry your friend if I have to."

"You will not," he replies, turning up his nose.

"I have to deal with you sleeping with my friend. Why shouldn't you have the same?"

Kent folds his arms. "Do you know where Toby has been? Because I do."

"Does Savannah know where you've been?"

LIE TO ME

Laughing at Kent's death glare to his sister, I grab my bag. "I don't think I want to know where he's been."

Kent's parents walk out of the restaurant, shaking their heads in amusement. We follow, filtering out behind.

"Hey, I'm not that bad!"

I link my arm with Kent's, and he bends down a fraction, placing a kiss on the top of my head. I close my eyes, taking a breath.

"Really?" I say. "I'll ask Max and see what he thinks."

"No, you won't. Everything I've done with other women is in the past."

Leaning my head on his shoulder, I reply, "I know. I'm only messing around. I don't want to know about the other women. Not any of them."

Not even Freya anymore. I hate what that bitch did to him. And I hate that, after he revealed his past betrayal, I still couldn't reveal mine. It wasn't the right time. But we're getting closer, and things are moving forward, actually steaming forward, and I don't want to keep it from him anymore.

After this weekend, I will have to open up. Whatever it does to me to go back there, I have to. Kent deserves the truth. I just have no idea how I'll be able to re-close that wound once it's been ripped open again.

I lost everything, including myself, when it all blew up, and I'm terrified of starting that process again. I've worked so hard. It's exhausted me to rebuild my life.

It's different now.

"What happens next then?" I ask Kent as we walk … somewhere.

"Well, next, we go out and do something. When we were young, it was theme parks and zoos. Actually, to be fair, it's still that, but Mum has something different planned for your birthday."

"Yeah?"

He nods. "Cocktail class."

"Well, the sound of that does not suck. I'm going to learn how to make cocktails?"

"Yep." He rolls his eyes. "We all are."

"Awesome."

The dark look he gives me shows he doesn't think it's very awesome, but who cares? Because today isn't about him. What better way to spend your birthday than with lots of cocktails?

"After that, I've told her she's done, and I'm stealing you."

My tough guy who takes no shit still listens to his mum. If he had his way, we would probably be in bed.

"What are we doing when you've stolen me?"

Arching an eyebrow, he grins. "Oh, I couldn't possibly tell you that."

"No fair."

"Never said I was going to play fair."

"Can you give me a clue?"

"You'll need a change of clothes for two nights. No pyjamas. We're sleeping naked."

We're going away together?

"You can't leave it there. Where are we going?" It's not the Maldives. That's too far for just two nights.

He stops us in the middle of the street, his family still walking ahead.

Pressing his forehead to mine, he whispers, "Somewhere romantic where I can have you all to myself for a whole two days."

"I love the sound of that."

"Me, too. Today is proving to be rather ... crowded."

"No, it's been lovely. Kent, your family is great."

His eyebrow lifts. "Hmm. They're meddling."

"They love you. You're lucky."

Wincing, he holds me close. "I'm sorry. Have you heard from your parents?"

"They don't even have my number. It's fine. Believe me, I'm better off without them."

LIE TO ME

"I'm still sorry."

"Don't be. Just be *really* nice to me this weekend."

Laughing, he presses a soft kiss to my lips. "Oh, I plan to."

After cocktail-making, which was awesome, Kent's family insisted on walking us both back to mine after we left the bar in the city, so I could pack, but Kent made them promise to leave immediately. I love his family, but I'm ready to be alone with him, too.

I'm going to tell him about Simon and my family in the week, so I want to soak up every moment of perfection with him before things get messy for me, before I have to tear open my heart again.

Kent squeezes my arm and grins down at me. He's looking forward to being alone, too. Heidi is ahead of us with her parents, and Kent and I are behind. Freddy and Brooke have already gone home.

We turn the corner, and my building comes into view.

My heart stops, and my feet plant.

Simon turns around and spots me.

No.

Shit, I can't breathe.

No, not now!

"What's wrong?" Kent asks.

His family hears and turns around.

"Sav," Simon calls.

No, no, no.

I'm free-falling. The floor whips away, and I plummet into darkness.

"Savannah, what's going on? Who is he?" Kent presses.

Simon is walking toward me.

Kent tugs my arm, so I'm facing him. "Savannah!"

"Hey, get off her," Simon orders.

My back stiffens, catapulting me back to a reality I hoped would never happen. "Shut up, Simon!" I snap, clenching my trembling hands.

"What the hell is going on? Who the fuck are you?" Kent shouts at Simon.

"I'm Sav's guy."

I glare at him. "No, he's not. He's *nothing*. Get out of here, Simon. I don't ever want to see you again."

"I'm not going anywhere until we sort this out."

"Hey!" Kent snaps. "She said get out of here, so fuck off."

Kent's dad holds his arm up, trying to calm him down. Kent's face is red, and the way he's glaring at Simon makes me nervous.

My heart falls to the floor. My old world and my new world weren't ever supposed to meet. They don't work together, like gin and Coke.

"You don't know what you're talking about, mate, so back off," Simon says.

"Stop it!" I shout. God, we have a crowd watching now. "Simon, go. There's nothing you can ever say to me to make me stop hating you. I want *nothing* to do with you."

"Don't say that. We all miss you. Your parents are still devastated. What happened was a mistake, Sav."

Kent tenses beside me.

Fuck.

Please go, Simon, please.

"A mistake? You were sleeping with my sister for *six months* before I found out, and you're trying to claim it was a mistake!"

"Can we go somewhere and talk?" he asks.

"No." I almost laugh. *He's insane.* "Leave!"

"You need to go right now," Kent says, taking a step closer to Simon. His dad is right there, ready to stop Kent if he tries to punch Simon or something.

"This isn't over," Simon says, turning around. He walks back down the street, leaving my life splitting apart.

LIE TO ME

Kent turns to me, eyes wide, chest puffed. He doesn't look like he's breathing.

Tears sting my eyes. *What have I done? I should have dealt with this properly.*

"Kent, I'm sorry," I whisper.

He doesn't like lies. Not after Freya and what she did to him. He opened up and told me everything, and I kept my mouth shut.

"He's your ex. The one who was nothing?"

My heart rips. "Yes."

"Jesus," he seethes, turning his body away from me.

"I'm sorry. I wanted to tell you, but …"

"But what, Savannah?" he snaps, spinning back.

Judy steps in. "Let's go inside and talk. The street is no place for this."

"I'm not going anywhere. *She lied.* We're done, Savannah." Kent starts to walk away, and his dad follows him, calling his name.

He's walking away from me.

His back is hunched. He's angry, defeated, and betrayed.

I did that to him. This is all my fault, and I have no idea what to do or how to fix it.

I look desperately between Judy and Heidi, unable to move. *Someone, do something! Stop him!*

I'm just standing here, like a frozen idiot, while the best thing I've ever had walks away. My heart shatters as he walks around the corner and out of sight.

Pressing my hand against the searing pain in my chest, I take a ragged breath.

Think, Savannah.

Heidi steps in front of me. "Dad will talk to him. You need to let him cool off before you try."

I know that. He's not in the mood right now. It's just happened, and he's going to be obsessing over the lie. I have to give him time, but, God, I don't want to. I want to chase him down and beg for forgiveness.

"Let's go inside. I have questions."

Of course she does. This time, I'm not going to be able to talk my way around them either. Everything is out in the open. Well, almost everything.

"Come on, darling," Judy says, wrapping her arm around my back.

I look up at her. "You're shaking."

She smiles. "That's you."

"Oh."

I'm shaking.

We slowly climb the stairs. Each one feels like it's taller than the last. Heidi takes my keys from my bag and lets us into my flat.

"Take a seat," Judy says, leading me to the sofa.

I drop down, and that's when I feel a tear roll down my cheek. "I didn't mean to lie. I swear, I didn't."

"Why did you? There's no shame in being cheated on," Judy asks.

Dropping my eyes, I reply, "I couldn't talk about it. Hurts too much." But I'm going to have to tell them now.

Heidi leans closer to me. "Because he cheated with your sister?"

"Not just that, but because …" I take a breath as pain slices through my chest. "Because I found out about their affair while I was in the hospital, m-miscarrying our baby."

"Oh my God," Judy whispers, scooting closer and wrapping me tightly in her arms. She lays her head against mine, like she's trying to take the pain away.

"I was only nineteen. We didn't plan to get pregnant, but the pill didn't work one month. I found out when I was seven weeks pregnant, and I was petrified. It took me two weeks to get used to it, and I started to believe that I could do it, you know. I was young and didn't know anything, but I would learn how to be a good mum. I think I even started to get excited, but two days later, I woke up, haemorrhaging blood."

The words, my story, bleed from every pore, screaming as I reveal the most heartbreaking thing I've been through. I can't believe how fast everything pours from my mouth, but if I can make them understand, then Kent has to.

"Hon, I'm so sorry," Heidi says, taking my hand.

A tear rolls down my cheek. I feel it slide and curl under my jaw. "Simon wasn't over that night. He said he was working late. I shouted for my mum, and she took me to the hospital. We all tried to call Simon, but his phone was off. My sister wasn't answering either. A friend of Simon's, who we'd rung to try to get ahold of him, came to the hospital. He told me he wouldn't cover for him anymore, and he told me where they both were."

Judy shakes her head against mine. "I can't believe it."

"They were at a hotel. While I was losing my baby, my boyfriend was sleeping with my sister." My hands curl into fists, and I cross my arms, pressing them into my chest. My baby died, and they weren't there.

"I hate them both," Heidi says.

"Yeah, me, too," I reply with a ragged breath. "My parents were so angry with Isla to begin with, but it didn't take them long to want to forget it all had happened. I couldn't do it. I couldn't go back to the way things were. Simon and Isla kept seeing each other, and my parents said nothing."

There was no way I could be around them. They were both a reminder of the miscarriage. I was so young, and I had no idea how to grieve for a baby.

"And that's why you're estranged from them," Heidi says.

"Yeah. They ruined everything, I lost so much, but I was the one who ended up getting blamed for the family rift."

Heidi shakes her head. "I cannot believe they took her side."

"I need to speak to Kent."

Judy grimaces. "Darling, I don't think that's a good idea yet. Give him an hour. Let his dad talk to him first."

I turn my head, and she moves back a fraction. "He hates me. I have to fix that. I have to try."

"He's angry. He loves you. Since Freya fucked him over, he's been obsessed with total disclosure. It's the one breaking point he has. Right now, he's just going to be pissed off that you lied, and until he calms down, he won't see reason," Heidi says.

I turn to her. "But I can explain to him."

"Savannah, he's not going to listen yet. Trust us, we've seen him when he's like this. He shuts down cold and won't hear anything. You had very good reasons not to want to talk about your past, but until he's chilled the hell out, he's not going to hear what you're saying. Don't do that to yourself. When you explain, he needs to be in a place to understand."

"How am I supposed to wait for that?" I rasp, dipping my head as the tears flow more freely.

How am I supposed to wait for him when missing him hurts so much that I can't breathe?

I curl into Judy and sob until my throat is raw.

30

Kent

I SHOVE MY FRONT door open so hard, it slams back against the wall. My heart is racing a million miles an hour, pumping adrenaline around my body like it's blood.

Fuck it! Fuck every-fucking-thing!

Dad's arm shoots out, catching the door on the rebound. It could have fallen off, and I wouldn't have cared. Storming through to the kitchen, I head to the alcohol cupboard.

"Kent, you need to calm down," Dad orders.

I can't fucking calm down!

Grabbing a bottle of Jack Daniel's, I unscrew the lid and drink from the bottle. "Fuck!" I bellow, slamming it down on the counter. My knuckles turn white as I grip the neck of the bottle in my fist.

"Do you feel better now?" he asks.

"No, I fucking don't. She *lied* to me. How the hell did I not see it?"

"There's a reason, son. The guy, Simon, slept with her *sister*."

"And that's a reason to run away from home, pretend you don't have an ex, any siblings, or a relationship with your parents?"

He shrugs. "I don't know the details, and that's why you should let her explain before you do this. We all have our reasons for doing certain things, Kent. At least allow Savannah to give you hers."

I tighten my grip, my heart ripping to shreds. "I don't want to hear her reasons for shit. I told her all about Freya, everything that happened, and how it changed who I was. Fucking hell, I held nothing back. *That* was the time for her to tell me."

"Maybe she wasn't ready yet. You told her about Freya in your time. You should at least grant her the chance to do the same."

"Why the fuck are you taking her side?"

"Son, I'm taking *your* side. You love this girl, but if you're not careful, you're going to ruin the best thing that's happened to you."

"*I'm* going to ruin it? I'm not the one who lied!"

He raises his hands. "Give her the benefit of the doubt. Please, don't do anything rash that you'll regret later."

"I thought she was different." I swig. "Fuck me, I was going to propose."

Dad's eyes widen.

"Yeah. If that bastard hadn't turned up, I could have been engaged to the liar next weekend."

"Kent, watch what you say."

"I'm not going to regret calling her a liar, Dad."

"Yes, you are."

Sighing, I close my eyes and then take another swig. *Fuck me, this is a new pain I haven't experienced before.*

"I didn't know you were planning on proposing," he says after a long stretch of silence.

"Yeah, well, I was."

LIE TO ME

I know we haven't been together long, but that doesn't matter to me. Savannah is everything. She's all I see, all I feel, all I want.

Now, I'm back to being burned and alone.

Fucking bitch.

"I'm sorry, Kent."

I look away and swig. The liquor burns so good on the way down.

"I love her," I whisper. "It's nothing like it was with Freya."

Dad steps closer and opens a cupboard. He takes two tumblers out and puts them down on the counter. "I know you love her, and I know it's different. That's why you can't let the same thing happen again. Freya and Savannah are nothing alike. She must have been severely damaged by this guy and her sister's betrayal to not want to talk about it."

"I don't care."

He takes the bottle from my hand, prying it from my curled fingers, and pours two small measures. "You will care when you've calmed down."

"I'm going to need more than that," I say, taking a deep breath that feels like knives are digging in my chest.

He glances at me out of the corner of his eye and then shakes his head. He pours a little more into my glass and hands it over. "What's the plan now, Kent?" he asks.

"Move on."

Tilting his head, he gives me a look that makes my heart die. He knows it's not going to be that simple either. I would love to press a button or flip a switch and turn off my feelings for her. If I could stop being in love with her right now, I would.

But I can't, so I have to feel agony until my heart repairs.

Fucking great.

"Do you not think you should speak to her?"

"I will have to eventually. Some of her stuff is here."

Her shit is all over my house, and I'm trying really fucking hard not to look at any of it.

"I'll rephrase, Kent. Do you think you should talk to her about what just happened? She deserves the opportunity to explain, and you deserve the explanation."

"She doesn't deserve anything, and I don't want it."

"That's not true."

"Yes, it is!"

"It won't be when you've calmed down."

I've had enough of his input now. "Why are you still here, Dad?"

"Why do you think, son?"

Growling, I walk away. There's nothing he can say or do to make this better, so I don't know why he's trying. She lied and then lied some more. She *knew* I couldn't take lies after Freya.

Savannah fucked this up all on her own.

"Fuck!" I bellow and drop to the sofa. *What the fuck am I supposed to do now? I love her.* Resting my elbows on my knees, I tug my hair.

I take a deep breath.

She's still here. A lot of her stuff is in my apartment. She even has house things all over the place. Fucking little hair slides that seem to multiply are littering my bathroom along with the coconut shampoo that brought me to my knees, her face powder, and clothes. She has flowers in a vase on the dining table that I just want to throw out the window. My apartment needed softening apparently.

God, how stupid was I for letting her in to every part of my life?

The sofa cushion beside me caves. Dad has sat down. I don't look up though because I don't want to see his expression. He'll probably look at me with pity. Or he'll tell me to go back there and speak to her, and I can't deal with either of those right now.

"It's going to be okay, Kent."

I laugh despite there being nothing funny here. "No, it's not. I'm not going to get over her as fast."

"I understand that."

LIE TO ME

Dropping my arms, I sit back and stare ahead. "She lied about everything. Do you think the fucker has been in contact with her?"

Was that while she was with me? Did she reply to him while she was in my apartment, when we were out together? God, that's going to drive me crazy.

"I don't think there's been anything going on between them, Kent."

"Of course there's not. That's not the point though. He's clearly been hassling her if she didn't want him around, but she didn't tell me. I could have helped. Why couldn't she tell me about her past? It doesn't make sense. None of it was her fault, so why couldn't she talk to me?"

"It was painful for her; you could see that. Sometimes, it's easier for us to try to forget or to ignore what causes us the most harm. This wasn't just her ex who hurt her, but also her whole family. She cut *everyone* off and moved away from all that she knew. That must be so painful."

My blood turns to fire. "I don't care! She knew she could talk to me. I gave her so many opportunities. I asked, but I didn't push, and I gave her space when I thought she needed it. What did I get in return? A load of bullshit about parents who just never gave a shit, no serious ex, and no siblings."

"Not everything is as black and white as you would like it to be. I understand your need for honesty after Freya, but not being ready to open up about something and purposefully deceiving isn't the same thing."

"Might as well be."

He sighs. "Tell me this, did she ever offer any information about her family or anything about her past, or was it when you asked?"

"Asked," I growl. *Where is he going with this?* "Just because she didn't sit me down and offer the bullshit doesn't mean it's not bullshit."

"It means that she didn't want to lie, but she wasn't ready to be honest."

Shaking my head, I close my eyes and take a breath. *He's not getting this.* "I think you should go."

"Is that because I'm making sense?"

"No, it's because you don't get it."

Dad stands up, and although I don't look at him, I know he's looking at me. "Kent, I will love and support you always, but I'm going to leave because, right now, *you* don't get it, and I know the best way for you to get to grips with the situation is to be alone."

I wait until he closes my front door, and then I allow the weight of the grief I feel to swamp me.

"Fuck!" I shout, jabbing the heel of my palm into my splitting chest.

It hurts so fucking bad; it takes my breath away.

Gripping my glass, I launch it at the wall and bellow, "Fuck!"

31

Savannah

MONDAY LIVES UP TO its reputation by being massively shit. And it's only seven a.m. I was supposed to be okay after the weekend. Obviously, I wasn't going to be, but it was nice to have the hope. Now, I have nothing.

I'm empty.

I walk down the street toward work. Although it's a little chilly, the sun is shining, and the sky is blue. Inside, I feel ice cold. No amount of sun is going to lift my spirit. My stomach churns with nerves of seeing Heidi again. She was so nice to me on Saturday, but I haven't seen her since—my choice. I needed to be alone.

She would have had time to speak to Kent, and she might be angry with me now, too.

That doesn't sound like Heidi, but he's her brother, and family is the most important thing to her.

I check my phone as I walk. No messages from Kent.

Taking a deep breath and swallowing heartache, I open the three texts from Simon. Two from last night and one from this morning.

Simon: You can't ignore me forever. I need to talk to you.

Simon: Call me! I'll meet you anywhere, but this will happen.

Simon: Fucking call me, Sav!

My pace slows, the closer I get to the studio. People behind me tut and shift around, walking off ahead. I would usually apologise, but today, I'm not feeling very British. They can all go to hell for all I care.

The studio door opens, and Heidi steps out.

I stop as she looks around. *Is she stopping me before I go inside? Am I out of a job now?*

No, it's too early for me to officially be there, so she wouldn't have known I was coming. She's probably just getting some air.

Frowning, Heidi gestures with her arm for me to go to her.

Shit. I place my feet on the floor but don't feel like I'm moving as I take the last few steps. I need this job.

"Hey, how are you?" she says when I'm in earshot.

"Um … " *Awful.* I just want to go home, curl up, and give in to the pain.

She tilts her head to the side. "Come on in and talk about it."

I step through the door. On her desk are two drinks and a plate of pastries. Kent used to bring me pastries in bed.

"You didn't have to do this," I say, dropping my bag down on the floor beside my desk.

"I wanted to. I figured you'd probably not eaten much over the weekend."

No, nothing actually. The thought of food makes me feel sick.

I sit down opposite Heidi's seat and pick up the coffee. "Thanks."

LIE TO ME

Heidi sits and rests her elbows on the desk. "Have you spoken to Kent?"

Shaking my head, I drop my eyes. "I tried but ..."

"He's stubborn, and it sometimes takes him a while to come around, but he *will* come around."

"I just want him to talk to me, let me explain."

Heidi hands me a paper plate and points to the pastries. I put my drink down and take a cinnamon swirl. My stomach rumbles at the thought of food.

"I saw him yesterday," she says, tearing apart a croissant.

"How is he?"

She purses her lips, thinking about how honest she should be.

"You can tell me, Heidi."

"He's ... I've never seen him like this. He was upset when everything came out with Freya, but I think that was more the betrayal. This time around, he's a mess, and he misses you."

Okay, maybe I don't want to hear it.

Closing my eyes, I whisper, "Heidi, I'm so sorry. I never meant to hurt him."

"I know, and he'll understand that soon, too. I can't believe you kept it all in for so long though. How did you cope?"

"I ..." Frowning, I search my mind to think of what I did. What did I do? Besides moving away and cutting all ties, I didn't do anything. What is there to do anyway? There's no single action that can repair a broken heart. Over time, scar tissue glues the pieces back together, but it's never the same.

"You haven't dealt with it?"

"I'm over my family, believe me."

"I don't mean your family, Savannah. I mean, the miscarriage."

No, I haven't thought much about that.

Shrugging one shoulder, I rip another piece of pastry. "There's nothing I can do."

"Do you think you should talk to someone?"

"No, I'm fine. It was a long time ago, and I let myself cry and be sad at the time. I'd rather not go back now." I raise my eyes.

Honestly, that's kind of bullshit. I haven't really dealt with it, I guess. I mean, ignoring something probably isn't classed as dealing. There's nothing I can do now though. I can't change what happened any more than I could have stopped it from happening back then. I have to accept that and move on.

"Fair enough. Will you tell me more about your parents? I thought you were estranged."

They only got the basic details on Saturday because I was having a hard enough time with breathing under the crushing grief of Kent breaking up with me and talking about my baby.

"We are."

She smiles. "You know what I mean."

"They were as shocked and heartbroken as I was when they found out about Simon and my sister. They were angry with her, disgusted that she could do that to me, and while I would never ask them to choose between us, not even after she did that, I did want them to back me up."

"They didn't at all? You said they were angry with them at first."

"Yeah, at first, they were. They supported me when I cut her out of my life, but I think they assumed it would be temporary—like, if they waited a few weeks, everything would go back to normal. Two weeks later, they started talking to me about forgiveness. We found out shortly after that they were still seeing each other."

"What did your parents do then?"

Despite the total lack of humour, I laugh. "Nothing. I don't know if they spoke to her about it, but they never let on if they did. I was told that I should get past it, or I would break the family apart."

"Fuckers."

This time, I laugh for real. "Yeah, I thought that, too."

"So, what happened then?"

LIE TO ME

Smirking, I shake my head at her. "My old life is like a soap opera to you, isn't it?"

She sits back in her seat, unaware that she was inching in with every question. "I'm sorry."

"No, it's okay. Talking about it actually isn't as bad as I thought. I wish I'd realised that weeks ago when Kent was telling me about his ex."

Heidi waves her hand. "Forget him for now. What happened?"

I pop some pastry in my mouth and chew fast. "Well, a month after we found out they were still together, it all got to be too much. My parents had accepted them, even going out to dinner with them. I couldn't get my head around it, and no amount of talking to them made them understand, so I left."

"How?"

"Walked out the door."

She deadpans, dropping her hands to the desk. "Not funny."

"I packed my bags while my parents slept and my sister was at Simon's, and I left."

"You didn't tell anyone?"

"I left a note. There's no way I could have had that conversation with them; it would have gotten messy. I had to go without anyone knowing. It was the best decision I ever made."

"And you've had no contact since? How did Simon know where you lived?"

I turn my nose up. "I think he must have hired a private investigator. Before that, it was only messaging on my old Facebook account. Then, he started calling me a couple of months ago, even after I changed my number. I texted him back, very clearly telling him that I wanted him to leave me alone and to never contact me again. He turned up once, but I thought I got through to him that I'm done. Then, he turned up on my doorstep again, and you know the rest."

She slowly shakes her head. "Unbelievable. Do you know what he wants?"

"He said on the phone that he wants to talk. I thought telling him to bugger off would do the trick, but apparently, he's fucking stupid."

"The fact that he cheated on you makes him fucking stupid."

Yeah, I'll give her that.

I pop another piece of cinnamon swirl in my mouth.

"How long should I leave it before calling Kent again?"

"When did you call him?" she asks.

"Saturday after you and your mum left … and Sunday," I reply, wincing. "I know you said not to, but I had to let him know that I was sorry and that I wanted to explain. Anyway, he didn't answer, so I sent a super-long text."

"You explained everything over text?"

"No, not all the details. I just told him how much I regret not being braver and sharing my past with him and that I would tell him everything if he gave me the chance."

And I told him I loved him. I've never loved anyone the way I love him, and it will kill me if he can't forgive me. How do you get past something like that? It was stupid of me to allow him all of my heart, but he has it, and there's nothing I can do now. If he doesn't forgive me, I'll just have to accept the fact that he will always have some of it.

"He's always been headstrong. We never could tell him something; he had to realise it by himself."

"There an average timescale for that?"

Heidi's eyes fill with sympathy. "Hard to tell, as it varies. What are you going to do next?"

"I don't know. I don't want to give him space. I want to show him how sorry I am. It feels wrong not to call or text."

"I get that."

"Do you think I should go to his?"

Heidi opens her mouth and then closes it.

I slump back in my chair. "I'm guessing that's a no."

"Well, he's never been in love with someone he's angry with, so it might work."

"You don't sound sure of that at all."

LIE TO ME

She shrugs, eyes filling with sympathy.

I lay my head back and give in to the crushing ache in my chest. Only Kent can heal me now.

32

Savannah

I WALK HOME FROM work on Friday, and everyone around me is buzzing for the weekend. It's been approximately one hundred forty-four hours since I last saw Kent, and each one of those has been a struggle.

Now, I'm facing a whole weekend on my own, missing him again. I had the briefest taste of what a relationship should be, and I suppose I should just be grateful for that. But I can't be when I know we should be together. Kent isn't supposed to be the one who got away. If I can't manage to fix this, nothing will make it right. I won't get over him even if I do learn to live without him.

Before Kent, I didn't really do much anyway, so I should be used to being alone and spending my time indoors reading or binge-watching TV, but I'm not.

It's even harder than adjusting my time from when I was with Simon.

It's a lovely autumn evening, too, even if a little chilly. The sun is still shining, and on the opposite side of the road, people are already sitting outside bars, having drinks. Soon, the clock will change, and the nights will draw in earlier. I welcome it right now.

I speed up, almost keeping pace with a man in front of me, jogging. I want to be home where I can curl up and not see anyone until Monday.

Jesus, I'm such a loser.

Letting myself into my flat, I slam the door behind me and bolt it. Pressing my forehead against the wood, I close my eyes. Tears sting behind my eyelids.

Missing Kent hurts so bad; it takes my breath away.

Thankfully, I have food, so I don't have to go out or have anyone deliver anything. My heart tightens the way it used to. I can feel myself sinking to a place I fought so hard for so long to drag myself out of. Darkness storms my mind, reeling me in.

He's not going to forgive me. I'm going to be alone.

Why did I ever think it was a good idea to start a relationship with him?

Things were so much easier when I had nothing. I shouldn't have let myself be happy again. I was perfectly fine before Kent, but I got greedy, wanting more.

Some people aren't supposed to have more.

I open my eyes, stand up straight, and kick off my shoes by the door. Walking straight to my bedroom, I peel off my clothes to get changed into something comfortable enough to slob around the apartment in.

Kent still has a few things at mine, and I'm tempted to put his T-shirt on, but that's asking for trouble. It would be nice to get through the day without breaking down like a baby.

Though I cried for a solid hour when I woke up this morning, so I've already failed.

I have a clean pair of leggings and an oversize T-shirt, which isn't Kent's, so I throw those on and chuck my work clothes on the end of my bed. I can't be bothered to do any washing right now.

LIE TO ME

My apartment is eerily quiet as I head back to the kitchen to find alcohol and food. I have a couple of bottles in my fridge that don't need to still be there come Monday.

I'm so sad, spending my weekend eating, drinking wine, and watching Netflix alone.

But those are the weekends I was used to, and I liked them perfectly fine before.

I open a bottle and pour a large glass. In the freezer is a microwave meal that'll do, so I chuck that in and watch the little black container turn around through the door.

Max and Toby wouldn't let Kent do this. He's probably out or at the very least having the two of them over to his to drink. I hope he hasn't gone out. He's hurt and angry, and if he's drinking in a bar, he might find someone.

Shit, that hurts.

If he doesn't forgive me, that will happen eventually, but I'm definitely not ready to hear about him shagging some girl anytime soon.

He wouldn't.

I know he did before—he's slept with a lot of women—but I honestly don't think he could right now. Or maybe I'm just hoping.

The microwave beeps at the same time someone knocks on my door. My buzzer never rang, so I guess it's either Heidi or someone already downstairs had opened the door. Or Kent. It's unlikely, but my heart thuds at the hope of it being him on the other side or the door. It's been six days, and he might have cooled down enough to at least want to talk.

If I could just get him to listen, maybe we could sort all of this out. So far, he's not returned any of my calls or replied to the daily messages I send.

I don't dare think about the worst-case scenario. He has said before that he wouldn't forgive being lied to. It's the one thing he wouldn't do.

Don't think about that.

I put my glass down on the counter and pad slowly toward the front door with my heart in my throat. My hands tremble as I unbolt the door and open it. I hold my breath, but then my shoulders sag.

"What do you want, Simon?" I ask, folding my arms as my stomach sinks. This is the first time he's tried to see me. I deleted my Facebook account the night Kent walked away from me.

"I want to talk. Please can I come in?"

"No."

"Come on, Sav."

"There's nothing I want to say to you."

"I don't care. You knew that, eventually, this would catch up with you. We have a lot to talk about, and I'm not going anywhere until you let me in."

"Then, I guess you're going to have to live in that hallway."

I drop my hands and grip the door, ready to slam it in his arsehole face, but he kicks his foot out, blocking me.

"Ten minutes is all I'm asking. You must have questions," he says, leaning a little closer to me.

I had questions, but at the time I needed answers, he wasn't talking. My sister was the one shouting her mouth off about how she was sorry but that they had fallen in love. Apparently, neither had wanted to hurt me. Like, what the hell did they think would happen? Even if Simon did want her and not me, why didn't he break up with me first? I could have gotten past that in time. It wouldn't have been easy, watching my ex move on to my sister, but that would have been a hell of a lot better than them cheating.

My chest burns, filled with fresh anger for an old pain. "Fine, fucking come in, and explain it all," I find myself saying.

I'm breaking a rule I made the day I left, but I realise I actually want to hear this. I want to know what excuse he has for why he treated me so badly.

It must be good.

Simon walks into my flat and looks around my open-plan living/kitchen area. I don't want him to look at my stuff, and I really don't want him looking at Kent's things. I haven't moved his zip-up hoodie, DVDs, or hair gel, so I have to see little parts of him everywhere.

"This place is nice, Sav."

"Quit the small talk. I don't give a shit what you think of my flat. Just talk."

"You don't have to be so hostile. I came here to have a discussion as adults."

"And, as an adult, I'm telling you to fucking say what you came here for." I laugh. "And you're telling me to act like an adult when you were the one sneaking around with my sister?"

Sighing, he runs his hands over his face. "I am sorry for the way I handled my attraction to your sister."

I swallow bile as my stomach rolls.

"I was weak. At first, it was flattering when she flirted with me. You and I had been together for a while."

"That makes it okay then."

He ignores my snide comment. "The longer it went on, the more I wanted her. Then, one night, we kissed. It was wrong, and I know that, but I couldn't help it. We ended up in bed."

"Literally don't think I want to hear this," I mutter, wishing I hadn't put my wine down.

"I hated myself in the morning, and she did, too. We vowed to never let it happen again."

"You sucked at that."

"We tried for weeks, but we couldn't stop it."

"Why didn't you break up with me? You didn't have to cheat."

"Because I love you."

I stare at him. There are so many things I want to say. The words are spinning around my mind, but the stupidity he's showing right now has blocked my mouth.

He steps closer, and I hold my ground. "Whatever you think of me, I do love you."

"Can you start using past tense, please? You're making me want to vomit."

"I still love you."

"You don't have a clue what love is." I could never, ever cheat on anyone. The very idea of being unfaithful to Kent is unthinkable. "You put yourself first time and time again, and you didn't care if you hurt me. You're a selfish prick, and honestly, you and my sister deserve each other. I hope you have both spent the last three years worrying that the other one will cheat."

Simon's eyes narrow. Either she cheated on him or I'm just dead on the mark. I don't care which one it is really.

"When I found out you were pregnant, I told her it was over."

"That went well," I mutter sarcastically.

"I stayed away from her until …"

I freeze, already guessing what he's about to confess. "Until when?" I ask.

"Until that day. I'm so sorry I wasn't there, Savannah. You should have never had to go through that alone."

He started sleeping with my sister again the day we lost our baby. Bile burns my throat.

I fucking despise him.

"You need to go," I growl.

"Not yet, please. I need you to believe me when I tell you how sorry I am. I've grown up a lot since then, and I realise exactly what I did. It was selfish, you're right, and it was the worst thing I could have done."

My hands ball into fists as my heart thumps against my rib cage. I want to punch him. "Great. Now, go."

"Savannah."

I throw my hands in the air. "Don't *Savannah* me. You came here and asked to explain, and now, you have."

"I didn't want to be with her when everything came out. You were angry, rightly so, but it made me wake up. The whole thing with your sister was so wrong, and I didn't want it to continue."

LIE TO ME

"Then, why did you? You stayed with her, Simon. You came around my house with her, expecting me to be fine with it. Why do that if you didn't want to?"

He shrugs. "I don't know. Everything was so out of control. You hated me, my parents and your parents hated me, and I hated me. She didn't."

"You stayed with her because she didn't hate you? Are you still together?"

He drops his eyes.

"Oh my God, you've actually stayed in a relationship with her for three years."

"You were gone."

"You fucking coward."

His head snaps up, and he grinds his teeth. That hit a nerve, but how could he deny it? "You don't understand."

"Nope, and I don't want to. I actually think it's Karma, to be honest."

"Who was that guy with you last week?"

"I'm not talking about him with you."

"Are you together?"

"You have no right to ask me that."

"I was young and idiotic, Savannah, but I'm not the same person I used to be, I swear."

Turning around, I take the few steps to the kitchen and get my wine. This is definitely a conversation requiring wine.

"I won't ask if you're going to offer me anything to drink," he mumbles like a petulant child.

Good.

"Does my sister know you're here?" I take a sip.

"No."

"Ah, so if I say I'll come home, what will happen?"

He scratches his jaw, his eyebrows drawing closer together.

"Have you not thought this through? Why do you want me to come home, Simon?"

"I love you."

"Hilarious. So, you want us to get back together?"

"I've always wanted that. I've spent three years trying to look for you."

"While you're with my sister. Does she know you've been looking?"

"She knows about the private investigator I hired."

Not about the attempts before that.

"If I agreed to go home and be with you again, what would happen with her?"

"Nothing. Our relationship is dead. She feels it, too."

I lift my eyebrow. "You think she feels that, or you know?"

"Look, forget what could happen. I know we can rebuild what we had. It won't be easy, but it's all I want."

Am I actually really drunk and imagining all of this? Or asleep? A nightmare is probably more accurate for this.

"And, if I say no, you're going to go home and pretend to live happily ever after with her?"

Simon turns his head, looking out my window.

"Oh my God, that's what you're going to do. Simon, grow a pair, and leave her if that's what you want, but leave me out of it because that's never, ever going to happen."

"That guy is your boyfriend then."

"He could be my boyfriend, my friend, or my long-lost brother, and it wouldn't change a thing. I don't want you, and I'm stunned that you think I could. After everything that happened, you honestly think I could find anything I like about you again?"

"We were good together."

I throw the hand not gripping my wine in the air. "Until you fucked my sister!"

What world does he live in? Delusional, colossal wanker.

"I'm sorry! I made a mistake and let everything spiral, but if you come back with me, I promise to be the man you fell for again," he pleads with wide green eyes.

"Leave, Simon. Go home, and forget about me."

He walks over until he's right in front of me. "I can't forget about you."

LIE TO ME

"Try harder because we aren't going to get back together. I can't forgive you, and I don't want to forgive you. I would rather die alone." If Kent doesn't forgive me, that might actually happen, but it will still be a lot better than being with a cheater.

He takes a deep breath, making his nostrils flare. "Is that what you really want, Sav? Because, if I go now, I'm not coming back."

"Don't let the door hit you on the arse."

"Fine." He steps around me and walks out of my life, hopefully for good.

My front door bangs as he exits, and I breathe a sigh of relief. My wine ripples in the glass where my hand shakes. I take a bigger sip.

I go to sit on my sofa to collect my nerves before I eat, but someone is shouting outside. I peer out the window, and my free hand clutches my throat.

Oh no.

Kent and Simon are fighting in the street.

What is Kent doing here?

I slam the glass down on my coffee table and fly out the door. Taking the communal stairs two at a time, I get down fast. My legs carry me forward where I barge into the door to open it.

Kent's arm extends and punches Simon in the face.

"Stop!" I shout.

Both look up at me, and Simon uses Kent's distraction to his benefit. He plants his fist into Kent's stomach.

I scream, "No!"

But it's too late, and Kent is doubling over. He recovers fast though and stretches back up. Turning, Kent faces Simon. I dash over and grab Kent's arm.

"He's not worth it," I say, tugging him to try to get him to look at me. "Please, just let it go, Kent, and come inside."

"Thanks for last night, Sav," Simon says as he backs away.

Kent's body tenses at Simon's words.

"No. Kent, nothing happened with him. You know me."

A pair of my favourite turquoise eyes finally looks at me. "I *thought* I knew you."

He pulls his arm out of my grip, and tears sting my eyes.

"Please, come inside."

"There's nothing to say," he seethes.

"Then, why are you here?" I ask, stepping forward, desperate to get him to stay. "You came for a reason."

"It doesn't matter."

"Yes, it does. Simon came over, like, five minutes ago. He wanted to explain, and I wanted to hear his version. But then I told him to leave. I don't want anything to do with him. Please believe that. You're the only person I could ever want."

"How do I know you're telling the truth, Savannah? I thought I knew you."

"You do. You're just being stubborn right now. If you give me a second, I'll tell you everything."

"I know everything."

"From Heidi. That's not the same as us sitting down and discussing it. I only kept it from you because I didn't know how to talk about it without breaking down. It's the most painful thing I've ever been through—well, second now. I didn't know how to deal with it, so I tried to do what I'd been doing since the day I left, and I mostly ignored it all."

Kent's eyes close as I ramble about my past and how much I miss him.

When he opens them again, they're vacant.

"Take care of yourself, Savannah," he whispers, stepping back.

"Kent, please."

He turns around and unlocks his car that's parked up the street.

He did come here for me, but instead, he found Simon leaving my building.

My heart fractures all over again, and I reach for the brick wall beside me to steady myself.

He's not going to forgive me.

33

Kent

IF MY MUM WITNESSED my driving right now, she would call the DVLA and get them to revoke my licence.

After everything Simon did to her, Savannah let him back into her life. He was in her fucking flat. When I saw him, smirking at me in the middle of the path, I lost it.

My fist screams in pain as I clench the steering wheel. I don't even know where I'm going. I'm driving in the opposite direction to my house. I could call Toby and Max and get them to meet me somewhere, but they would have questions.

Wherever I go, I'll have to talk though, and I think I would rather that than go home alone. I make a left, and Toby's house is up ahead. He's more mature than Max, and although I know, if I want a serious conversation, I can talk to Max, too, it's easier with Toby.

I park the car in his drive and get out. Max's car is here, too.

Fuck's sake.

I'm just heading up the path when Toby opens the door.

Smirking, he cranes his head over his neck and shouts into the house, "Put some clothes on, Heidi! Your brother is here."

His face falls when he sees me approach, fists clenched and jaw tight. I guess I look as shit as I feel.

"What's happened, dude?"

"I need a drink," I bark.

Toby steps aside while I head into his kitchen. He has a full-height larder cupboard full of every alcoholic drink you could ever want. I scan the cupboard and grab a bottle of Southern Comfort.

"What's going on?" Toby asks behind me while I unscrew the lid and drink straight from the bottle. "Did something happen with Savannah again?"

I've already had a lengthy conversation with them after I broke up with Savannah. Neither of them seems as angry with her as I am.

I turn to him, my fingers digging into the glass. "Something happened with her ex."

"Fuck. Sit down, buddy." Max grabs a bottle of Jack Daniel's and three glasses even though he knows I won't use a glass.

I sit on the brown leather sofa in the large open-plan living/kitchen area. The back of Toby's house looks out onto a field, so he has the entire wall made of glass.

"Go on," Toby prompts, placing the glasses on the chunky oak coffee table.

His eyes are filled with sympathy. He thinks she's back with her ex. Not that it's any of my business anymore, but I can't see that happening. The dude is a snake.

"I went to her flat to see her, and he was walking out of the building just as I arrived."

"He was? I thought she didn't want to see him again?" Toby asks.

You're not the only fucking one. "Me, too."

He leans forwards. "Well, maybe she didn't want him there. She can't control him coming over."

LIE TO ME

"She let him in to explain what had happened. He took great pleasure in telling me that they'd talked."

He also said he'd spent the night, but that's untrue. Savannah's reaction was honest. At least I know she has it in her.

Toby nods and pours Jack Daniel's into a glass. So far, Max has been quiet, probably because he knows this isn't the time for jokes yet.

"So fucking what? She might have talked to him, but she loves you. Mate, you can't blame her for wanting answers. Didn't you say that she left without a word? So, she probably didn't get to ask everything you would want to know in that shitty situation."

I take a deep breath through my nose. He keeps defending her. Toby always tries to see the good in people. He was the one telling me that Freya probably wasn't up to something right until the point where we found out she'd stolen all of my money.

"I don't know what was going on, but I saw red. Savannah came out just as I was punching him in the face."

Toby grins. "Nice. Let me guess what happened next. You didn't give her a proper chance to explain his second visit either."

"Fuck off. I didn't come here to be judged."

"You want to talk, man, we'll talk, but I'm always going to be honest. You fucked up again."

"People keep saying this shit, but how did *I* fuck up when she's the one who's been lying? And not just once. She's been lying the entire time I've known her."

"You went over there to let her explain, but instead, you let your own feelings control you." Toby shrugs. "You're fucking everything up."

"Thanks again for that, dickhead."

Max laughs. "We're not trying to piss you off—that's usually just a bonus—but what kind of mates would we be if we weren't honest?"

Now, he's vocal.

"Good ones."

He holds his finger up. "Untrue. Right, Toby?"

Toby nods in agreement. "Untrue," he confirms. "You ain't ever going to get a girl like that again, so you need to think about what will happen if you let her go."

"I don't want another woman lying to me, so that's fine." In fact, from now on, I should just stay away from women altogether. Two burns, one that's fucking gutting me, and I'm done.

My phone rings in my pocket. Max and Toby exchange a look. They want me to answer because we all know it's going to be Savannah calling. She's tried to get ahold of me hundreds of times since last week, but I've never picked up. I'm surprised she keeps calling.

And, deep down, although I hate to admit it, I love that she hasn't given up. How sad is that?

Toby points to my ringing pocket. "Not answering?"

I take a breath. "No."

"What's the plan now?"

"Work."

"Work?"

"Yeah, I run a business, and I've not been in the office as much recently. Now that I'm no longer distracted, I can work on expansion."

Toby sits back in the seat. "That's not always the answer, Kent. Savannah can't be replaced with work."

My chest tightens, twisting painfully until I have to breathe deeply just to get oxygen. Fuck this, I need to leave. I shove the bottle of Southern Comfort down on the sofa and stand up. "See you later."

It's Monday morning—nine days since Savannah and I broke up. Nine days since I found out about her betrayal and had my heart ripped to shreds.

LIE TO ME

I stare at my laptop, willing myself to do something productive.

"All right, fucker," Max says, letting himself into my office. He sits down on the opposite side of my desk and kicks his legs up.

Both he and Toby gave me space over the weekend after I stormed out of Toby's house on Friday, but apparently, Max is over that now.

"What do you want, Max?"

"What are you doing here?" he asks.

"Working. This is my company."

"Yeah, so why are you here? You own the place; people do the work for you. Go home or go out. That's what I'd do if I were the boss."

Sighing, I close my laptop. "What do you want?"

"To talk about Savannah."

"No," I snap, balling my fists on the desk.

"Heidi told me what happened—*all* of it. I don't think Savannah meant to hide anything, not for malicious reasons anyway."

"I don't want to talk about her."

"Dude, you're going to have to. She's nothing like Freya; you've said so yourself. The longer you continue with this, the worse you're going to feel. Then, you're not going to be able to get back with her because it will have been too long, and neither of you will want to lose face. You're going to die alone."

"Did your parents never think to get you tested?"

He grins. "Kent, stop being a stubborn prick, and go sort this out with your girl."

"She's not my girl."

"Bullshit she's not."

I grind my teeth. "Go away, Max."

"Nope. Your receptionist is making me coffee. Do you know if she's single?"

"Fuck's sake," I mutter, looking up to the ceiling.

"Unless you want to go find a pub?"

"No, I want to work." I want to be able to work.

Right now, my mind can't focus on anything for longer than three seconds. Savannah is still everywhere. I can smell her hair and feel the softness of her skin. My head thuds back against the chair. I didn't know pain could take on a life of its own.

"No one wants to work, man."

"Where does your boss think you are?"

He tilts his head to the side. "My boss is my dad."

Yeah, and his dad only continues to employ him because he's his son. Max is good at what he does; it's just that he rarely does it. Though I imagine, if I were his employer, I would want him out of the office as much as possible, too.

"Max, honestly, I just want to try to get something productive done."

"Can that something productive be talking to Savannah and sorting this mess out? We both know you're not going to be able to focus until you do."

"I'll focus just fine when I don't have you talking to me."

Mia, the receptionist, walks into my office with two coffees.

Max twists around and smiles. "Thank you, darlin'."

Really?

She puts the mugs down.

"Thanks, Mia."

With a nod, she retreats out of the room.

"I'm going to marry that chick."

"She's already married."

Max throws his hands up in the air. "Damn it. Now, I'm sad. We should go out and make me feel better."

My phone vibrates on the table.

Savannah.

Max lifts his eyebrow. "I think it's time you answer the phone, Kent."

"I think you should fuck off, Max."

"Look, let's get real here for a minute, shall we? I know feelings aren't something we often discuss, but you are my guy, and I hate to see you like this. You look like shit, mate, and you're no fun. She kept something big from you, and that sucks, but she had her reasons for that, just like you had your reasons for going all tech geek after Freya."

"I'm not a tech geek."

"You built a business around computer security or some software thing or some shit, so no one could be hacked the way she hacked your account. Whatever. You're good with computers now."

The vibrating on my phone stops.

"Call her back." Max picks up his drink.

"Put the fucking coffee down. We're going out," I snap.

"Yes!" He slams the mug down, spilling coffee all over the fucking desk. "I knew you would come around."

"Clean this up."

"I'll go grab a towel while you call Savannah back."

I take a breath. I'm not going to call her back.

Max cleans up his mess, and we take our mugs into the kitchen, thankfully not passing Mia, as we didn't drink anything.

"Which pub, buddy?" Max asks as we walk out onto the street.

"The closest one."

"I'll take you to the closest one that's open at ten in the morning."

As promised, Max takes me to a pub very local and very open. I sit down while he gets the beers. He's going to talk about Savannah more; I know he is. Or he's going to feed me beers until I'm drunk, and everything comes spilling out. Since talking to my parents and sisters, not long after I found out about her past, I've managed to not talk to anyone at all about her.

Heidi and Brooke have sent countless text messages, begging me to open up, but I don't want to talk. I want to forget that I ever fell in love with Savannah, and I definitely want to forget that I still have her engagement ring sitting in my coat pocket.

I would take it out, but that would involve touching it.

"There you go, mate," Max says, putting a beer in front of me.

"Thanks." I immediately pick it up and take three long gulps.

That's better. *Getting wasted always helps, right?* The more I drink, the less I remember. At least, that's how it all worked out when Freya fucked me over. Something tells me, it's going to take a lot more alcohol to forget Savannah.

I must be some sort of magnet for bitches looking to screw someone over. Savannah might not have stolen my money and done a runner, but she's worse. She made me fall in love with her, see a future, want to settle down, get married, and have kids.

All along, she was hiding an entire life.

That's much worse than being a thief.

"Are we going to sit here in silence?" Max asks.

"Yeah, sounds good to me."

"Come on, buddy."

I put the glass down as my fingers start to itch to launch at him. "Max, leave it."

"You're being stubborn and letting Freya run your emotions. Don't give her that power. She *can't* have that power. Not after everything you've been through and how far you've come. Right now, you're only thinking of you and how you feel hurt, but look at it from Savannah's point of view."

I raise my eyebrow.

"Not only did her boyfriend cheat, but he also cheated with her *sister*, and the rest of her family blamed her for the problems they were having. She went through one of the worst things a person could go through when she lost her baby, and she had no one to help her. Everyone who was supposed to pick her up wasn't there in the way she needed. Can you imagine how lonely she must have felt? She ran away from everything she knew because she couldn't stay."

He throws his hands up. "You're too busy thinking about you that you've forgotten to think about her. How do you think she feels, having to talk about that again?"

Max's words scrape against my skin like sandpaper.

I let out a breath I didn't even realise I had been holding.

She must have felt so alone, so scared, and so betrayed. She was in too much pain to talk about her past.

Fuck, she was only nineteen, too. What the fuck is wrong with me? The thought of Savannah broken, alone, and in pain is fucking intolerable. And I'm part of her pain. I've hurt her, too.

"Stop letting your feelings about your ex cloud your judgment over this situation. They're nothing alike. Freya was a gold-digging whore; Savannah's lie was self-preservation."

The chair scrapes along the floor as I stand up. *I need to get to her.*

Max leans back in his seat. "About fucking time."

I barely hear his words because I'm heading out the door, my legs moving faster by the step.

I've been such a fucking idiot.

34

Kent

I TURN RIGHT OUT the door and break into a sprint. Savannah will be at work, and Heidi's studio isn't far from here. I feel like I'm about to walk into the lion's den. She has every right to be angry with me—my sister, too—but I hope she will listen.

My heart pounds as my feet hit the pavement.

Outside the studio, Heidi is talking with the postman.

When he nods and walks off, she looks up and places her hands on her hips. "What do you want?"

I plant my feet in front of her, breathing like I just ran a marathon. My lungs feel like they're going to collapse. I'm in good shape, damn good shape, but I sprinted faster than I'd thought was humanly possible to get to my girl.

"Savannah," I say.

"You want Savannah?"

"Yes," I confirm.

"You'd better mean that. If you go in there and end up upsetting her, I'm going to bash your mindless head in."

What a lovely picture she paints.

"Jesus, Heidi, violent much?"

"I mean it. She's had enough heartache."

"I know that." My chest tightens as I think about what she's been through. I just need to hold her.

"I'm going to go for coffee then," she says, turning on her heel and stalking off.

The door to the studio suddenly looks a lot bigger and a lot heavier. Walking through it will either get me everything I've ever wanted or leave me with nothing.

My stomach rolls with nerves as I push the door open.

I step inside.

"Heidi, we have an order of twenty Hayley T-shirts."

I close my eyes. *God, I've missed her.*

She turns around when she gets no reply. She freezes, only her mouth parts. "Kent," she whispers.

Her hair is tied up today, high and messy. Her eyes are glossy, like she's not had much sleep.

"Hi."

"Hi," she replies. "Um, Heidi isn't here at the minute. I'm not sure where she went."

"She's gone to get coffee."

Savannah blinks, realising I'm here for her and not my sister. "Is everything okay?"

I shake my head and take a tentative step closer. "No, it's not."

"What ..." Her lips press together, as she knows what's wrong.

"Savannah," I say, her name rolling from my lips. I take another couple of steps, and I'm right in front of her. "I'm sorry I reacted so badly."

Her shoulders sag. "No, it's not your fault. I should have told you and—"

"Stop." I reach out and brush my fingers along her jaw. My body instantly reacts at the touch. I feel myself getting hard, and my heart beats wildly as I long to wrap myself around her. "Max was right—amazingly. I wasn't angry with you. Everything from Freya came flooding back and how I felt then. I'm sorry," I say, leaning in and pressing my forehead to hers.

She doesn't push me away. Her grey eyes flit closed, and she whispers, "I didn't want to lie to you, not ever, but I had no idea how to talk about what had happened. I find it hard to relive that time. I'm sorry I was dishonest."

Sighing, I drop my hand and hold hers. She grips me hard, curling her fingers into my palms, and looks up.

"I wouldn't have judged you, and I wouldn't have made you go into details you weren't happy to discuss. I just wanted to know."

"I'm sorry. God, I'm so sorry, Kent. You were incredible. I've never been happier. I never intended to lie, but I wasn't ready. Then, you opened up and told me all about Freya. You welcomed me into your family with open arms and made me feel special. That kind of made it harder to come clean because I was scared to lose everything. You're perfect, and I've never truly felt like I deserve that because you have so much more to give."

I blow out a breath. That's some heavy shit she's just put on the both of us. I'm not sorry for making her the centre of my fucking universe. I love her!

"What do you want me to say, Savannah?"

A smile touches her lips. "Lie to me."

I pull her in close and wrap my arms around her back, trapping her in, not that she was trying to get away. "I can't forgive you, I don't love you, and I don't want to spend every day for the rest of my life waking up beside you."

Tears well in her eyes, and her smile grows. "I don't love you either."

Thank God for that.

"I'm so sorry I let my ex affect us."

She closes her eyes and breathes. "No, it's okay. I understand. It's not always easy to let go of the past."

"Please tell me I haven't completely ruined everything. I need to know you don't want us to go our separate ways."

Her hands find their way to my stomach. She brushes her fingers up my chest and stops by my heart. "Definitely not. I'll never want that."

"Good, because I'm still crazy in love with you, Savannah."

When she opens her eyes, her face breaks into the most stunning smile that makes my heart ache. "I'm crazy in love with you, too, Kent."

I can't wait. There is a proper way to do this—with candles and flowers and massive romantic gestures that I would have to ask Heidi and Brooke about—but I can't wait.

The ring is still in my pocket.

I sink to the floor, and her arms drop away.

Frowning, she asks, "What are you doing? We can't do that now. Heidi will be back in a minute."

Barking a laugh, I arch my eyebrow. She hasn't seen that I'm on one knee. She thinks I'm about to go down on her. Not that I'm not totally up for that, but right now, I have something more important to do.

Reaching into my coat pocket, I tightly grip the ring box and take it out.

"Kent, come on, we can't do—" She stops talking. Her stormy eyes round like saucers when she sees the little black box.

I flip the lid open, presenting her with the most beautiful diamond I could find that I thought she would love. "Savannah Dean, I fell in love with you when I thought loving was impossible. I can't imagine spending one more day without you. I promise to love you for eternity."

She drops to both knees in front of me, gripping my forearms. "Yes!"

"You didn't even let me ask!"

Pressing her lips together, she zips her mouth and tries miserably to hold back a smile.

"Savannah, will you marry me?"

"Nah," she replies, her lips parting in a grin.

I narrow my eyes. "You know, the only person who thinks you're funny is you."

Laughing, she wraps her arms around my neck, and my heart soars.

"Of course I'll marry you!"

I prize my arms out from where she wedged them between us and hold on to her tight. "I love you," I whisper into her ear.

"I love you, too." She pulls back, a tear leaking from her eye. "Now, put that on my finger!"

I salute, grinning like a fucking fool. The ring slips onto her finger.

"There, now, I officially own you," I tease, but she doesn't hear me.

She's too busy staring at the ring like she's not sure if it's real or not. My fucking bank balance knows how real that rock is.

"It's perfect," she says, finally lifting her tear-filled eyes to mine.

I bend down and kiss those soft lips. She tastes just how I remember.

"I don't want a long engagement, babe."

She tilts her head to the side. "Okay. I don't care when it is."

"Do you want to reach out to your family?"

"No."

"Good, because I'm too fucking angry with them."

She sinks into my arms again. "Let it go, Kent. That's all in the past, and I only want to focus on the future."

We're going to have to have a proper conversation about her past at some point—she must know that, too—but it definitely doesn't have to be on the day we've sorted things out and gotten engaged.

The studio door slams shut behind me.

"You two all right?" Heidi asks.

Yeah, we must look fucking weird right now, down on the floor.

Savannah lets go of me and stands up. She holds her hand up, the rock on her finger facing my sister.

The most deafening squeal rips from Heidi's mouth, making me jump out of my skin.

"What the fuck was that?" I snap, getting to my feet.

Neither of them acknowledges me at all as they run and hug each other.

"Oh my God, I can't believe it!" Heidi shouts.

I don't think Savannah can reply because my sister is squeezing the life out of her.

I stand back from them like a third wheel.

Heidi lets go and grips Savannah's upper arms. "You're going to be my sister-in-law! I can't believe my brother proposed! This is amazing!"

"I know!"

Heidi turns to me. "Mum and Dad are going to freak! In a good way. My baby brother is getting married." She runs at me—like proper runs.

I brace myself, so she doesn't knock me on my arse. "Glad you're happy about this, too, sis," I say as she slams into me.

"Congratulations! Oh my God, I only have coffee." On her desk are three drinks. She backs away. "I'm going for champagne, and then Savannah is getting the rest of the day off."

"You don't have to do that, Heidi," Savannah says before I can thank my sister.

I look over Heidi's head and frown at Savannah.

I don't know why she is saying that when we can have all day to go back to mine and celebrate ... naked.

"As if you're working on the day you get engaged. I'll be back in ten." Heidi runs out the door like a lunatic.

"She's excited," Savannah says, stepping closer to me.

"She's very excited." I wrap her in my arms. "I can't wait to get you alone. We have lost time to make up for as well as this."

"Hmm, I'm looking forward to that."

"We might have to see if Heidi will give you the rest of the week off."

"You want to keep me in bed for five days?"

"Longer than that, but I know my mum is going to make us go over there this weekend. There will be a party—and, no, there's nothing I can do to stop her."

Savannah laughs, and the sound hits me right in the chest. "I don't mind a party. A small one."

I smile at her because there's also nothing I can do regarding the size of this party. At least we'll have control over the wedding, but a party my mum is throwing is going to be exactly as she plans it.

But I don't care what my mum plans on doing. I don't care if it's just family or the whole town. All I care about is having Savannah back and feeling like I can breathe again.

35

Kent

LAST NIGHT, SAVANNAH AND I ignored the rest of the world and focused on making up for lost time. Now, she has to go to work because she refuses to ask for more time off, but I'm not ready to let her go just yet. I know how that sounds, like I'm some pussy, but I've missed her more than I thought it was possible to miss a person.

We're both dressed and standing in her kitchen. Her head is resting on my chest as she awkwardly sips her coffee. She's almost burned my chest at least a dozen times, but I'll take a little burn when it's because she doesn't want to let me go.

Bending my head, I kiss her hair. "We should go soon."

"Yeah, I know," she murmurs. "We're getting together tonight, yeah?"

"Savannah, we're engaged. You're moving in."

Her stunning grey eyes peek up at me. "As much as I love my little apartment, I really like the sound of moving in with you."

"Good. We'll get you packed up tonight. For now though, we should get to the studio before you're late again."

That gets her moving. She backs away and puts the mug on the counter. "Come on, I'm not being late." Savannah is obsessed with being on time, which I do get.

I grab my phone, wallet, and keys and then slip on my shoes. Then, we head out the door.

She locks up and takes my hand as we walk down the communal stairs. "I can't wait for the lift in your building."

"You have a lift here, babe."

"I know, but it feels too lazy to take a lift up one floor."

Yeah, but I would probably still do it.

We head onto the street where it's just starting to get busy, crowds of people dashing to work. We join them, falling in line behind two businessmen in tailored suits. I should make more of an effort at work really. I usually rock up whenever I want in my jeans and shirt. Probably won't though.

Savannah's phone beeps in her pocket. One of her hands is in mine, so she uses the other to grab it.

When her steps falter, I know something is up.

"What is it?"

"My mum," she whispers.

Her hand is visibly shaking as she lifts the phone to her ear. I tug her to the side, in the doorway of a building, so we're out of the way.

"Hello?" Savannah says, her voice cracking. I can't hear what her mum is saying with the background noise, but Savannah is frowning. "We don't need to meet. There's no point. You took her side. I don't care."

She tightly squeezes my hand, the longer she's on the phone.

"There's nothing to talk about. It's done. No, you put Isla first. I needed you!" Her voice rises as anger begins to eclipse the shock of her mum's call. "No, don't bother coming here. Just take care of Isla. Whatever." She lowers the phone and taps the End Call button.

I hate her parents. They have two daughters, so I get that it was a tough situation, but they backed the one in the wrong, and that's unforgivable in my eyes.

Savannah must have felt so lonely, going through a miscarriage and double betrayal at the same time. Her parents should have been behind her all the way.

"Babe, are you okay?" I ask.

"Let's just get to the studio," she mutters, pulling me as she power-walks.

We're not far off, and I can understand that she doesn't want to discuss this in the street, but I'm worried about her.

I reach out to open the door as we approach the studio, but she shoves it open first and lets go of my hand.

"Savannah, wait," I say, shutting the door.

Heidi rises to her feet from her sewing table. "What's wrong?"

"My mum called me," she says, slamming her handbag down on her desk.

My sister looks at me at the same time my eyes slide to her for help. I'm not sure what to do to make this better for Savannah. I wish there were something, but I can't take back the past, and I can't force her parents to make her a priority.

She's shaking. Her body is trembling like she's freezing.

"I'll put the kettle on," Heidi says, rubbing Savannah's arm as she passes. "You want tea or coffee?"

"Tea, please," Savannah replies softly. She turns to me. "I didn't think I'd hear from her again. I mean, it's been three years, and besides messaging me, she's not tried to find me."

"They've only emailed?"

"Actually, not they, just my mum, and she messaged on my old Facebook page. She told me to come home and sort it out, but she couldn't have been that bothered by my absence since she didn't try finding me. So, I figured she only sent those messages to ease her own guilt—you know, so she could tell herself she tried."

"Fuckers," I growl. How can anyone do that? I don't have kids yet, thank God, but I don't know how someone could turn their back on them. I couldn't even leave a pet. "I didn't know you had Facebook?" I ask.

Max and Toby couldn't find her.

"I don't now. I deleted it the day after we broke up. Sav Dean is no more."

Sav. No wonder we didn't find her then.

She deleted her old life when I walked out on her.

I stroke her hair out of her face, my fingers lingering on the soft skin over her cheek and down her jaw. "What do you want me to do?"

A frown slips on her face. "What do you mean?"

"Do you want me to try talking to them? I want to do something. Tell me how I can fix this." I pull her into my arms.

"I love that you want to help, Kent, but there's nothing you can do."

"But that's unacceptable. You're hurting. There must be something I can do."

Laughing, she presses her chest against mine. "You're sweet. They'll stop contacting me soon."

"You don't want to try talking to them again?"

She pulls back and stares into my eyes. "No, I have all I need right here."

"Tea," Heidi announces, popping her head around the partition wall.

"Thanks, Heidi," Savannah replies, dropping me to head for her caffeine.

Charming.

I follow her and sit at the small table in the kitchen area.

"Okay, I'm going to say it," Heidi announces, wincing as she locks eyes with Savannah. "I think you should speak to your parents and get everything out in the open before you tell them to stay away."

I think so, too, but I don't want to agree with Heidi now and make it seem like an ambush.

Savannah sighs and looks down at the table. She runs her finger along the handle of her mug. "I've thought about that many times over the last three years. In fact, I've almost driven back there to do it, but I don't think it will change anything. I still won't want a relationship with them."

"You don't have to have anything happen from it. All you need is to say what you want, and then you can properly put this in the past."

"It's already in the past."

Heidi tilts her head. "Savannah, you kept all of this to yourself for years because you couldn't talk about it."

"I've told you all about it now."

"And we're glad you have because we want to be there for you, but can you honestly say you've dealt with all of the betrayals?"

Savannah taps her finger on the table. "I've not really thought about it."

"Because you've been ignoring it, babe," I say.

She presses her lips together, refusing to look at Heidi or me. I exchange a glance with my sister, and she now seems as lost as I am. What Savannah wants to do and what she needs are two different things, and she's battling herself.

No one can make her face her family again even if we all think she should. I don't want to push because she might not be ready, and I'm not risking losing her again for anything.

"Would you be there?" she asks after a long second, twisting her head to me.

"You even have to ask?"

I'm not letting her go alone. Not when they still think they did the right thing three years ago. Savannah is my universe, and she won't ever have to face anything alone again. I wouldn't risk them getting inside her head or making her feel worse about this. They blamed her for the rift in the family, and as long as I'm breathing, I won't allow her to believe that.

Smiling, she dips her head. "I'll see if they'll meet us this weekend then."

"You don't want to do it now?" Heidi asks.

"I'm working now."

"No, you're not. Make the call, hon. I've got things here if they can meet you now."

She shakes her head in protest. "No, you've already given me plenty of time off. I wasn't here yesterday, and I know how busy things are getting."

"Savannah, you're my best friend and future sister-in-law. I want these people out of your head and out of your life ASAP. Make the call, and then you and Kent can move forward … to making me nieces and nephews!"

Why are people so obsessed with me and Savannah reproducing?

I narrow my eyes at her. "Not happening anytime soon."

Savannah nods in my direction. "What he said."

"Fine, whatever. Call them now and get this sorted."

She doesn't want to. When she takes her phone out of her pocket, she hesitates.

"I can call if you want?" I offer. I'm not fucking afraid of a conversation with them. In fact, I damn well crave it.

"That's okay. I'll do it." She unlocks her phone.

Heidi and I watch as she calls her mum and presses the phone to her ear.

With a deep breath, she addresses her mum and asks her to meet.

Where? she mouths to me.

"My place," I reply.

She gives them my address and agrees she can meet them there in thirty minutes, giving us plenty of time to get there first.

They're already in the city?

When she hangs up, I put my coffee mug down. "They're here?" I ask.

"Yeah. Arrived this morning apparently." Savannah turns to Heidi and smiles. "I'll be back as soon as I can. Thank you."

"Anytime. Give them hell."

Laughing, Savannah nods in agreement. "I plan to."

We walk to her place to get my car, and then I drive us back to my apartment and park underground in my spot.

"Thanks for this, Kent. I know we're having to go back and forth a lot at the minute."

"There's no one else I'd rather drive around the city for." I'm sure as hell not walking, even if it would be faster. Leaning over, I kiss her. "Ready to get this over with?"

She gets out of the car. "I think so. You need to stay calm. I know what you can get like when you're pissed off."

I fake gasp. "How dare you."

"Please, Kent, you're fiery when you get worked up." She rolls her eyes. "You can tell them to fuck off when they're on their way out the door. All I ask is that you let me do some talking before that happens."

I hold my hands up, and then we walk toward the lift. "Babe, I don't know why you think I'm going to call them useless wankstain parents the second they walk through the door."

Hitting the button to call the lift, she laughs. I've missed that sound so much.

"Wankstain?"

"You've not heard that one before?"

"No, and it's kind of gross, but I like it." She steps closer to me, pressing her tits against my chest. "I think I would like you to say that to them when they're leaving."

"I think you need to move these away from me before I take you to bed and leave your parents outside, knockin' on my door," I say, pushing my hands between our bodies to circle her nipples with my thumbs.

Closing her eyes, she moans, and I jump back like she's electrocuted me.

Grey eyes flick open. "What?"

"Nothing," I mutter, adjusting myself in my jeans. Damn hard-on ten minutes before her dickhead parents' arrival. "Just need to take a breather."

The lift doors ping open, and we get in.

"You're always horny, Kent."

"Well, stop being so fucking sexy, and I won't be." I frown. "Hold on, you're the one pressing those perfect tits up against me like you want me to get hot and take you to bed. *You* are always up for it, too."

She lifts one shoulder in a lazy shrug. "Not denying it. I want you inside me."

"You're doing this on purpose, so I'll carry you to my bedroom, and neither of us will hear your parents knocking over the sounds of your moaning."

"Take me," she whispers.

"Savannah." Her name is a warning. My dick is painfully hard, balls tightening with the need to empty inside her. My control isn't great around her, but I need to keep a clear head for this conversation.

"I want to feel your big cock stretching me."

Fuck.

I slam my fist against the stop button on the lift and launch myself at her. Savannah's back slams against the side of the lift with a thud, and my mouth swallows her cry. Her hands find my hair. She grips and lifts herself up, wrapping her legs around my waist.

Her mouth fights mine for dominance, tongues wrestling. It's hot and wet, and I'm so fucking close, it's unreal.

"Savannah," I mutter as my lips devour hers, "I need to be inside you."

I unzip my trousers, shoving them and my boxers down. Hitching her skirt, I pull her underwear to the side and enter her in one sharp movement.

Her lips leave mine, and her head thumps back against the wall. "Fucking hell, Kent."

"God, you feel too good, Savannah. You're so tight, so ready ... fuck." I thrust, and my eyes roll back in my head.

Savannah's fingernails cut into my shoulders as she holds on tight while I pound her into the mirror on the wall behind her.

"I'm so close, Kent."

"Good, because I'm about to go," I grit out. "Fuck. Fuck."

LIE TO ME

Savannah calls out my name, her voice strangled and so sexy, and I explode inside her. Riding out the orgasm that has my knees about to give up, I press my head against hers.

"I love you so much," I confess.

Slumping in my embrace, she whispers, "I love you, too, Kent."

I plant a kiss on her lips. "We have five minutes until your parents are due to arrive," I say.

I slip out of her, and her feet hit the floor. I move her underwear back in place and straighten her skirt, all while smirking at her lying against the wall with her eyes closed.

"You okay?" I ask, humour lacing my words.

"Yeah," she replies, flicking her eyes open. "I want to do that again."

"Later, nympho." I tug my boxers and jeans up and start the lift.

We glide up to the top floor, grinning at each other like fools.

I let us into my apartment and pull Savannah to the bathroom to clean up. "You have a change of clothes in my room," I say, wiping her down.

Since sex in the lift, she's been on a high and absolutely useless.

"Am I going to have to dress you?"

With a laugh, she stands up as I drop the flannel. "No, I've got this. My legs are back to normal now."

"I love it when you come like a train."

"It doesn't suck for me either," she says, heading out into my room to get changed. Her skirt and underwear lay on the floor in my bathroom. She's never normally messy, so although her legs are normal now, her mind is still in that lift.

There's no better feeling than knowing how much I affect her.

When I enter my bedroom, she's fully dressed in a pair of skinny jeans and long black top. She rubs her palms on her hips and chews on her bottom lip. "It's going to be okay, right?"

"Savannah," I say, moving close, "it's always going to be okay. I'm here, so lean on me whenever you need to."

"Am I cheating by not doing this alone?"

"You don't have to do something alone to prove your strength."

A smile sweeps across her lips. "I really do love you."

"Good, because you're stuck with me."

My doorbell rings, and she freezes.

"Don't do that. You've got this."

Her expression changes, and her forehead smooths over. "I have. They're the ones in the wrong, not me." She sounds like she's been rehearsing that in her head.

"Exactly. Now, do you want me to get the door?"

With a deep breath, she shakes her head. "No, I'll do it."

36

Kent

I WATCH SAVANNAH WALK out of my room with her head held high and back straight. She's ready for this, and I'm so proud of her. When Simon cheated with her sister and her parents took their side, it stole so much from her. She's spent three years hiding and keeping her past to herself. It's eaten away at her confidence, but today, she's fully taking that back.

I follow as she struts right up to the door and swings it open.

"Mum, Dad," she addresses. Her posture falters when she sees a woman who must be her sister behind them. Before they notice, she recovers herself. "Isla." Her sister's name sounds like a swear word coming from her mouth.

I take an instant dislike to her, too.

Moving aside, Savannah lets them all in.

Isla looks around my apartment with wide eyes, similar to Savannah when she first walked in here. But, besides the same shade hair and similar eyes, they look nothing alike.

"This is a nice place you have," her mum says.

I'd exchange pleasantries, but I don't want to.

"Let's sit down," Savannah says.

I follow her to our sofa and park my arse right beside her. Pressing her arm against mine, she sinks back into the cushion. I love that I'm the one she leans on. I always want to be that person to her.

Her parents sit opposite us, and Isla sits on the single armchair facing the view of the city.

"I wanted to clear the air and get everything out there before we go our separate ways once and for all. Maybe I should have done this before I left, but I'm doing it now, and I think that would be best for all of us," Savannah explains.

Her mum's face falls. "We want more than that. I don't want to live the rest of my life without my youngest daughter in it."

"That isn't your decision, Mum," Savannah replies. She gets straight to the point. "When I lost my baby, I was devastated. You were the one with me because my boyfriend was off having an affair with my 'sister.'" She uses air quotes when addressing Isla as her sister, and I bite back my amusement.

Isla's jaw tightens.

"I don't understand how you could witness how devastated I was from losing that baby and *then* finding out about *them* and not be there for me."

"I was there for you," her mum argues.

"For a couple of weeks. I wasn't over it when you told me it was time to move on. I didn't stop grieving for the little one I'd lost, grieving for the end of my relationship with Isla, and I sure as hell wasn't over the betrayal from Simon. You tried to push me into papering over it because *you* didn't like that I was still angry, and we couldn't have fucking family dinners anymore. God, you're so selfish."

"That's a bit harsh," her dad says.

"Harsh?" Savannah's voice hitches. "It's the truth! And where were you? Not once did you come and sit with me. You didn't try to comfort me or even ask how I was doing."

"I didn't know what to say, Savannah," he replies, dropping his chin.

LIE TO ME

Fucking coward.

"You're my *dad*. You should have tried. I didn't need you to do more than hold me and tell me that everything would be okay."

He looks away from Savannah, and I want to grab his fucking head and make him face this. She puts her hand on my leg, sensing my rising temper.

"Simon and I never planned on getting together. You act as if we tried to hurt you," Isla says.

"Why are you even here?" Savannah asks.

"Because I think we can move forward. It's been a long time."

"Like I told Simon, I have moved forward."

Isla's face falls.

Oh, the wanker hasn't told her he's visited Savannah.

My girl didn't miss it either.

She tilts her head. "Maybe you should leave now and go have a conversation with your man."

Isla doesn't react. "I don't need to."

"No, I suppose he came straight home and told you all about turning up at my flat and coming to see me when I agreed to have it all out."

Isla's eyes narrow, and their parents look at her and then at each other.

This is getting good.

"He didn't? What a shock. It's so unlike Simon to tell a lie."

"Savannah, let's not talk about him right now," her dad says.

"You're doing it again," I spit, unable to keep quiet now. "You're putting Isla before Savannah, protecting the wrong daughter."

Squeezing my leg, Savannah lets me know it's okay. I hate the thought of her being hurt over this shit though. They're her parents, and they clearly favour Isla. I have no idea why.

"I'm not doing anything of the sort," he argues.

"Bollocks you're not."

"Kent," Savannah warns, "it's okay. I know the drill by now, and it stopped hurting a long time ago. I don't need validation from them anymore."

Her parents watch our exchange with curiosity. They don't like me any more than I like them. In any other circumstances, I would care what my girlfriend's parents think, but these people don't deserve to call Savannah their daughter.

"We are not trying to diminish what you went through or how devastating it was for you to lose your baby, but we couldn't lose our whole family," her mum says. "I'm sorry we didn't do enough for you."

"Why did you forgive them so quickly?" Savannah asks. "It was only a matter of weeks."

Her mum wrings her hands. "It wasn't easy. I was so angry with Isla and Simon for what they'd done. But, when it came down to it, I had to try to preserve the family. I had to try to fix things between you all, so we could be a family."

"But they were together. I don't understand how you could go from watching him with me to watching him with her."

"Like I said, it wasn't easy. I wish none of it had happened, but I can't control anyone's behaviour, Savannah."

"No, you can only control yours, and you chose to forgive what they had done to me so fast. How could you look them in the eye, knowing what they'd done? That cheating arsehole was flitting between us both, but you invited him back into your house."

"You make it sound like we had a one-night stand," Isla says. "We fell in love. I'm sorry that happened, but it did."

Savannah looks at her sister and rolls her eyes. "Don't be naive, Isla."

I frown. "What's that supposed to mean?"

Laughing, Savannah waves her hand. "Nah, actually, don't worry. It doesn't matter. Believe him all you want."

Isla sits forward. "No, you finish what you were going to say!"

"Isla, enough," their mum says. "We didn't come here to argue."

"She's trying to tell me something about Simon, Mum."

Simon wants Savannah back. That's never happening.

"I don't care about Simon!" her mum snaps.

"Can I applaud?" I whisper to Savannah.

She nudges my arm, trying to hide a smile.

"I don't care about Simon either," Savannah adds. "So, let's move on."

The look Isla gives Savannah, eyes narrowed and chin pointed, has me straightening my back. I will kick this bitch out of my apartment if she's going to be a dick to my girl.

"Whatever," Isla mutters.

Savannah ignores the world's worst sister and turns back to her parents. "Were you as angry with me as it seemed when I wouldn't get on board with your new happy family plan?"

Her dad drops his head further and leaves it to her mum to answer. "At the time, when we were all hurting and couldn't see things clearly, yes. I'm so sorry, Savannah. We know it was wrong. As soon as the dust settled, we realised what we'd done, but by then, it was too late because you'd gone, and all we had was a note."

"Did you look for me?"

"Of course we did. We tried getting through to you first, then family, and then your friends. We drove to hostels, and then we went to the police. We knew there wasn't anything they could do though. You were nineteen and had left a note."

She folds her arms. "Yes, I did leave a note. One saying not to try to find me, which you clearly ignored."

"We're your parents. We could never honour that request."

"I'm not surprised really. You've not done anything that I wanted in the past."

"You're being purposefully difficult," Isla snaps.

"You were purposefully unfaithful," Savannah replies.

She's doing a much better job of keeping cool than her spiteful sister, and Isla is getting frustrated by that fact.

"You and Simon weren't right."

"Maybe not, and maybe you two did fall for each other, but I'm your *sister*, and you never should have gone there. The little coward should have ended it with me first. Instead, you decided to go behind my back, even after you learned I was pregnant. I don't really know how you justify that to yourself, Isla, and to be honest, I don't care, but don't pretend like you're innocent, and don't act like what you did was okay."

"You don't know what you're talking about," Isla spits.

Savannah rolls her eyes. "Of course I don't."

"Girls, please," her mum says. "Savannah, we came here to try to settle our differences and to apologise for letting you down."

"Well, you've apologised, and as far as I'm concerned, our differences are settled."

"I don't think you mean that unless you're willing to let me and Dad back into your life."

She shrugs. "Fine, I don't mean it then. We won't agree here, so I think you should all leave. Maybe shoot me a text occasionally if you want, but beyond that, I don't want anything to do with you."

Savannah's mum holds her heart. "I want a relationship with you again."

"It's too late for that." She sighs. "Look, I'm not trying to hurt you, but this is most certainly a case of too little, too late, Mum. I got tired of being angry and wishing for things that weren't going to happen. I've moved on, and I'm happy." She squeezes my leg. "Really happy."

Yeah, fuck you, I make her happy!

"Savannah …" her dad says.

"Don't, Dad. There are no hard feelings. Let's just leave it at that."

Isla snorts. "And me?"

"Definitely no hard feelings with you. You're with Simon, and that's punishment enough."

I press my lips together tight, so I don't laugh. Isla's eyes become slits as she glares so hard at Savannah. Her parents don't say anything. I cut them a look in case they suddenly get any ideas.

Savannah stands up.

I blink up at her before rising to my feet. *Where is this going?*

"You okay, babe?" I ask, touching her back.

Her grey eyes peek up at me, and a smile touches her lips. "I'm great actually." She turns back to her parents and sister. "I'm glad we got to clear the air, but I think we should leave it there, and you should go."

Her parents stand. Isla gets up too, and she looks longingly at the door.

"Honey, I don't—"

"Mum, my offer to message occasionally stands, but that's it."

"Right. Okay," she replies, wiping a tear from her cheek.

Savannah doesn't react to her mum crying.

"Let's go. This was a waste of time," Isla says, folding her arms.

Looking at her sister, Savannah smiles sarcastically. "Take care, and good luck."

Her parents turn to leave when a hammering on my front door has us all freezing.

Savannah tilts her head up. "What the hell is that?"

I move around her. "I don't know. You stay there."

The banging rattles the door until I swing it open.

"What the fuck do you want, prick?" I growl at Simon as he stands before me, breathing heavily with his hands clenched.

In the background, I hear Isla say Simon's name and the sound of footsteps closing in.

"Where is she?"

"Isla's inside."

"Not her!" he snaps.

Savannah. He's here for Savannah right now.

37

Savannah

ME? SIMON WANTS TO see me?

Kent turns back to me from the door, and Simon uses that as the perfect opportunity to let himself into the apartment.

"What the hell is going on?" Isla shouts to Simon.

She heard him admit that he was looking for me and not her.

"Why won't you answer my calls?" Simon asks me, totally ignoring his girlfriend.

I fold my arms. "Because I'm done talking to you."

"Well, I'm not done!" he snaps, saliva spitting from his mouth.

Isla steps forward and throws her arms in the air. "Simon, what the hell is this?"

His head snaps to her like he's just noticed she's in the room. He's not at all focused on my sister; it's all about trying to get me back. He doesn't have a hope in hell of that. This is going to be good since Isla has just realised exactly what's happening.

Karma, you beauty.

"You don't understand," Simon says to Isla.

"Understand what? What can you possibly want from my *sister*?" Isla shouts.

I laugh because I've been there. "I used to ask myself the same question."

Isla growls and takes a step toward me. My back instantly straightens. I won't back down to her. But Kent still steps forward at the speed of light and puts his body half in front of me.

I love him.

"Isla, that's enough," Mum says, sobbing at the exchange. "Let's go. You can sort this out with Simon later."

Simon growls. "I don't need to sort this out with Isla. I need to sort this out with Savannah."

"You're crazy if you think you need anything from my girl," Kent snaps at him. "Now, get the fuck out of my apartment."

His apartment. Wait. How does he know where Kent lives? Unless Isla told him. I did give Mum the address. Or the little weasel followed us. That sounds more like The Colossal Wanker's style.

He turns his nose up as his beady little eyes take Kent in.

Good luck, knobhead. Kent could crush him with one hand.

"Try it," Kent warns, his shoulders broadening.

Okay, so, as much as I really do love Kent backing me up, I need to do this. They only know the strong Savannah. They weren't around for the last three years when I lost myself to grief, so I don't want to show them I need a man to fight my battles. And *I* don't want a man to fight my battles.

I touch Kent's arm and step around him.

I've got this.

"Enough," I snap. "This is Kent's apartment, so you'll play nice, or you'll leave right now." I step forward. "I'm going to say this one last time, and I'll be very clear, so you understand. I don't want anything to do with you. Don't call me, don't message me, don't stop by. Our contact ends here today, so go home with Isla, and get on with your life."

Isla's face turns red, like she's been holding her breath for the last five minutes. "Simon!" she screeches. "What is going on?"

Surely, he has to come clean now. He has to tell her that he's not happy. It wasn't that long ago that he admitted that Isla was a mistake, and he would ditch her for me. Not that I would ever have him back. There's no way out of this for him.

Sighing long and hard, he throws his hands up. "We're wrong."

Kent looks at me at the same time I turn to him. Even though Kent wouldn't piss on Simon if he were on fire, he still winces at how badly Simon's explaining things to Isla.

"We're wrong," she repeats, tilting her head like she's testing the words to see if they make sense.

They do to me.

"Everything. What we did, the fact that we stayed together. It's all wrong."

Mum and Dad move closer to Isla. I remember what that feels like, though I doubt they'll move away from her after a few weeks.

"Maybe you could take this outside," I say. "We're done here. You can work on your relationship or your breakup elsewhere."

"Shut the fuck up, Savannah!" Isla snaps. "What did you say to him? You've gotten in his head."

She's angry, so I'll ignore her telling me to shut up, especially since she followed it by a question. "Hmm, let me think. What did I say to him? I told him to leave, and I told him never to contact me again. Did you fall asleep for that part?"

"Let's calm down," Dad says.

"First, I am calm, and second, I never asked for this. I didn't want any of you to come here, so for Isla to accuse me of anything is ridiculous. Simon is all hers. Believe me, I do *not* want him."

"How can you say that after everything?" Simon asks.

I deadpan and twist my body to face him. No one else speaks either because, despite what anyone thinks of the situation, we all know he and Isla are ultimately to blame here.

"Did those words actually just come out of your mouth? Are you high or drunk? It's *because* of everything that I don't ever want to see you again."

His eye twitches, and he shakes his head.

Is there something wrong with him? A breakdown maybe?

He doesn't seem to register his place in this. For him not to understand where I'm coming from is ludicrous.

"It was always us," he says.

"Until it was you and my sister. Leave, Simon."

"This is un-fucking-believable!" Isla shouts. She lunges forward and pushes Simon.

Mum dashes toward her and pulls her back while my dad does nothing. No shock there.

"Isla, don't," Mum pleads. "Let's just go and talk."

I roll my eyes.

"I'm sorry," Simon says to her. "I tried, Isla, but it never felt right. I only realised that when Savannah left. Everything got so serious, so quickly. Savannah and I were talking about moving in together when we finally went away to uni, and you were there. Then, Savannah got pregnant and lost the baby."

Savannah got pregnant. Yeah, I did that all on my own.

I grind my teeth. He's never said that he blames me for losing the baby, and I always assumed he wouldn't, but he kind of put it all on me there.

You know what? No. I'm not going there.

I've only just stopped blaming myself, so I'm not going to allow him to throw me ten steps back.

He can fuck right off.

"You got her pregnant." Kent folds his arms and raises his eyebrow.

So, I wasn't going to bite, but apparently, he's not letting that go.

Simon looks like he wants to kill Kent. "Who the hell asked you?"

LIE TO ME

"Okay, you need to leave. Right now. Get out."

Simon takes a step back and pulls something out of his pocket. A knife.

My eyes widen, and I open my mouth to shout at him, but Kent tugs me back behind him.

"What are you doing with that?" Isla asks.

"Son, you need to put that down," Dad says.

"Savannah, I need to talk to you on your own." He holds the knife higher.

It's long, and it has a serrated edge. I didn't notice it until he was holding a knife, but he looks tired and run-down. His eyes are red and sunken, hair a mess, and his clothes are wrinkled from days of use.

"Not happening," Kent snaps.

I ignore everyone else in the room because the only person I seem to think is capable of remaining calm is me. Well, my dad, too, but he's unlikely to do anything.

Raising my hands, I say, "I'll talk to you if you put the knife down."

"Savannah—"

I cut Kent off before he can say any more. "Shh!" I hush sharply. "You've got my attention, Simon. Put it down."

He holds the knife higher. "We belong together."

I want to correct him because we most certainly do not, but I'm not looking to piss off the guy wielding the knife.

"Why now, Simon? After all this time, it doesn't make sense."

His wild eyes dart to Isla and then back to me. "She ..."

"What?" I repeat.

"She wants a baby."

"Oh." *Good luck to that kid, having them as parents.*

He runs his hand over his face. "All I could think about was how it should have been with you."

Isla gasps, taking a step back like she's been slapped.

Definitely no way back now.

"We were a long time ago, Simon. You made your choice the second you allowed things to go too far with her. There was never going to be any way back, not even if we hadn't lost the baby."

"That's not right. It's not right. We belong together, Savannah. It's always been us, right from when we were fifteen."

I look at Isla for—dare I say it—help. But she's just staring at him with tears in her eyes, devastated. I'm not sure what she expected really. He's hardly going to be the most reliable since he's done one of the crappiest things to a girlfriend that you could do.

There's a shift in the air, a kind of desperation that has the hairs on the back of my neck standing up. Simon breathes deeply. His knuckles turn white around the handle of the blade.

It makes Kent sidestep, so he's protecting more of me.

"We belong together, Savannah."

Isla snaps, "Okay, Simon, just calm down a minute."

She's changed her tune. As angry as she is that he's just admitted he doesn't want her, she's still trying to appease him.

Because she thinks he's about to do something stupid.

He's not paying any attention to her though. He's watching me like no one else is around. I fucking hate it, but again, he has a knife.

Kent's forearm muscles flex as he clenches his fists.

He wants to finish this. He wants to grab Simon and punch him. I do, too. I'd love nothing more than to whack Simon around the head with his own knife—handle end, of course, as I'm not a monster—but that wouldn't be smart.

"What we did wasn't right, Isla." He turns toward her and points the blade at her chest. "It wasn't right. You kept telling me it was, that it was okay because we had fallen in love, but it wasn't okay."

My heart drops. She's a bitch, but I don't wish her dead.

"Simon, look at me," I say. "It is okay now. A lot of time has passed, and I know you're sorry. Please put that down and talk to me."

He turns his head but keeps the knife pointing at Isla. "You don't want me."

My body tenses. I can't lie. "No, I'm sorry, I don't."

"No. No, no, no, no!" he raves, the veins in his neck popping through the skin. He walks toward the door.

No one moves because none of us really knows what to do. I've never seen him like this before.

When he stops, his back hunches, and he slowly turns around. There are tears in his empty eyes.

"I can't live without you," he rasps.

His words turn my blood to ice.

"Simon, don't!" I shout, lunging forward as he turns the knife to himself.

Kent's arm wraps around my waist and yanks me back. Simon looks up, his vacant eyes burning into Kent, his lip curling, furious that Kent thinks Simon is a threat to me.

"Let her go. She's not yours," Simon says, voice low and chilling.

I am Kent's in every way possible, but that's only going to add fuel to the fire.

Kent's arm tightens around my waist.

Simon raises the knife, so it's pointing in the air.

"Can you put that down, please?" I say, holding my hands up. I nudge Kent, and he lets go, but he doesn't move even a millimetre away from me. "Simon, give me the knife, and we'll talk."

His eyes flit between everyone in the room, spending a fraction longer each time he reaches me again. He looks lost, scared, and empty. Like he has nothing left to lose.

"Simon," I repeat, "can you give me the knife?"

Turning from Isla, he looks at me and nods. "It's really over." His voice is a whisper. He's talking to himself, finally realising that there's no way back for us.

"Simon, hand Savannah the knife, son," Dad says.

I want to roll my eyes. I've almost defused the situation, so now, he talks up. *Where was he when Simon turned the knife on himself?*

Everyone ignores my dad, besides Kent, who I feel tense even more beside me.

I focus on Simon because he's so close to handing the knife to me. He shuffles forward a step, eyes staring into mine like he's trying to tell me something. I don't know what it is because he's so emotionless. His facial expression is blank.

"That's it," I reply and hold my hand out.

Kent takes a step forward, so he's slightly closer to Simon than I am. I don't even think Simon noticed, as he's not looked away from me.

"Sav," Simon breathes, "it's never over."

In the blink of an eye, Simon lunges at me. Kent shouts something and grabs me, but it's too late. Simon is in my face. I feel the sharp coldness of the blade in my abdomen.

There's a flurry of reactions, but I seek Kent.

Oh God.

His eyes are wide and mouth parted as he grips my upper arms. "Savannah!"

Pain blasts through my stomach, and my legs go weak. Kent catches me as my knees give way.

"It's okay, babe," he whispers, kneeling down and cradling me against his chest. His hand pushes down on my stomach.

"Ahh!" I cry out, pushing my face into his chest as my abdomen catches fire.

"Shh, I'm sorry, baby. I need to stop the bleeding. Look at me."

The pain is overwhelming, stealing my breath and slowing my heart, but with effort, I still manage to tilt my head.

I instantly wish I hadn't bothered. Kent's beautiful turquoise eyes are glazed with unshed tears. My mouth drops, ready to tell him to stop, to convince him that I'm fine, but I can't speak. Nothing will come out.

"Don't. It's okay," he says, noticing the battle I'm having. "Don't talk. Focus on me. Stay with me. Your mum is calling for help. Paramedics will be here soon."

I nod, but the action is agonising.

"You're going to be fine, babe. I promise."

My eyes are heavy. The blistering pain is tugging me toward sleep. I want to go. Right now, I would go willingly, but I'm too scared that I won't wake up. I don't want to leave Kent.

"Hey, hey," he says. His face blurs out of focus. "Savannah, listen to me."

I can see him better again. I raise my arm and grip his chest, needing something to hold on to.

"That's it. Keep your eyes open, okay? When we get out of the hospital, we're going to the Maldives."

His eyes flick to my belly, and for a nanosecond, they portray blinding fear. I feel more pressure as he pushes his hand harder on my stomach.

How long until the ambulance is here?

Where is everyone else?

All I see is Kent.

He looks back up and smiles. "It's not that bad."

Now, you're the one lying to me.

"They're going to fix you up, Savannah, and then I'm bringing you home. I'm going to look after you, and I swear on my life, no one will ever hurt you again."

It's so cold in here. My body is heavy. I can feel Kent's arm tightening under me as he takes more and more of my weight.

"Baby, hey," he says, pressing his forehead to mine, "stay with me. I need you to do that."

He's out of focus again.

Kent? Come back.

My heart races. I don't want to leave him, but everything is slowly turning black.

"Savannah!" he snaps. "Look at me."

I'm trying.

Kent!

"Hey, come on, you can do it. I'm here. Listen to my voice. Help is on the way. I can hear them. Baby, please, look at me."

I can't.
Darkness.
I don't know if my eyes are closed, but I can't see.
Cold creeps up my spine and branches out to each limb.
"Savannah!"
I love you, Kent.

38

Kent

"SAVANNAH!" I SHOUT.

She's limp in my arms. Eyes closed.

My world stops.

"Savannah!"

Her dad and sister are holding Simon down on the floor, but he's not even tried to move. Her mum is on the phone by my front door, waiting for help.

"Wake up, baby. Savannah, wake up!" I shake her because I can't move my hand to tap her face. "Fuck, Savannah, wake up!"

My heart races, hands shaking. Her chest is rising and falling still, but she won't wake up.

Why the fuck won't you wake up?

"Savannah, can you hear me? I know you can."

She's breathing, so I have to believe that she can hear me.

"I know I've said it a thousand times before, but I really do love you. I've always known what love is. My parents shower me in it, I have two sisters I'd do anything for, and I have friends who are more like brothers. But then you came along. Fuck me, Savannah, I was not prepared for it. Falling in love with you hit me so hard."

Her blood is warm and slippery against my hand, leaking through my fingers. I've stemmed the flow considerably, but I can still feel it dripping further down my wrist.

Is that why she's out of it? Because of the blood loss? She just needs a transfusion and she'll be okay.

"There's supposed to be a very fine line between love and hate. Before you, I never believed that. I thought that love was love, and hate was hate. Stupid of me to be so black and white about something really, but you came along and threw a whole bunch of stormy grey in there.

"You changed my world, Savannah, and there is still so much I want to show you, so many places I want to take you. And I still need to marry you. So, you'd better just be taking a fucking nap right now, babe. I'm not doing this without you."

I can feel her stomach moving where she's breathing. I don't know if it's fear talking, but it's getting shallower.

My muscles bunch.

"Savannah."

"They're here!" her mum shouts. I hear her run out the door, ready to meet them off the lift.

Thank fuck.

"Did you hear that? The paramedics are here. I need you to hold on, babe. Stay with me. Keep listening to my voice. I'm not going anywhere, not ever, so you can't either."

If she dies, my life will be over. That might sound dramatic, but some types of love you can't carry on without. I wouldn't even know how to live without her anymore. She is the centre of my world. Everything I now do is built around her—what I think she'd like, when I'm going to see her, or where we want our future to be.

I don't want a tomorrow if she doesn't finish today.

"I found a house," I tell her. "I was going to surprise you. It happened completely by accident. It's my parents' neighbour. Don't worry; they're still a mile away, but their house is only a few years old. It's modern, the way you like, and I'm already planning to attach a tyre to a tree over the stream."

I pull back a little to look at her. To make sure she's still with me. My breath catches. Her skin is pale, lips tinted the tiniest bit blue.

"Savannah, fight," I whisper.

Fuck.

Savannah's chest stops moving.

"No!" I shout. "Help!"

My arms shake. I lay her down. She needs CPR.

"Fuck no, don't do this to me, babe." I look over my shoulder and shout, "Help!"

Isla leaves Simon, still being pinned under her dad, and runs over. "Oh God."

"Put pressure on the wound," I snap, placing my palms over her chest.

I push down hard. Really hard. Bringing my hands up and down in succession, I pump her chest, willing her heart to start beating again.

Come on, baby, come on.

I pump.

She can't leave me.

My eyes well. I blink tears. Fear wraps around my lungs and squeezes.

I pump. Down. Up. Down. Up.

Please, Savannah. Please breathe.

She can have mine. I'll trade places with her in an instant. She's so sweet, so strong, and so independent. All she needs to do is believe in herself more, and my girl could conquer the world. Savannah can't be the one to leave. Not her.

I pump.

Isla chants, "Oh God."

In the distance, I can hear their mum frantically relaying information to whoever has arrived first. Police or paramedics. I need it to be the paramedics.

Savannah's life is in my hands, and it's agony.

Come on, breathe.

I pump.

I love you. Don't leave me.

My palms force down into her chest, and with each compression, each time my hands get close to her heart, I'm begging her to fight as hard as I am.

"Savannah," I mumble as my efforts seem to have no effect.

Footsteps thud toward us.

Paramedics. Through tears, I see clothes.

One of them, a female, fires questions that I'm unable to answer.

How long have I been doing chest compressions?

I don't know. Forever.

Isla has the answers and relays the information they need.

I can't see anything but her still chest.

I can't hear anything other than the sound of my own pulse. And I wish I could give it to her.

I'm being moved. Slumping back, I brace myself on my hands and stare dumbly at my future fading in front of me.

My heart is beating too fast.

I'm fucking overheating.

She's going to die.

They're going to tell me there's nothing more they can do for her.

There will be a funeral.

I can't go to her funeral.

My fingers cut into the wooden floorboards under me.

I can't fucking breathe.

Is this how she felt before she stopped breathing?

They're shocking her. Her chest jumps up.

Nothing.

Jump.

Nothing.

39

Kent

SAVANNAH, COME ON.

Jump.

"There it is," one of them says. "Okay, let's get her out of here."

Closing my eyes, I drop my head back and breathe in relief.

Oh fuck. Thank fuck.

She's alive.

She's alive, and she's going to be okay. She has to be.

I stand as they carefully put her on the gurney and lift her up, my tears not yet drying but falling for another reason.

As I turn, the police run into my apartment. I ignore them as they head for Simon on the floor, and I go with Savannah.

Neither one of her parents asks if they can go in the ambulance. There is no way in hell I would allow that to happen anyway. Savannah wants them out of her life for the most part, so the person she needs to see when she wakes up is me.

We head down in the lift, both paramedics focused on her, checking her pulse.

I can't keep my eyes off her. She's so beautiful. I don't know how I got so lucky. When she wakes up, I won't waste another second. I won't ever let anything get in the way of us again.

"She's going to be okay, isn't she?" I mutter, not able to tear my eyes away from her face.

"It's looking good right now, but we can't promise."

I press my lips together. They can't promise. Of course they can't, but that's not good enough.

The lift doors slide open, and we race out toward the ambulance parked right outside the building. They load the gurney in, and I jump up, too.

One of the paramedics slams the back door shut and goes to drive.

"Can I hold her hand?" I ask, desperate to touch her, to feel warmth.

He looks up from where he's checking her pupils. "Of course. Talk to her as much as you can."

I reach out, hesitating for a second because I'm fucking scared that she won't be warm. When my hand touches hers, I feel the connection in my whole body. Closing my eyes, I savour the moment and how she makes me feel.

"Hey, babe," I say, flicking my eyes open and giving her hand a squeeze. I rub my thumb over her knuckles. "We're on our way to the hospital, so they can take care of you. Once they're finished, it's over to me. And you know that means my mum, too. You think she's over the top on birthdays; you wait and see what she does when someone's unwell."

Mum is going to love fussing over her, almost as much as I am.

"Don't worry; I'll rein her in. She's going to want to move in with us until you're better, but I'll get Dad on board. It'll just be you and me, the way it's supposed to be."

I continue to talk to her for the next ten minutes about absolute bullshit. The ambulance pulls to a stop.

The back door is opened, and I'm suddenly struggling to keep up. She's wheeled into Accident and Emergency, the

LIE TO ME

paramedics relaying the information that Isla gave them. I follow, but once we reach the double doors inside, I'm stopped.

"You can't come any further."

I can't go any further.

She's on her own now.

Who's going to make her fight?

She nearly died back there.

The paramedic in the ambulance told me to keep talking to her.

Shouldn't I keep talking to her?

I watch the double doors swing gently until they stop. The receptionist who took Savannah's details when she fractured her wrist comes over. She gives me information about where to wait because Savannah is going straight into surgery.

The hospital seems a lot bigger than before. The corridors area is like a maze. I've been told there's a waiting room, and someone will come and find me there when there is news. So, I go because there's nothing else I can do for her now. I text my parents and Heidi on the way. I fucking need them right now.

My parents are the first ones to burst through the door, shortly followed by Heidi and Brooke.

I've not relied on a fucking hug from my mum since I was a kid, but the second her arms wrap around me, I almost collapse into them.

"I thought she was dead," I rasp, trying to ignore the very real fact that she might still leave me.

"Shh, I know. It's okay, Kent. She's going to be fine," she coos into my ear.

I want to believe that, but there's this masochistic part of me that can't help thinking about her dying.

"Let's sit, son," Dad says, leading me and Mum to seats in the corner.

Heidi and Brooke give me a hug before sitting down, too.

"What happened?" Brooke asks.

My mind flashes back. The knife. My scream. Savannah falling in my arms. The fear that I thought might cripple me.

I tell the story, almost robotically, relaying the facts and trying to keep the emotion out. I can't talk about how scared I was.

"She's going to be okay," Heidi says. She sounds so sure of herself. "Where are her parents now?"

I shrug. "I don't know, and I don't care."

They could be talking to the police. They're probably making sure Isla is okay.

Pushing my arms out, I try to relieve the ache.

"What's wrong?" Mum asks, watching me stretch out my muscles.

My arms are fucking killing me. *Why haven't I noticed that?* As soon as I do, they throb.

"Nothing," I grit through my teeth, my heart tying in knots.

"Tell me, Kent." She puts her hand on my forearm.

"I had to …" *Fuck.* Breathing deeply through my nose, I manage to say, "She stopped … I had to do chest compressions." And, now, my arms ache like fuck. It's a bitter physical reminder of the worst fucking moment of my life.

Dipping my head, I close my eyes. More tears fall.

"Oh my God," Heidi gasps.

I'm swarmed by more than one set of arms as my family pulls close.

We wait. One hour. Then, two.

Time is supposed to be the one consistent thing. A minute is always sixty seconds. An hour is always sixty minutes. But, when you're waiting for something, when your whole future is suspended in the air, time crawls.

"Do you want to talk about it?" Heidi asks.

I know what she's asking. And, no, I don't want to talk about trying to revive my girlfriend after she technically died.

I couldn't do it. If the paramedics hadn't turned up, she would be dead.

LIE TO ME

The sting in my chest intensifies. I roughly rub over my heart with the palm of my hand.

I'm about to leave the room and get some air because the walls are closing in, and my nerves are burned, but the door swings open.

My heart stops. "How is she?"

The doctor smiles. "She had an internal bleed, but we've managed to repair the damage. She's been in recovery and doing really well. I can take you to her now."

My back straightens, heart soaring. "I can go now?"

She smiles again. "She's just been transferred to the ward. Only one for now though."

"That's fine," I say.

Everyone else can wait.

"We'll follow you to the ward and wait outside until we can see her, too," Mum says as they gather their things.

I'm already out the door with the doctor and following her down the corridor. She leads me somewhere around the other fucking side of the hospital. My pulse quickens as she swipes her card and pushes the door open to Ward E.

Savannah is in the first room. The lighting is low, like it's nighttime. She's lying in bed, her head slightly raised.

Her eyes flick to me, and I feel like I've been punched in the chest.

"You're awake," I breathe.

"Hi," she rasps, blinking heavily.

I stride to her bed and sit down. Stroking her cheek, I say, "You're okay."

"I'm okay," she repeats. Her voice is low, almost a yawn. "I love you."

"Savannah." Her name is a whisper. "Babe, I love you so much. You scared the shit out of me back there."

"Scared me, too." Her eyes tear as she stares at me like she's seeing me for the first time again. "I didn't want to go to sleep. I could hear your voice, and I wanted to stay like you said, but I couldn't—"

"Shh." I lean over and kiss her lips. "None of that matters now. You're here, and I'm never leaving your side again."

"Not ever?"

"Not even while you pee."

She scrunches her nose, making me laugh.

I kiss her again.

Epilogue

Savannah
One Year Later

"I WANT MORE," KENT murmurs into my ear as he rolls beside me.

I flop my arm over his chest, facing him. He's lying on his back, chest rising and falling heavily, but his head faces me, like always.

"You literally just came."

He narrows his eyes. "Tell me you don't want another orgasm."

I glue my lips together. Only crazy people don't want lots of orgasms. "I cannot lie to my husband."

His eyes flit closed. "That's the first time you've called me that."

"We've been married for only a few hours, Kent."

He shrugs and pulls me into his arms. I lay my head on his chest and listen to the sound of his heart racing. Kent kisses the top of my head. He's been amazing this last year.

After the showdown and Simon stabbing me, I've not seen my family. Occasionally, my mum and dad send a message to let me know they still love me, but for the most part, they respect that I don't want them in my life.

Simon is in prison still—thankfully. Mum said he's receiving help, but I shut her down because I don't want to hear it. I don't want to waste a second thinking about him ever again. When he gets out, I'll get a restraining order.

I recovered quickly from the surgery, though Kent kept fussing over me for a lot longer. Can't say I didn't love every second of it though. We both had three weeks off work, and we spent it on the sofa, not letting go of each other.

Since everything came out, I feel so much lighter. Kent knows it all, and there's no need for me to worry about someone from my past turning up. Looking back, I wish I'd come clean straightaway, but I wasn't sure that Kent really wanted a relationship, and I wasn't ready to talk about the miscarriage.

He's been amazing with that, too. Once my family was out of my life, I started to grieve properly for the baby I'd lost. Kent took me to the stream at the end of his parents' garden where he handed me flowers to send down the flowing water and a yellow balloon to let go. We lay on the grass until the balloon disappeared. It was really lovely to do something to say good-bye.

I hadn't realised how important that was until he took me out that day. I broke down for the last time, and now, I'm able to look up at the stars and imagine my little angel flying high. It still hurts when I think about the one I lost, and sometimes, I have a cry, but I'm so much better now.

"Can we blow off our own reception and stay in bed?" he asks.

Three hours ago, we had our ceremony, followed by dinner. Now, we're waiting until eight p.m. to have a massive party with family—not mine obviously—and friends.

"You know, I think they would notice."

"That's not what I asked, babe. I don't give a shit if we're missed tonight. I'm asking if we can do it."

"No."

"But this is *our* wedding night."

"Your mum spent a lot of time, energy, and money on this reception, and we're not missing it. Besides, I want to cut my cake and have my first dance. Those are things I've dreamed about since I was little."

Sighing, he replies, "Why couldn't you have dreamed about fucking your husband senseless?"

"When I was a kid?" I say flatly.

He frowns, pouting like a baby. Reaching forward, I bite his bottom lip, and he laughs, pulling his head away.

"I love it when you bite." Pulling me closer, he presses his slick body against mine. I'm definitely going to have to redo my hair and makeup before we leave this room. "Now, how about you put that mouth to good use?"

"I will if you will."

His nostrils flare at my suggestion. "You have no fucking idea how much I love you, Savannah."

"Ditto."

Though I think I have some idea. Every day, he proves by little things or big things he does or says. I've never been happier.

Kent scrambles down to the end of the bed and lies on his back. "I'm ready, sweetheart. Come sit on my face."

Sighing with a little dramatic flair, I get on all fours and shuffle down. There really is no elegant way to do this, but Kent groans in response to me backing up. He seems to think everything I do is sexy, and I sincerely hope that never stops.

He makes me feel sexy, to be honest, so I very slowly lower myself down and then wrap my hand around the base of his cock. His moan is muffled as his lips cover my clit.

Holy fuck.

I circle my hips, grinding against his tongue, as I take his erection into my mouth. Kent's fingers grip my thighs, and I press my lips together and suck. Kent thrusts upward, trying and a little bit failing to control the movement so that he doesn't choke me. Secretly, I love it when he loses control.

My lips are stretched around his erection as I take him deeper. He groans loudly and flattens his tongue. It's intense as fucking hell.

I pump his cock and run my tongue over the tip. He grows, tightening his grip.

Kent rolls his tongue harder, faster, and keeps hold of my thighs, so I can't move. It's maddening, as I need to move. I need the friction because I'm so close. The throbbing between my legs is getting unbearable.

My body bursts into flames down to my toes. I'm too hot, too close. I just want to come, and the way he's flicking my clit, I know it won't be long.

He's so good at this.

I hollow my cheeks and pump the base of his cock with my hand as my body builds and then falls apart. Kent lets go of my thighs, and I rock, riding out my orgasm at the same time he groans against my flesh and spills into my mouth.

Swinging my leg over, I collapse onto the bed, breathing heavily.

He chuckles. "You're perfect, babe. That was perfect."

"Yeah, it was."

I'm sensitive as hell down there now. My body is still floating on an orgasmic high, legs like jelly and heart pounding. He makes me feel this way every time we're together, and I can't get enough.

"Are you sure I can't convince you to stay here?" he asks, clambering up and flopping back down beside me.

He tugs me into his arms, and I lay my head on his chest, throwing my leg over his.

This is where I belong.

"Nope."

Well, obviously, he could. It wouldn't take much because since we said, "I do," I seem to want him even more, but we have a lot of people celebrating with us this evening.

Sighing hard, he runs his fingertips over my stomach. "Fine."

"KENT!" Max shouts from outside our room. Toby is also there—at least, I assume the wolf-whistling is him. It's unlikely to be anyone else. "Get it, boy!"

"Your friends are idiots."

"Yeah," he agrees, chuckling at their antics. "I did get it though."

Rolling my eyes, I push myself up. He's smiling like he's got everything he could ever want or need, like there's nothing out there that could top how life is right now. I feel it, too. My heart beats fast in my chest at the knowledge of having this man for the rest of my life. And it's really nice, knowing we can both "get it" over and over again whenever we want.

"I love you, Kent."

"I love you, too, babe."

Acknowledgments

AS ALWAYS, THERE ARE a few people I couldn't do this without.

To Zoë, Kirsty, and Kim, thank you for having my back when I'm fighting a deadline and not thinking that every word I write is complete nonsense. Natalie, thank you for beta reading! You ladies will never know how much I appreciate your support.

Sofie, I rarely have any ideas for my covers. I send you a very vague description of the book, and from that, you somehow know exactly what to do. I love your covers, and you've really outdone yourself with this one.

To my husband and our two boys, thank you for being there.

Jovana, you are amazing. Thank you for always fitting me in your schedule and finding things in my manuscripts that I would never see!

And thank you, readers, for reading Kent and Savannah's story.

About the Author

UK NATIVE NATASHA PRESTON grew up in small villages and towns. She enjoys writing contemporary romance, gritty Young Adult thrillers, and of course, the occasional serial killer.

Follow Natasha on social media:

Goodreads: https://goo.gl/nWsYRC

www.facebook.com/authornatashapreston

https://twitter.com/natashavpreston

www.instagram.com/natashapreston5

Made in the USA
Columbia, SC
20 October 2018